ALSO BY STEPHANIE PERKINS

Anna and the French Kiss
Lola and the Boy Next Door
Isla and the Happily Ever After

THERE'S SOMEONE INSIDE YOUR HOUSE

THE WOODS ARE ALWAYS WATCHING

TWO THRILLING NOVELS IN ONE VOLUME BY
NEW YORK TIMES BESTSELLING AUTHOR

STEPHANIE PERKINS

DUTTON BOOKS

DUTTON BOOKS

An imprint of Penguin Random House LLC, New York

There's Someone Inside Your House first published in the United States of America
by Dutton Books, an imprint of Penguin Random House LLC, 2017
The Woods Are Always Watching first published in the United States of America
by Dutton Books, an imprint of Penguin Random House LLC, 2021
This omnibus edition published by Dutton Books,
an imprint of Penguin Random House LLC, 2024

Dutton is a registered trademark of Penguin Random House LLC.
The Penguin colophon is a registered trademark of Penguin Books Limited.

Visit us online at PenguinRandomHouse.com.

LIBRARY OF CONGRESS CATALOGING-IN-PUBLICATION DATA IS AVAILABLE.

ISBN 9780593858073

1st Printing

Printed in the United States of America

LSCC
Edited by Julie Strauss-Gabel
Design by Anna Booth
Text set in Minion Pro

THERE'S SOMEONE INSIDE YOUR HOUSE

THE WOODS ARE ALWAYS WATCHING

TWO THRILLING NOVELS
IN ONE VOLUME

THERE'S SOMEONE INSIDE YOUR HOUSE

A NEW YORK TIMES BESTSELLER

STEPHANIE PERKINS

For Jarrod, best friend & true love

People live through such pain only once;
pain comes again, but it finds a tougher surface.

WILLA CATHER,
The Song of the Lark

CHAPTER ONE

THE EGG-SHAPED TIMER was on the welcome mat when she came home.

Haley Whitehall glanced over her shoulder, as if expecting someone behind her. Far in the distance, a red combine rolled through the sallow cornfields. Her father. Harvest time. Her mother was still at work, too, a dental technician at the only practice in town. Which one of them had left it here? The decaying porch boards sagged and splintered beneath Haley's shifting weight as she picked up the timer. It rattled in her hand. The day had been cold, but the plastic eggshell was warm. Faintly so.

Her phone rang. It was Brooke, of course.

"How's the blood?" Haley asked.

Her best friend groaned. "A nightmare."

Haley went inside, and the screen door banged closed behind her. "Any chance that means Ms. Colfax will drop it?" She marched straight to the kitchen, slinging her backpack onto its black-and-white checkerboard floor. *Sustenance.* This afternoon's rehearsal had been particularly grueling.

"Never." Brooke snorted. "She'll never drop it. Who needs common sense when you have ambition?"

Haley set the timer back on the countertop—where it belonged—and opened the refrigerator. "Normally, I'd argue for ambition. But. I'm really not looking forward to being drowned in corn syrup."

"If I had the money, I'd buy the professional-grade stuff myself. Cleaning up the auditorium will be hell, even with all the tarps and plastic sheeting."

Most theatrical productions of *Sweeney Todd* used at least some amount of fake blood—razors with hidden squeeze bulbs, gel capsules in the mouth, false clothing-fronts to conceal bloodstained doubles underneath. Additional mayhem could be implied with red curtains or red lights or a frenzied crescendo of screaming violins.

Unfortunately, their high school's musical director, Ms. Colfax, had an unquenchable zeal for drama by all its definitions. Last year's production of *Peter Pan*, for which she'd rented actual flying harnesses all the way from New York City, had resulted in the broken bones of both Wendy and Michael Darling. This year, Ms. Colfax didn't just want the demon barber to slit his customers' throats. She wanted to shower the first three rows with their blood. She referred to this section of the auditorium as the "Splatter Belt."

Brooke was the stage manager. An honor, for sure, but it came with the impossible task of trying to steer Ms. Colfax toward sanity.

It wasn't going well.

Haley held the phone to her ear with her shoulder as she loaded her arms with packages of deli-sliced turkey and provolone, a bag of prewashed lettuce, and jar of Miracle Whip. "Shayna must be flipping her shit."

"Shayna is definitely flipping her shit," Brooke said.

Shayna was their temperamental—often volatile—costume

designer. It was hard enough to find decent costumes in rural Nebraska with a budget of zero, but now she had to deal with bloodstain removal on top of it.

"Poor Shayna." Haley dumped the ingredients onto the counter. She grabbed the closest loaf of bread, wheat with some kind of herb, which her mother had baked the night before. Her mother baked to relax. She used a bread maker, but still. It was nice.

"Poor *Brooke*," Brooke said.

"Poor Brooke," Haley agreed.

"And how was Jonathan today? Any better?"

Haley hesitated. "You didn't hear him?"

"I was running splatter tests in the parking lot."

Haley was playing Mrs. Lovett, and Shayna's boyfriend, Jonathan, was playing Sweeney, the female and male leads. Still only a junior, Haley had been getting leads in drama club and solos in show choir for the last two years. Both as a performer and powerful contralto, she was simply *better* than her peers. A natural. Impossible to overlook.

Jonathan was . . . above average. And he was charismatic, which helped his stage presence. However, this particular musical was well beyond his capabilities. He'd been struggling with "Epiphany," his most challenging solo song, for weeks. His transitions held all the smoothness of someone stumbling across a bull snake in a tool shed, but even those were nothing compared to the way that he'd been massacring his duets.

Brooke seemed to sense Haley's reluctance to gossip. "Oh, come on. If you don't spill, you'll only make me feel guilty for venting about everybody else."

"It's just . . ." Haley spread a gloppy coat of Miracle Whip onto the bread and then tossed the dirty butter knife into the sink. She'd wash it off later. "We spent the *entire* rehearsal on 'A Little Priest.' And not even the whole thing! The same few bars, over and over and over. For two freaking hours."

"Yikes."

"You know that part where we sing different lines simultaneously? And our voices are supposed to be, like, tumbling over each other in excitement?"

"When Sweeney finally figured out that Mrs. Lovett wants to dispose of his victims by baking their flesh into her pies?" Brooke's voice was a wicked grin.

"It was a disaster." Haley carried her plate into the living room, but she didn't sit. She paced. "I don't think Jonathan can do it. I mean, I seriously think his brain *can't do it*. He can sing in unison, he can sing harmony—"

"Sort of."

"Sort of," Haley conceded. "But if someone else is singing different words? He keeps stopping and restarting. Like he's trying to work through an aneurysm."

Brooke laughed.

"It's why I left early. I felt like such a bitch, but God. I couldn't take it anymore."

"No one would ever call you a bitch."

Haley swallowed a huge bite of turkey. It was a balancing act—cradling the phone, holding the plate, eating the sandwich, pacing the room—but she didn't notice. She was worried. "Jonathan would."

"Jonathan shouldn't have gotten the part."

"Do you think I should call him and apologize?"

"No. *No.* Why?"

"For being short with him."

"It's not your fault he can't handle Sondheim."

This was true, but Haley still felt ashamed for getting so frustrated. For walking out of rehearsal. She plopped onto the ancient corduroy couch, one of the many relics from when the farmhouse had belonged to her grandparents, and sighed. Brooke said something else in best-friend solidarity, but Haley's phone chose that moment to do its usual thing.

"What'd you say? My connection is going in and out."

"So call me from the landline."

Haley glanced at the cordless, which was perched on an end table only a few feet away. Too much effort. "It's fine now," she lied.

Brooke circled the conversation back around to her current hardships as stage manager, and Haley allowed herself to drift away. She could only hear a third of Brooke's ranting, anyway. The rest was static.

She stared out the windows and finished her sandwich. The sun hung low on the horizon. It shone through the cornfields, making the brittle stalks appear soft and dull. Her father was still out there. Somewhere. This time of year, he didn't let a single ray go to waste. The world looked abandoned. It was the opposite of the loud, colorful, enthusiastic group of people she'd left behind at school. She should have stuck it out. She hated the quiet isolation that permeated her house. It was exhausting in its own way.

Haley made sympathetic noises into the phone—though she had no idea what she was sympathizing *with*—and stood. She walked her plate back to the kitchen, rinsed off the crumbs, and popped open the dishwasher.

The only thing inside it was a dirty butter knife.

Haley glanced at the sink, which was empty. A frown appeared between her brows. She put the plate into the dishwasher and shook her head.

"Even if we *can* get the sprayer working," Brooke was saying, their connection suddenly clear, "I'm not sure enough people will even *want* to sit in the first three rows. I mean, who goes to the theater to wear ponchos and get drenched in blood?"

Haley sensed that her friend needed vocal reassurance. "It's Halloween weekend. People will buy the tickets. They'll think it's fun." She took a step toward the stairs—toward her bedroom—and her sneaker connected with a small, hard object. It shot across the floor tiles, skidding and rattling and clattering and clanging, until it smacked into the bottom of the pantry.

It was the egg timer.

Haley's heart stopped. Just for a moment.

An uneasy prickling grew under her skin as she moved toward the pantry door, which one of her parents had left ajar. She pushed it closed with her fingertips and then picked up the timer, slowly. As if it were heavy. She could have sworn she'd set it on the countertop, but she must have dropped it to the floor along with her backpack.

". . . still listening?"

The voice barely reached her ears. "Sorry?"

"I asked if you were still listening to me."

"Sorry," Haley said again. She stared at the timer. "I must be more tired than I thought. I think I'm gonna crash until my mom gets home."

They hung up, and Haley shoved the phone into the front right pocket of her jeans. She placed the timer back on the countertop. The timer was smooth and white. Innocuous. Haley couldn't pinpoint *why*, exactly, but the damn thing unsettled her.

She trekked upstairs and went directly to bed, collapsing in a weary heap, kicking off her sneakers, too drained to unlace them. The phone jabbed at her hip. She pulled it from her pocket and slung it onto her nightstand. The setting sun pierced through her window at a perfect, irritating angle, and she winced and rolled over.

She fell asleep instantly.

●   ●   ●

Haley startled awake. Her heart was pounding, and the house was dark.

She exhaled—a long, unclenching, diaphragm-deep breath. And that was when her brain processed the noise. The noise that had woken her up.

Ticking.

Haley's blood chilled. She rolled over to face the nightstand. Her phone was gone, and in its place, right at eye level, was the egg timer.

It went off.

CHAPTER TWO

THE NEXT MORNING, the entire school was buzzing about two things: the brutal slaying of Haley Whitehall and Ollie Larsson's newly pinkened hair.

"You'd think they'd care less about the hair," Makani said.

"This is Osborne, Nebraska." Her friend Darby sucked up the last drops of his gas station iced coffee. "Population: twenty-six hundred. A boy with pink hair *is* as scandalous as the death of a beloved student."

They stared through Darby's windshield and across the parking lot to where Ollie was leaning against the brick wall of the front office. He was reading a paperback and pointedly ignoring the whispers—and not-whispers—of the other students.

"I heard her throat was slit in three places." Makani paused. The car's windows were down, so she lowered her voice. "Carved up to look like a smiley face."

The straw dropped from Darby's mouth. "That's *awful*. Who told you that?"

She shrugged uncomfortably. "It's just what I heard."

"Oh God. And the day hasn't even begun."

A long face with kohl-blackened eyes popped up beside the passenger-side window. "Well, *I* heard—"

Makani jumped. "Jesus, Alex."

"—that Ollie is the one who did it. And that he used her blood to dye his hair."

Makani and Darby stared at her, agape.

"I'm kidding. Obviously." She opened the back door, tossed in her trumpet case, and slid inside. The car was their morning hangout. "But someone here will say it."

There was too much truth in her joke. Makani winced.

Alex kicked the back of Makani's seat with a royal-blue combat boot. An exclamation point. "I don't believe it. You still have a thing for him, don't you?"

Unfortunately, yes.

Of course she still had a thing for Ollie.

From the moment Makani Young arrived in Nebraska, she couldn't keep her eyes off him. He was, without a doubt, the strangest-looking guy at Osborne High. But that also made him the most *interesting*. Ollie had a skinny frame with hip bones that jutted out in a way that reminded her of sex, and cheekbones so prominent they reminded her of a skull—the illusion of which was enhanced by his blond, invisible eyebrows. He always wore dark jeans and a plain, black T-shirt. A silver ring—a thin hoop in the center of his bottom lip—was his only adornment. He kind of looked like a skeleton.

Makani tilted her head. But maybe less so, now that his white-blond hair was a shocking hot pink.

"I remember when *you* had a thing for him," Darby said to Alex.

"Yeah, like, in eighth grade. Until I realized he's a full-time loner. He's not interested in going out with anyone who attends this school." With a rare and embarrassed afterthought, Alex grimaced. "Sorry, Makani."

Makani and Ollie had hooked up last summer. Sort of. Thankfully, the only people who knew about it were sitting here in Darby's car.

"It's fine," Makani said, because it was easier than saying it wasn't.

There were a lot of rumors about Ollie: that he only slept with older women; that he only slept with older men; that he sold opioids stolen from his brother's police station; that he once almost drowned in the shallow part of the river. That—when he was rescued—he was both blind drunk and buck naked.

Then again, their school was small. There were rumors about everyone.

Makani knew better than to believe any of them outright. Rumors, even the true ones, never told a complete story. She avoided most of her classmates for that very reason. Self-preservation. Recognizing a similarly dismal soul, Darby and Alex had taken her in when she'd been forced to relocate from Hawaii midway through her junior year. Her parents were embattled in an ugly divorce, so they'd shipped her off to live with her grandmother for some normalcy.

Normalcy. With her *grandmother.* In the *middle of nowhere.*

At least, that's how Makani told the story to her friends. And, much like a rumor, it did contain a kernel of truth. It was just missing the rest of the cob.

Her parents had never paid much attention to her, even in the best of times, and they'd only recently separated when the incident at the beach occurred. After that . . . they couldn't look at her at all anymore. She didn't like looking at herself, either.

She deserved this exile.

Now it was mid-October, and Makani had been in Osborne for almost a year. She was a senior, and so were Darby and Alex. Their mutual interest was counting down the days until graduation. Makani wasn't sure where she'd go next, but she certainly wasn't staying here.

"Can we return to the important subject?" Darby asked. "Haley is *dead*. And no one knows who killed her, and that freaks my shit out."

"I thought you didn't like Haley," Alex said, pulling her dyed-black hair into a complicated twist that required a large number of chunky plastic barrettes. She was the closest thing their school had to a Goth, if you didn't count Ollie.

Makani didn't.

Their exteriors were both comprised of black clothing and thin, pointy body parts, but Alex was hard and aggressive. She demanded to be noticed. While Ollie was as soft and silent as the night sky.

"I didn't *dislike* Haley." Darby tucked his thumbs under his suspenders, which he wore every day along with a plaid shirt and sensible trousers. He was short and stocky, and he dressed like a dapper old man.

Darby had been assigned female at birth, and though his legal name was still Justine Darby, he'd socially transitioned during his freshman year. If their school didn't like a boy with pink hair, Makani could only imagine how long it'd taken for them to get used to the "girl" who was actually a boy. They mostly left him alone now, though there were still side-glances. Narrowed eyes and pinched mouths.

"I didn't know her," Darby continued. "She seemed nice enough."

Alex snapped in a barrette that resembled an evil Hello Kitty. "Isn't it weird how the moment someone dies everyone becomes her *bestest* friend?"

Darby scowled. "I didn't say that. Jeez."

Makani let them bicker it out before stepping in. She always did. "Do you think one of her parents did it? I've heard in cases like this, it's usually a family member."

"Or a boyfriend," Darby said. "Was she dating anyone?"

Makani and Alex shrugged.

All three stared at their passing classmates and fell into an unusual silence. "It's sad," Darby finally said. "It's just . . . terrible."

Makani and Alex nodded. It was.

"I mean, what kind of person would do something like that?" he asked.

A sickening wave of shame rolled throughout Makani's body. *It's not the same*, she reminded herself. *I'm not that kind of person*. But when the warning bell rang—three sterile chimes—she bolted from the cramped hatchback as if there were an actual emergency. Darby and Alex groaned as they extricated themselves, too caught up in their own gloom to register her odd behavior. Makani exhaled and readjusted her clothing to make sure that she was decent. Unlike her friends, she did have curves.

"Maybe it was a serial killer," Alex said as they headed toward first period. "A long-haul trucker on his way through town! These days, serial killers are always truck drivers."

Makani felt the welcome return of skepticism. "Says who?"

"The FBI."

"My *dad* is a truck driver," Darby said.

Alex grinned.

"Stop smiling." Darby glowered at her. "Or people will think *you* did it."

By lunchtime, Alex's tasteless joke about the source of Ollie's hair dye had spread. Makani had heard more than one student whispering about his possible guilt. It infuriated her. Ollie was an anomaly, sure. But that didn't make him a killer. Furthermore, she'd never seen him talk to, or even look at, Haley Whitehall.

And Makani had studied *him* a lot.

She was upset, despite understanding that the rumors were

exactly that—fabrications created to distract them from the unknown. The unknown was too frightening. Makani had also overheard a group of academic overachievers gossiping about Zachary Loup, the school's resident burnout. She didn't think he was guilty, either, but at least he was a better suspect. Zachary was an asshole. He wasn't even nice to his friends.

Most students, however, were agreed on the real suspects: Haley's family. Maybe a boyfriend. No one *knew* of a boyfriend, but perhaps she'd had one in secret.

Girls often had secrets.

The thought churned inside Makani's stomach like a rotten apple. As Darby and Alex speculated, she pushed away her paper boat of French fries and glanced around.

Nearly all of the 342 students were here in the nucleus of the campus, completely surrounded by brown-brick buildings. The quad was plain. Dreary. There were no tables or benches, only a few stunted trees scattered about, so students sat on the concrete ground. Unwind a spool of barbed wire, and it could have been a prison yard, but even prisoners were given tables and benches. A dry fountain filled with dead leaves—no one could remember ever having seen the stone lion shoot a stream of water from its open mouth—rested in the center like a mausoleum.

This time of year, the weather was unpredictable. Some days were warm, but most were cold. Today was *almost* warm, so the quad was crowded and the cafeteria was empty. Makani zipped up her hoodie, shivering. Her school in Kailua-Kona was always warm. The air had smelled like flowers and coffee and fruit, and it had tasted as salty as the Pacific, which glistened beside the parking lots and football fields.

Osborne smelled like diesel, tasted like despair, and was surrounded by an ocean of corn. Stupid corn. So much corn.

Alex grabbed a handful of Makani's uneaten fries. "What about someone in show choir? Or drama club?"

Darby scoffed. "What, like, Haley's understudy?"

"Isn't that the person the *Masterpiece* detective would investigate?" Alex asked.

"The what-now?"

"Sherlock, Morse, Poirot. Wallander. Tennison."

"I only know one of those names." Darby dipped his pizza into a glob of ranch dressing. "Why don't you watch normal television?"

"I'm just saying, let's not rule anyone out yet."

Makani was still staring at the fountain. "I hope it's not a student."

"It's not," Darby said.

"Please," Alex said. "Angry teenagers do shit like this all the time."

"Yeah," he said, "but they show up at school with an arsenal of automatic weapons. They don't go after people in their *homes*. With *knives*."

Makani muffled her ears with her fists. "Okay, enough. Stop it."

Darby ducked his head, abashed. He didn't say anything, but he didn't need to. School shootings were real. With real murderers and real victims. Haley's death felt one step removed from reality, because it didn't seem like something that could happen to them. The crime was too specific. There must have been a reason for it. A horrible and misguided reason, but a reason nonetheless.

Makani turned to look at them, backpedaling the conversation in an attempt to downplay her reaction. "Well . . . Jessica didn't do it."

Alex raised her eyebrows. "Jessica?"

"Jessica Boyd. The understudy." Makani rolled her eyes when Alex smirked. "I only know she's the understudy because I heard somebody else say it. But can you honestly imagine her killing anyone?"

"You're right," Alex said. "That does seem unlikely." Jessica Boyd was a delicate wisp of a thing. It was difficult to imagine her even flushing a dead goldfish. "But did you guys notice that Haley's best friend didn't come to school today?"

"Because Brooke is in mourning." Darby was exasperated. "Like *I* would be if this happened to one of *you*."

Alex leaned forward conspiratorially. "Think about it. Haley was one of the most talented students here. Everybody knew that she'd leave us for someplace bigger and better—Broadway, Hollywood. Whatever. She was the kind of person who should be totally stuck up, but . . . she wasn't. People liked her. Which always means someone *didn't* like her. Resented her."

Makani's nose wrinkled. "And you think it was her best friend?"

"No one even knew Haley," Darby said, "unless they were in the drama club or Vocalmotion." Vocalmotion was, regrettably, the self-chosen name of the show choir. Osborne High only had three re-spectable organizations: the drama and choral departments, which had a nearly one-hundred-percent overlap, and the football team.

It was Nebraska. Of course their school took football seriously.

"But that's exactly what I'm saying," Alex said. "Nobody else knew her. So doesn't it make sense that one of her friends did it? Out of jealousy?"

"Should we be worried? Are you plotting to kill us?" Makani asked.

"Ugh," Darby said.

Alex sighed. "You guys are no fun."

"I believe I warned you this morning," Darby said, "not to appear so excited."

The wind picked up, and it shook a paper banner on the other side of the quad. An advertisement for *Sweeney Todd*. Each letter dripped with garish, hand-painted blood, and two long swaths of dark red tulle draped down from opposite corners like theater curtains. A gust heaved the tulle into the air, where it danced and writhed. Makani felt a chill touch her spine. Her name meant "wind" in Hawaiian, but she wasn't superstitious about it. Except when she was. They should stop talking about Haley.

"It's tactless," she said, unable to help herself. She nodded toward the banner. "The Splatter Belt. Do you think they'll cancel it?"

Alex swallowed the last greasy fry. "They'd better not. That was the first school function that I've ever planned on attending. Willingly," she added. She was in the marching band, which meant she was forced to attend the football games.

Darby stared her down until she made eye contact.

"What? It seemed like fun," she said. "Getting covered in fake blood."

Makani snorted. "There's that word again. *Fun.*"

Faux wistfulness spread across Darby's face. "I remember when you used to collect plastic horses and Pokémon cards, and your life goal was to work for Pixar."

"Lower your voice, dickpunch." But Alex grinned.

A back-and-forth taunting of childhood hobbies and idiosyncrasies ensued, and Makani, as it so often happened, found herself excluded. Her attention waned, and her gaze drifted across the quad. It was almost time. Any minute now, and . . .

There.

Her heart plummeted as Ollie appeared from the depths of the locker bay to throw away an empty plastic grocery bag. This was his daily routine appearance. He always ate a packed lunch in an uninhabited nook behind the old lockers, and then he always disappeared into the main building. He would finish this hour in the library.

Makani felt a familiar pang of sorrow. Ollie was so alone.

A small group of football players stood beneath the *Sweeney* banner, blocking the entrance to the building. Her muscles tensed as Matt Butler—Osborne's golden boy, its prize running back—said something as Ollie approached. Whatever it was, Ollie didn't react. Matt said something else. Ollie didn't react. Matt flicked his thumb and index finger at Ollie's hair. His friends laughed, but Ollie still didn't react. It was agonizing to watch.

A meaty guy with an absurd name, *Buddy or Bubba,* she thought, jumped up and snatched at the tulle, and the right half of the banner ripped and collapsed downward. He laughed even harder as Ollie was forced to duck, but the pleasure was short-lived.

Matt gestured angrily at the wreckage. "Hey, man! Show some respect."

The outburst carried across the quad. It took Buddy or Bubba several seconds to make the connection between the ruined banner and Haley, but as his expression transformed from confusion into humiliation, he was faced with a choice—either admit to a wrongdoing or double down. He doubled down. Shoving Matt's shoulder, he set off a furious chain reaction of even more shoving until they were no longer blocking the entrance.

The escalating action held the student body in rapt attention. Only Makani was staring elsewhere. Ollie still hadn't moved. He'd kept it together, but it was clear that the football players had unnerved him. She was on her feet.

"No," Darby said. "Makani. *No.*"

Alex shook her head, and her barrettes clicked against one another. "Ollie doesn't deserve your help. Or pity. Or whatever it is you're feeling right now."

Makani smoothed the front of her hoodie. She was already walking away.

"You never listen to us," Darby called out. "Why don't you ever listen to us?"

Alex sighed. "Good luck, gumdrop."

This *thing*—this unbearable weight and pressure—that had been boiling inside Makani for months was about to erupt. Ollie might not deserve her help, but she still felt compelled to try. Maybe it was because she wished someone at her previous school had helped her. Or maybe it was because of Haley, a horrific situation already beyond anyone's help. Makani glanced back at her friends with a shrug.

When she turned forward, Ollie was staring at her. He didn't look nervous or angry, or even curious.

He looked wary.

Makani strode toward him in a bold path. She always stood out among their peers. Their skin was several shades lighter than her brown complexion, and her surf-inspired wardrobe was several shades brighter than their Midwestern sensibility. She wore her hair big—in its natural curly coils—and she moved with a confident sway in her hips. It was a false confidence, designed so that people wouldn't ask questions.

Ollie glanced one last time at the jocks, still shouting and posturing, and pulled aside the dangling tulle. He went into the building. Makani frowned. But when she opened the door, he was waiting for her on the other side.

She startled. "Oh."

"Yes?" he said.

"I . . . I just wanted to say, they're idiots."

"Your friends?" Ollie deadpanned.

Makani realized she was still holding the door open, and he could see Darby and Alex through the tulle's transparent weave, spying on them from across the quad. She released her grip. It slammed shut. "No," she said, trying on a smile. "Everyone else."

"Yeah. I know." His face remained impassive. Guarded.

Her smile dropped. She crossed her arms, her own defenses rising as they sized each other up. They were almost eye level; he was only an inch or two taller than she was. This close, she could see the *newness* of his hair. His scalp was hot pink. The dye would need more time to wash out of his skin. There was something vulnerable about seeing him like this, and her body re-softened. She hated herself for it.

She hated herself for so many things.

Makani hated that she'd gotten carried away with Ollie, even though she'd been warned about his reputation. She hated that she'd tricked herself into believing she didn't care for him, when she'd always known that she did. And she hated the way it had ended. Abruptly. Silently. This was their first conversation since the end of summer.

Maybe if we'd talked more to begin with . . .

But that was it, wasn't it? There had never been a lot of talking. At the time, she'd even been grateful for it.

His pale eyes were still fixed on her, but they were no longer passive. They were searching. Her veins throbbed in response. Why did it suddenly feel like they were back behind the grocery store, preparing to do what they did on those hot, summer afternoons?

"Why are you here?" he asked. "You haven't spoken to me all semester."

It made her angry. Instantly. "I could say the same thing about you. And I *said* what I wanted to say. About our classmates. Being idiots and all that."

"Yeah." His posture stiffened. "You did say that."

Makani let out a singular laugh to show him that he wasn't getting to her, even though they both knew that he was. "Fine. Forget it. I was just trying to be a friend."

Ollie didn't say anything.

"Everyone needs friends, Ollie."

He frowned slightly.

"But, obviously, that's impossible." With one violent thrust, she pushed the door back open. "Great talk. See you in class."

She stormed straight into the curtain of tulle. She swore as she struggled to pull it aside, growing more and more ensnared in the dark red netting. A thunderous uproar surged across the quad—a chaotic mob of excited, agitated spectators.

The fight had finally broken out.

Makani stopped thrashing. She was trapped, imprisoned even, in this miserable town where she hated everything and everyone. Especially herself.

There was a quiet stir, and she was surprised to discover that Ollie was still behind her. His fingers carefully, gently untangled her from the tulle. It dropped back into a sheet, and they watched their classmates together, in silence, through the blood-colored haze.

CHAPTER THREE

"DID YOU KNOW that Haley girl?" Grandma Young called out from the sofa.

Makani waved goodbye to Darby as he drove away. He honked twice. Her grandmother's house was only a short walk from school, but he always picked her up and dropped her off anyway. Makani lived in Osborne's oldest neighborhood, and Darby lived in its newest. Alex lived on a muddy cow-calf operation near Troy, one town over. She had band practice in the afternoons and carpooled with a girl who played tenor sax. They could all drive, but Darby was the only one with full-time access to a car.

Ollie lived . . . in the country. Makani wasn't sure where. When the fight had ended, he'd gone to the library, and she'd gone back to her friends. Later in Spanish, she'd felt the faint pressure of his stare—it had thrilled her, even though she wished it hadn't—but nothing had actually changed. It felt like it never would.

Makani's heart sank as she locked the front door, further enclosing the scope of her world. "Yeah, I knew Haley. Sort of. Not really."

She kicked off her sneakers and socks and placed them at the bottom of the stairs to carry up to her bedroom later. Shoes were another thing Makani disliked about the Midwest. Apart from the summer months, it was too cold to wear slippers, but her feet always felt heavy in the necessary sneakers and boots. It had taken ages to build the callouses so that they didn't rub her heels into blisters.

Flip-flops, she corrected herself. *Not slippers.*

Regionalisms still tripped her up. *Flip-flops* weren't a big deal. But she cringed every time she heard someone order a *pop* instead of a *soda.*

Her grandmother was perched in front of the television, streaming *Scandal* on Netflix and separating out the edge pieces of a new jigsaw puzzle. Makani flopped into a well-loved easy chair. It had belonged to her granddaddy. Tucking her feet under her legs to keep them toasty, she picked up the cardboard lid. The puzzle was a folk-art design that featured a folksy pumpkin patch, a street of folksy houses, and a stream of trick-or-treaters dressed in folksy costumes. Grandma Young liked to keep things seasonal.

"I'm waiting for the local news to come on," she said.

Makani tossed the lid back onto the coffee table and glanced at her phone. "You still have another hour and a half."

"I want to hear what Creston has to say about all this." Creston Howard was the handsome, black half of the five o'clock news team, and Grandma Young believed his word to be infallible. "The whole thing is *awful.* I hope they catch whoever did it."

"They will," Makani said.

"She was so young, so talented. Just like you."

That last part wasn't true, but Makani knew better than to correct her. She could already hear the beats of their ensuing argument: Makani would deny it; her grandmother would accuse her of negative thinking; Makani would explain that she was simply being honest; her grandmother would press; and then Makani would explode with something like, "You aren't my mother! My own mother is barely my mother! We're not talking about this, okay?"

Instead, Makani scrolled through her phone. She no longer hoped for a text or message or email from Jasmine, her former best friend. And she no longer hoped that, for some miraculous and unlikely reason, everything would go back to the way it had been before. Those hopes had perished a long time ago. It was difficult to pinpoint the exact moment, though perhaps it began when she'd signed the official government document that changed her surname from Kanekalau to Young.

She hadn't taken her mother's maiden name because of the impending divorce. She'd taken it because it wasn't safe to be the easily Google-able Makani Kanekalau anymore, and she'd needed a fresh start in Nebraska.

Still . . . Makani checked her phone.

As usual, there was no word from back home. At least the messages of hate had long stopped. No one there was looking for her, and the only people who still cared about it—*the incident,* as she self-censored that night on the beach—were people like Jasmine. The only people who mattered. Makani would have never guessed that her friends' permanent silence would be infinitely more painful than those weeks when thousands of uninformed, condescending, misogynistic strangers had spewed vitriol at her. It was.

Even without the repeat of their most frequent fight, Grandma Young's voice turned disapproving. "You left the kitchen cabinets open again this morning."

Makani stared harder at her phone. "I'm not the one leaving them open."

"My memory is fine, hon. You'd already left for school when I got out of bed. It's basic manners to tidy up after yourself. I'm not asking for much."

"I didn't even *have* breakfast this morning." Makani couldn't conceal the swell of her frustration. "Have you called your doctor? Like I asked you to?"

"As you're well aware, I haven't had an episode in almost a year."

Makani looked up, and Grandma Young immediately lowered her gaze. It was hard for her grandmother to discuss her weaknesses . . . or have anyone question her version of the truth. They shared this trait. Grandma Young snapped two puzzle pieces together in a way that signaled the end of it as Makani kept staring, wishing that she could push the discussion while recognizing the depths of her own hypocrisy.

Her grandmother was taller than most women of her generation. She had short hair that she had allowed to age, gray with white speckles. It looked beautiful, like the negative of a snowy owl. Makani's paternal grandmother, back in Hawaii, still dyed her hair black. Grandma Kanekalau even used the same color and brand as Alex.

Grandma Young wasn't so harsh. She had soft dark brown skin, a soft figure, and a soft voice, but she spoke with the firmness of a commanding authority. She used to teach American history at the high school. She'd been retired for half a decade, and though Makani was thankful that she would never be subjected to a class taught by her own grandmother, she imagined she'd probably been a good teacher.

Grandma and Granddaddy Young had always been kind in a way that the rest of her family was not. They asked questions. They were attentive. Even before the divorce proceedings began, Makani's parents had been selfish. As a child, Makani had wanted a sibling to keep her company, to adore her, to *care* about her, but it was for the best that her parents had never had another child. They would have ignored him or her, too.

But Makani's banishment to Osborne wasn't just because of her own unspeakable mistake. Grandma Young had also done something bad. Last Thanksgiving, her neighbor caught her sleep-pruning his walnut tree at three in the morning, and when he'd tried to rouse her, she'd lopped off the tip of his nose. She'd been having trouble with sleepwalking since the unexpected death of Makani's grandfather the summer before. Doctors were able to reattach the fleshy nub, and the neighbor didn't sue, but the escalation had alarmed Makani's mother, who persuaded her father that the best solution— to *all* their problems—would be to dispatch their daughter to watch over Grandma Young.

Makani's parents couldn't agree on anything, but they had agreed to send her here. They probably believed the lopping had been serendipitous.

For the most part, Makani didn't think her grandmother needed a babysitter. Not a single hazardous episode had occurred since Makani's arrival. Only in the last few months with the return of these mundane, low-key episodes—open cabinets, misplaced tools, unlocked doors—had Makani realized that she was, indeed, needed.

Usually, it felt good to be needed.

It had backfired only once.

She'd been needed in July. The heat that afternoon had been stifling, the kind of oppressive humidity that lends itself to tank tops, short shorts, and bad decisions.

Makani already had all three covered.

It was the first anniversary of Granddaddy Young's death, and her grandmother wanted to spend the day alone. It was also Wednesday, double-coupon day, so Makani offered to do the weekly shopping in her stead. Greeley's Foods was less than two miles away, on Main Street. It was as plain and boxy as the high school, but with the added charm of lower ceilings and cramped aisles.

Makani couldn't understand why these places didn't expand their premises. There was plenty of room to do it. Unlike coastal Hawaii, rural Nebraska had an abundance of land. It had nothing *but* land. It was a completely different country.

She entered the store with a handwritten list and a recycled envelope stuffed with coupons. They noticed each other right away. He was wearing the green Greeley's apron and restocking the plum tomatoes. Only Ollie Larsson could make an apron look sexy.

Makani wanted to say something. By the way he stared back, she knew *he* wanted to say something. Neither of them said anything.

She wheeled around a rickety cart and filled it with healthy food. Her grandfather had died of a heart attack, so her grandmother had been recently consumed by the gospel of nutrition. As Makani hunted down boxes of steel-cut oats and bags of dried beans, she prickled with the knowledge of Ollie's movements throughout the store. When he switched from stocking the tomatoes to the squash. When he hustled over to aisle five to clean up a broken jar of sweet relish. When he drifted back to produce.

They had never spoken in school. They'd had several classes together, but he kept to himself. Makani wasn't even positive that he'd been aware of her existence before that afternoon. She'd hoped he might switch to working one of the store's three registers, but as she headed toward the checkout lanes, he vanished into the back room.

She couldn't help it. She felt disappointed.

Makani was piling grocery sacks into Grandma Young's early-nineties gold Taurus wagon when she heard the laugh—singular and derisive. She slammed the trunk closed angrily, already knowing that it had something to do with her.

Ollie stared at her from the alleyway beside the store. He was perched on a plastic milk crate, giving all the appearance of a smoke break, except instead of a cigarette, he was holding a book loosely between his fingers.

"You think my grandma's car is funny?" she asked.

An unorthodox smile grew on his lips. He let it sit between them for several long seconds before speaking. "I'm not sure why I'd make fun of yours when *that's* mine." He pointed at a white vehicle parked on the other side of the lot.

It was a decommissioned police cruiser. The force's crest had been scraped off, and it didn't have the light bar on top, but Makani recognized it from school. Everyone knew that Ollie drove a police car—a gift most likely bestowed upon him by his older brother, a cop—and their classmates ragged him about it mercilessly. Makani suspected he kept driving it just to prove that he didn't give a shit.

"So, why were you laughing at me?" she asked.

Ollie rubbed the back of his neck. "Not you. Me."

Makani didn't know if it was the summer swelter or the culmination of seven months of unrelenting tedium, but she sensed . . . *something*. She walked toward him, slowly. Her bare legs shone. "And why were you laughing at yourself, Ollie?"

He watched her approach, because it was clear that she wanted him to watch. He waited to reply. When she stopped before him, he tilted up his head and shielded his eyes from the sun. "Because I wanted to speak to you earlier, but I was too nervous. *Makani.*"

So, he knew who she was.

She smiled.

Ollie stood up from the milk crate, and his silver lip ring glinted in the sunlight. She wondered how it would feel between her own lips. It had been too long since she'd kissed anyone. Since anyone had wanted to kiss her. *Get a hold of yourself.* Makani took a physical step backward, because it was impossible to converse when they were standing that close. Chest to chest. And she was, above all things, intrigued by Ollie.

She nodded at his paperback. "I never see you without a book."

He held it up so that she could see its cover: a cluster of men hanging out the doors and windows of a moving train. She didn't recognize it, so he explained. "It's about an American who travels from London to Southeast Asia by train."

"Is it a true story?"

He nodded.

"Do you read a lot of true stories?"

"I read a lot of travelogues. I like reading about other places."

"I get it." Her smile returned. "I like thinking about other places."

Ollie stared at her mouth for a moment, distracted. "Any place but this one," he finally said. But it was clear that he was referring to the greater Osborne, and not this very specific place beside Greeley's Foods—this place that contained her.

"Exactly," she said.

He leaned against the brick wall and melted back into the shade. She couldn't tell if he was trying to regain his disinterested cool or if he was simply shy. "You're from Hawaii, right? Are you going back there after graduation?"

Makani's heart stuttered. She searched his eyes—such a searing blue—but it was unlikely that he knew. The Hawaiian media had withheld her name, though that hadn't stopped *social* media. It hadn't stopped her from needing to change her name.

"I'm not sure," she said cautiously. "What about you? Where do you want to go?"

Ollie shrugged. "Doesn't matter. Anywhere, so long as it's not here."

"What's keeping you from leaving now?" She was genuinely curious. A lot of their classmates never made it to graduation.

"My brother. And the money." He gestured at his apron. "I've been working here since I was fourteen. That's when they'll let you bag groceries."

She'd never heard of someone her age holding down a job for that long. "Jesus. That's . . . three years? Four?"

"I would have started earlier if they'd let me."

Makani glanced behind them at the desolate Main Street. Greeley's Foods faced a meager row of mismatched awnings—a tanning salon, a real estate office, an upholsterer, and a bridal shop that still had prom dresses in its window display. She'd never been through any of their doors. "I wish I could get a job."

"No," he said. "You don't."

His conviction irritated her. She'd wanted to apply at the Feed 'N' Seed, where Darby and Alex both worked, but she'd been firmly denied. "I do. But according to my parents, my job is to take care of my grandmother."

Ollie frowned. "Does she need help? She's always seemed fine to me."

Makani was startled . . . until she realized that he must see her grandmother here at the store. Grandma Young was notable enough; few black people lived in Osborne. His brother had probably even had her as a teacher. "She *is* fine," she said, sliding into her usual half-truth. "My parents are just using her as an excuse."

"For what?"

"For sending me four thousand miles away. Parents are the fucking worst, you know?" Her regret was instantaneous. It wasn't fair to say things like that in front of someone who didn't have any parents at all. She winced. "Sorry."

Ollie stared at the asphalt for several beats. When his gaze returned upward, his expression was detached, but she could still see a struggle underneath. It wasn't difficult for her to imagine how awful it would be to live in a town where everyone, even the new girl, knew that a drunk driver had killed your parents when you were in middle school, and that your brother had moved back home from Omaha to raise you.

He shrugged. "It's okay."

"No, I'm really sorry. It was a shitty thing to say."

"And I'm sorry that your parents are the fucking worst."

Makani wasn't sure how to respond—*Was that a joke?*—so when Ollie's mouth split into a grin, her heart skipped like a scratched vinyl record. She didn't want to ruin the moment. "All right, all right. I'd better get home." She strolled back to her car and shook her head. But as she opened the door, she called out, "See you next week, Ollie."

Ollie bit his lip. "See you next week, Makani."

There was nothing else to think about, so, for the next six days, Makani thought exclusively about Ollie. She thought about his lips and her lips and pressing them together. Pressing *more* than their lips together. She entered a fever state. She hadn't had a boyfriend since moving to Nebraska. Makani pleaded with her grandmother to let her take over the grocery shopping. She tested out words like *responsibility* and *maturity* and strung together other words like *valuable, learning,* and *experience.* She won.

When Makani pulled back into the lot, Ollie was sitting on the same milk crate. He was reading a book and eating a red Popsicle. Makani went straight toward him. He stood. His expression didn't give anything away, but she felt the truth of it in her bones: Ollie had been waiting for her.

She stepped inside his personal space.

Ollie bit his lower lip over the silver ring. It slowly slipped back out.

When he wordlessly offered her the Popsicle, she went for his mouth instead, because she'd long ago—six days ago—decided that being forward was the best way to approach a guy with his sort of reputation. Their first kiss was wet. Cold tongue and sugary fruit. *Cherry,* Makani thought. His piercing was warm from the summer sun. The surgical-steel hoop pushed against her lips. It felt dangerous.

The Popsicle hit the asphalt behind them in a frozen, quiet *thump.*

They made out there, in the alleyway, every Wednesday for the next three weeks. The fourth week, it rained. They moved into the backseat of her grandmother's car. This additional barrier of privacy led to the next natural stage.

"Hands," she explained later to her friends. "Not mouths."

"Could you make it sound any more disgusting?" Darby said.

"But it's an important distinction," Alex said. "They got each other off, but their clothes were still on. And their heads were still above sea level."

Makani made a face. "Never mind. I'm not even sure why I told you."

On the fifth Wednesday—the last before school began—the sky was clear, but Ollie slid into her car anyway, and she drove them someplace private.

It was a cornfield, of course.

They had sex, of course.

"Are you guys ever gonna go out? You know, for real?" Darby asked her that night. "Or is this just going . . . to end?"

It ended the next week. Before the first bell on the first day of school, their eyes locked across campus. Ollie's expression was unreadable. That purposeful, standoffish blankness. The truth hit Makani like an ugly slap. *No,* they had never discussed going out. She didn't even have his number. This summer had been a secret thing, a *dateless* thing, which meant that one of them—or both of them—was ashamed of it.

Makani wasn't ashamed. Confused, yes. But not ashamed.

So, it was Ollie, then.

Makani narrowed her eyes. Ollie narrowed his. *Did he know?* Had he somehow found out about that night on the beach? Now he'd act as if they'd never known each other. Shame returned to Makani full force.

So did humiliation. And rage. She refused to look at *him* anymore, and she never returned to Greeley's. She pleaded for her grandmother to resume grocery duty, claiming that school took up too much of her time. It didn't. Makani had been judged and put back in her place, but she was still bored as hell.

As she pointlessly rechecked her phone, battling two measly bars of pitifully weak service, Makani wondered if boredom had also contributed to her reapproaching Ollie at lunch. Had she really sunk that low?

Probably. Shit.

"Oh, shoot," Grandma Young said. A spinning circle blocked the television screen, and Olivia Pope had stopped talking mid-sentence. "I called the cable company just last week, but they said we're already getting their highest-speed package."

Makani pictured her beachside bungalow in Hawaii, where the internet only went out in the worst tropical storms. Where her phone always had full bars. Why couldn't landlocked Osborne figure this out? Why was *everything* so damned difficult here?

They turned off Netflix, and Makani grabbed her shoes and trudged upstairs to do homework. When she returned downstairs at five, Creston Howard said nothing new in a way that reassured Grandma Young but made Makani want to punch him in the jaw. It was all very unsurprising. They'd both already seen the footage online: the Whitehalls' crime-scene taped farmhouse, Haley's father stumbling, head down, into the police station for questioning, and Haley herself, flying around the stage last year as Peter Pan.

"Tonight, Osborne grieves for Haley Madison Whitehall," Creston said, ending the segment with a solemn head tilt. "It's a sad day for a sad community."

Grandma Young nodded as Makani's nose wrinkled with distaste. Neither her grandmother nor Creston seemed to realize that he'd insulted the entire town. At least he wasn't wrong. Sad *did* describe it.

But then she felt bad again, because a girl was dead, and it really was sad.

CHAPTER FOUR

MAKANI'S MIND CHURNED with restlessness as she helped her grandmother cook dinner. It was one of her daily chores. When Makani moved in, Grandma Young had posted a list of daily and weekly chores on the refrigerator under a magnet that read: YOU CAN'T SCARE ME. I TEACH HIGH SCHOOL. She claimed Makani needed structure. This was true, even Makani knew it was true, but it still sucked. Sometimes she felt like a child. Sometimes she felt like a caregiver. She didn't want to be either of those things.

Tonight, they prepared a heart-healthy meal of baked turkey meatballs and a simple salad with vinaigrette. It was beyond depressing. Makani lusted for flavor and fat. *Lime-topped papaya. Kalbi ribs. Poi with lomi salmon.* If she could, she'd spend her every cent on a plate lunch—steamed rice, mac salad, and an entrée. *Chicken katsu. Teri beef. Kalua pig.* Her mouth watered, and her soul ached.

Sometimes dinner was the hardest.

They'd only just sat down at the table when her phone dinged. Grandma Young aimed a lethal sigh at the heavens. Makani yanked the phone from her pocket to silence its ringer, and a text from an unknown number lit the screen: *I could say the same thing about you.* Her chest cavity froze into spiny shards of ice.

A second text appeared: *What did you mean when you said that?*

"How many times do I have to tell you? No phones at the dinner table."

Makani's head shot up. "Sorry," she said automatically.

But her grandmother was taken aback by her expression. "Who was that?"

"Mom," Makani lied.

Grandma Young examined the bait. She would have never okayed a dinnertime chat with Makani's father, whom she'd never particularly liked, but she remained hopeful that her daughter would make amends with her granddaughter. "Do you need to call her now or can it wait?"

"I'll be right back, sorry." Makani stumbled from the dining room into the kitchen, where her grandmother couldn't see her, and reread the texts. Her heart floundered, trapped in the narrow space between fear and hope. She couldn't imagine this was *him,* but . . . it couldn't be anyone else. Could it?

who's asking?

The reply was instantaneous: *Ollie.*

Her heartbeat exploded into a race. She stared at the screen, waiting for him to say more. Finally, she texted: *don't remember giving you my number*

Another quick reply: *Tell me what you meant.*

It figured that Ollie was the sort of exasperating person who would text in complete sentences *and* ignore her question.

what do you THINK I meant??

I think you feel slighted, which means there's been a misunderstanding.

Slighted. Seriously, nobody normal talked like this. But he had her attention. Makani texted back a single question mark. She watched the three dots appear and disappear on her phone as Ollie typed, paused, and then resumed typing.

The text arrived: *I thought you were ashamed of me. And I'm guessing you thought that I was ashamed of you.*

Makani's eyebrows shot to her forehead. Directness like this was rare. Admirable, even. The eternal question reemerged from the gloaming. *Does he know what I did?* It was impossible to tell without more information, but a disconcerting inkling crawled through her gut, prodding her forward. Maybe he knew. But maybe she'd been wrong. Maybe, out of the two of them, she was the one who had cast judgment.

Makani replied: *why did you think that?*

Well. We never exactly talked, did we?

didn't think you were the talking type

I didn't think you were, either.

Makani paused. Her grandmother cleared her throat—a little too loudly—in the next room. Makani texted: *so . . . you want to talk*

I want to talk if you want to talk.

She should be annoyed, but she wasn't. Not in the least.

"Makani," her grandmother warned.

"I'll be right there. Almost done."

"You aren't even talking!"

"We're texting."

"That's not talking. You need to *talk* to your mama."

Makani grinned as she sent another message: *texting isn't talking*

Her phone rang, and she jumped. "Shit!"

"MAKANI YOUNG."

Makani winced as she answered. "This isn't a good time. I'll call you later, okay?" She hung up before Ollie could respond and slunk back to her dining room chair.

Grandma Young tracked every movement. "That wasn't your mother."

Makani shoveled an entire dry meatball into her mouth. Like a child.

"Give me your phone."

Makani stiffened in alarm. "Why?" she asked, muffled through the ground turkey.

"You heard me. I want to see who you were texting."

"Fine, it was Alex." She swallowed. "I was texting Alex."

Her grandmother held out her hand, palm up.

"Fine! It was a guy, okay? Are you happy now?"

Her grandmother paused, considering her options. "What's his name?"

"Grandma—"

"Don't *Grandma* me. What's his name?"

"Ollie. Oliver Larsson." Makani already knew to add his last name. People in this town always wanted a last name.

Her grandmother frowned. "Larsson. Isn't he that young cop?"

"That's his brother, Chris. Ollie is in my grade."

Grandma Young considered this, and Makani prayed that she'd never heard the rumors about Ollie. Prayed that being the brother of a cop was a *good* thing in this town. At last, her grandmother relaxed. The slightest bit. "He was my student, Chris. A nice young man. It's such a shame what happened to their parents."

Makani also relaxed. The slightest bit.

"If you want to continue seeing Oliver, I'll have to meet him."

"*Grandma.* We were only texting."

"And then your phone rang." She pointed her salad fork at Makani, a statement and an accusation. "That boy is after you."

• • •

Makani sent the text after her grandmother had gone to bed: *is now a good time?*

Curiosity fed her anxiety. The prospect of talking to Ollie was the first exciting thing that had happened to her since, well, *fooling around* with Ollie. She stared at her phone as she paced the carpeted floor, willing it to make a noise. Who didn't keep their phone beside them at all times? But it stayed silent on her dresser.

The dresser and the rest of the furnishings had once belonged to her mother. Makani had moved into her mother's childhood bedroom. The matching set of bulky oaken furniture was an unappealing shade of golden orange. The bed was too tall, its bedposts too severe. They spiraled toward the ceiling like sharpened tusks. The dresser was heavy and long, and the mirror was equally large and repulsive. But the desk. The desk was a behemoth. It made Makani's laptop look avant-garde, as if the wood had been joined together so long ago that it had never before known a personal computer.

It was the opposite of how her mother lived now. Despite the laid-back beach environment, her house was streamlined and stainless steel. Makani had always felt that her mother's tastes left something warm to be desired, something *comforting,* but this wasn't any better. It was completely void of personality.

Her grandparents must have selected the furniture, and in the years since her mother had left, they'd removed any pictures or posters that might have provided insight into her mother's teenage years. In their place were framed elementary- and middle school–aged photographs of Makani and bland paintings of prairie lands. The solitary lingering trace of her mother was an old carving inside the desk's top drawer: SOS.

It wasn't often that Makani understood her mother, but she certainly understood the quiet desperation behind this lone act of vandalism.

Since moving in, Makani had taken down the photos of herself—*hideous*—and shoved them under the bed. Only a few items from her former life were on display. She kept a pretty bowl of coral pieces and cowrie shells on the desk, her stuffed bear and stuffed whale on the bed, and her jewelry on the dresser, neatly hung on a stand that looked like a tree. But mainly she kept things in drawers. Hidden away.

Makani checked her phone again, in case she'd temporarily lost her hearing. Still nothing. It was getting late.

A sudden rustling outside disturbed the quiet night.

She moved to her window and peered down into the shadows. The next-door neighbor's sleek tomcat—not the neighbor who'd lost the tip of his nose, the one on the other side—often hunted in their yard. Makani had never been allowed to have a cat or a dog. Someday, when she had her own place, she'd have both.

More rustling. Makani squinted through the darkness.

The sound was coming from the overgrown viburnum below her window. She craned her neck, trying to see the bush, trying to see *through* it. A burst of furious, quick agitation startled her. And then . . . silence. The cat must have found a vole.

Makani pressed her face against the glass, cupping her eyes with her hands like binoculars, shielding them from her bedroom light. She waited for the cat to trot across the lawn with its prize, but the lawn, illuminated by a triangle of orange streetlight, remained empty. It held nothing more interesting than falling leaves.

She returned to her phone. Nothing had changed there, either.

Makani glanced back at the window. For reasons she couldn't explain, she felt an unsettling tingle of exposure. She crept toward the glass and peeked out from the side.

The neighborhood was still deserted.

Hello, paranoia, my old friend.

She closed the curtains, grabbed her phone, and carried it to bed, where she laid it beside her on the ivory-colored eyelet comforter, another relic from her grandparents. She tried to study for a Spanish test, but she was distracted. Why did Ollie think that she'd be ashamed to be seen with him? Because of those rumors? If that were the case, then he probably *didn't* know about her own transgressions, otherwise he would have known that she wasn't in a position to point fingers.

Maybe they stood a chance. Maybe they'd even have a real date. After all, he'd been desperate enough to hunt down her phone number.

Even though he'd ignored her question about how he'd gotten it.

Her brow was still pinched as she pushed aside her textbook for the latest issue of *Rolling Stone*. Makani didn't normally bother with paper magazines, but she'd been unable to resist when she saw Amphetamine on its cover. Their scandalous song about an underage girl who'd broken the heart of the lead singer—supposedly based on someone real, according to the article—was a huge hit. Makani felt both the anger and the ecstasy of the song's catchy lyrics. She wondered if she'd broken Ollie's heart last summer. Had he broken hers? Or had it already been too broken to make a difference?

Her phone dinged. She scrambled to pick it up, dropping it twice in her haste and excitement.

It was a picture of an enormous, hairy, white male ass. Makani groaned and tossed the phone aside without replying. She didn't feel like indulging Alex in one of her favorite games. Alex liked to steal her and Darby's phones, type "hairy butts" into Google Images, and then slip their phones back to them. When they weren't at school, Alex texted the pictures at random.

Her phone dinged again at 11:31. It was him.

I was at work, but I'm home now. Are you still awake?

A primal panic flooded her system. Should she wait before

replying? *No,* that would be stupid. Silence got them into this mess
in the first place.

Ollie answered after the first ring. "Hey, sorry about that call earlier. I was on my break, but I guess that was a bad time?"

Makani's voice was cool. "How did you get my number?"

"Oh." Ollie sounded startled. "Uh, yeah. Sorry. My brother. He
can, you know . . . get things. Information."

It was his second apology in seconds. And he'd asked Chris for
help, which meant he'd at least told his brother *something* about her.
A smile grew on her lips, but she said, "That's a little creepy."

There was a long pause.

"I'm kidding." Makani laughed, pretending to be more composed
than she actually was. "I mean, don't get me wrong. It's still creepy.
You should have asked *me* for my number. But . . . I'm glad to be
talking to you."

His voice loosened on the other end. "Me too."

"So."

"So."

Her fingers picked at the comforter's eyelets, but she spoke her next
line flirtatiously. "So, you still work the Wednesday shift at Greeley's."

He laughed once. "I do. Though I can't help but notice that you
don't come around anymore."

"Yeah, there's this real asshole who works there. He acts like I'm
invisible whenever I see him at school."

"Interesting. Because there's an asshole at school who's been ignoring me, too."

Makani thrilled at the ease of their banter, but her laughter dwindled with an uneasy twinge of regret. "That was pretty lame of us,
huh? Assuming."

Ollie agreed without elaboration. "Monumentally."

"Could we speak clearly for a moment?" she asked.

"I'd like us to speak clearly for all moments—present and future."

Makani almost smiled, but the gesture vanished before fully arriving. Her voice hardened. "Look, I only want to keep talking to you if you want this to happen in a real way. If you want to, like, hang out with me. If you only want to fuck me, I'm out."

"Whoa." Ollie exhaled. "No. *No.* That was never *only* what I wanted. It just happened. I have no idea how that happened."

"We're equally to blame. I think that's been established," she said wryly.

Their phones filled with another tense silence.

"So," he ventured, "speaking clearly . . . you like me?"

"Speaking clearly . . . yes."

A respectful pause. Or perhaps Ollie was catching his breath again. "Speaking clearly . . . I like you, too."

It had been so long since Makani had felt any amount of genuine, unadulterated happiness that she'd forgotten that sometimes it could hurt as much as sadness. His declaration pierced through the muscle of her heart like a skillfully thrown knife.

It was the kind of pain that made her feel alive.

CHAPTER FIVE

THEY TALKED FOR hours. Until Makani's hands were cramped from gripping her phone and even the singing crickets had gone to bed. His obliviousness to her past was a relief. They needed to speak clearly, yes. But only about the things that needed to be spoken about.

His parents had been farmers, and the family had been tight-knit. About a month after the accident, the police gave his brother, who'd just been hired, the old cruiser to replace the car that had been totaled. It was a generous gift. When Ollie turned sixteen, Chris had given him the cruiser as a birthday present. Ollie despised the Crown Vic and the loss that it represented, but he drove it out of respect for his brother. And his need for a car. He talked about his relationship with Chris—strained, parental, loving, frustrating—and she talked about her relationship with her grandmother. Which was the same.

"What happened to your grandparents?" Makani's house was dark and filled with old shadows. She curled up under her covers. "Why didn't they take you in?"

"Half of them are dead, and the other half are drunks." The timbre of Ollie's voice was lower than usual. It was quiet and gravelly with the night. "So, when a guy with a blood-alcohol concentration that was twice the legal limit killed our parents . . . you can see why Chris fought to be my guardian."

Makani didn't like her parents. But she did love them, and she could only imagine how shattering it must have been, must *continue* to be, for Ollie to have lost both of his in the same senseless act. They'd been on their way home from an errand at the Feed 'N' Seed, the same location where Darby and Alex now worked. Their car was struck in the broad daylight of a random Tuesday afternoon. Something about it being daytime heightened the tragedy in Makani's mind.

"How did your mom wind up in Hawaii?" Ollie asked.

"She left here right after graduation. She had this *grandiose plan*— that's what she always called it—to travel through all fifty states before picking a new home. She even had this foldout map that she'd stolen from a bookstore in Norfolk. She still has it. She showed it to me once, and there was just this big, black X through Nebraska."

"So, what happened?"

"She used all her savings to go to Hawaii first. She got a job at a resort, enrolled in community college, and then met my dad."

"A *grandiose plan*. Maybe that's what I need."

Makani made a sound between a huff and a snort. "Only if you can follow through. To me, it's just another story about my mom's failures."

"It's not about Hawaii being so great that she didn't need to see her other options?"

"No."

"I always follow through on my plans," he assured her.

•   •   •

He proved it only a few hours later. Makani was slumped inside Darby's car before school, seething with sleep-deprived irritation. She'd been excited to tell her friends about the call, but they weren't reacting in the way that she'd hoped.

"Of course he *gets* you," Alex said from the backseat. "You're both poor little orphans."

"I'm not an orphan," Makani grumped.

"I still can't believe you have to introduce him to your grandma," Darby said. "How did he react when you told him?"

"I didn't." Makani tried to ignore the squirming in her gut as she scanned the parking lot for Ollie. A trail of students was heading toward the corner by the road, where a memorial for Haley—flowers and cards and playbills and candles—had appeared overnight in front of the school's sign. In black changeable letters, its marquee read: WE LOVE YOU, HALEY. YOUR STAR STILL BURNS BRIGHT. "I wanted to make sure everything was okay first," she said. "You know, in person."

"It's every grandmother's dream." Alex raised her palms into sarcastic jazz hands. "A social outcast who screws her granddaughter, ignores her for months, and then illegally obtains her phone number!"

Makani winced. "You know it's not like that."

"It's exactly like that," Alex said.

"It *is* creepy how he got your number," Darby said.

"You don't think it's romantic?" Makani asked.

"No," Darby and Alex replied together.

"He should have asked you for it," Darby continued. "You would have given it to him."

"Well, I'm just glad I didn't wake up my grandma. You're right that she wouldn't have liked discovering me on the phone with a guy in the middle of the night." Makani paused, detecting the ideal opportunity for a subject change. "Although, a part of me wishes I actually *had* woken her up. I think she's sleepwalking again."

"Oh, man." Alex arched her back in a catlike stretch and yawned. "What'd your g-ma do this time? Use the hair dryer as a toaster?"

Darby laughed at the word *g-ma*. Alex gave him a wink in the rearview mirror.

"It was the kitchen cabinets again, all of them," Makani said. "I found them wide-open this morning. That's two days in a row and the fourth time this month. She needs to go to a sleep clinic, but I don't know how to convince her."

"Ever wonder what she's looking for at night?" Darby asked.

"A book on self-defense for her granddaughter," Alex said.

A loud rap on the window behind Darby made him shriek. They jumped in their seats. When they realized who it was, Darby and Alex goggled at Makani.

Makani's skin flushed with heat. "Let him in, let him in."

The locks weren't automatic, so Alex leaned over to open the door. Ollie popped in beside her with a blast of cold morning air.

"Sorry," he said. "I didn't mean to scare you."

Three sets of eyes blinked at him. Somehow, Makani had already forgotten that his hair was pink. She'd been picturing him last night in bed as a blond.

He glanced between Darby and Alex with visible nervousness. "I thought . . . Makani would have told you?"

"She did," Darby said, though he still sounded baffled.

Alex smiled like a witch in a fairy tale. "We know everything."

The undertone of Ollie's skin began to match his hair as Makani continued to gape. "What are you *doing* here?" she asked.

The pink bloomed until his entire head became a single color. It was the rare moment in which she could read his expression with complete certainty: Ollie wanted to rewind this video until he was out of the car and safely back on the other side of the lot. His hand crept toward the door handle. "You said you wanted . . . to hang out."

"I did." Makani shook her head before changing it to an emphatic nod. "I did."

She felt her friends staring at them with wide, soap-opera eyes as she emerged from the stupor of confusion. For the first time, Makani realized that Ollie's appearance and demeanor weren't merely acts of rebellion. They were armor for his shyness. It must have been so difficult for *him* to have approached *her*—without the protective barrier of his phone and in the company of her friends, no less.

Makani infused her next words with as much kindness as possible. "You just caught us off guard. That's all." And then she flashed him her fullest, most high-wattage smile. A long time ago, she'd been known for it. "I'm glad you're here."

"Me too," Darby said. Because he was good like that.

"Next time," Alex said sharply, "bring doughnuts."

Ollie risked a glance at her.

"I like the ones with chocolate frosting," she said.

Ollie settled back into the version of himself that he shared with the rest of the world. His eyebrows rose slightly, and his voice flattened. "Who doesn't?"

"Makani likes maple. Darby likes plain glazed."

Ollie jokingly booed his response, which made Alex kick the back of Makani's and Darby's seats. "See? I've always told you, you're crazy."

It was an olive branch, of sorts, and Makani was able to breathe again. Until Alex refocused her attention.

"So, Buscemi," Alex said. "What's the inside scoop?"

Ollie's eyebrows rose a little further.

"Steve Buscemi played Mr. Pink in *Reservoir Dogs*."

"I'm familiar with it," he said. "But the character wasn't named after his hair color."

Alex didn't care. "What's the scoop, Buscemi?"

He seemed wary by her vagueness. "About . . ."

"*Haley.*"

He shifted. Almost imperceptibly. "Why would you ask me about her?"

Alex punched his shoulder, and Ollie grimaced, unused to her intense style of questioning. "Your brother is a cop," she said. "So, what are the police saying about her case?"

Darby sighed. "Ignore her. She has no tact."

Ollie rubbed the offended shoulder. "Chris doesn't discuss his work with me."

"But he does give you the very personal and private phone number of our dear friend Makani Young?"

"*Alex,*" Makani warned. Sometimes it was difficult to be Alex's dear friend.

Alex scooted closer to Ollie, ignoring his physical discomfort. The knees of her ripped fishnets pressed against his thighs. "Just tell us this. Was your brother at the scene?"

Ollie forced his body into a wider position, which forced Alex back to her side. "Actually." His voice remained measured. "It should have been the sheriff's jurisdiction, because it happened out of city limits. But her dad's a hunting buddy of Chief Pilger, so he contacted him directly. The whole department was called out an hour later."

Makani imagined dozens of uniformed officers storming the cornfields. "The whole department?"

"The whole department is five people," Ollie said.

"Is it true about her throat?" Alex asked. "Three slashes in a smiley face?"

Makani fought the urge to scold her again.

"Worse," Ollie said. "Five deep cuts. The eyes of the smiley were Xs."

Darby shuddered. "Like . . . dead cartoon eyes?"

Ollie nodded once. "The killer probably took a lot of pleasure in the act. Her vocal cords were slashed. The police think it might have been intentional."

Miniscule hairs rose on the back of Makani's neck. *Dead cartoon eyes.*

But Alex straightened as she recalled a favorite theory. "They think the killer was angry because Haley could sing? That it was someone who was jealous of her talent?"

"Or," Ollie said, "maybe she said something that she shouldn't have said."

"Drugs." Darby bounced as he turned toward the backseat. "It's always drugs. Maybe she stumbled across someone's meth lab and was going to rat them out!" And then he immediately looked appalled with himself for encouraging the conversation.

These same opposing energies—guilt and curiosity—were also twisting inside Makani, but Ollie only shrugged. "They don't know much of anything yet. And there wasn't any evidence left behind. At least, none that they've found so far."

Curiosity won. "Was she . . . was Haley . . . violated?"

"No," Ollie said.

"Thank God." Makani and Darby said it together. Makani was relieved that Haley hadn't suffered through that, too.

"She was found in bed, but it doesn't look like the killer physically touched any part of her," Ollie said. "Or that she touched him. The police aren't even sure if the person was male. She didn't have any bruises, and there wasn't anything under her fingernails—no skin or fibers snagged from scratching or fighting."

Makani considered this. "So, Haley was taken by surprise."

"Maybe. Or maybe she knew her killer."

"Or maybe both," Alex said, and they all nodded like sages. She crossed her arms, triumphant and smug. "I *knew* you'd have insider information."

The wrinkles deepened in Ollie's brow. "That's *all* I know. Seriously. And you're aware that you can't tell anyone any of this, correct?"

"Please." Alex brushed him off. "The only people I'd tell are already in this car."

Darby reached into the backseat and squeezed Alex's chipped-black, nail-polished hands. "I love you, too."

Something else was bothering Makani. "How do you know all this if your brother doesn't discuss his work with you?"

Ollie shrugged. "Overheard conversations." But when she didn't look convinced, he added sheepishly. "And . . . I read his files when he's asleep."

Her eyebrows lifted in surprise.

Alex scooted back toward him. "Does Haley's dad have an alibi?"

"I have no idea," he said.

"Sure you do."

"I told you that's all I know."

"Okay, so find out."

Ollie finally laughed, glancing at Makani. "Yeah. Sure."

Laughter was the best response whenever Alex was this relentless. Makani dared to feel a cinder of hope. Through the windshield, two fragile-looking girls passed by carrying a bundle of white balloons. Tears streamed down their cheeks.

"Are they in the musical?" Makani asked.

"I don't think so," Darby said.

Makani's heartbeat stumbled with an uncomfortable realization. "Did any of you guys bring something?"

Ollie and Alex shook their heads as Darby removed a sheet of cardstock folded in half from his backpack. He'd drawn a heart on the front of it with a glittery red pen. "I made this last night, but I left room for your names, if you want."

Always reliable, Darby had remembered. Alex fished out a ballpoint and scribbled her name beside his. She offered the card and pen to Ollie. Taken aback—perhaps even touched—he printed his name at the bottom in small capital letters.

Ollie held out the card and pen to Makani.

As she stared at the glittery heart, guilt oozed through her brain's every fold and crevice. She'd never spoken to Haley when she was alive. Makani hated gossip, yet she'd been speculating about the girl's life and dissecting her death as if they were seated at the table of one of those murder-mystery dinner parties. She didn't deserve to sign the card, because it had never occurred to her that Haley might *need* a card.

"Makani?" Ollie sounded concerned.

Her vision swam as she accepted the card and pen. She signed because her friends were watching. The signature felt fraudulent.

They abandoned the car and joined the crowd. As Darby placed their card atop the mound of depressing tokens, Makani wondered who would collect these gifts, and when. Would Haley's parents feel pressured to bring everything home, or would it all stay here so long that the cards and posters and teddy bears became weather battered, only suitable for the landfill?

Students from every social group paid their respects: the drama and choir geeks, of course, but also the athletes and academics, the gamers and techies, the FFA and rodeo kids. Multiple youth groups prayed together as a single unit. The student-council president handed out flyers for a candlelight vigil, while the burnouts hovered along the edges, stoned and uncomfortable, but needing to mourn with the rest of their community.

Meanwhile, Makani pretended to be upset for the same reasons as her classmates. She pretended that the local news van, parked near the flag at half-mast, hadn't broken her into a sweat. She pretended that she was cold when she put up the hood of her hoodie and angled her face away from the cameras. She pretended to belong.

Despite unbelieving glances from the student body, Ollie rejoined them at lunch. Makani had invited him, but she was still astonished when he sat down, cross-legged, beside her. He was making an effort. It lifted her mood, even though the ensuing conversation was awkward. Ollie ate his sandwich in silence. Makani could only hope that her friends would be as patient with him as they'd been with her.

At least his presence released her from being the third wheel. Darby and Alex had never purposefully treated Makani like a charity case, but she was still the intruder on their decade-long best friendship. It didn't matter that this new fourth wheel was shaky. Makani felt steadier with Ollie there, because he was there for her.

He didn't stay. With ten minutes left in the period, he mumbled an excuse and took off for the library. His exit was so hasty that Makani didn't even get the chance to say goodbye. She shot an apologetic look to her friends and then chased after him.

"Hey. *Hey.*" Makani grabbed his sleeve. "Are you okay?"

Ollie searched for an excuse. "Yeah. I just . . ."

"No worries. I get it." And Makani was pretty sure that she did. Sometimes the pressure of a situation was too much, and you just had to run.

Ollie fidgeted with the zipper of his black hoodie. He glanced at the mostly male group of gamers and techies sitting nearby on the ground—staring at them, whispering—and narrowed his gaze. They stopped talking. He turned back to Makani and nodded.

She rolled her eyes.

He smiled.

Her confidence resurged. The anxious fog slipped away. She smoothed down his sleeve where she'd grabbed it and looked up at him through her dark lashes. "So, what are you doing after school today?"

His eyebrows lifted. "Giving you a ride home?"

Makani flashed another smile as she strutted away. "Good answer," she called out. It was the perfect parting line. Until the jerks beside them had to ruin it. "Good answer," one of them mimicked, and the others laughed.

Makani stopped. "Excuse me?"

Rodrigo Morales, a shortish guy with intense eyes and enormous headphones draped around his neck, seemed startled to be called out. His recovery was quick. "I'll give you a ride home, sweetheart."

"Ugh," one of his two female friends said.

"She's right." Makani crossed her arms. "Ugh."

"Oh, I can give you *both* a ride," Rodrigo said with misplaced swagger, and the other female threw a hamburger bun at his head.

"That'd be the only thing worse than walking," another friend said drily. His name was David, and he was a scrawny senior in an oversize T-shirt with a bright green Minecraft Creeper on it. The whole group burst into howls of laughter.

"Aw, shut up." But Rodrigo's embarrassed anger was directed at David, and it prompted a volley of outrageous insults between them.

Makani wasn't sure when Ollie had returned to her side. She was grateful that he'd noticed and was willing to help, but she was even more grateful that Rodrigo had already forgotten. They glanced at each other, self-consciously.

"See you later?" she said.

"Later," he agreed.

She escaped to the other side of the quad and inclined her head in the gamers' direction. "What do you see in that guy, anyway?" she asked Alex, who'd been harboring inexplicable feelings for Rodrigo since August.

Alex shrugged. "What? He's cute. And he's really smart."

"He's immature."

"He'll grow up." She grinned and added, "I'll help him."

"That requires speaking to him first," Darby said.

"We *speak*. We speak to each other all the time in physics."

Darby scoffed. "Like yesterday, when you blasted him for miscalculating that one equation? That had to be the first answer he's ever gotten wrong."

"Thus, the blasting."

"Poor Rodrigo." Makani's curls bounced as she shook her head. "It's hard being the unrequited crush of Alexandra Shimerda."

"I'm telling you, there's something between us."

Darby patted her leg condescendingly. Alex slapped his hand away, but they were laughing as the bell rang. Its shrill waves reverberated off the flat buildings, and they groaned as they collected their belongings.

Makani tossed her empty soda-fountain cup into the recycle bin. "Darby, I won't need a ride today. Ollie's taking me home."

Darby paused, mid-putting on his backpack, to exchange a look with Alex.

That was all it took. Makani's jaw clenched. She was the third wheel again, and it was clear that the first two wheels had been talking about her. "What? *What?*"

For once, Alex was reluctant to speak. Darby cleared his throat for the delicate attempt. "It's just . . . you haven't lived here as long as we have," he said. "We don't know if Ollie *really* almost drowned, or if he *really* sleeps with the lowlifes at the Red Spot, but there's definitely something . . . not right there. Not since his parents died."

Alex tugged on her skirt's frayed hem. "We don't want you to get hurt."

"Hurt again," Darby said.

Makani's hands trembled. "You don't know him."

"Neither do you," he said.

"So, what? A fucked-up thing happened to him, and then maybe he made some mistakes. But maybe he didn't. And if he did, who cares? Does that mean he doesn't deserve a second chance?"

Alex took a step back. "Whoa. Where's this coming from?"

Makani shoved her hands in her pockets and balled them into fists. "He's driving me five minutes to my front door. I'll be fine." She wasn't sure if they could hear her as she stormed away, or if she even wanted them to hear her. She rephrased it, wrapping the words around herself against the chill of the October wind. "I'm fine."

CHAPTER SIX

OLLIE HELD OPEN the passenger-side door of the Crown Vic. The gesture was sweet and old-fashioned. "I feel like I've done something bad," Makani said, patting the cruiser's frame as she climbed in.

Ollie gave her a wry smile. "Now you know how I always feel."

It was a truth land mine—the exact reason why they were drawn to each other, told in the form of an obvious joke—but since Makani was the only one who recognized it, she kept the unintentional epiphany to herself. She watched him walk in front of the hood and then around to the driver's side. The way his body moved reminded her of something else old-fashioned: *Rebel Without a Cause*. James Dean was never so pale or so pink, but Ollie walked like a cool guy who was still deeply unsure of himself.

The interior of the car was clean and empty. The upholstery in the front was cloth, but the backseat was vinyl. Probably so that officers could clean up more easily—sweat, vomit, urine, blood. The steel-mesh divider had been removed, and there were no special radios or computer equipment, only a short handle beside the driver-side mirror that controlled a spotlight. Everything else looked normal, but she felt apprehensive. Her memories of the police were not fond. Ollie tossed his bag into the back and slid inside.

"So, have you?" she asked. "Done something bad?"

It was meant to be a flirtatious continuation of their joke, but it didn't come out sounding that way. Warnings from her friends rattled in her head. She wondered which of the rumors about Ollie might be true, at least partially, and felt guilty for snapping at Darby and Alex. She'd have to send them an apology text later. Maybe even a reconciliatory hairy ass.

Ollie paused, his hand on the ignition, to look at her square. "Have *you*?"

"Yes," she said. It was the most truth that she could admit.

"Yeah." He turned the ignition. "Me too."

They inched into the dusty herd of American-made cars and trucks headed for the exit. Bumper stickers and vinyl crosses on rear windows proclaimed their driver's devotion to Jesus Christ. Trademark Browning deer heads marked others as hunters, and more vehicles than not had something star-spangled or a faded SUPPORT OUR TROOPS magnetized ribbon. The dirt parking lot looked nothing like the parking lots back home, and it always made Makani feel as foreign and unwanted as a Toyota.

Ollie, lost in his own ruminations, didn't speak again until they were next in line to exit. "Which way?"

For a split second, Makani was surprised that he didn't know where she lived. But why would he? "Take a right. And then in two blocks, you'll take another."

The energy in the car deflated even further. "So, this won't be a *long* ride home."

His disappointment made her feel better. She gave him a coy smile. "I never told you," she said, "but I like your hair."

Ollie glanced at her as he maneuvered onto the street. "Yeah?"

"It's empowering. A big middle finger to gender stereotypes."

He glanced at her again, checking to make sure that she wasn't making fun of him. She wasn't. Makani hadn't been positive until this moment, but the pink was angry and defiant. It was sexy.

Ollie tried to shrug it off. "It's not like I'm the first straight guy to do it."

"But I'll bet you're the first guy, straight or gay, to do it in Osborne." This seemed to please him, so she continued. "Any particular reason?"

"It was just . . . something to do. Chris gave me hell for it."

She scrunched her nose. "That sucks. I'm sorry."

"Don't be." He touched the hair at the nape of his neck, and a devilish smile broke through his inscrutable expression. "Now I'm glad I did it."

Makani laughed, throwing back her head.

"There." Ollie sounded so certain. "That's how I know."

"Know what?" she asked, amused.

"That you aren't from around here."

Makani's heart pounded as she waited for him to expand on the thought. She would wait forever, if she had to.

"No one who grew up in this town has a laugh like yours."

Her bated breath exhaled as a disbelieving snort. "There's a line."

But his voice didn't change, and he didn't grow defensive. "I'm serious. You stand out."

"I stand out because I'm not white." She pointed at her street. "It's this one."

Ollie slowed, turned onto Walnut, and shrugged. "That, too."

He didn't deny it. Nor did he ask the dreaded follow-up, *So, what are you?* Only Darby—who also innately understood the concept of otherness—had successfully avoided this pitfall. Just as it was rude and invasive to ask him about his genitalia or sexual preference, it was equally rude and invasive to ask her about her ethnicity. It was the sort of information that should only be volunteered. Never asked for.

But people always asked. It was less common back in Hawaii, where the majority of the population was multiracial, but it still happened. Makani loathed their furrowed brows as they attempted to place her inside a recognizable box: Light brown skin. Hair somewhere between loose corkscrew curls and the tight coils of a 'fro. Chin, nose, and eyes . . . something vaguely Asian.

Where are you from?

No, where are you from originally?

I mean, where are your parents *from?*

Sometimes, she asked why they cared. Sometimes, she lied to confuse or annoy them. Usually, she told the truth. "I'm half African American, half Native Hawaiian. *Not* like the forty-fourth president," she'd be forced to add, sensing their eagerness. Obama was only born in Hawaii. His mama was a white girl from Kansas.

Ollie tapped an index finger against the steering wheel. "Which one is your house?"

"It's a few blocks down, just past those trees. On the right-hand side."

"All right turns."

"Hmm?" Her mind wasn't fully back to the present.

"To get to your house from school. That's satisfying."

It was true. This afternoon, at least, the short drive had been satisfying. She wanted it to continue. "Do you have to work today?"

"No. Do you?" But he quickly corrected the mistake. "I mean, do you have to take care of your grandma today?"

"Nope." She drew out the word. Hinting.

Ollie stared ahead, index finger still tapping. "Should we . . . do something?"

A thrill spiked through Makani. Only one final and unpleasant hurdle remained. She tried to keep her voice relaxed. "Well, I'd love to . . ."

"But?"

She braced herself. "But first, you'll have to meet my grandmother."

"Okay," he said.

Makani was flabbergasted. "Seriously?"

"Yeah." He took in her expression as they passed beneath the oak-lined, shadow-dappled portion of the street. "Wait. Weren't *you* serious?"

"Of course. But I didn't think you'd be this okay with it."

The corners of his mouth lifted into a smile. "You're forgetting you're in the Midwest. This is how we do things here." When she raised a skeptical eyebrow, he actually laughed. "It'll be fine."

She had a hard time believing that, but his confidence was reassuring. Somewhat.

"It figures that you live here," he said.

Once again, she was taken aback. "What's that supposed to mean?"

He craned his neck to look at the branches overhead. "Beautiful girl. Beautiful neighborhood."

She frowned. "For real, Ollie. I'm not into lines."

"I'm just saying, you live on the best street in town. When I was a kid, I always wished I lived under these trees."

"Until you discovered the rest of the world has way better streets and way better trees?" She pointed out a white two-story with a large porch. "That's mine."

Ollie pulled into the driveway and turned off the engine. Makani waited for him to expand upon her remark—to agree about preferring anywhere else to Osborne. When he didn't, she worried that she'd pushed him too far. He'd complimented her twice, and she'd dismissed him both times. And even though she had the impression that he was desperate to move away, it still sucked to hear someone talk shit about your hometown.

"You're right, though," she said. "It *is* the best street. I guess I'm lucky."

It wasn't a lie, and it felt strange to admit. It had been a while since Makani had felt lucky, or even grateful. Most of the towns around here had brick-paved streets in their oldest districts, which seemed both anachronistic and genuinely charming. Main Street and her grandmother's neighborhood contained the only brick pavers in Osborne. The houses here were more attractive, and they also had better landscaping. This time of year, the leaves turned comforting shades of yellow and gold, cornhusk scarecrows dotted the yards, and sacrificial pumpkins sat on porch steps, waiting to be carved.

In September, Grandma Young had filled her planters with sunny round mums, and last weekend Makani had raked the fallen leaves into those orange trash bags printed with jack-o'-lantern faces. They were tacky, but Makani liked them anyway.

She cocked her head. "I've never asked, I've only assumed. Do you still live on your parents' farm?"

Ollie nodded. "We're not selling the house until I'm done with school, but we've already sold most of the land to our neighbors. They've incorporated it into their giant-ass corn maze. Perhaps you've seen the billboards?"

This last sentence was sarcastic. The fluorescent advertisements for the Martin Family Fun Corn Maze were everywhere. The Martins were a sizable clan of longtime residents. Every single family member had a different shade of red hair, and three of them—two siblings and a cousin—went to Osborne High.

"Yikes," Makani said. "That must be weird for you."

Ollie shrugged. She'd noticed that he was a frequent shrugger. "It's not bad."

"MAKANI YOUNG."

They jump-flattened into the upholstery. Wincing, Makani looked out the window and found Grandma Young. She was standing on the steps that led to the back door, and her hands were positioned on her hips.

"*Christ,*" Ollie said in a low voice. "How long has she been staring at us?"

"Probably for all eternity." Makani steeled herself as she exited the car. "Hey, Grandma—"

"I thought you'd been brought home by the police!" Grandma Young hustled down the rest of the stairs to meet her. "Nearly frightened me to death when I looked out the kitchen window and saw you sitting there."

"Oh, it's not—"

"But it's not a cop car, is it? It doesn't have any decals. Unless it's undercover!" Her panic bubbled back to a boil. "Are you okay? What happened?"

"I'm *fine,* Grandma. Everything is fine. A friend drove me home, that's all."

"That's not Darby's car."

"A new friend."

Grandma Young wrapped Makani into a constricting hug. She seemed enraged but on the verge of tears. "I thought something had happened to you. Something like what happened to that poor Haley Whitehall."

An unexpected lump rose in Makani's throat. Her grandmother's first thought was that she had been attacked—not that she'd done something wrong. Makani fought to keep her voice steady. "Well. Clearly nothing happened, because I'm standing right here."

Ollie's door opened, and his feet crunched into the gravel driveway.

Grandma Young's death grip loosened. And then her arms fell away completely. As Makani turned around, she realized with a flush of horror what her grandmother was seeing: a skeleton-like boy dressed in all black.

With hot-pink hair.

And a lip ring.

"I'm sorry, Mrs. Young," the skeleton boy said. "We didn't mean to scare you. I'm Makani's friend, Oliver Larsson. Ollie." He stepped forward to shake her hand.

Grandma Young gingerly accepted the outstretched hand as she examined every square inch of his appearance. Makani was glad when Ollie didn't flinch or look away, which her grandmother might have deemed weak. He only smiled, which helped to soften his sharper features. "You're the young man who works in the produce department at Greeley's," she said, finally letting go of him.

"Yes, ma'am. I've been working there for almost four years."

"How old are you?"

Makani's stomach warped, but Ollie replied with ease. "I just turned eighteen."

Grandma Young nodded toward his car. "That's some ride you've got there."

Ride, Makani thought. *Ohmygod no stop stop stop.*

Ollie held the smile. "It gets me where I need to go."

Grandma Young considered him for another excruciating moment. And then she scolded her granddaughter. "Don't just stand there. Show him inside."

Mortification followed Makani into her grandmother's original, unironic, midcentury-modern kitchen. At least it was clean.

"Would you like anything to drink?" Grandma Young asked Ollie.

"No, thank you," he said.

"We have water, skim milk, iced tea, Sprite—well, it's not Sprite, it's the off-brand Sprite—orange juice, cranberry juice, tomato juice—well, it's the low-sodium kind, so it doesn't taste as good, but it's healthier—"

"Water would be great, thanks," Ollie said.

"Tap water? Or we have a jug in the fridge. It keeps it cooler."

Makani dug her nails into her palms. "We all know how refrigerators work."

"Tap is fine," Ollie said.

"Ice?" Grandma Young asked.

"Yes, please."

"The square kind from a tray or the round kind from a bag?"

"Oh my God, Grandma. You are literally killing me."

"Either is fine," Ollie said. "Whichever's easier."

Grandma Young opened the freezer and reached into a clear bag of ice. "Oliver, I apologize for my granddaughter. For her rudeness, but also for her misuse of the word *literally*. I've corrected her at least a dozen times."

Makani made a choking motion with her hands. Ollie shared a secret smile with her as Grandma Young turned back around. Without breaking a beat, she placed the ice-filled glass between Makani's clenched fingers. Ollie and her grandmother laughed.

But the atmosphere remained unnaturally formal in the living room as Grandma Young inquired about Ollie, and he inquired about her. Makani sat with her grandmother on the sofa. Ollie sat in the easy chair. The grandfather clock beside the staircase ticked and ticked the agonizing seconds. After a conversation about Grandma Young's church dwindled to an end, Ollie pointed at the coffee table.

The edge of the jigsaw puzzle had been completed along with sections of the pumpkin patch.

"My mom liked those, too. Sometimes during the holidays, she'd pull one out from the back of the linen closet, and we'd work on it together. My dad and my brother couldn't stand it. They thought puzzles were boring. But I've always thought they were satisfying, you know? Each piece having its exact place."

Makani was stunned. Excluding their phone call last night and the badgering from Alex this morning, she'd never heard Ollie speak so many sentences in a row. He tended to use the minimal amount of words possible to express himself.

Grandma Young gestured at her with an ice-free glass of off-brand Sprite. "This one thinks they're boring, too."

Ollie shook his head at Makani. "You're missing out."

"Isaac, my husband, he didn't care much for them, either," Grandma Young said. "But they calm me down. Keep my mind occupied."

There was a pause as something like an acknowledgment of sorrow passed between Ollie and her grandmother. Unable to bear it any longer, Makani glanced at her phone and jumped up from the sofa. "Sorry! We need to get going."

Grandma Young set down her drink on an L.L. Bean catalog. "Oh?"

"Ollie has a late shift tonight, so we wanted to hang out a little before then."

"I was gonna take her to Sonic for slushes." As Ollie stood up from the easy chair, its springs gave a muffled squeak. "Last ones of the season, before it gets too cold."

"I like their limeade." Grandma Young's ankles cracked as she rose to her feet. "It was nice meeting you. And feel free to join me anytime." She nodded at the puzzle.

Ollie tucked his fingertips into the pockets of his jeans. "Thanks."

Makani marched him to the back door in the kitchen, leading them toward freedom and calling over her shoulder, "I'll be home before dinner!"

When they were tucked safely inside his car, they exchanged the same sly grin. "You're good at that," Makani said. "At lying."

"So are you."

"Yeah. Sorry about that." She laughed in an attempt to hide her embarrassment. "I promise I won't make you come back and do a jigsaw puzzle with my grandmother."

His grin held. "Who says I don't want to?"

Makani laughed again. "Okay, weirdo." She was relieved that he'd gotten along with her grandmother and spoken to her like a normal human being. But the companion emotion was that same inescapable shame. No matter how many times she'd stuck up for him with her friends, she couldn't stop underestimating him herself.

"Just promise me Sonic was a lie," she said.

"God, yes," Ollie said. The Sonic Drive-In was the only name-brand restaurant in town. It was where the football crowd hung out. "I'm taking you to the ocean."

They drove through Osborne—past Greeley's Foods and the Red Spot, past the bustling Sonic and the deserted shell of an old Sinclair gas station, past the gigantic Do it Best hardware store and the shed-size Dollar General—and out of town.

They didn't talk much, but their silence was companionable.

They crossed the railroad tracks and went over the river. The countryside was flat. Stiff vegetation, muddy fields, round bales of hay. Modest farmhouses and monstrous tractors. The view was uniform in every direction, broken only by the long, dinosaurian contraptions that Makani had learned were center-pivot irrigation systems.

The grass and dying corn plants were the same shade of drab golden brown. The occasional trees, dressed for autumn, added pointillistic yellow dots to the landscape. Everything was yellow and gold, except for the sky. It was gray.

It didn't seem like they were traveling anywhere specific, yet Makani felt a change, a tremulous sort of anticipation, as they approached their destination. Ollie turned off the highway and onto a nondescript dirt road surrounded by cornfields. It looked like any other nondescript dirt road surrounded by cornfields, but as they drove farther, Makani realized how secluded it actually was. There were no other people or houses in sight. Darby and Alex would be livid if they knew she was here.

Makani composed a text, apologizing for earlier, but the connection was too slow for the message to send. A pellet of discomfort lodged in her stomach as the car dead-ended in the middle of another field. Or maybe it was all one field.

"What's this road even for?" she asked.

Ollie turned off the engine. "I have no idea. *Literally.*"

Makani laughed with tension-releasing surprise. "Ollie Larsson. Was that a joke?"

He raised his eyebrows and smiled. "Never."

Her heart somersaulted. They weren't parked in the same location where they'd had sex, though it looked similar. That particular memory was tinted with loneliness and desperation. Now she only felt the nervous thrum of excitement.

"Careful stepping out," Ollie said, unlocking the car. "It's always muddier than you think."

Makani tucked away her phone, opened the door, and peered down. The ground was a thick marsh of wind-stiffened mud. She tested it with a sneaker toe. It seemed solid enough, so she climbed out—and tromped straight into it, three inches deep. "Shit!" But she laughed again. "I thought you said you were taking me to the beach."

"The ocean," he corrected.

The temperature had dropped. The brisk air smelled like decaying leaves, distant woodsmoke, and chilled terrain, a reminder that Halloween was around the bend. Makani pulled up the hood of her floral-printed hoodie and zipped it up. She should have worn a coat, but she still sucked at this cold weather thing. Most people here didn't even consider it cold yet. Just nippy.

She plodded forward to join Ollie. He was leaning against the front of the car, its engine ticking lightly as it cooled. But the metal was still warm, almost hot, and it felt good against her jeans. The leggy corn encircled them, two feet overhead. She turned pointedly to Ollie. He was staring straight ahead into the vast golden nothingness.

"It's not the Pacific," he said, "but it's the best I can do."

Ollie must have registered her confusion in his peripheral vision, because he met her gaze with another smile. "The fields. I know you miss Hawaii."

As her mind absorbed this thoughtful gesture, her eyes lingered on the curve of his lips. She wanted to kiss them again. She forced her head away and tried to focus on their surroundings—she really did try—but she felt him still watching her.

He slid back and up onto the hood of his car. "Here."

She hopped up beside him, metal thumping, her left leg touching his right.

Ollie pulled up the hood of his own hoodie. It was tight against his head—hers puffed out a bit with her hair—but a shock of hot pink flashed out from underneath the black cotton fabric. It looked like the only bright thing in the universe.

"Okay," he said. "Now look again."

The wind rustled the brittle cornstalks. It sounded like a spitting, crackling fire. The dry tassels reached for the open sky while the dead silks pointed down to the muddy earth. Slowly, ever so slowly, the wind strengthened and changed course, and the fields swayed as a single element, rippling outward in a current of mesmerizing waves.

Something hidden inside Makani lifted its head and blossomed. The sensation was sublime. Makani often complained that she was drowning in corn, but she wasn't gasping below the water. She was perched on the edge of the horizon.

She felt Ollie trying to gauge her reaction. She smiled, letting it linger on the fields before inclining her head toward his. "Thank you," she said.

And then she kissed him.

Makani was surprised at the familiarity of his mouth, the *taste* of it, how natural Ollie's lips felt when pressed against hers. She remembered how to work both around his piercing and with it. His breath caught, and she felt the thrill of having invoked the reaction. His hands slipped under her hood, on each side of her neck, and it was the first time that his fingers had touched her skin since the end of summer. She gasped. Her arms wrapped around him. Their hips slid against each other, digging into the metal of the car. It was painful, and Makani would have bruises, but it didn't matter. She didn't care.

They kissed—they made out like this—until the setting sun ripened the clouds into peaches and apricots. Until his phone interrupted them.

Ollie scooted back as he removed it from his pocket. "Shit. It's probably Chris, wondering where I am, oh—" He hopped off the car to answer it. "Hello? *Hello?*"

The connection must have been weak. Makani thought it was

odd when he went inside the cruiser for privacy, using it like an old-fashioned telephone booth. Wouldn't the connection be stronger outside? She could hear the rumble of his voice but none of his words.

Her blood still pulsed with heat, but she shivered. After they'd had sex, he'd turned into a ghost. She wanted to believe that he wouldn't disappear again.

Ollie hung up.

They stared at each other through the windshield. His eyes were heavy. Whatever it was, it wasn't good news. With an ominous knot of dread, Makani slid down the hood, trudged the few feet through the mud, and rejoined him in the car.

She left the door open.

"Work," Ollie said. His body was slumped into his seat. "One of our cashiers was just fired for stealing. I can't believe it. It doesn't sound like her at all. They want me to go in and run her register."

Relief rushed over Makani. She'd assumed that something worse had happened. Haley's school photo, plastered across the local media, flickered through her mind like a harbinger. *Enthusiastic smile. Bright eyes. Neatly parted hair.* She looked so wholesome, so undeserving. Not that anyone deserved her fate.

Ollie's slump deepened. "Sorry. This sucks."

"Don't worry about it." Makani scraped the mud from her sneakers against the bottom of his car. His boots weren't nearly as caked. "Besides, now we only half lied to my grandma. I promised her that I'd be home for dinner."

He didn't respond, so she asked before losing her nerve, "Why did you take the call in here? You didn't want me to hear you talking to your boss?"

It nudged him back into the present. "Sometimes I get a stronger signal in here. Something to do with the old police wiring, I don't know."

"I couldn't even get a text to send earlier."

He shrugged. "Maybe we need CB radios, like the jocks and ags."

She pointed an accusing finger. "Bite your tongue."

Leaning forward, he lightly took her finger between his teeth. She smiled. "I could call my manager back," he said, a few minutes later. "Make an excuse."

But Makani needed to believe that Ollie would return. She kissed him twice, one kiss on each temple, and closed the door. Haley's school photo vanished from her thoughts.

"Drive," she said. "We'll have plenty of time for that later."

CHAPTER SEVEN

THEY WERE UNDEFEATED. The best team in the state. And they were playing one of the worst tomorrow night. So why was Hooker being such a fucking dickweed?

For the last forty minutes, Matt Butler had been standing in the locker room showers with his eyes closed. Practice was over. The sun was down. Everyone was gone. He'd told the guys that he'd catch up with them at Sonic, but he wasn't even sure if that was true. He wanted to be alone, enveloped in water and quiet and steam, forever.

It had been a rough week. The pressure of the playoffs, pressure of the recruiters, pressure of his parents. Haley. That stupid fight in the quad and the disappointed lectures from Principal Stanton and Coach Hooker that followed. Lauren. She'd been ragging on him again for not texting her back fast enough. Worse, she was acting like she'd known Haley—like she'd been personally devastated by the tragic loss of a dear friend—when, as far as he knew, Lauren and Haley had never hung out. Not once. It was okay to be upset about someone's death, even if you never really knew the person. But Matt hated the way his girlfriend was making the tragedy about herself.

He couldn't stop thinking about Haley's parents. The media was placing ample suspicion on her father, but every time Matt saw him in the news, Don Whitehall looked gutted. His eyelids were so swollen that he could hardly keep them open. Only a psychopath could fake that kind of reaction. Then again, only a psychopath could commit that kind of murder. Haley's mom had issued a televised statement. She'd begged anyone in the community to step forward if they knew the perpetrator's real identity, but she could barely speak through her grief. Something about her physical appearance reminded him of his own mom. That made it worse.

He still felt the shock of when Buddy had ripped down the *Sweeney Todd* banner. His best friend hadn't known what he was doing—Matt could see that now, they were cool—but it had made the entire team look like assholes.

Both Hooker and his father grilled him constantly about the importance of appearance. And Matt was trying to keep up appearances, but the stress of everything, of everyone *relying* on him, had been getting to him all semester. It was making him pick these fights. Obsess over the Whitehalls. Misplace his belongings. Matt had been losing his essentials (phone, keys, wallet) in the strangest places (sock drawer, vegetable crisper, patio table) with no memory of having moved them there.

Unless . . . it wasn't the stress.

Matt's muscles clenched as three letters chorused in his mind: CTE.

Chronic traumatic encephalopathy was a disease caused by repetitive blows to the head. Early symptoms included memory loss, disorientation, and erratic behavior. Later symptoms included dementia, impeded speech, and suicide. Basically, it destroyed your brain, and football players everywhere were suffering and dying from it. Mostly old guys, who'd played pro. But plenty of young guys, too. Even high schoolers.

It was the disease that the NFL and universities didn't want to discuss, because it hurt their bottom line. Matt's teammates didn't want to talk about it, either. Ignoring it made it easier to pretend that it wasn't serious, made it easier to keep playing ball. No one wanted to ruin the game they all loved.

But Matt thought about CTE. He thought about it a lot.

Professional football was the only future he'd ever wanted. It was what his father, whose own dreams were shattered when he tore up his left knee on the field at Memorial Stadium, had always wanted.

His mother, on the other hand. She used to want it. Now every time a story hit ESPN, he'd find a printed-out article sitting on his place mat at the breakfast table. Her silent plea. To Matt's everlasting shame, he always made a show of crumpling up the articles in front of his dad. They'd been working so hard for this, for so long.

But, secretly, Matt had started pocketing them.

The first article he'd kept was about Tony Dorsett, a college and pro Hall of Fame running back. Matt was a running back, too. He was the best in the Midwest, with the Division I FBS recruiters serenading his front door to prove it, but every time he found his phone in the wrong place, he broke into a cold sweat.

CTE? Is that you?

Because what would he do if he couldn't play football?

On the mantelpiece in his living room, a framed photograph was prominently displayed. It was taken on the day he was born, and he was swaddled in a scarlet Huskers blanket. Now, only a few short months remained before he had to officially commit to one school. Because he *would* commit. He would keep playing.

The choice wasn't an actual choice.

Matt turned off the water. He examined his hands, which were pruned and gelatin white. The weak showerhead dripped water onto the tile floor. Somewhere during this exhausted mulling, Matt had decided to join his friends at Sonic.

Tomorrow was the last game of the regular season, and it was important to keep focused on their opponent and not look past them into the playoffs—even though everybody knew it was a win. It's why practice had been so frustrating. Hooker had drilled them harder than ever, yelling in an unparalleled, spittle-faced volume that they were getting too comfortable. Matt was confident, but he wasn't comfortable. He wouldn't feel *comfortable* until he'd made it through playoffs without injury.

Buddy liked to joke that Hooker yelled because of a deep-seated resentment of being forced to listen to them shout his own terrible name. Matt always laughed, but he knew the head coach's motivations came from a better, smarter place. Hooker cared.

Matt toweled off and then wrapped it around his waist. He grabbed his combination shampoo/body wash, stepped over his dirty practice clothes, and strode through the cloud of steam. His wet footprints trailed behind him. The lockers smelled like male sweat and old rust, and they were in alternating colors of scarlet and gold. Osborne proudly wore the same shade of scarlet red as the Huskers, but Matt's locker was gold, because a team superstition asserted that the scarlet lockers were unlucky. Seniors always claimed the gold lockers.

Matt ground to a halt. His combination lock was missing.

CTE? Is that you?

He shook his head, pissed at himself, as he swung open the metal door. His helmet and deodorant were on the top shelf. The larger bottom space, which normally held his backpack and mesh duffel bag, was empty.

"Aw, fuck." Matt muttered it. But then he slammed down the

bottle of shampoo/body wash so hard that the entire row of lockers quivered in shock.

He glanced around the room. Nothing appeared to be out of place. He jerked open the gold door closest to his. Despite keeping it permanently unlocked—Buddy could never remember the combination—their teammates rarely stole or hid things from him. The usual items were still inside of it. Nothing else.

Matt looked under the row of benches. More nothing.

"Fuck. *Fuck.*"

He stalked toward the showers, annoyed that his own absent-mindedness had led to this irritating prank, which was forcing him to re-dress in his soiled practice clothes. It meant that he'd have to stop by his house before Sonic to change. He'd also have to shower again, or Lauren would complain about the smell.

Matt rounded the corner, and his practice clothes were gone.

Perfect.

"All right, guys." His voice was loud and deep, and it resonated against the steel lockers. "You got me."

There was no reply.

"What do you want? A dick pic or something?" Matt kept the tone jocular. He was *done* with this week, but he refused to give his friends the satisfaction of knowing it. "Guess you should have taken my towel, too."

The steam evaporated. The room grew cold.

He rubbed the hair on his arms. "Hello?"

The question echoed.

Even more than the silence, Matt *felt* his aloneness. He headed for the coaches' offices. As expected, their windows were dark, and their doors were locked. Hooker and the assistants usually went home straight after practice, especially if it'd been a tough one. School rules required them to stay until the last student was gone, but they liked to give the guys an opportunity to vent and decompress without the fear of being overheard.

The entrance to the locker room was located beside the assistant coaches' shared office. Matt readjusted his towel and cracked open the door. He peered into the dusk, half expecting—and very much hoping—to find the team waiting outside, phones raised to capture him in all his humiliated glory.

Nobody was there.

In the distance, a crowd murmured. It was the candlelight vigil for Haley. Parents and students and teachers were already gathering at the front of the school. His stomach dropped as he realized that he'd have to walk past them to reach the parking lot. He couldn't do that in a towel. It would be disrespectful.

Matt closed the door and tried again. "Hello?"

Doubt crept in.

Did he see his practice clothes when he got out of the shower? The most logical explanation was that the guys had stolen them at the same time as his regular clothes, and that all his shit was currently in the back of someone's pickup.

Matt weighed his options. He could call Buddy and beg for it back. He could call his mom and ask her to bring him something else to wear. Or he could call Lauren. *No way. She'd tell her friends.* The only other option was to wait for the vigil to end, but how long would that take? Two hours? And then he'd still have to drive home in his towel.

Wait.

Drive.

His keys and phone were in his pockets.

Matt shouted a long, lethal expletive. Anger coursed through his veins as he threw open every non-locked locker. Crouched on his knees and peered below the benches. Jumped onto the benches and peeked on top of the lockers. He looked in the showers, urinals, stalls, and under the sinks, but his belongings were nowhere to be found.

This was it, then. He'd have to walk home.

Matt lived in the newer neighborhood across town. He had never walked it, but it was probably only thirty minutes away. Still, the temperature would be below forty by the time the vigil ended. And he'd be wearing a goddamn towel.

Defeated, he sank onto the bench outside Hooker's office. His body was a weary sack. Everything ached. Matt leaned against the cinder-block wall—right beside a telephone. He grabbed the receiver off its hook, scanning his brain for numbers.

It's not CTE. No one memorizes them anymore.

The only number he knew was his parents' landline, but when he called, no one picked up. He tried again. "Goddamn motherfucking answer the phone!" he said, and a cry emerged from the locker bay.

Matt froze.

Everything was silent. And then . . . someone whimpered.

Before this moment, Matt would have guessed that the sound of another human—no matter how distressed—would have launched him to his feet in fury. But something else kicked in. Instinct, perhaps. It was the only explanation for the overwhelming trepidation triggered by that single whimper. Why his internal sensors lit up on high alert.

His body was stone. He listened.

The person had gone silent again, but their presence was unmistakable. Matt gripped his towel and stood. He felt exposed and vulnerable, an animal lying belly up. He pressed forward without sound, yet his footsteps were still too loud.

He reached the lockers.

At the far end of the bay, at the far end of the bench, a slender figure sat with their back to him. Their hoodie was up, and their head was down. Their shoulders shook in a way that suggested crying. Matt couldn't tell if it was a girl or guy, but it wasn't one of his teammates. They were too small to play football.

"Hey." He didn't mean for it to come out so angrily.

The figure flinched.

Matt tried to calm his voice. "Who are you?"

The figure didn't move.

Matt retightened the towel, keenly aware of his genitals. "Hey," he said again, stepping forward. His tone was softer. "Are you okay?"

The figure sniffled, and Matt realized that it might be one of the special-needs kids. The second-string quarterback had a sister in the after-school program, so he knew they met in a classroom nearby. This might even be her. Sometimes Faith showed up near the end of practice and watched them run drills from the bleachers.

Matt approached with caution as he circled the wooden bench. Their face was still aimed at the floor. Matt kneeled before them, trying to get at eye level. "Do you need help? Can I help you?"

The figure raised their head. Slowly. Deliberately.

Matt frowned. It wasn't Faith, it—

The knife slid into his abdomen with shocking ferocity and immediately back out with equal vigor. Matt collapsed forward, knocking his head against the bench, while his mind remained a step behind. *What just happened? Was that an accident?*

The figure stared down at him in hatred.

Matt's mind scrambled to make sense of it. He was half on the bench, half on the floor. He couldn't find their name. "You. What the hell did you do to me?"

The reply was swift—a powerful downward thrust into his skull.

Matt screamed. His attacker yanked with gloved hands on the hilt until the knife tugged back out, and the rest of Matt's body fell onto the hard ceramic tile. He was still conscious as a crumpled piece of paper materialized from the pocket of his attacker's hoodie.

The figure kneeled before him. Held out the paper in front of his eyes. Smoothed it down.

It was an article that his mother had printed out several weeks ago. Matt had carried it around in his backpack for a few days before it had disappeared.

His eyes widened with a deeper fear.

The figure, content that Matt understood what he was seeing—the personal *violation* of it—returned the paper to the hoodie's pocket.

Matt wanted to speak. He couldn't. The last thing he saw was an arm, splattered with his own blood, as the sawtooth edge of a large hunting knife carved around the circumference of his head. With a squelch that signaled the release of suction, it popped open like the lid of a jack-o'-lantern. His brain was slashed into mush. And then the top was placed back on.

Nice and tidy.

CHAPTER EIGHT

THE COPS WERE removing students from the classrooms, one at a time, for questioning. It had taken twenty-four hours for Haley's memorial to appear, but the front corner of the school was already blanketed in fresh roses, poster-board collages, and footballs. Dozens of small red flags, normally affixed to cars and trucks on game day, had been planted in the ground and were flapping in the wind. Tonight's game—the final game of the regular season—had already been forfeited. It was the first forfeit in team history.

The entire campus was stunned with disbelief. Half of the students were dressed in school colors. Several openly wept. A dozen stuffed-animal lions had also appeared overnight at the memorial, because Matt's team number was twelve and their mascot was Leo the Lion. Last year, the youth groups had protested to change his name—*Leo* was too astrological—but this morning, their most vocal objector had led a prayer by the flagpole while wearing a LION PRIDE sweatshirt.

A custodian had found Matt's body. The nearly two hundred

mourners at Haley's candlelight vigil had witnessed the cops and ambulances scream onto the scene.

Makani had been home for less than an hour, the taste of Ollie still tingling on her lips, when the cavalry of lights zoomed past Grandma Young's front window. It looked like every emergency vehicle that Osborne had to offer. The news hit social media first, as it always did: *There'd been an accident at the high school.*

UPDATE: *There was a body.*

UPDATE: *It was a student.*

UPDATE: *It was Osborne's favorite student.*

The town climbed from local to statewide news, and the obligatory journalists had swarmed in, swelling their presence. *Matthew Sherman Butler. Haley Madison Whitehall.* When people died, the media turned them into three names. Makani had hardly known either of the victims. It felt wrong to have this much information.

The reporters clustered along the perimeter of the campus, nabbing strays for exclusive interviews. Makani had bolted around the feasting horde, but plenty of other students were willing. One news crew even had the nerve to duck beneath the crime-scene tape to film the trash bins where Matt's backpack and duffel bag had been discovered, presumably stashed there by his killer. Makani had heard the furious shouts of the police officers all the way from the quad.

Haley had been murdered at home, and Matt had been murdered at school.

Haley had been beloved in drama, and Matt had been beloved in football.

One victim, two victims.

These things made a difference.

A rumor circulated about canceling school, but Makani assumed it didn't happen so that the questioning could take place more easily.

It seemed probable that the cases were connected; there were too many similarities. Everyone, including the teachers and administrators, would be required to face an officer by the end of the day. Students were called out individually. The order was supposedly random, but it was clearly alphabetical.

Justine Darby, Oliver Larsson, Alexandra Shimerda, Makani Young.

She would be the last to go.

When Darby returned to their second-period physics class, he grabbed an empty seat beside Makani and Alex.

Makani pressed him for details. "What kind of questions did they ask?"

"Easy things," he said.

They didn't bother to hide their conversation. Everybody else was already talking. Phones, normally forbidden, were on full display as students grieved and searched for new information. It was difficult enough to pay attention on an average Friday, but even the teachers knew that no lessons would be taught today as they adopted the dual roles of counselors for the students and secretaries for the officers.

Mr. Merrick, the physics teacher, was engaged in a discussion with two football players whose heads were down. Breaking another school rule, he had a hand gripped on one of their shoulders. Comforting. Underneath Mr. Merrick's bushy and uncultivated eyebrows, it looked like he was trying not to cry.

"They asked if I knew the victims," Darby said. "If I'd ever heard any rumors about them, if I knew anyone who might not have liked them, where I was last night between six and seven. That sort of thing. The officer was really nice."

"Did you get Chris?" Makani had glimpsed him in the hallway

before class. With his pale skin and white-blond hair, it was easy to identify him as Ollie's brother. Chris was a bit broader, though, despite being more slender and less muscular than most cops.

"No, it was the lady. Officer Gage. Kinda hot, actually."

"And *good at her job*," Alex said, not looking up from her phone.

Darby waved a dismissive hand. He was a feminist, too. "You'll be fine," he told Makani, because her head was cowering and her elbows were burrowed against her sides. Unconsciously, she was making herself smaller.

Makani hated the idea of talking to the police. Answering their questions. What if they looked into her record and discovered her expungement in Hawaii? She'd always dreaded that someday, something would happen that would prompt a closer inspection of her files. *And this was it. Today was the day.* What would her friends think of her?

If Ollie were here, maybe his stillness would be a comfort. But they only had one class together and since the previous evening, they'd only spoken over text. Ollie had lain awake, afraid of getting a knock on the front door—the chief of police coming to say there'd been a third attack, and now his brother was dead, too. Chris hadn't come home until after four in the morning. Ollie had slept in and barely made it to school on time.

"Do you think the team will bow out?" Darby asked Alex.

Makani realized they'd been talking for several minutes.

"Of the playoffs?" Alex shook her head. "Their spot was already secure. And Matt wasn't the only one being scouted. The team *can't* stop playing—"

"Because this is Nebraska." Makani filled in the blank like a robot. Most conversations about football ended with that phrase.

Alex loved playing the trumpet, but she preferred concert season to marching band. She nodded her displeasure. "The boosters sent out a text-blast this morning. We're taking tonight off with the team, but practice resumes on Monday."

Darby glanced around to ensure their privacy. "I heard the coaches might be suspended, because they left school grounds immediately after practice. Someone was supposed to stay behind with the team. And if someone *had* stayed behind . . ."

Alex grimaced. "Twenty bucks says the only coach suspended is the lowest-ranking assistant."

"I didn't think Haley and Matt even knew each other," Darby said, returning to the most baffling question. "Do you really think they were dating?"

The tone of the rumors had shifted. Haley's father was taking a backseat while the secret lovers theory came under scrutiny. Suddenly, their classmates swore they'd spotted Haley and Matt sharing a banana shake at Sonic or groping beneath the bleachers.

"I mean," Darby said, "Matt's been with Lauren Dixon for two *years.*"

"Which is why it was a secret." Alex leaned in, wafting them with her favorite perfume. Her skin smelled floral and spicy. "Maybe Lauren found out and killed them both in a jealous rage."

"You seriously think a girl could've done that?"

"Of course a girl could've done it."

Darby scowled at her. "I meant, physically. Matt was a big guy."

"You don't think Lauren has bitch strength?" Alex asked.

When Makani moved to Osborne, Lauren had been the first to ask: *What* are *you?* Makani gave an honest answer, and Lauren had laughed. *So, you're a mutt!* She thought she was being cute, and everyone within earshot had laughed. Makani had despised her ever since. But even with their history, she was glad that Lauren had stayed home and would be spared—for a time, at least—what was being said about her.

"Maybe the killer doesn't even go here," Darby said. "Maybe it's someone from a rival team. Someone competing for the attention of the same college recruiters."

"But then why kill Haley?" Alex asked.

He contemplated it for a few seconds. "Love triangle?"

They startled as a voice in front of them laughed with condescension. It was Alex's tempestuous crush. As Rodrigo turned around to face them, Alex glared at him witheringly. But her posture perked up.

Rodrigo laced his fingers behind his head, cocky and relaxed. "Though, I suppose a love triangle is as likely as your secret lovers' scenario."

"It is so"—Alex pointed at his chest—"not."

David, who was sitting beside Rodrigo, rolled his eyes. Makani understood. Their friends needed to get over themselves and suck face.

"What about Buddy?" Darby asked. "In the love triangle?"

Rodrigo's expression grew even more skeptical. "Buddy Wheeler?"

"No, the other Buddy who plays football," Alex said.

Darby ignored them. "Remember last year when his girlfriend dumped him, and he punched her locker so hard that his skin got caught in the metal grate? Shit required stitches. Now there's someone angry enough to kill, *and* he's Matt's best friend."

"Buddy is too dumb to be the killer," Alex said.

"On that, alone, we agree," Rodrigo said.

Makani glanced at the classroom door. Would anyone notice if she left?

"Are you gonna throw up?"

Makani looked back to find David staring at her. He seemed more bored than interested, but that might have just been his face. It was long and plain with an odd swoop of sandy hair across his forehead. "You're clutching your stomach," he said.

"I guess I'm just ready to talk about anything else."

He shrugged. "Is there anything else to talk about?"

It was a valid question, but it made her feel even more alone.

In addition to the most obvious—and outlandish—suspects, speculation about Ollie and Zachary was also on the rise. *Ollie and Zachary. The loner and the asshole. The bullied and the bully.* Plenty of people had noticed Matt messing with Ollie only two days earlier, and several others had witnessed Zachary taunting Matt last month after the announcement that Matt would be crowned Homecoming King.

Makani had spent the homecoming game watching a werewolf movie in Darby's basement. When the game ended and her duties to the band were over, Alex had joined them. None of them went to the dance the following night. They hadn't been asked. Now the Homecoming King was dead. It was impossible to believe.

"Who do you think did it?" David asked.

Makani stared at the door. She couldn't keep her eyes off the exit. "I don't know. Maybe their deaths aren't even connected."

Darby's, Alex's, and Rodrigo's attention snapped back to her.

"I m-mean," Makani said, "of course they're connected, but what if Haley and Matt were *exactly* who we thought they were? What if there's no great conspiracy, and they were chosen simply because they were both popular?"

Alex shook her head. "Haley wasn't popular."

"She was well liked and respected. It's almost the same thing."

"Okay," Rodrigo said, "so your theory is that someone *un*popular killed them? Someone jealous of their status?"

Makani bristled. "I don't have a theory. I'm just saying we don't know."

"They wouldn't have to be unpopular," Alex said. "Just *less* popular."

"At least it means we'd all be safe," Rodrigo said.

Up until then, Makani hadn't been sure if Rodrigo was aware that he wasn't universally admired. It made her like him a little more. She would prefer to go unnoticed altogether. Unfortunately, the sharp end of her anonymity seemed to be rapidly approaching.

The police came for her during the last period of the day. It was Makani's only class with Ollie, but they'd hardly spoken before Señora Washington asked her to step into the hallway. The young, decidedly not Hispanic, Spanish teacher looked despondent with a touch of relief. It was the final name that she would have to call out.

"Best for last," the officer said as the door closed behind her. He wore a stiff, dark blue uniform, and his name tag read LARSSON.

Right. Because it had to be him.

Makani lifted a hand in acknowledgment. She was afraid that her voice might betray her nervousness, if her clammy skin didn't do it first.

"Hope you don't mind that I requested your interview." The grin was uncannily familiar. "I was curious who my little brother has a crush on."

She had no idea how to respond, so she didn't. The word *crush* was an invigorating jolt. But this easily ranked as one of the worst ways to meet a potential boyfriend's family. She'd been praying for any other officer.

Chris—Makani decided to think of him as *Chris* rather than *Officer Larsson,* because it was moderately less intimidating—led her to an empty room filled with electric typewriters. It was the keyboarding classroom. Freshmen were taught on typewriters, because it was too easy to cheat on computers. Copy and paste. Chris gestured to the hard orange chair that was stationed beside the teacher's desk.

Makani sat down obediently. The buzzing fluorescent lights were so harsh and stark for a room that felt so neglected and out of time. They made her feel naked. She crossed her arms, worried that it looked disrespectful, and then sat on her hands instead.

Chris rolled the comfortable teacher's chair toward her and took a seat. He examined her appearance, not unkindly. "How're you holding up?"

Makani knew she didn't look right. She looked twitchy and disturbed. It was better to admit it and hope that he assumed it was for normal reasons. "Not great."

"Yeah, I hear you. Everyone's shaken up pretty bad. Even us," he said, and she assumed he meant the police. "We've never seen anything like this in Osborne. Have your teachers given you the information about counseling?"

Ollie had been so good with her grandmother, yet here she was, completely failing with his brother. She'd spoken two words and could barely look at him, and he already thought she needed counseling.

Still, all she could do was nod. At least it was true. *Every* teacher had given them the information. The counselors would be slammed for months.

"Good. That's good." Chris removed a flippable notepad from his breast pocket and clicked a pen to the ready. "Now I just have a few questions. They're totally standard. We're asking everyone."

Another nod. Her hands began to sweat underneath her jeans.

His voice remained friendly, though it grew a touch sterner. *Cop voice.* "I know you're new around here, but were you acquainted with either of the victims?"

It was a peculiar thing. Makani had lived here for almost a year—plenty of time to have gotten to know the victims—but in a town like this, she would always be made to feel like the new girl. "No," she said. "I've never spoken to Haley."

I've never spoken instead of *I never spoke*. As if there were still a chance that they might bump into each other buying iced mochas at the gas station.

She adjusted her verbs. "Maybe I spoke to Matt once or twice in government class, because he sat near me, but I'm not even sure. If I did, it wasn't memorable."

The interrogation continued: *Do you know anyone the victims might have had trouble with? Were they ever bullied? Did they ever bully someone else?*

Makani answered each question in the negative, wondering how many of her classmates had possessed the audacity to mention Ollie. They would have all known that they were talking to his brother— same last name, similar appearance, infamous car.

Sergeant Beemer had interviewed Ollie during lunch. Ollie hadn't told Makani much, only that it'd taken the entire hour. Everybody else's interviews had taken just a few minutes. Was Ollie questioned about the episode with Matt in the quad? And had there been other episodes before it?

"Sorry." Makani shrugged at the industrial linoleum. "I'm not much help. I don't hang out with either of their crowds."

"That's okay. Everything helps." His tone had softened, and she looked up. Having successfully nabbed her attention, he broke into a mischievous smile. "Where were you yesterday between the hours of six and seven p.m.?"

Her cheeks exploded with heat.

His grin widened.

"I was with your brother." Makani cringed and crossed her arms. "He drove me home at six thirty, and then I made dinner with my grandma."

"And where had Ollie driven you?"

She moaned somewhat dramatically.

"Might I remind you that I'm an officer of the law?"

He was flat-out teasing her, so Makani steeled herself with a wry, defeated smile. "I honestly don't know. It was some random cornfield off 275, between here and Troy. We made out. He got a call from work, and then we left."

Chris made another notation on his notepad.

Makani sat up a bit straighter. "Why? What did *he* say?"

"Same thing." He looked pleased with himself. "I just wanted to hear you say it."

She actually laughed, which made him laugh, too. "Can I go now? Is this over?"

He waved for her to remain seated. "Almost."

Makani rebraced in anticipation of the inevitably awkward next question—*What are your intentions with my brother?*—which she would *not* answer, so she was caught off guard when Chris asked, "How much hunting experience do you have?"

"None." Her brow furrowed. "My dad used to take me fishing sometimes, but I was never really into it. Does that count?"

"Did you ever help him gut the fish?"

"No."

"How much experience would you say that you have with a knife?"

The blood drained from Makani's face. "W-why would you ask me that?"

Chris looked up from scribbling. He cocked his head. "Because the person we're trying to find has a certain level of skill with a knife and knowledge of anatomy."

"No." Her voice trembled. *"No."*

Thankfully, he must have jumped to the conclusion that she was upset by the reason for the question rather than the question itself. "You're okay," he assured her, tucking away his notepad. "That's all we needed to know."

Her heart was racing as he led her back into the hallway.

"I still have to interview the administrators, but at least you get to go home soon, huh?" Chris held out his hand. "Until we meet again."

Makani shook it. She wanted to say that it was nice to meet him. Instead, she rushed into the restroom.

She was already crying as she burst into the first stall—not for a specific reason, but for all of them. She wished that she were in Hawaii having a normal senior year. She wished that she could have been the appropriate blend of charming and sad for Chris. She wished that there weren't psychopaths who killed for pleasure and made the world feel unsafe. She wished that Ollie were her boyfriend, and that she could make out with him again, preferably as soon as possible. And she wished that she weren't so selfish to wish for a boyfriend when two of her classmates were dead.

If she stayed here any longer, people might wonder. Makani swallowed her tears, dried her face with a scratchy paper towel, and exited the bathroom.

Ollie was leaning against the wall beside the drinking fountains. His eyes were dark with under-eye circles. "You got my brother." It wasn't a question.

"Officer Larsson requested me specifically."

Ollie sighed.

"It was fine. He was nice." Makani glanced around, but the hallway was empty. "Were you . . . waiting for me?" And then she noticed her backpack on the floor near his feet. "Why do you have that?"

"I asked Señora Washington if I could use the bathroom. She

didn't even notice when I grabbed our bags. I saw you go inside, so I waited."

She'd been in there for over ten minutes. Panic floated to the surface, instantly accessible. "I was sitting. Just sitting. I didn't want to go back to class."

Ollie nodded.

"You should have knocked," she said.

He raised his eyebrows. They both knew that he would never have dared to knock on the door to the women's restroom. Too many potential embarrassing outcomes.

"No, sorry." Makani was exhausted and confused. None of this was making any sense. "But . . . *why* do you have my bag?"

"Are you okay?" he asked.

"What?" She shook her head. It was like they were having two different conversations. "No, I'm not okay. Are you okay?"

Ollie smiled. "Not at all."

Makani stared back at him until she erupted with helpless laughter. Tears returned to the corners of her eyes. "I have no idea what's happening."

"There are still twenty minutes until the final bell, but I'm leaving now." Ollie picked up her backpack and held it out. "Want a ride?"

CHAPTER NINE

THE ONLY PEOPLE who noticed their early departure were the reporters. They hovered like vultures between the campus and parking lot, waiting for the students to be let out for the weekend. Waiting for carrion. As Makani and Ollie neared, Makani's spine stiffened. She lowered her head and walked faster. Ollie adjusted his speed to match.

The reporters erupted all at once: *Did you know the victims? How would you describe the atmosphere inside the school today? Will this hurt your team's chances in the playoffs?* Microphones and cameras were jammed in their direction, and Makani angled her body away from the intrusion in the clearest possible signal, but a woman with a wall of hairsprayed bangs chased behind them anyway. "How does it feel to have lost two of your classmates in only three days?"

Makani focused on Ollie's car at the far end of the lot.

"How does it feel to have lost two of your classmates in three days?"

Car, car, car, car, car, car, car—

A hand touched Makani's shoulder, and she screamed. Her eyes looked manic with fright. The reporter stumbled backward into her cameraman, and Makani screamed again. The woman exclaimed something in confused anger, and suddenly Ollie stood between them shouting, "Get away from her! Get the fuck away from her!"

The cameraman placed a hand on the reporter's arm, urging her back, but she wasn't ready to yield. "You," she said. "Pink hair. How does it feel—"

"How the fuck do you think it feels?"

The cameraman pleaded with the reporter. "They're probably minors—"

Through the haze, Ollie reached for Makani. An arm slid around her back as he hustled her toward his car. *Car, car, car,* she thought. *Car.* He opened the passenger's door, helped her inside, and ran to the driver's side. All five of her senses were overloading. Instead of trying not to cry, Makani just tried not to sob.

She expected—maybe even wanted—him to tear out of the lot, but he exited cautiously and stuck to the speed limit. He turned left, away from the direction of her house, and drove until they reached the park near the elementary school.

The cruiser pulled over to a stop. Makani felt him trying to decide whether or not to lay a comforting hand on her arm. "I'm sorry," she said. Her overreaction was blatant and humiliating. She had to lie. "I don't know why . . ."

"You don't have anything to apologize for."

She sniffled, rummaging through her backpack for tissues.

Ollie leaned over her to pop open the glove compartment. It was lined with crumpled napkins from an out-of-town KFC.

She accepted a wad and blew her nose. There was no attractive way to do it. She felt like a monster. "It's been such a shitty day."

"*Such* a shitty day." He laughed once.

They sat in silence for a full minute. Makani stared out the window. The park was empty apart from a mom and toddler on the swings. "I don't want to go home." Her voice was weak and dispirited. "She'll want me to rehash everything that happened at school today, but I don't wanna talk about it. I can't think about it anymore."

Ollie nodded. He understood that she was talking about her grandmother. "Where would you like to go?"

"Someplace quiet."

So, Ollie took her to his house.

It was a twenty-minute drive, halfway between Osborne and East Bend on Highway 79, another lonely road of cornfields and cattle ranches. Every mile, they'd pass another highlighter-yellow billboard for the Martin Family Fun Corn Maze. A smiling family of cartoon redheads beamed at them from the top corner of each advertisement.

NEBRASKA'S LARGEST CORN MAZE! 5 MILES AHEAD!

PUMPKIN PATCH! 4 MILES AHEAD!

HAYRIDES! 3 MILES AHEAD!

PETTING ZOO! 2 MILES AHEAD!

CORN PIT! 1 MILE AHEAD!

"What's a corn pit?" Makani already felt lighter, knowing that she had a few hours' respite ahead of her. She'd texted Darby that Ollie was driving her home, and she'd texted Grandma Young that Darby was taking her to his house. Neither seemed pleased, but they'd each correctly assumed that she needed a distraction from the news.

"Exactly what it sounds like," Ollie said. "A giant pit of corn kernels."

"Okay. But what does one *do* with a corn pit?"

He glanced at her with a smile. "You know those ball pits at

McDonald's? It's like that, but bigger. A lot bigger. It's pretty fun," he admitted. "Now, the petting zoo. That's what I could do without. When the wind blows just right . . ."

Makani laughed as circus-like flags appeared through the fields. They passed the sprawling maze and a massive dirt parking lot, which was mostly vacant. "Does anyone actually come here?"

"It's packed on the weekends. People drive in from Omaha and Lincoln. And it's loud. You can hear it in my house. On Saturdays, they even have a polka band. When our windows are open, I'll often find my feet tapping to the belch of their tuba."

She laughed again. "I'm still imagining you swimming in the corn pit."

Ollie kept his eyes ahead, but they twinkled. Or maybe gleamed.

He turned onto the next road. A gentle hill broke up the flatness of the surrounding earth. It was the hushed, eerie beauty of Willa Cather country, a century later. Sophomore year, she'd been assigned to read *O Pioneers!* in English class, and the familiar descriptions of the land had comforted her. They'd reminded her of visiting her favorite grandmother. Little did she know that, soon enough, she'd be living here.

The novel no longer held any appeal. It wasn't fictional anymore.

A house in the distance grew bigger, and Makani realized that the road was Ollie's driveway. His house was white, like hers, but peeling and weatherworn. It was a Victorian Gothic Revival—a style that was growing obsolete in these parts—with three dramatically arched windows under three steeply pitched roof points. Twin columns framed a modest covered porch. The expansive yard was unkempt and overgrown.

Makani was grateful that she didn't believe in ghosts; she only believed in the ghostlike quality of painful memories. And she was sure this house had plenty.

Not everything about it was gloomy, however. As she stepped out of the car, a set of wind chimes jangled in the breeze and two large ferns swayed on chains from opposite ends of the porch. They were dead from the early frosts. But proof of recent habitation.

Ollie shot her a nervous glance. "Home sweet home."

Had he ever brought home a girl before, or was this something new for him? Something potentially vulnerable? On the disintegrating coir welcome mat, a single word was barely visible: LARSSON.

The younger Larsson unlocked the front door, which opened into a large, dim, and dusty room. "I know." He sighed. "It looks like a haunted house."

Makani held up two innocent hands. "I didn't say a word."

He led her inside with a tight smile. The floors were old hardwood, and the boards groaned with each step. Makani waited in the threshold while Ollie threw open the curtains. Sparkling dust motes caught in the sudden light as the living room was revealed to be more homelike, more *normal,* than anticipated. She couldn't help feeling relieved. The rugs, lamps, and hardware seemed to be a mixture of Victorian reproductions and actual Victorian antiques, but the sectional sofa was firmly from this century.

Though . . . there *was* something about the space. It possessed an unnatural amount of stillness. Everything appeared unruffled. Unused.

"Would you like something to drink?" Ollie asked. "We have water, orange juice, Coke—well, it's not Coca-Cola, it's the off-brand Coke—"

Makani laughed, because he'd remembered. "Water's fine."

"Tap water? Ice? No ice?"

She trailed behind him through the adjoining dining room, which was also murky and untouched. Ollie moved like a creature of habit. "Whichever's more work for you," she called out, even though the temperature inside wasn't much warmer than it had been outside. She didn't want ice.

At least the kitchen was brighter. Much brighter. Curtainless windows looked out upon the sweeping fields, and the maze's flags waved merrily in the distance. Ollie's kitchen, though not as clean as Grandma Young's, was less dusty than the other rooms, and the dishes had been recently washed and were drying on a rack. And while the cabinetry and furniture didn't look exactly modern, they didn't look Victorian, either.

A shadow lurched out from the floorboards.

Makani shrieked as a small dog with a speckled, bluish-gray coat skittered and stumbled toward Ollie.

Laughing, he kneeled to greet the intruder. "Hey, Squidward."

For the second time in an hour, she'd completely lost her shit. Makani felt embarrassed, all over again. "Sorry. I didn't know you had a dog."

"Blue heeler." Ollie smiled as he rubbed its head. "Back when we adopted him, I was a big *SpongeBob* fan. Now he's deaf and almost blind. He sleeps most of the day—that's why he didn't notice when we came in." Squidward leaned against him, as if he were using Ollie to keep himself upright. "How are you, buddy?"

Makani squatted to pet him. "Is he friendly?"

"If you let him sniff your hand first, you'll be fine."

Squidward himself kind of smelled, but Makani didn't mind. His fur was coarse, almost waxy. But it felt nice to be petting a dog and even nicer to be this close to Ollie.

"Do you have a dog? Back home?" Ollie looked aside as he added this second question, aware of how infrequently she spoke of her past.

But dogs were a safe subject. Makani shook her head as Squidward rolled onto his back. "My mom claims she's allergic. Really, she just thinks they're too messy."

"We have a cat, too. She's probably outside right now."

"Sandy Cheeks?"

He grinned. "Raven."

"Ah. A *much* cooler name."

"Not necessarily. At the time, I had a massive crush on Raven-Symoné."

Makani laughed.

Ollie rubbed Squidward's belly. "I have no idea why my parents let me name our pets."

"Because, clearly, your parents were awesome." But she flinched as soon as it came out. Was it okay to mention them? Although, he was the one who brought them up.

And now he was nodding in agreement.

It occurred to her that perhaps Ollie appreciated the acknowledgment of his parents. Perhaps it was harder when people went out of their way to avoid talking about them—when they pretended like his parents had never existed in the first place.

Makani often pretended like hers didn't exist. At her grandmother's insistence, she called her mother once a week and her father every other week. They didn't even know what was happening here, because, until this moment, she hadn't thought to tell them. Her parents always spent the too-long calls complaining about each other.

Ollie washed the dog off his hands and grabbed two burritos from the freezer. He held them up for her. They were both bean and cheese. "One or two?"

Makani longed for a piping hot bowl of saimin, a noodle dish so common back home that it was on the menu at McDonald's. Osborne didn't even have a non-saimin McDonald's. But burritos were decent. Better than whatever she'd be making for dinner with her grandmother. "One, please," she said. "Thanks."

He slipped off their wrappers, hesitated, and then grabbed another burrito for himself. All three went into the microwave.

As she scratched behind Squidward's ears, Makani stared at a faded photograph on the refrigerator. Ollie's parents stood in front of Old Faithful. Their arms were around each other, and they were smiling as the geyser sprayed above their heads like a whale's blowhole. His father's smile was farmer-stiff, but his mother looked carefree.

Beside it was a photo of Ollie and his brother. Ollie looked old enough to be in high school, but he was still younger than she'd ever known him. His hair was an odd, streaky green, and he was wince-laughing as Chris pulled him into a forced hug. She wondered if their parents were already dead and who had taken the picture.

"I tried to dye it blue." Like always, Ollie had been watching her. "One of the first lessons that you learn in school—yellow and blue make green—and I forgot."

"You look like a mermaid. A sad, pubescent mermaid."

Ollie froze. And then he covered his face, shaking his head in disbelief. "That might be the actual worst thing that anyone has ever said to me."

"No!" As Makani burst into laughter, she smiled with all her teeth. "I mean, I stand by my assessment. But I swear I have pictures that are just as bad. Worse, even."

"I demand proof."

"Fair enough. The next time you're at my house, take a peek under my bed."

Ollie blinked. And then his eyebrows rose, perhaps at the mention of her bed.

"Seventh-grade swim team." Makani shuddered as she recalled her flat chest, gawky posture, and unflattering suit. "Let's leave it at that."

The microwave let out an extensive series of beeps. As Ollie removed the steaming burritos, he glanced at her. "You're a swimmer?"

Shit.

She couldn't believe it had slipped out. Since the age of seven, she'd dived competitively, but her grandmother was the only person here who knew it. Osborne didn't even have a swim team. And even if it did, those days had passed.

"I used to swim." She looked away. "A little."

Her eyes snagged on a brown file folder. It was sitting in the center of the breakfast table. She didn't have to open it to know what it contained.

Ollie followed her gaze. "See? He's practically asking me to read it."

"Why didn't he take it with him?"

"I'm sure he just forgot. Happens all the time."

The case file was thick. "Isn't a good memory kinda important for an officer?"

Luckily, Ollie didn't take offense. "That's why they write everything down. Cops do shit-tons of paperwork." He shrugged. "Memories aren't reliable, anyway."

Makani wished that she could forget. In the darkest hours of the night, her own memory was keen and cruel.

"You can look if you want." Ollie's voice tensed. "It isn't pretty."

Of course she wanted to look—sheer human curiosity demanded it—but there would be no *un*looking once she'd done it. Her fingertips crawled toward the file anyway. They recklessly flicked it open to reveal a stack of photographs and papers. A female body lay on her back, right arm hanging limp from a bed. Her neck had been carved open by five crude slices. One for the mouth, two for each eye. X and X.

Dead cartoon eyes.

In Makani's imagination, this scene, this smiley face, had been tidy and precise, but in reality . . . it was a bloodbath. The head was tilted too far back to see Haley's real eyes. The longest cut was deep and vicious, and her neck skin flapped open in a jagged, ugly gash. Her hair, clothing, and bedsheets were soaked with enough blood to curdle a butcher's stomach. Blood had dried inside her nostrils.

Makani closed the file with a shaking hand.

"Bad, right?" Ollie said.

It wasn't just bad. It was horrific.

A real dead body looked different from the ones on television or in the movies. There was nothing artful about it. Nothing positioned. Haley's body looked lifeless—but not like life had been taken away from it. Like it had never had life.

Ollie pressed his fingers to his temples. "I should have warned you."

"You did." Makani hugged herself. Was Matt in that stack of photos, too, or did he have a separate file? The brutality of the crime overwhelmed her. *Someone did this.* A real person had crept into Haley's house and murdered her in her own bed.

"Any chance the police have a lead?" she asked.

Ollie shook his head. "But they do think it's probably someone a lot smaller than Matt."

"So, not another football player."

"Right."

"Why?"

He waited for her to meet his eyes. "Are you sure you want to know?"

Makani nodded.

"Before the killer did . . . what they did, they stabbed Matt in the gut. But his abdomen had nothing to do with the final display of his brain. So, he was probably attacked by someone who physically *couldn't* go straight for his head. They had to weaken him first. Bring him down to their level."

Perhaps the killer was female, after all.

Dead cartoon eyes. Blood inside her nostrils.

Makani became aware of a dinner plate being pushed gently against her stomach.

"Hey," Ollie said. "It's nicer in my room."

She stared down at the warm plate. Was Matt stabbed once in the abdomen or had it taken multiple jabs for him to go down?

Wordlessly, she accepted the burritos. Ollie carried their water glasses. As the stairs creaked beneath their feet, Makani wondered how many gruesome pictures he'd seen since his brother became a cop. Sure, there had never been deaths in Osborne this violent before, but people died by accident all the time. People like his parents.

Did it get easier to look at the photos? Or did it get harder, knowing that so many people died so young—and in such awful ways? Did seeing the proof of this make you more paranoid or more careful? Or did it just harden you?

Old photographs were everywhere. A framed studio portrait of his whole family hung at the top of the upstairs landing. Ollie was so little that his mother held him on her lap. What was it like for him to look at this one every day?

"It's this one," he said, pulling the phrase from her mind.

Makani had assumed that his bedroom would be as black and unembellished as his wardrobe, so when he opened the door, she blinked in surprise.

The room was filled with sunlight and signs of life. Even the kitchen clung to a whiff of abandonment, but here, Ollie's ubiquitous paperbacks were spread across every surface. There were too many for his shelves, so they'd spilled onto his rug, been stacked on top of his desk and under it, and even lay in messy piles on his unmade bed. With its heap of mismatched blankets, the bed looked like the coziest spot in the entire house.

Makani set down the plate on his desk and picked up the closest book, *Jupiter's Travels*. "Four years around the world on a Triumph," she read aloud. On the cover, a man in an old-fashioned leather jacket rode an old-fashioned motorcycle. The paperback smelled old, too, like dusty shelves and faint mildew. She used it to gesture around the room. "I knew you liked to read, but . . . wow."

Ollie shrugged with his hands in his pockets. "I get them from garage sales and the used bookstore in East Bend. I haven't read them all. I just keep picking them up."

"I wasn't making fun of you. My last boyfriend read a lot, too."

Shit. Double shit.

Ollie wasn't her boyfriend. They barely knew each other. She wanted to know more about him—she *wanted* him to be her boyfriend—but they were each still standing behind a wall of unspoken history. She decided to act like she hadn't meant anything by it and casually picked up another book. Glanced at him. His pale skin was unable to hide an emotional flush. At least he didn't seem turned off by the idea.

Makani had been surprised in Darby's car yesterday morning when she'd realized that Ollie was more shy than he was rebellious, but she was even more surprised now to realize that she found his shyness attractive.

She held up a travel guide to Italy. "Mind if I go with you?"

"We'll leave tonight." Ollie stepped toward her, and her heart spasmed. But he had only come closer to remove his keys from his pocket and take the plate to his bed.

Disappointed, she flipped open the guidebook. "Positano. Hotel Intermezzo. Excellent value in this charming, family-run hotel overlooking the sea." She carried the book to his bed and plopped down beside him. "Shall I call for a reservation?"

Ollie smiled as he bit into a burrito. He held out the plate with his other hand. She accepted one. It was strange sharing a plate, but she liked it. It made her feel close to him.

"Tell me," he said.

Makani swallowed before speaking. The cheap burrito was thoroughly mediocre but immensely satisfying. "Tell you what?"

"About your last boyfriend. The reader."

She smiled. Caught. And then she nudged his leg with her kneecap, pleased by his obvious jealousy. "I thought I'd steered us away from that conversation."

"You tried. Usually, you're good at that. At steering away."

It was the first time that it had been acknowledged out loud. She felt chastised but rose to the challenge. "Okay, here's my offer. I'll tell you about my last boyfriend if you tell me about your last girlfriend."

Ollie considered it for a few seconds. "Deal."

Makani steeled herself to remain honest. "His name was Jason Nakamura, and we dated for seven months." She tried to gauge Ollie's expression. It remained maddeningly enigmatic. "He was a swimmer, too. Freestyle."

But then he wouldn't talk to me anymore.

"But then I moved away."

"Did you try to make it work long distance?" Ollie asked.

She discarded her final bite back onto the plate, an end piece of freezer-hardened tortilla. "That would be a *very* long distance." When he waited for elaboration, she selected her next words carefully. "No. We didn't like each other enough."

Ollie nodded with understanding.

She braced herself. "Your turn. Last girlfriend."

He set the plate onto the floor with a hollow clunk. "No one."

It wasn't the answer she was expecting. She stared at him, searching for comprehension. He stared back as he repeated it. "No one."

"Explain. Use more words."

A smile tugged at his lips. "I've never had a girlfriend."

Makani had made out with him. Makani had had *sex* with him. She found this statement to be highly improbable. He knew what she was thinking, and he shrugged, but it wasn't a shrug of indifference. It was a shrug that was hiding some measure of embarrassment. "I've never had a girlfriend, but, yes, obviously I've had sex before you."

Makani couldn't let that one sit. "Obviously."

Ollie squirmed and glanced up at the ceiling. "Not *obviously* because I was *amazing. Obviously* because . . ."

"Oh, no. No, no, no." Her hair bounced as she shook her head. "I need to hear you finish that sentence."

His expression deadpanned. "Because I lasted more than thirty seconds."

She burst into raucous laughter, which made him smile. Ollie always smiled when he saw that she was happy. Makani leaned into the space between them. "So, are you gonna tell me about this non-girlfriend? Non-girlfriend*s*?"

His smile widened into a grin. "Yes."

She moved in closer, beckoning. "But not today?"

Their lips were an inch apart.

"Not today," he said.

They went for each other at the same time. Mouths clashed. Jackets peeled off. She lowered herself onto her back, and he moved above her, pressing down. The weight of his body made her feral. Her fingers clawed under his shirt and up his back as his hands slid over her bra. Her hands moved to the bottom of her shirt, ready to strip it above her head, when suddenly . . . they were aware.

A third person was in the room.

CHAPTER TEN

CHRIS STOOD IN the doorway and swore. And then swore again. "Damn it, Ollie!"

Ollie scrambled to sit up, scrambled to make sure that Makani was covered even though they hadn't gotten that far. "What are you doing here?"

His brother rubbed his forehead. "Nice to see you again so soon, Makani."

Her skin burst into flames as she shielded herself behind Ollie, who tried again. "Why are you *home*?"

Chris dropped his hand and crossed his arms, drawing her eyes to the holster on his belt. "Chief sent me away to get some rest." He glanced warily at the empty plate beside the bed. "When did you get here? Did you ditch again?"

Ollie didn't reply.

"Shit, Ollie. You can't . . . you can't *do* that."

Makani wished that she could run. She wished that she were anywhere but here.

"We missed zero schoolwork," Ollie said. "Nothing was happening."

"If nothing was happening," Chris said, "then it shouldn't have been so hard to keep seated until the bell." When Ollie tightened his mouth, Chris groaned and collapsed into the desk chair. He followed it with a long sigh. "Listen. There's a killer on the loose, and we don't know who or where he is. Or if he's even a he. That means *your* ass needs to be where it's supposed to be at all times. I need to know where you are."

"Why?" Ollie sounded remarkably incredulous for this reasonable request.

"Because it's dangerous out there!"

"They murdered the star of the musical and the star of the football team. Tell me what I have in common with those victims."

"You know that's not the point. Shit," Chris said again. He turned his attention to Makani. "You've gotta stop hanging out with this kid. He's a bad influence."

Makani felt a wave of gratitude that he didn't view *her* as the bad influence. She ventured out from behind Ollie.

"Does your grandmother know you're here?" Chris asked.

She wanted to lie, but he was a cop. "No."

Chris shook his head. He picked up Ollie's keys from the desk and held them out, staring at the hardwood floor. "Ollie, drive her home."

"Chris—"

"*Ollie.*"

Ollie stomped over, snatched the keys in a way that made Chris wince, and then stalked out of his bedroom.

Makani followed, but she glanced back to lift a hand in goodbye.

Chris raised a weary hand in return. "Sorry. But I have to."

It was a strange thing for a parental figure to say, and it reminded her of the unnatural relationship that he'd been forced to play in his brother's life. In that moment, she felt sorry for Chris. Ollie hadn't made it easy for him. Then again, nothing about Ollie's life seemed to have been easy, either.

That night—when Haley and the drama club were supposed to be in the middle of their first dress rehearsal, when Matt and the football team were supposed to be winning their final game of the season— Darby sent a text to Makani: *Can we talk?*

She'd just finished loading the dirty dinner dishes into the dishwasher. Grandma Young was watching a Marvel movie in the living room. She didn't know that Makani had been to Ollie's house, and Makani planned to keep it that way.

"Will Chris tell her?" she'd asked on the somber drive home.

Ollie tried to assure her, despite the crease in his brow. "I doubt it. His weakness is that he still wants to be my cool older brother."

To be safe, they made Saturday plans in full view of Grandma Young. He was going to come over before his shift at Greeley's.

I mean, phone-talk?

Makani frowned at the second message. It was always ominous when someone asked to talk instead of text. She told her grandmother that she'd join her in a minute and waited until she was safely enclosed in her bedroom before hitting the call button.

Darby picked up after the second ring. "Thanks."

"Yeah, what's up?"

An awkward silence followed. Another bad sign.

"Darby?"

"I—I just want you to know that as your friend, I love you, and that's why I'm telling you this."

Makani felt her body temperature drop. "Tell me what?"

"And you know I would never say this if it weren't important. If Alex and I weren't genuinely concerned."

"*What*, Darby?"

He mumbled something rapidly that contained the name Ollie.

A surge of hot anger replaced Makani's chill, but she tamped it down and asked him to repeat that last sentence.

The accusation spewed forth in a torrent. "Discounting rumors, it's still a fact that Matt and his friends have been bullying Ollie for years, and his alibi isn't strong for either murder, and we think he might be taking advantage of you, and Alex said I had to be the one to call, because you'd just tell her to screw herself, or you'd think she was joking, but I swear we're not." He took a breath. "Not that we think he's guilty! But that *was* creepy how he got your phone number. You have to admit it."

Makani didn't have to admit anything. It was misguided and insulting. "So, what? You and Alex just sat there at the Feed 'N' Seed all afternoon, selling cattle supplements and talking shit about me?"

"No!" Darby sounded miserable. "I'm sorry. We're worried about you."

"Yeah. You mentioned something along those lines yesterday, re-member?"

His voice dropped into a meek whisper. "It didn't seem like you were listening."

Fury overtook her like an explosion from a pressure cooker. "And what about Haley, huh? What did Haley ever do to Ollie? Why would he kill her?"

"In eighth grade, he asked her out, and she said no. She was a seventh grader. He was humiliated. It wasn't long after his parents had died, and it was the last time I heard of him asking out someone from school until . . . this weird thing with you."

It shocked her into speechlessness. She hadn't expected Darby to have a real answer. But it was still a colossal leap.

"Makani? Hello? Are you there?"

"That was four years ago." She forced her voice into a normal volume, despite the outrage swelling inside her again. "That's a long time to wait for a petty grudge."

"Just consider this: Ollie snubbed you for months. You guys hadn't talked since the end of summer. It's possible . . . he might want revenge on you, too."

She sucked in her breath.

"Regaining your trust could be a part of his master plan—"

"*Master plan?*"

"I only meant—"

"I was mad at him, too! It was mutual. A stupid misunderstanding."

"You're right, it's probably nothing." Darby backed down to plead with her. "But you have to understand that I could never live with myself if he turned out to be the bad guy, and I'd kept my mouth shut."

Makani's indignation dissipated. Flared back into raging life. And finally re-extinguished. Darby was trying to be a good friend. He was just getting it wrong. On paper, fine, Ollie looked suspicious. But he wasn't a murderer.

She couldn't prove it. She just knew it.

Ollie was shy and helpful, and he looked happy whenever she was happy. Darby's confrontation hurt, because he was supposed to be the thoughtful friend. Alex was the impulsive one. And it confirmed her fears; they really did talk about her behind her back.

Darby sounded distant through her buzzing eardrums. "Makani?"

"I appreciate your concern." It was a lie and not a lie. "But you're wrong."

And then she hung up.

•   •   •

All night long, Makani tossed and turned. The house creaked like it was alive.

Ollie, Haley.

Ollie, Matt.

Ollie, Me.

All morning long, she ignored the apology texts from Darby and the jokey texts that acted as apologies from Alex.

Ollie, Haley.

Ollie, Matt.

Ollie, Me.

At noon, she was surprised to discover yesterday's shoes still at the bottom of the stairs. She grabbed them before Grandma Young could scold her.

Ollie, Haley.

Ollie, Matt.

Ollie—

NO.

Makani threw the sneakers, hard, onto her bedroom floor. Yesterday's socks were already lying beside the closet door, but the strangeness of this did not register to her.

She had to believe that the mistakes of Ollie's past didn't guarantee that he would make even worse mistakes in his future. She had to believe that every mistake was still a *choice.* She had to believe that Ollie was a good person, because she had to believe it about herself.

He arrived in the early afternoon. After the cycle of beverage options, they settled into the living room, because—as Makani learned—it was against house rules to have a boy in her bedroom. As her friend,

Darby was the only exception. Back in Hawaii, she'd spent plenty
of time in her bedroom with her ex-boyfriend. Her parents either
hadn't noticed or didn't care.

The television was tuned to the closest physical station, which
was broadcasting a basketball game. Neither Makani nor her grandmother followed the NBA, but Grandma Young was anxious to see
the local news bumpers. Makani slouched beside her on the sofa
while Ollie resumed his position in the easy chair.

Ollie hadn't been kidding. He really did like jigsaw puzzles. A
countryside harvest festival was spread across the coffee table, and
its repeating autumnal patterns held him and Grandma Young in a
matching trance. Perched on their seat edges, they bonded over eti-
quette and strategy: start with the border. Then any sections that contain printed words. If someone is searching for one specific piece, but
the other person finds it, it must be handed over, because it means
more to the first person. And always save the sky—the hardest part
of any puzzle—for last.

Makani tried to join in, but the tediousness made her hungry, so
she brought out snacks and ate snacks and brought out more snacks.
She wondered if her ex would have entertained her grandmother
without complaint. Before the incident, she would have said yes.
Jason was wild, but she had been wilder. And he was a decent guy.

He was also a coward who'd never bothered to ask for her side of
the story. A coward who'd ignored her instead of dumping her outright. A coward who'd treated her like the highly contagious carrier
of a deadly plague. Though, in a way, she was. Makani was a social
plague. She hated Jason for his cowardice, but she understood it.

"You know, we've just been praying for their families, day and
night."

They looked up at the sound of the young, country voice. A square-
faced boy with a cross necklace and LION PRIDE sweatshirt—the de

facto spokesperson for the various local youth groups—was on television. The text at the bottom of the screen read: CALEB GREELEY, FRIEND OF THE VICTIMS.

The bumper cut to a blandly handsome man in a navy-blue suit. "Osborne reacts to the slayings and to a killer still at large. Details at six." Creston Howard enunciated with the practiced air of a professional, managing to sound both solemn and upbeat.

The basketball game resumed. Grandma Young turned to Ollie. "That was Pastor Greeley's boy, wasn't it?"

Ollie nodded. "He works with me at the grocery store."

It was a familiar conversation, Ollie and her grandmother swapping information about mutual acquaintances. Makani hadn't recognized many of the names until now. "Oh. *Greeley*," she said. "Caleb is related to the owner?"

"Caleb is the grandson of the original Mr. Greeley," Ollie explained. "His uncle runs Greeley's Foods now."

"And what does Caleb do there?" Grandma Young asked.

"Weekend supervisor."

Makani couldn't hear it in his tone, but she wondered if Ollie was bitter that Caleb was a supervisor when Ollie was the one who worked more hours. If it were her, she'd be bitter. "Caleb wasn't actually a *friend* of the victims, was he?"

Ollie smirked. "As friendly as I was."

Makani nudged her grandmother. "See? You have to turn off the news. It's not even telling you the truth."

"You grieve in your way," Grandma Young said, "and I'll grieve in mine."

Despite the outside world, their living room was at ease. Makani wondered why discussing a tragedy—consuming every single story about it—*was* often comforting. Was it because tragedies manifested a sense of community? *Here we are, all going through this terrible thing together*. Or were tragedies addictive, and the small pleasures that came from them the signal of a deeper problem?

Ollie handed over a puzzle piece to Grandma Young. She exclaimed with delight and snapped it into place. They high-fived.

No, Makani decided. It was impossible that this boy who was so kind to her grandmother could ever be a murderer.

CHAPTER ELEVEN

THERE WAS A machete wedged behind the empty watercooler. He couldn't believe that someone had hidden it here, of all places. He yanked out the large plastic bottle and threw it at the woman, gaining the precious seconds necessary to reach back and fumble for the weapon. The bottle hit her head with a satisfying *thonk*. As she staggered, his hand clasped around the wooden handle. The machete came loose with just enough time to thrust it forward between her ribs. She fell against the copy machine. Planting his boot on her chest, he tugged out the blade before lifting it over his head and swinging it back down through her neck in a single, swift motion. Her head splattered against the cubicle and then dropped into a recycle bin. He held out the machete to admire it.

Yes. This will do nicely.

But to keep it, he had to discard one of his other weapons, so he placed the tire iron behind the watercooler for someone else to find. That made him smile.

Rodrigo Morales paused the game and tossed aside the controller. He took off his headphones. Rubbed his eyes. It was midnight.

His parents were carousing in Vegas for their silver wedding anniversary, and he wasn't about to let a single minute of this glorious weekend go to waste. He'd spent Friday night and all today fighting the zombies in *Battleground Apocalypse* with only one short nap, and he'd fight them all Sunday, too.

He was the youngest of four children and the only son. His last sister had moved out in mid-August, and now with his parents out of town, this was the first time in his entire life that he'd ever been truly alone. He relished it.

Rodrigo stood, and his spine cracked from bottom to top. He rolled his neck in a methodical circle. Stretched his arms toward the ceiling. *Wake up*, he ordered himself.

He slumped out of the living room and into the kitchen for an energy drink. It was a new brand—JACKD, in aggressive all caps—and it came in a lurid green can. Despite the marketing campaign's flagrant promises, it wasn't better than any of the others. He'd been building up his tolerance for years. He chugged a full can. Half a sausage pizza had congealed on the stovetop from earlier, so he finished it off while checking his phone.

Kevin still uses Ubuntu lol

It was a text from David. He was binging classic anime with their other friends at Kevin's house. Anime sucked, and Rodrigo was glad to be missing it. Except, he didn't *totally* think it sucked. He liked *Attack on Titan* when they forced him to watch it last year, but he couldn't help it. Something inside him made him pretend that he didn't.

I wouldn't even put that distro on mi abuela's computer, Rodrigo replied.

David lol'd again. Their friends were a joke when it came to operating systems. Not that David was much better. He tried to keep up with Rodrigo, but nobody around here could. In elementary school,

Rodrigo had jailbroken iPhones and Kindles for extra cash. Now he had eight different PAYware games on all the app stores. His latest—a dumb game about popping rainbow bubbles—was raking it in.

Binge so lame you need me to keep you entertained? Rodrigo asked.

Nah we're watching cowboy bebop. It's cool.

Rodrigo had vaguely heard of it, but he researched its plot as he moved into the bathroom to take a piss. It was some space cowboy bullshit. He didn't bother replying. He checked his favorite message board, but the usual torch-and-pitchfork crowd were still up in arms over this new company of video game developers that was run entirely by women. His insides shrank with a familiar shame as he quickly left the page. Not that long ago, he'd been one of them.

He cringed as he remembered what he'd said to Makani Young. *I'll give you a ride home, sweetheart.* If his sisters had heard it, they would have kicked him in the cojones. But the line had just slipped out. A knee-jerk, base-level wisecrack. He wasn't that guy anymore. He still didn't understand how he'd ever been that guy.

He walked back into the living room and found that his gaming rocker was facing the wrong direction. Strange. He didn't remember tripping over it.

Rodrigo turned it around, plopped down, and put on his headphones. The game's death-metal pause music blasted in his ears. Had Makani told Alex what he'd said? Probably, which sucked. Alex was smart and sexy and kind of mean, but mean in the same way he was. And sometimes it seemed like she might like him back.

A powerful buzz hit his system. At first, he thought it was from imagining Alex in her torn fishnets, until he realized it must be the energy drink. His bloodstream glowed electric.

Rodrigo unpaused the game. A zombie shot out from the closest cubicle, but he was ready, and he hacked off its emaciated head. He ran through the dilapidated office with his machete aimed high. He was invincible.

An hour later, Rodrigo was asleep.

Somehow, he'd managed to pause the game before he crashed. But he didn't get up. He fell asleep with his headphones still on, the music still pulsing and thrashing.

The sunlight streamed in through the glass back doors. It was so bright that it was painful. Rodrigo squinted, blocking the assault with his hand, and knocked over a full can of JACKD. The chartreuse liquid spilled across his mother's immaculate Mexican rug.

"Shit!" Rodrigo uprighted the aluminum can, but the liquid had already stopped beading. It was seeping into the threads. He lurched to his feet, but the headphones cord yanked him back down, and he fumbled to throw off the whole contraption.

His ears rang in the emptiness of the house. Death metal pumped quietly from the headphones on the floor. He didn't even remember grabbing another energy drink. He only remembered the one that he'd chugged in the kitchen.

A headache ruptured his brain. Was it possible to get a hangover from energy drinks? He turned off the music, and the silence was a cathedral. Rodrigo rubbed his eyeballs through his lids with the palms of his hands. When he opened them, the pinpricks disappeared but . . . something wasn't right.

He was in his living room. Except he wasn't. Or was he turned around? Instead of facing the television, his gaming rocker was facing the couch. Rodrigo looked behind himself. The television was sitting on its stand in the middle of the room. Dead center.

There was a pause of incomprehension.

And then his mind snowballed with panic.

All at once, his gaze absorbed the rest of the room. The two chairs that flanked the couch had been switched. The coffee table was blocking the sliding doors. The fiddle-leaf fig had been moved from beside the doors to the opposite wall, and the floor lamp, usually nestled beside the couch, had been placed beside the fiddle-leaf fig.

His rocker was the only piece of furniture in the correct place.

Rodrigo's heartbeat pounded inside his ears as he tried to piece everything together. Tried to make *sense* of it.

David. It seemed like the sort of prank he'd pull. He had a weird, unpredictable side that Rodrigo didn't always like. Or maybe Sofía, his youngest and most irritating sister. The one who'd finally moved into an apartment at the end of summer.

"Sofía?" He rose to his feet. "David? Are you still here?"

The house didn't answer.

"Ha-ha. Very funny. You got me."

The house still didn't answer.

"What the *shit*," Rodrigo mumbled as he stepped straight into a puddle. In his shock, he'd forgotten about the spilled drink. He jogged to the kitchen for paper towels, but they weren't in the holder underneath the high cabinets.

They were sitting on the center of the island.

Rodrigo knew that he should laugh—whoever this was, they'd gotten him again—but he couldn't. Not yet. Maybe because no one had jumped out to yell gotcha and point their finger.

Had *he* moved everything last night?

It was possible. Maybe.

He checked all the doors, just in case. They were locked. He jogged a little faster as he checked the windows. The one in the guest bathroom was open. His blood turned cold.

Not Sofía, then. She still had a key.

David? Or Kevin? Rodrigo released a foul stream of expletives, realizing it was probably *all* his friends, those fucking assholes, getting revenge on him for turning down their stupid animefest. That's why David had texted him at midnight. They were checking to see if he was still awake. Rodrigo circled the interior of his house, waiting for them to appear. But the rooms were empty.

Rationally, Rodrigo knew that this prank was genius. Breaking into someone's house in the dead of night to rearrange their furniture while they slept? He wished he'd thought of it. It would have scared the hell out of Sofía.

But the reality of it wasn't funny. There were no silly notes, no *Are you awake?* texts, no red-lipsticked warnings on his bathroom mirror. The whole situation felt off.

Instinct told him to call the police, but . . . that was dumb. Wasn't it? He checked his phone for the hundredth time, and when there weren't any messages, he sent a text to the whole group. *LOL you got me. Who did it?*

There was an electronic *ding*, and Rodrigo spun around, yelling and tripping over his feet as he stumbled backward in fear. A slender figure stood motionless in his kitchen. Their slouched back was facing him, and they were wearing a hoodie with the hood up.

"H-hey." Rodrigo's voice came out as a croak.

The figure didn't move.

Rodrigo hated that he felt so terrified. Whoever this was, he was about to be *pissed* at them. The person was too skinny to be one of his sisters.

He crept forward. "David? Is that you?"

The figure didn't move.

"Emily?" She was the smallest in his group of friends. He felt ashamed to think about her hearing the tremor in his speech, but the figure . . . it was so unnaturally still.

What if it *wasn't* someone he knew?

His white socks touched the edge of the kitchen floor. His T-shirt was damp with sweat. He reached out to touch the figure's shoulder—

The killer spun around and lunged. The knife went straight into Rodrigo's heart and back out, a *shuck-shuck* that sunk him to his knees, and then the blade stabbed him in the back again and again and again. Rodrigo gasped. And then gurgled.

And then nothing.

The body lay on the floor like a slaughtered calf. Blood pooled beneath it. The white cabinets were sprayed with a gory red, and the thickest drops trickled down the doors like tears. The killer lifted the deflated carcass under its arms and dragged it to the living room. Propped it in the rocker. Sawed off its ears. The ears were stuffed into the headphones, and then the headphones were placed onto the head.

The killer sat on the rug—crisscross applesauce—picked up the abandoned controller, and unpaused the game. There was no hurry.

No one would be home for hours.

CHAPTER TWELVE

RODRIGO MORALES CHANGED everything. In the early hours of Monday morning, the students of Osborne High were instructed not to come to school. Classes were canceled until further notice. Students were urged to stay home or, if their parents would be at work, stay in the home of a trusted friend. It wasn't safe to be alone.

In the wake of this developing tragedy . . .

The official texts, emails, and voicemails all repeated this same illogical and clunky phrase. No information was provided regarding the third victim, but the town's collective mind was many tentacled and far-reaching. The Morales family had neighbors, several of whom had been startled awake by flashing police lights shortly after 2:00 a.m.

At breakfast, everybody followed the story on two screens—phone and television. Makani jumped as a plate was set down in front of her. She'd only been tangentially aware of Grandma Young, still in her pajamas and plush robe, mixing ingredients and cooking on the stovetop. Makani blinked at the short stack of pancakes.

"Oatmeal pumpkin," her grandmother said.

Their usual breakfast was whole-wheat toast or a bowl of fiber cereal. Makani didn't need to ask why the change. Pancakes kept her grandmother occupied while they waited for information. Pancakes gave her a task to do with her hands in a world that seemed more and more out of her control. And pancakes showed Makani that, even though the world was frightening, she was loved.

If only Makani had an appetite. The cloying sweetness of the maple syrup made her nose ache and her stomach turn.

Rodrigo.

That was the rumor. The guy who'd insulted her five days ago on the quad. The guy she'd spoken to three days ago in physics class. Alex's weird crush.

Rodrigo.

He couldn't be dead, because he was still so alive in her mind.

Makani had already texted Alex. It was her first attempt to contact her since Darby's confrontation, and she had yet to receive a reply. Now she felt guilty for ignoring their texts over the weekend.

"Well?" Grandma Young asked.

"Thank you," Makani said automatically. She'd forgotten about the pancakes.

"I meant, is there anything new?"

"—just in, we *can* confirm a third victim in the Osborne slayings . . ." Creston Howard said from the living room, and they lunged toward him. ". . . a seventeen-year-old senior, Rodrigo Ramón Morales Ontiveros."

His full name. Makani's knees buckled.

He would never be just *Rodrigo* again.

"Oh Lord." Grandma Young covered her mouth with both hands.

The news showed live footage from the crime scene. Two officers in heavy coats stood outside of a one-story rancher with a frosted lawn, discussing something with crossed arms. Neighbors huddled in the foggy street behind a banner of yellow tape.

Creston spoke over the feed. "The boy's parents discovered his body in the early hours of the morning after returning home from a weekend trip to Las Vegas. Police say it appears that he died from knife-related trauma, which has led them to believe the case is connected, though they have yet to disclose if his body faced similar mutilation."

Makani lowered herself, stunned, into the easy chair.

Her grandmother placed a hand on her shoulder.

"Hang on," Dianne Platte said, and the screen cut back to Creston's coanchor in the studio. "We've just received word that *all* Osborne schools are now closed for the day. Parents of middle and elementary school students are being asked to pick up their children immediately, and the police have issued a warning for them to not be left unsupervised until whoever is responsible has been taken into custody."

Grandma Young's willowy hand clenched into a hard grip.

Makani stared at the television in despair, but she could no longer see it. Her vision swam. *His family. His friends. Alex.*

Oh my God, Alex.

"I taught his sisters." Her grandmother's voice cracked. "I can't—"

Makani stood to embrace her, choking back tears as Grandma Young collapsed into her arms. Creston and Dianne repeated their updates. Makani peered over her grandmother's shoulder and out the large window that looked across their front lawn. She scanned the yards for the boogeyman, the Babadook, Ted Bundy.

The street was empty.

A misty chill radiated from the windowpane. Had it been this cold when the killer slipped away from Rodrigo's house? Had the killer finally left behind some evidence in the frost? Makani's bare feet were almost numb. Her hope felt even colder.

The ice crystals melted from the vegetation, but the morning remained bleak. Businesses switched their open signs to closed. Parents stayed at home and locked their doors. Fear clouded the air as panic threatened to storm.

Everyone had known Matt, and plenty had known Haley, but few had known Rodrigo. He wasn't popular. Most people remembered him as a smart-ass who actually happened to be smart. He'd never had a girlfriend, and his small group of friends rarely socialized with other groups.

Overnight, every student had become a potential target.

The story went national. Three murders had given Osborne a serial killer. And not just any serial killer, but the media's favorite kind—someone who committed heinous acts on attractive teenagers. The news spread like wildfire. Makani heard Chief Pilger's official statement during a rundown on CNN: *The Osborne PD is pursuing several leads. The killer will be apprehended, and he or she will face the full punishment of the law. If anyone has any information regarding these crimes, please call this number . . .*

Ollie called around noon. Grandma Young was in her bedroom on the phone with a church friend, and Makani was still parked in front of the television. Ollie was at the police station, performing menial tasks for his brother. Chris didn't want him to be alone, but it was also a punishment for ditching school on Friday. Ollie was stuck there until his afternoon shift at Greeley's. Assuming the grocery store stayed open.

Makani pressed him for details. "Is it true that they have some leads?"

"Sort of," Ollie said. "The police don't want to reveal too much to the public, but the killer left behind two imprints in the blood on the Moraleses' living room rug—a partial of a boot and a partial of the seat of his jeans, which included fibers."

He paused. Makani could tell he was holding something back.

"It's sick," he said, lowering his voice, "but after the murder, he stayed to play *Battleground Apocalypse* on Rodrigo's PlayStation."

Makani's heart picked up speed. "He?"

"Sorry. That's still speculation. It's just the most likely possibility."

Backtracking, her mind finally absorbed his previous statement. "The killer stayed at the crime scene . . . to play a video game?"

"Yep. They sat in Rodrigo's blood—right beside his dead body— and played Rodrigo's game for five hours."

"Five *hours?*"

"Five hours."

"Oh my God. Oh my *God.*" It was impossible to imagine. "That might be the most fucked-up thing I've ever heard."

"At least it means the killer was finally careless and left something behind."

"There weren't any fingerprints on the controller?"

"No. And most of Rodrigo's were smudged off. The killer probably wears gloves, but the police had already guessed that."

Makani was still thinking about the type of person who could sit beside a hacked and slashed body for five hours. "If the killer stayed there for so long, they must not have been concerned with getting caught. They must've known that Rodrigo's parents were out of town. They must've—"

"Known Rodrigo before the attack." Yeah. All three murders have been so personal—not to mention that killing someone with a knife is significantly more intimate than using a gun," he added, sounding like his cop brother, "so it doesn't seem probable that the killer is some random, crazy drifter. It's probably someone they all knew."

"Someone *we* know."

An unintelligible voice in the background interrupted their conversation. "Okay, okay," Ollie said with his phone pulled away from his mouth. "Sorry." He was back on the line. "Chris wants me to get back to organizing his files."

"Oh. Yeah."

Neither of them said goodbye.

"Hey." Her stomach tore open like a buzzing wasp nest. "I miss you."

His response was silence. The wasps dropped dead. But then he spoke, and she could hear him smiling. "I miss you, too."

When they hung up, she clutched her phone against her chest. It vibrated, and the sensation startled her. A long, garbled text had arrived from Darby: The Feed 'N' Seed was open, he was meeting Alex there for work, and he'd update her again after seeing Alex in person. All morning, they'd been pretending like their fight had never happened. It was more important to make sure that Alex was okay. She still hadn't texted Makani, but she'd made contact with Darby. Makani tried not to feel hurt by this.

A crocheted throw materialized over her legs. "You looked cold," Grandma Young said. She sat down on the sofa, on the side nearest to Makani's chair.

Makani pulled up the blanket with a shiver. "Thank you."

"Have you spoken with your parents yet?"

"No." She shook her head. "But I will."

Grandma Young had given strict instructions to call them both when they were awake, to let them know that she was safe. Makani dreaded it. She wanted sympathy and crocheted throws. Not her parents. With the five-hour difference, it was 7:30 a.m. on the Kona Coast. People were out of bed and checking their phones. Would her old friends notice Osborne in the news? Even if they did, they wouldn't make the connection. No one would recognize the name of the town. No one except for Jasmine.

Makani and Jasmine had once been as close as Darby and Alex, but now Makani knew that even the strongest of friendships cracked under pressure. And her bedrock with Darby and Alex wasn't nearly so thick. She had to see Alex. She had to make the effort, because, otherwise, Alex might stop making the effort in return.

"Can I borrow the car this afternoon?" Makani's question seemed loud and abrupt. "I'd only be gone for an hour."

"*May* you borrow." Despite her alarm, Grandma Young still had to correct Makani's grammar. "And what, in heaven's name, is so important?"

Her best chance of succeeding was to tell the truth. She did.

The heavy *tick* of the grandfather clock permeated the house as Grandma Young weighed her decision. "I can't let you take the car and go alone." She held up a hand to stop Makani's protests. "But I will drive you there myself."

Ollie went to work at Greeley's Foods, and Darby and Alex went to the Feed 'N' Seed. Even in times of crisis, humans and animals needed to eat, and teenagers earning minimum wage needed to be there to ring up the sales.

The sky was dim and overcast. The Feed 'N' Seed was located on the outskirts of town, and Makani arrived shortly after her friends had begun their shift. The store smelled grainy with a fetid, tangy undertone of livestock, though it contained no animals.

Alex's eyes were smeared and wholly rimmed with charcoal eye-shadow and black mascara. Evidence of crying. Darby sat beside her on a stool behind the long sales counter, as somber as a grave.

It was less embarrassing to be in public with her grandmother than Makani had expected. Grandma Young made her feel safer. The Osborne Slayer, as the media had dubbed the killer, wasn't stalking Makani—apart from Ollie, her only local connections were here, surrounded by enormous bags of food pellets—but her nerve endings were frayed, all the same. The musty scent of foreboding clung to the town like mold on a decaying house. It was impossible not to breathe its stench into her lungs.

Near a display of pasture pumps, two middle-aged men wearing Carhartt overalls and matching frowns spoke in low, tense voices. They were the store's only customers. Normally, the Feed 'N' Seed would be bustling, and the ranchers and farmers would be booming jovially as they swapped stories. Makani didn't need to hear what the two men were whispering to know that they weren't talking about football or the weather.

Darby's posture lifted when he noticed Makani and her grandmother.

"Hey," she said awkwardly. She wasn't sure where else to start.

"What're you doing here?" And then, remembering his manners, he added, "Hi, Mrs. Young."

Grandma Young nodded hello.

"We came to see how you're doing," Makani said to Alex. She corrected herself. "How you're *both* doing."

"Pretty. Shitty." Alex drew out the rhyme.

Makani glanced at her grandmother, but Grandma Young didn't blink. It was neither the time nor place to criticize. Sometimes, swearing was acceptable.

"I'm sorry." Makani reached across the counter to squeeze Alex's limp hand, injecting as much compassion into it as she could. They conversed with their eyes. Alex didn't say anything, but Makani could tell that the gesture was meaningful to her.

Grandma Young had engaged Darby in a series of questions. "Yeah, my parents are freaking out," he said. "They didn't want me to come here today."

"Oh!" Grandma Young's posture changed like she'd remembered something important. She pivoted back toward Makani. "Your parents called while you were in the shower. Both of them."

Her tone was accusatory, but Makani's avoidance had turned into genuine forgetfulness. Momentarily, she was surprised that her parents had seen the news, though she wasn't surprised that they'd called her grandmother—asking *about* her, instead of asking her directly. They'd met humanity's minimum requirement.

"Sorry, Grandma," she said.

Grandma Young cocked an eyebrow. "What about Oliver? I'm sure you didn't forget to call him. Is he all right?"

Alex's hand grew rigid.

Makani released it and stuffed her fists into her coat pockets. "He's fine," she mumbled. *I shouldn't have let go. I should have pretended like this wasn't a thing.*

But Grandma Young wouldn't stop talking. "I'm glad he came over this weekend. I don't know why he'd put that thing in his lip, but he's a nice boy."

It was the worst possible moment for her to defend Ollie's character. Makani cringed, holding her breath, as Darby and Alex exchanged a dark look. They hadn't known that she'd seen him again. She neutralized her expression and prayed that they wouldn't use this opportunity to report their insane suspicions to her grandmother.

They didn't. After another silent communication and a warning glance at Makani, Darby changed the subject. "Do you think school will be canceled again tomorrow?"

Her legs weakened in relief. "They should cancel it for the rest of the week."

"Matt was killed on school grounds." Alex kicked her toe against the counter, pointedly avoiding Makani's gaze. "They should cancel it until someone is arrested. Assuming the police are looking at *every* suspect."

Before Makani could respond, or even decide how to respond— anger, guilt, and defensiveness warring with her knowledge that Alex was truly suffering—an old man with a cowboy hat and sun-worn wrinkles appeared in the doorway of the manager's office. He was checking to make sure that his employees weren't gossiping instead of helping customers.

Grandma Young gave him a nod. "Good afternoon, Cyril."

He nodded back. "Sabrina."

"We'll let you get back to work," she said, as pointedly to Makani as it was to Makani's friends. "Please don't hesitate to call us if you need anything. Anything at all." This, she directed toward Alex with tenderness.

Alex wilted. Darby placed an arm around her shoulders. Makani and her grandmother left. And as the door's decorative cowbell gave its plaintive *clang* goodbye, the first snowflakes of the year began to fall.

Evening crept into town. Patches of white snow gathered in the blue shadows, but the flakes were still melting on the roads and sidewalks. Makani imagined the soft powder drifting onto the memorial at school, dusting the flowers and cards and stuffed lions. Because of classes being canceled, no one had been able to place any tokens on the mound for Rodrigo. It was almost unbearable.

The official texts, emails, and voicemails arrived after dusk. All Osborne schools would be closed the following day. Classes would resume on Wednesday, and deputies outsourced from the Sloane County sheriff's office would be stationed on each campus.

The sky blackened. The snow began to stick.

Grandma Young stared out the front window at the quiet street. "Maybe the killer won't strike tonight. They'd leave behind tracks in the snow."

Makani tasted fear in the wind. "Maybe."

They closed the curtains and double-checked the locks.

CHAPTER THIRTEEN

SCHOOL WAS BACK in session, but the classrooms were half empty. Even Grandma Young had debated whether or not to send Makani, and, as a former teacher, she never let her stay home. Makani had to have a fever or be vomiting, neither of which had happened since moving here. Her attendance record was perfect. Her grandmother had only decided in favor of school because of a last-minute call from a sleep specialist in Omaha. They'd had a cancellation and could get her in that afternoon. Apparently, she was more concerned about her sleepwalking than she'd been letting on.

"My appointment wasn't for three more months," Grandma Young had said. "It's impossible to get in. I should go."

Makani had agreed. And when her flustered grandmother had rushed her off to school, Makani didn't mention that she could have gone with her. She'd wanted to go to school. Something about *not* going felt cowardly, like they were letting the killer win. But as she sat in her deserted first-period class, she wondered if she'd lobbied for the wrong choice. Neither Darby nor Alex was here. Darby's parents hadn't let him, and Alex had asked to stay home. A morose spell had been cast over the campus. It felt otherworldly in its emptiness and melancholia.

After three minutes of silence during the morning announcements, one minute for each loss, Principal Stanton—who *never* did the morning announcements—broke the news that *Sweeney Todd* had been canceled. He claimed that the decision had been made out of respect for the victims with special regards to Haley and her family. This was true enough, although everyone understood that a musical about a barber who kills his customers with a straight razor was far too grisly for their grieving community.

Makani felt bad for the drama kids who'd been working so hard and looked so crestfallen. Two desks ahead of her, Haley's best friend, Brooke, lamented. "Haley would have wanted the show to go on."

Everywhere. They were everywhere.

Those who had left them and those who had been left behind.

In second-period physics, Makani stared at Rodrigo's empty seat as if it contained a phantom. David sat beside the physical vacancy in hollow silence.

The rest of their group—Rodrigo's other friends who'd decided to brave school—kept her focus at lunchtime. Through the strange osmosis of tragedy, she suddenly knew their names: Kevin, Emily, and Jesse. They shared David's anguish, though their body language expressed it in different ways from his numbness.

Kevin, *fear*.

Emily, *devastation*.

Jesse, *helplessness*.

Everyone's reaction was unique, including the football players. On game days, they always dressed in button-downs, khakis, and ties, and that's what they'd chosen to wear today. Still a team. But their pressed clothing couldn't disguise their emotional upheaval, or how similar their mourning was to the gamers. Hulking Buddy even clapped gangly Kevin on the shoulder as he waited behind him in the pizza line. They'd never been on equal terms before, but now they would forever have this terrible October in common.

Social boundaries were being crossed everywhere. Students still ate with their own kind, but each group sat a little closer to the other groups, and they weaved in and out of one another's conversations. They were all talking about the same thing, anyway.

It was sad that people only got along when everybody was unhappy.

Makani and Ollie sat beside each other in the back corner of the cafeteria. Last night's snow had almost completely melted, but no one wanted to be outdoors. It didn't matter that the murders had all taken place indoors. Walking through the open quad felt like wearing a bull's-eye. It seemed safer to remain in the thick of the crowd, although *thick* was still relative. They were the only two people at their table.

Makani hoped this was because of the low attendance as opposed to a general distrust of Ollie. It was growing in all the students, not just Darby and Alex. Ollie hadn't revealed any outward signs of acknowledgment, but it was impossible for Makani to believe that he hadn't noticed the darted glances and heated murmurs. It had never been so clear that he didn't fit in—and how much that rankled them.

Zachary Loup, asshole burnout and the other frequently rumored suspect, had been smart. He'd stayed at home.

"I spent the afternoon watching the news with my grandma," Makani said. She slid her fries toward Ollie and hoped that he'd take some. His apple, Ziploc of Cheetos, and peanut-butter sandwich seemed especially sad today. "It was depressing. All of those parents and siblings and grandparents and aunts and uncles and cousins. All of them being shouted at. 'How does it feel to know that your son's killer is still at large?'" She shook her head. "And yet, there we were. Waiting to judge and analyze their responses."

Ollie dipped a French fry in ketchup. "Thanks."

She felt an urgent need to engage him in conversation, aware of the eyes that judged *them*. They needed to look normal. Or, at least as normal as was possible today. Ollie's usual demeanor might appear suspiciously calm. Though, if he seemed happy, that would look inappropriate, too. Makani hated that she had to worry about what other people thought of him.

"What about you?" she asked. "Were you at the station again?"

"Yeah, but Chris didn't make me work. He wasn't even there. He had to drive to Tecumseh, so I hung out with Ken."

"Ken?"

"The dispatcher."

"Oh. Is he . . . cool?" The question felt dumb, but Makani wanted to know more about Ollie's life. Truthfully, she wanted to know *everything*. They'd exchanged a few texts yesterday, enough for her to know that he'd be coming to school today. Perhaps, if she were still being honest, it was the main reason why she'd wanted to come, too.

Ollie's mouth twitched with a smile. "He's a fifty-something, thrice-married divorcé who owns two ATVs. His favorite show is infomercials."

Makani laughed.

His smile turned into a grin.

"So, what's in Tecumseh? Was Chris interviewing a suspect?" She paused. "And *where's* Tecumseh?"

"About two and a half hours away, past Lincoln. It's the site of the state's only maximum-security prison. He was called out for something unrelated. Unexciting."

"Your whole day sounds—"

"Unexciting," Ollie repeated.

She laughed again. "You know, the next time we have a day off, you're welcome to stay at my house instead." It was both a practical suggestion and a flirtatious offer, but Makani quickly realized what else she'd implied. *Why* they would have another day off. Her expression collapsed. "I didn't mean . . . I hope another person doesn't . . ."

Ollie nodded. He understood.

"Ugh." Makani thumped her head dramatically against the table. "Everything is the worst." She turned her head, cheek against tabletop, to look at him.

And then he did the best thing.

He laid his head against the tabletop, too.

They stared at each other—cheeks squashed, noses inhaling the funk of an old cleaning sponge. She wished that she could reach under the table and take his hand, but they'd never shown a public display of affection. That was for boyfriends and girlfriends. She still wasn't sure what this was, she only hoped it would continue. It would feel good to be close to someone again. It would feel good to be close to *him*.

Her phone dinged. Makani swore as they lifted their heads, and she checked the screen. "Grandma. Just making sure everything's okay."

An odd look appeared on Ollie's face.

"What is it?"

He shook his head. "Something my brother said."

She waited for him to elaborate, and he glanced around before lowering his voice. "Chris told me that they worked in silence at Rodrigo's house, because they were still in shock. The only sound was

Rodrigo's phone. It was blowing up with friends who'd heard the rumors and were trying to check in." Ollie shuddered. "Chris said that was the worst part, the part that kept them all on edge. The sound of those unanswered calls and texts."

"Oh, man," Makani said softly. "That's bleak."

"If we could have your attention . . ."

Caleb Greeley and someone else from the religious crowd, a tall, mousy girl that Makani recognized as a junior, were standing on the cafeteria's modest platform stage. Caleb spoke into a microphone. Makani knew what was coming next.

". . . we'd like to lead you in a short prayer for Haley, Matt, and Rodrigo."

Yep. Makani couldn't think of a single instance of prayer during school back in Hawaii, but it happened all the time here. And *everyone* was expected to participate. That was the part that bothered her. Makani genuinely hoped that others, including her grandmother, found peace and strength through prayer. But she wasn't religious herself, and it made her uncomfortable whenever it was forced upon her.

She bowed her head and listened to Caleb and the girl not so much *pray* as *preach.* They recited many, many Bible verses. Her annoyance at Caleb rose. First, there was the prayer at the flagpole. Then, the interview on television. Now this. Was he getting something out of the attention? Was he enjoying the spotlight a little too—

Makani stopped herself. She was doing to him what everyone else was doing to Ollie. Anyone could look sinister when viewed through the lens of fear—even an overly zealous, deeply sincere boy like Caleb. She pushed her suspicions aside. But as another minute dragged by, Makani realized that she could appreciate his goodwill while simultaneously wishing that he would also suggest something they could actually *do* to help support the victims' families or catch the killer. Prayer alone wasn't action.

Underneath the table, someone took her right hand from her lap. Her eyes jolted open.

Ollie stared back. She glanced around, but everyone else, even the cafeteria ladies, had their eyes closed. Ollie laced his fingers through hers. She tightened the grip and leaned in.

They kissed.

Heat and electricity and life spread throughout her body. They opened their mouths and kissed deeper, without sound, surrounded by the prayers of the frightened. When Caleb said, "Amen," their lips pulled away, and they smiled quietly. No one any wiser to their indiscretion.

Near the end of the last period, Principal Stanton returned to the loudspeakers to thank everyone for coming today, to remind them that the school would still be open tomorrow, and to announce a small piece of good news: Rosemarie Holt won the barrel race last weekend at the Sloane County Championship Rodeo.

Makani didn't give a damn about the rodeo, and Rosemarie was a junior in none of her classes, but she cheered along with the rest of her Spanish class. Their universal joy was significantly overheightened. They felt grateful for any good news.

"Watch out, Rosemarie," Ollie said darkly.

The joke rang too true, and the happiness died in Makani's throat.

"The killer likes them talented," he said.

"Don't."

She hadn't meant for it to come out so sharply. Ollie looked startled, and the space between them grew awkward. "Sorry," he said. "I only meant—"

"I know. It's okay." Makani shook her head, trying to smile. She'd understood his meaning instantly; she was upset because some-one might have overheard him. She attempted to mend the delicate breach. "Is that something the police are looking into?"

He nodded as her phone vibrated, rattling the top of her desk.

The noise rattled her, too. *Rodrigo's phone. Blowing up.* Thank-fully, it was more good news, this time from her grandmother: *Still in Omaha. Doc kept me waiting for over an hour just to tell me that I'll have to come back for more tests. I won't be home when school gets out. Would you please ask Darby to stay with you until I get there?*

Makani texted back: *sure! no worries.*

This time, her grin at Ollie was genuine. "Wanna come over to my place?"

CHAPTER FOURTEEN

THEY LEFT BEHIND Ollie's car at school and walked to her house, in case Grandma Young came home early and he needed to make a sneaky getaway. The irony was not lost on them that this behavior made them look suspicious, but the sun was shining, and the air was crisp with the magic of autumn.

Leaves pinwheeled from the sky and swirled across the sidewalk. Mums brightened the dull landscape with vibrant pops of yellow, lavender, and russet. Cheesecloth ghosts hung from invisible string on tree branches. Tombstones with joke names created temporary graveyards. And pumpkins—orange, white, tall, round, flat, and miniature—decorated every porch and door. Halloween was only three days away.

The afternoon felt like a gift. A respite from the ongoing stress.

Their plan was simple: Makani would encourage her grandmother to text updates regarding her arrival time, and, when she grew close, Ollie would duck out. Makani would say that Darby had *just* left, because they knew Grandma Young was around the corner, and Darby's parents were anxious to have him home. And then Grandma Young would get mad, but it wouldn't be anything an evening couldn't fix.

Puddles of melted snow still rested beneath the oak-lined portion of Walnut Street. The north-south roads in Osborne's oldest neighborhood were all named after trees: Cedar, Elm, Hickory, Oak, Pine, Spruce, Walnut, and Willow. They'd been christened in alphabetical order, so that the townspeople could always find their way home. Lately, Makani felt irrationally relieved that she didn't live on Elm Street.

"What'd you tell your brother?" she asked.

"That I'm going into work early," Ollie said. A moment of tension arose as they rounded the side of her house, and—

Yep. All clear.

Her grandmother's gold Taurus wasn't in the driveway.

They entered through the back door. The house was quiet. The only sound was its heartbeat, the hefty pendulum of the immense grandfather clock.

"It's such an old-people house," she whispered.

"I like it," Ollie whispered back.

They didn't have to lower their voices, but they did anyway. Energy crackled between them, intense and irrepressible. "I'm pretty sure the only items made in this century are the ones that moved here with me," she said.

He laughed quietly. She led him out of the kitchen and up the stairs.

"She hasn't finished it yet?" he asked.

Makani stopped, halfway up.

"The puzzle," he said.

She followed his gaze over the banister and into the living room, where most of the sky pieces—the blues and whites and grays—were still scattered around the coffee table. She shook her head and smiled. "I think she's been waiting for you."

"Next time, I'll visit when she's home."

Makani raised an eyebrow. "Sure you don't want to work on it now?"

Ollie bit his lip. Let the ring slip back out. "Positive."

As Makani led him into her bedroom, she sensed his eyes on the curves of her body. She felt his hunger, because it was the same hunger that she felt inside herself.

She locked the door behind them. Just in case.

It reminded her to check her phone, and a new text had arrived from Grandma Young. *Accident on Route 6. Stuck in West Omaha traffic.*

"Traffic sucks. We're in luck." Makani sing-songed it as she plugged her phone into a speaker and turned up the volume. The loud music was also just in case, but Ollie hardly seemed to register it. He seemed taken aback by his surroundings.

Uneasy, she crossed her arms over her chest. "What?"

Ollie took a moment to collect his thoughts. "It looks like the rest of the house. Not like you. This looks like . . . you're a visitor."

The shrewd observation stung more than expected. "I suppose I am."

Ollie nodded, and she was surprised that the gesture contained disappointment. Her arms uncrossed as she stepped automatically toward him, but he turned away from her. The emotional barrier slammed back into place. He kneeled beside her bed.

"What are you—"

"You once told me that I'd find something under here." At her baffled expression, he added, "A picture?"

Her eyes widened as she recalled the old swim team photo.

His smile gleamed with mischief.

"No, no, no, no, no, no, *no*." Makani threw her body between him and the bed, pinning down his arms as he struggled for something just out of reach. She couldn't let him see the picture now. Not while she was trying to seduce him. "Next time," she said, laughing. "I promise I'll show you next time."

Their chests touched. They breathed heavily.

Ollie stopped wriggling to give her another tempting smile. "And what good are the promises of someone who lies to her own grandmother?"

She kissed his lips—briefly—and pulled away. "Another day. I mean it." She kissed him again. "Just not today."

Ollie leaned forward and kissed her. Makani squirmed to shed her coat and got tangled in its sleeves. They both laughed as he helped her out of it.

"I'm curious—"

"Why I'm wearing a heavy coat? Because it *snowed,* and I grew up on the *beach.*"

"I'm *curious,*" he said, "why you're a winter Goth."

She was about to kiss him again, but this made her stop. "What?"

"Your summer clothes are colorful, and your winter clothes are black." He motioned at her coat and sweater to prove his point and then inclined his head for more kissing, as if he hadn't just initiated a weird conversation.

Makani pulled back so that he couldn't reach her mouth.

The summer clothes were her old clothes. In Hawaii, the warmest items she'd needed were jeans and a hoodie. Here, she'd had to ask her grandmother to buy her a coat, hat, scarf, gloves, and sweaters. They'd made a special trip to a mall in Omaha, and she'd selected everything in black. She couldn't explain *why* except that when she wore it, she felt a bit more protected. A bit more hardened. But that sounded dumb, and she didn't want Ollie to think she was copying him or Alex.

She teased him instead. "I like that you pay so much attention to what I'm wearing."

"I always pay attention to you. I always see you."

Her skin flushed as she held his gaze. "I see you, too."

Their bodies connected in a frantic crush. His hoodie disappeared, and then her sweater. And then his shirt. They were on her bed, and her jeans were off, and she was only in her underwear. She reached for his zipper.

Ollie placed a hand over hers. "Is this okay? Are you sure?"

These were the questions that required honesty. "Yes," she said. "Are you?"

"Yes."

She kissed him again, gently pushing aside his hand. "Yes," she repeated.

"Yes," he repeated.

The boy with the pink hair was asleep, and her grandmother had texted thirty minutes earlier that traffic was moving, but it was still slow. They had at least another hour.

Makani replied: *no prob! keep me updated.*

Her favorite song blasted through the speaker as she contemplated the rise and fall of Ollie's bare chest. His stomach was flat, much flatter than hers, and he looked more content in slumber than he did when he was awake. He looked soothed. The sex had been surprising, and not only because it had been quiet. (Just in case.) It had been different from their first time. It had been better. It had been *more*.

Makani watched Ollie until thirst overpowered her. She re-dressed, tugged a blanket over him, and went downstairs into the kitchen. The flatware drawer was open.

Her pulse spiked. "Grandma?"

Apart from the *tick* of the grandfather clock, the house was silent. Makani closed the drawer with a shaking hand. *She can't be home yet.* She rewound an hour to their arrival, trying to remember if the drawer had been open when they'd passed through the room. She didn't think so, but, admittedly, she'd been distracted.

It *must* have been open.

Her grandmother must have opened it before leaving for her ap-pointment. It was good that she'd gone to the specialist. Maybe they would finally get some answers.

Makani filled a plastic cup with tap water and chugged it. She refilled it for Ollie but then decided to use the downstairs bathroom, her grandmother's bathroom, before returning. With the loud music, she didn't *think* he'd be able to hear her peeing in the upstairs bath-room, but she was still self-conscious about it.

When she returned to the kitchen, the flatware drawer was open. Her body lurched to a halt. She gaped at it from the threshold.

The tracks must be loose. It's been rolling itself open this whole time.

But a lump thickened inside her throat.

Makani wasn't sure why she felt afraid. She glanced at the back door, but it was locked. She glanced behind her, but she was alone. Of course she was alone.

She crept into the kitchen and pushed in the drawer, just a few inches. Testing it. Waiting for it to roll back out.

It didn't.

She pushed in the drawer, all the way.

Waited.

Still nothing. *Maybe Grandma is right. Maybe I really am the one losing my mind.* The thought was unsettling, because it could be true. A period of time did exist that was difficult for Makani to remember. Perhaps these recent forgetful occurrences were remnants of her past trauma. Or perhaps, even worse, evidence of a new progression.

Shame poured through her as she stared at the drawer, willing it to open. She pressed her ear against its veneer and listened.

Nothing. The drawer held firm.

"*Shit,*" she whispered.

Makani shook her head. She went to grab the water, but the cup was empty.

"Shit," she said again, spinning around. She didn't know if she was searching for her grandmother or Ollie, but there was still nobody there. With trembling hands, she refilled the plastic cup and carried it toward the stairs, the water threatening to slosh over the sides. And that's when she noticed the jigsaw puzzle.

The sky was filled in.

The puzzle had been completed.

Makani dropped the cup. Water splashed onto her jeans as the cup bounced and spilled across the carpet. She scrambled to pick it up.

"Grandma?" she called out. "Grandma, where are you?"

Why had she sent those texts? Was this a test to see if Makani would lie to her? Did she know that Ollie was here? *Oh God.* She'd probably heard them upstairs, and now she was waiting for him to sneak out so that she could confront Makani. It was something her mother would do. She loved to set up Makani and then punish her for taking the bait. Was her grandmother more like her mom than Makani had realized?

Makani rushed back into the kitchen. "Grandma? Are you home?"

There was still no reply.

She slammed the cup onto the counter, grabbed a dish towel, and returned to dry the carpet around the base of the stairs. Her cheeks burned. Her heart felt as if it would burst from her chest. If Ollie had heard her yelling, he was being smart and remaining hidden. Clutching the wet towel, she headed back to the kitchen and stopped dead.

The cup was gone.

Her mind spun. Unable to process it.

"Grandma?" Makani sprinted toward her grandmother's bedroom at the back of the house. "Are you in there?" She pounded on the closed door, and when no one answered, she barged into the room. The bed was made. Everything was in its usual place. She even checked the closet—she didn't know why—but it was empty.

She hurried back to peer out the kitchen window toward the driveway and staggered backward. The cup was sitting in the center of the countertop. And every single drawer and cabinet was wide-open.

Makani felt paralyzed. The driveway was visible from here, but it held no cars.

"*Ollie?*" she whispered. She forced herself to turn around, half expecting, half hoping for him to be standing behind her.

He wasn't.

In a daze, she stumbled toward the stairs. Her eyes snagged on the completed jigsaw puzzle, and her body temperature chilled as a new horror settled in.

The killer had rearranged Rodrigo's living room furniture.

Makani remembered the drawers and cabinets—how many times they'd been left open in the last two months. What if the victims were toyed with before they were murdered? The acts against them could have been almost invisible. Gaslighting. Things that an officer would never notice while inspecting a crime scene.

The police had assumed that Rodrigo's furniture had been rearranged after his death as a part of the elaborate staging that the killer seemed to enjoy. But what if the killer had rearranged Rodrigo's furniture *before* his death?

A hooded figure stepped out from beside the grandfather clock.

CHAPTER FIFTEEN

MAKANI'S SCREAM REVERBERATED throughout the house. It rattled the pictures on the walls.

The figure jumped, startled by the volume of her terror, and dropped something. A knife thudded onto the carpet between them.

For a surreal moment, they were both frozen. A beige camouflage hoodie hung low over the killer's face, but Makani could see that he was male and white. He was also young, a teenager, judging from the slightness of his frame.

Makani glanced at his knife. It was large. The fixed blade was at least seven inches of steel, and it had two cutting edges—one regular and one sawtooth.

Its pointed tip was razor sharp.

She lunged.

Unfortunately, the killer was closer and faster, and as soon as his hand wrapped around the knife's black rubbery hilt, he thrust upward and sliced into her forearm.

She screamed again, stumbling backward. Suddenly, a yell arose

THERE'S SOMEONE INSIDE YOUR HOUSE **153**

from the landing. Ollie was barreling down to them, naked and at full speed.

Once more, the killer was caught by surprise, and Makani realized—in this millisecond—he had thought she'd been alone. Using his shock to her advantage, she slammed her body into his and knocked him to the floor. The hunting knife fell from his hand a second time as his hood flew back and exposed his face.

Makani blinked.

Recognizing him yet unable to place him.

He thrashed and kicked, and as she struggled to keep him pinned, a flailing limb rammed into her wound. She gasped. He clambered out from under her, snatched up the knife, and swiveled to attack. Ollie grabbed him from behind and hurled him aside.

A new battle cry rang out as a fourth person tore into the room.

Grandma Young launched herself at the killer. They hit the carpet together, and the knife plunged into her lower right abdomen. She cried out. The killer shoved the blade in deeper, wriggling it around. He kicked up his boots and pushed her off.

Makani threw herself over her grandmother's body.

Ollie chased after the killer, who was already running. The killer sidestepped and smashed into the grandfather clock. It crashed to the floor in a violent explosion of brass and tinder and glass. The carpet absorbed the cacophony into a swallowed silence.

Makani was perched on her hands and knees, panting. Blood coated the skin of her palms. It seeped through the legs of her jeans. Beneath her, Grandma Young's breathing was shallow and strained. Makani lifted her head cautiously.

Ollie and the killer were both still standing.

With a glance from Makani's narrowing eyes to Ollie's tensing muscles, the killer reassessed the situation. And then bolted out the front door.

Ollie shot off—straight through the shards and splinters—to lock it behind him as Makani leaped up and flew to the front window. "He's running left," she said.

"Where's your phone?" Ollie asked.

"Upstairs!"

"Mine too." He sprinted away. "Watch him!"

The hooded figure vanished behind a neighbor's detached garage. Makani moaned as she scoured the landscape for movement, any hint of movement. Her legs jiggled. Her arms trembled. There was a landline in the kitchen, but she didn't remember it until Ollie was already thumping downstairs with a phone at his ear.

"Ken," Ollie said to the dispatcher. He was still naked. "I'm at Makani Young's house on Walnut Street. The killer was just here."

Makani motioned for him to take the window. "He went that way! Around the corner of the garage."

"We need an ambulance. Her grandmother is seriously injured. She was stabbed in the stomach, and she's losing a lot of blood."

"Grandma? Grandma, stay with me!" Makani grabbed the nearest throw pillow and propped it beneath her grandmother's head. Her eyelids lifted open weakly.

"I'm fine," Ollie assured the dispatcher. "Makani is, too, but her arm was cut pretty badly. She'll need stitches."

Grandma Young's eyes grew worried.

"I'm okay. You're okay." Makani unbuttoned the bottom of her grandmother's blouse to get a better look at the wound. The shirt was heavy and wet.

"It's David Ware," Ollie said into the phone. "The killer is David Ware, and he's running in the direction of the school right now."

Makani peeled back the fabric, which shucked against her grandmother's stomach. Grandma Young inhaled sharply. Petrified,

Makani lowered it back into place as Ollie raced past her and up the stairs.

"Where are you going?" Makani shouted.

His voice carried down from her bedroom, and she realized he was standing at her window. "No, I can't see him anymore. . . ."

Ollie's phone call morphed into an unintelligible buzz. Makani's heart pounded with fear and adrenaline as she grasped her grandmother's hand, their skin slick with blood. She didn't know what to do. She didn't know how to help. The front window taunted her. At any moment, the killer might jump out from behind the bushes.

A gray shadow fell over her.

She shrieked.

"It's okay," Ollie said. But his eyes widened when he saw her arm.

She glanced down to discover that her left sweater sleeve was also soaked with blood. A diagonal slash had ripped open her flesh from elbow to wrist and exposed a throbbing gash of muscle. Her arm didn't seem like her arm. She barely felt the cut.

Getting on his knees, Ollie pressed a clean hand towel from the upstairs linen closet against her grandmother's wound. He nodded toward a second towel beside Makani. "Can you wrap that around your arm?"

He'd thrown on his clothes, but his feet were still bare. They were shredded from the glass. Frenzied trails of crimson footprints revealed his path across the carpet.

Blood. From his feet, her arm, her grandmother's stomach. It was everywhere.

"Here." Ollie gestured for Makani to take his place and to keep applying pressure.

Grandma Young's eyes were closed again. The instant Makani had instructions, the instant her grandmother's life was in her hands, her mind sharpened into focus. She held the towel in place as Ollie wrapped the other one around her forearm. She hissed with unexpected pain. A terrifying flash, a vision, accompanied it—a plain face with a dead expression.

Grandma Young tried to speak. "What did you say . . . his name?"

In the distance, the emergency sirens wailed their approach.

"David," Makani said. "That was Rodrigo's best friend."

David. David *Ware*. Had she even known his last name?

He'd never been mentioned in the speculation. Not once. He was someone who she and her friends—and Rodrigo—had even speculated *with*.

Who do you think did it?

He'd asked her that in physics class.

His pleasure must have been so perverse, asking when he already knew that he was going to kill her. Already knowing that he was going to kill his best friend.

The serial killers in her imagination, the fictional centerpieces of innumerable movies and television shows, were colorful and fascinating and impossible to keep her eyes off of. But her eyes had always glossed over David.

Who do you think did it?

She'd looked past him, even when he'd asked her.

She'd looked past him, even when he'd been sitting right in front of her.

Blazing lights. A rush of uniforms. Sense-memory panic swelled inside Makani as her house exploded into chaos. Paramedics in white shirts rushed toward her grandmother. The police swarmed Ollie, and Chris embraced him fiercely. Another officer rapid-fired questions at her. Makani's responses were a blur as Grandma Young was lifted onto a stretcher. A bearded paramedic peeked beneath Makani's towel, and she was hustled inside the same ambulance. Neighbors poured from their homes. News vans squealed onto the street. The last she saw of Ollie was a flicker of pink in the front window as the ambulance doors slammed closed.

You're in shock, they told her. As the nurses and doctor numbed, cleaned, and stitched her arm, the same police officer that had questioned her at home continued the interview.

Officer Beverly Gage. You can call me Bev.

She looked young for a Beverly, only a few years older than Ollie's brother. She had a large oval face, friendly eyes, and long hair pulled back into a ponytail. Was this the same officer that Darby had found attractive? It seemed so long ago.

Her grandmother had been rushed into an operating room, but the hospital wouldn't tell her if she was okay, and Officer Bev wouldn't tell her if David had been captured. Bev's timeline-related questions were mortifying. At least she saved the most prying inquiries until after the stitching was done, and they were alone.

Makani answered as truthfully as she could remember:

Yes, we had sex.

Um, ten minutes?

Then we talked for a while.

Maybe fifteen minutes?

I don't know. About music. And some guy who wrote a lot about Morocco . . . Paul something? I don't know.

Yes, and then Ollie dozed off.

I checked my phone, and then I watched him sleep.

I don't know. Fifteen minutes? Twenty?

It was humiliating. And now it would go on file, typed up on some kind of awful official document or digital record or both. As Bev made another notation, Makani's mind boomeranged back to her grandmother. She felt sick with guilt and helplessness. *Grandma might die because David wants* me *dead.*

Her thoughts spun again, and she imagined trying to explain herself when—*when* not *if*—her grandmother woke up. Makani had lied. Ollie had been naked. Illogically, these two facts felt so much worse than confronting the idea that someone had attempted to kill her.

I barely know him, she kept telling Bev. *No, I don't know why he'd target me.*

The first half was true. The second half was a lie.

Makani thought that she had suffered enough—she'd lost everything that mattered to her in Hawaii—but the karmic cycle of life had circled back around. This, at last, was her final punishment.

CHAPTER SIXTEEN

OFFICER BEV WAS gone, and Makani had been abandoned in the single-occupancy patient room to wait for news about her grandmother. She moved to an uncomfortable chair, not wanting to remain on the bed. The air smelled stale but sterile.

Makani didn't have her phone, so she couldn't contact Ollie or her friends. Or even her parents. The police and the hospital had been trying to contact her mom and dad with no luck. But a kind-hearted nurse with coppery hair kept checking in on Makani and brought her ginger ale and blueberry yogurt. She assured Makani that the surgical staff was brilliant, and their small hospital was fortunate to have them.

Every minute alone increased Makani's anxiety. She'd been in the hospital for nearly four hours. She turned on the television to pass the time.

This was a mistake.

Standing on her grandmother's lawn was the same hairsprayed reporter who'd chased her through the school's parking lot last

Friday. The graphic on the bottom of the screen read: FOURTH TEEN ATTACKED IN OSBORNE SLAYINGS.

"Did you hear any screams or unusual noises?" she asked an older man. He had a droopy but upturned mouth like a bulldog. It was the neighbor from two doors down.

"No, nothing at all. I was fixing my gutter when a boy tore across my yard in that direction." He pointed with a gnarled finger and then pressed the whole hand flat against his face in disbelief. "I shouted after him from my ladder, but he didn't look at me. He just shot around my carport and ran toward Spruce."

Back in the studio, the live footage was superimposed above Creston Howard's shoulder. Creston looked stiff and appropriately serious, though he couldn't resist a toothpaste-commercial smile as he led them into the break.

No one should ever have to see their own house on the news. Makani wanted to crawl into her bed and hibernate for the rest of autumn. But then it struck her that she might not even be able to go home. Her house was a crime scene.

"The suspect is eighteen-year-old David Thurston Ware," Creston said when the news returned, and goose bumps prickled her skin.

Thurston.

Now he had a middle name, too. It didn't seem right that a murderer should be allowed to have anything in common with his victims. Makani supposed it was for the sake of the world's non-homicidal David Wares, those few people unfortunate enough to share his namesake. It was like being a Katrina after 2005; it only brought one thing to mind. But at least no one could mistake a woman for a hurricane. Hopefully, the release of his middle name narrowed the inevitable misunderstandings of *which* David Ware.

Makani's name wasn't being reported, most likely because she was a minor. And a survivor. But Ollie wasn't named, either. Creston kept referring to him as a *male friend of the victim*. The police must be protecting him.

The news cut to a senior photo, and David's image leached through the screen like an odious stench. His smile was dopey and innocent, and his hair was brushed to one side as if he were a little boy. He had a faint mustache. There was nothing intimidating about his appearance, but Makani's stomach filled with caustic acid.

"The suspect was last seen wearing jeans and a camouflage hoodie," Creston said. "He's considered armed and highly dangerous. If you see him, do *not* approach him. . . ."

More footage of her house. More interviews with neighbors.

The man whose nose had been lopped off crossed his flannel-shirted arms. "Osborne, all of us, we're scared for our lives."

Makani wanted to change the channel, but fear held her hostage.

"It's like searching for a needle in the cornstalks," Creston said, and she loathed his inane glibness more than ever. But his coanchor nodded. Dianne's makeup was so unnatural and extreme that it looked airbrushed by a T-shirt vendor on a beach. "And a reminder that all Sloane County schools have been closed for the rest of the week. . . ."

Did she only report on school closings?

"Good news," a voice said beside her.

Makani startled at the jarring declaration. The coppery-haired nurse hugged her clipboard and said, "Your grandmother's out of surgery."

"Your grandma's a real trouper." The surgeon was a thickset man with dark, feminine eyelashes. "She's lucky. The knife nicked her vena cava, but it missed the aorta. If it had nicked that, well, we'd be having a very different conversation right now."

Through the room's windows, nighttime lights illuminated the buildings below—the squat brick library and a lofty brick church. Everything in Osborne was made out of brick. St. Francis Memorial Hospital was on the opposite side of Main Street, not quite a mile from her grandmother's house. It wasn't big, but it was the county's only hospital, and Makani was grateful that it was so close. Grandma Young had gone into surgery within emergency medicine's golden hour. The rapid intervention had saved her life.

"There was an injury to her intestines, which requires a long antibiotic therapy, and there was a cut to her right ureter," the surgeon said. "I've placed temporary drains, but when she's more stable, the ureter will need reconstructive surgery."

His words were a fog. Her grandmother was still in another part of the hospital, and Makani wasn't allowed to see her yet. She touched her bandaged arm for self-support. It was wrapped from elbow to wrist. "When can she come home?"

"She'll need significant rehabilitation here in the hospital. Three weeks, at least."

"Three *weeks*?"

"After that, we'll transfer her to a rehabilitation center . . ."

He was still talking as Makani, stupefied, lowered herself back onto the bed where she'd received the stitches. Three weeks . . . and then *more* rehabilitation . . .

The surgeon removed a pen from the shirt pocket of his green scrubs. He clicked it, and the finality of the sound made her look up. "Do you have any other family that you can stay with while she recovers?"

Her parents flitted in, and then straight back out of, Makani's mind as she shook her head. "It's just the two of us."

"That's okay." The nurse placed a steady hand on Makani's

uninjured arm. "Your grandmother will be awake soon, and we'll ask her where she'd like you to stay. I'm sure she has some friends who'd be happy to take you in for a while."

Makani's chest constricted. Grandma Young's church friends were *nosy*. They would ask so many questions. Maybe she could stay with Darby or Alex instead.

As the surgeon detailed the recovery process, he spoke with a brisk authority that Makani found difficult to follow. When he left, the nurse outlined it in simpler terms and reminded her where the call button was to ring for help. Makani glanced at her laminated ID badge—DONNA KURTZMAN, RN—and thanked her by name.

For the second time in a year, almost to the day, Makani was trapped inside a waking nightmare. Grandma Young had thrown herself at a serial killer to save her. The selflessness of this act was almost too big to comprehend. But equally astounding was that she'd made it home in time to do it. Makani should be the one in the operating room, not her grandmother. Her grandmother had done nothing to deserve this.

Two more excruciating hours passed alone with her thoughts.

At last, Donna led her to the ICU where Grandma Young was coming around from the anesthesia. Her enfeebled body was strung up with wire monitors and IVs and catheter tubes, and Makani had no idea what else. A reclining chair sat beside the bed. Makani perched on its cushioned edge and took her grandmother's hand. Her skin felt thin, her bones fragile. "Hi, Grandma."

Grandma Young's eyelids fluttered open. She tried to speak, but her voice came out as a whispered croak. *"What time is it?"*

"It's almost eleven. Do you know where you are?"

Her eyes closed again, groggily. She nodded.

"You had emergency surgery, but you're okay. Do you remember what happened?" There was a twenty-second pause. "Grandma?"

"What time is it?"

"It's eleven at night," Makani said. Donna had explained that the anesthesia would make her grandmother disoriented for a while.

Grandma Young gave another frail nod. "Are you all right?"

Makani had held it in since the attack. But this question, coming from this person, unlocked the dam. Warm tears spilled over, no longer containable. "I'm fine."

"Oliver?"

"Ollie's fine, too." Makani used her right sleeve to dry her cheeks. The left sleeve had been cut off. The rest of her sweater was encrusted with dried blood, and her jeans were stained with rust-colored pools. "We're all okay."

There was a knock on the door, which had been left ajar. Chris nudged it open. He was in his blue uniform and holding a small bundle of Mylar balloons. And beside him, as if summoned by their thoughts, stood Ollie.

Makani's heart cracked down the middle. But it was a good feeling.

Ollie looked pale—his skin tone even paler than its natural state—and weary. *No,* she corrected herself. *Bleary.* As if he'd been answering the same questions, over and over, for the last six hours. He glanced at her, skittish and apprehensive.

"I hope you don't mind, Mrs. Young," Chris said. "May we come in?"

If her grandmother had been anyone else, Makani guessed that he would have called her *ma'am.* This was the habitual *Mrs. Young* of a former student.

Grandma Young's eyes reopened, and her posture straightened the teensiest bit. She gained a modicum of strength as she regained the role of the adult. "Christopher. Officer Larsson," she corrected hoarsely. "Come in."

He grinned. "Christopher is still fine."

The brothers entered, and Chris presented Makani's grandmother with three balloons—a Get Well Soon, a blushing emoji, and an emoji wearing sunglasses. "There weren't many options at the hospital's gift shop," he said apologetically. "We bought flowers, but then they told us we couldn't bring them into the ICU." He turned to Makani. "They're in my car. One of the bouquets is for you, of course."

Grandma Young thanked Chris as he tied the balloons in a place where she could see them. Apart from the occasional lei and an orchid corsage at her ex-boyfriend's junior prom, Makani had never been given flowers. She smiled at Ollie, perhaps even glowed, but he wouldn't meet her eyes. Her expression faltered.

He knows. The police had opened her record, and now Chris and Ollie knew. Her heart withered. The muscle blackened into soot.

"I owe *you* the thank-you." Chris walked to her grandmother's bedside. "If you hadn't come home when you did . . ." He couldn't finish the thought out loud.

Grandma Young shook her head, barely. "They saved themselves. I only got in the way."

He smiled with a gentle laugh. "That's not what my brother said."

Ollie was staring at the floor, so Makani spared him the embarrassment of responding. "Have you caught him yet?" She didn't have to specify the *him*.

Chris's blond eyebrows pinched together, which darkened his appearance. "Not yet. There are a lot of places to hide around here, but he couldn't have gotten far. He's probably tucked up in someone's barn or grain bin." Chris sounded frustrated, and he paused to regain a measured control. "Everyone's looking for him, and everyone knows what he looks like. We'll get him soon. I promise."

He asked her grandmother how she was feeling.

Ollie knows. Chris knows. Everybody will know.

"How many stitches?" Chris asked.

It took a moment for Makani to realize that this question was for her. "Twenty-six." She was unaware that she was cradling her wounded arm. "It's nothing."

"Your nothing and my nothing are two very different things."

His tone was light, but her lungs tightened.

A nurse rolled something bulky past their door. The noise reopened Grandma Young's eyes. Her gaze locked on to Ollie, and she ushered him to her side.

Reluctantly, he complied. Each step seemed gingerly taken, evoking Makani's memories of his cut-up feet. He bit his lip ring, and the gesture revealed the truth: Her *grandmother* was making him nervous. Not her. He looked troubled because her grandmother had discovered him naked inside her house.

Makani felt a rush of temporary relief as Grandma Young reached for his hands. Ollie accepted them. *"Thank you."* She said it as emphatically as she could, meant with every cell in her body. "I'm so glad you were there."

Chris's eyes grew misty, betraying his professional stoicism.

Ollie nodded, but he lifted his chin. It quivered.

Grandma Young, still gripping his hands, shook them up and down. She inhaled deeply. "All right, then. That's that." And then she turned to Makani and asked, befuddled, "What time is it?"

•   •   •

In the hospital's unremarkable and unadorned waiting room, Ollie produced Makani's phone. It had been hidden in the pocket of his hoodie. "I grabbed it before the police could confiscate it. They'll pull your records and call logs, anyway."

Chris had to ask her grandmother a few questions, so they'd been banished. Makani's eyes widened as the precious object returned to her grasp. "Thank you."

"I think you have a few messages," he said wryly.

Entering her password revealed dozens of texts from Darby and Alex: *Are you okay? Where are you?! We are SO SORRY for suspecting Ollie!!!* Scrolling through their frantic apologies was comforting, until she remembered Rodrigo's phone. Had David texted him that morning to maintain the pretense of innocence? What kind of person could murder their best friend? Perhaps they'd never been friends at all.

Makani texted Darby and Alex to let them know that she was safe and that she'd call them later. She couldn't handle talking about it now. Not tonight. Not again. Even though she was staring at the call button beside her mother's name.

Ollie acknowledged her hesitating finger. "You should."

She moved near the elevators for privacy. There were three other people in the waiting room—a conservatively dressed elderly couple and a scruffy-faced man in an orange construction vest—and she didn't want them to overhear her, either. They were caught up in their own emergencies, and none of them had realized that they were sitting with the latest victims of the Osborne Slayer. Soon enough, the town would think of her and Ollie as nothing else. Makani wanted to hold on to this normalcy for as long as possible.

Her mother's voicemail picked up. "Hey, Mom. It's me. I don't know why you and Dad aren't answering your phones. The hospital and the police have been trying to call you for hours. Grandma and I are all right, but . . . just call me back, okay?"

The same thing happened when she tried her father. She left a similar message.

"No luck?" Ollie asked on her approach. He sounded numb.

She shook her head, slumping back into the chair beside his. They zoned out and watched the television mounted on the opposite wall. Blissfully, it wasn't the news. It was a rerun of *Friends*, and Chandler was in a box. Some kind of punishment for hurting Joey.

"They're using our names," Ollie said in a low voice.

Makani tilted her head as she turned to him. "Huh?"

"Snaps, tweets. The whole town knows that you and I were attacked."

He wasn't looking at his phone, so he must have seen it earlier. Outwardly, she remained blank and unsurprised. Darby and Alex had known, either from hearing it online or seeing her house on the news. But internally, the confirmation nauseated her. People Googled. People talked.

"At least they won't know that I was naked," Ollie said.

Sweat collected along her hairline. Behind her knees.

I should tell him.

"There are certain details that we, at the station, believe are best kept private," he said, in an accurate imitation of his brother. "Believe me, no one will know . . . the nature of your visit." Ollie switched back to his own voice. "Believe me, no one will know . . . until someone writes a book."

The image hurled her into the future and slackened her jaw. He was right. Someday, their story would be a chapter in one of those sleazy, mass-market, true-crime paperbacks that were shelved in the cobwebbed corners of used bookstores—the types of paperbacks that boasted about the number of crime-scene photographs inside.

Ollie winced at her expression. "So, we're not joking about it yet."

"Just tell me something good." She put her head in her hands. "I need to hear something positive."

He considered the assigned task, taking it seriously. "They've called in a team of dogs to help with the search. They think he went into the fields near the school. There's a huge manhunt happening right now—at least half of Osborne is out there searching for him." When she didn't respond, he added quietly, "It's almost over."

Her brain swayed inside her skull. "I won't feel better until it's *actually* over."

Ollie sank deeper into his chair. His long legs splayed out, and his hands folded over his stomach. "Yeah." He sighed.

"It's weird," he said, several minutes later. "I've known him my whole life. Our families went to the same church. We were on the wrestling team together in middle school. He didn't seem like a killer. He didn't seem like . . ."

". . . anything," Makani finished. Briefly thinking about Ollie as a wrestler.

"Yeah."

"Do you think that's why?" Ollie asked. "Because he feels invisible?"

She buried her head back into her hands and shrugged.

"I just don't understand why he would target *you*."

Her breath hitched.

I should tell him. I have to tell him. I can't hide anymore.

"Hey." A hand on her back.

She startled up with a gasp. Chris was stooped beside her chair. His and Ollie's faces were creased with worry. Behind them, the construction worker and the elderly couple were staring at her tattered clothing. The woman whispered to her husband.

Chris threatened them with a police officer's glare as he helped Makani to her feet. "Your grandma said it was okay to come home with us," he said. "Why don't you say goodbye, and we'll get the hell out of here."

CHAPTER SEVENTEEN

THE BROTHERS SWITCHED on the Victorian-style lamps throughout their house to maintain the illusion of safety. It had been less than a week since her previous visit, but the creaky loneliness of the old structure had already diminished in Makani's memories. Now, it felt intensified under the black coat of night. The crumbling plaster walls contained a crawling sort of dread. They were alive with hidden ghouls—ghostly and human.

Makani lay awake in Ollie's bed, underneath his cold window. The cloud-covered moon concealed the cornfields below. The floral bouquets had been brought in from the car and were bunched together inside the same glass vase on Ollie's desk. The yellow sunflowers, golden chrysanthemums, red gerbera daisies, and brown corkscrewed twigs were cheerfully autumnal, but the shadows they cast were inky and menacing.

Her attacker—it was intolerable for her to think his name right now—had reduced her to a child afraid of the dark. She wanted her stuffed animals. Perhaps they could have kept her tethered to these more simple fears as opposed to her current reality.

She wasn't at home, because she couldn't go home.

A serial killer wanted her dead.

The drugs for her arm were also supposed to help her sleep. Instead, she was paranoid and woozy. In the darkness, Makani became aware of her cut. It *hurt.* The tightly wrapped bandage was stiff, and it made her feel clumsy. Ollie had lent her a T-shirt and plaid pajama pants. The clothing and bedsheets smelled like his skin, musky and clean and arousing. But they were a constant reminder of where she was and why.

Chris had given his brother the choice of sleeping downstairs on the couch or upstairs on the floor of Chris's bedroom. Ollie had picked a third option, a sleeping bag in the upstairs hallway. The master bedroom remained empty. It belonged to the spirits.

Ollie's sleeping bag rustled outside her door as Makani's ears strained for sounds of the uninvited: Drawers opening. Puzzle pieces snapping. She tried to listen for the *tick, tick, tick* of the grandfather clock, but then she inhaled Ollie's scent and remembered, all over again, that she wasn't at home. Remembered that the clock had been broken.

A hooded figure lurched out at her.

She curled into a fetal position to protect herself from the blade. Everything was spinning. She screamed into the pillow.

"Makani," a voice said.

She scuttled into the corner in fright.

"It's okay," the voice said. In the moonlight, Ollie was crouched beside the bed. "You were having a nightmare." He climbed onto the mattress and coaxed her out from against the wall. Held her as she trembled in his arms.

Her heart was pounding in her throat, but as she stared at Ollie's thickly socked feet, her confusion reshaped into consciousness. "Do they hurt?" she asked.

"No," he said softly, and she knew it was a lie. "How's your arm?"

"Fine," she said.

They were silent for a long time. When he made a motion to leave, her night terrors surged back like an electrical storm. *"Don't."*

He didn't.

She lay down on the narrow bed and pressed her body against the wall. He slipped into the open space. He took out his phone, and his face illuminated in aqua blue. Makani was about to protest that she didn't want to see the news, when she realized he was setting an alarm. "So you can get back into the hallway before morning?" she asked.

Ollie smiled faintly as the light vanished.

With a muted thud, his phone was placed onto the hardwood floor. They pulled up the blankets. There was a gap between their bodies, slender enough for a shadow or a whisper. Makani heard it first. And then she felt it. His breath was warm and vital.

She closed the gap, and they nestled together against the darkness.

It took hours to fall asleep. Whenever her eyes closed, a hooded figure lurched out—an endless loop of the same harrowing second. Ollie shifted and rolled and twisted the sheets, but she was grateful for his presence. She was grateful not to be alone.

When her mind finally succumbed, the sleep was restless and sweaty. And then the alarm went off.

Makani gasped, jackknifing into a sitting position.

Ollie switched off the alarm and flattened the phone across his racing heart. Through the panes of the arched, church-like window, a rosy-orange dawn was breaking over the fields. The first birds of the morning sang to one another.

Makani dissolved into the blankets as Ollie's legs swung over the side of the bed. Her hand shot out. It clutched his upper arm—that sensitive place, where bare skin met shirtsleeve. He craned his neck to look at her. Her hand crawled up, grasped the cotton sleeve, and pulled him back down. They kissed.

Quiet. Hungry. Desperate.

Ollie broke away first, a few minutes later. She stared at him. Begging him to stay. He shook his head. *I can't,* he mouthed.

Please, she said.

"I'll be on the other side of the door," he whispered. *"I'm not going anywhere."*

Less than an hour later, they gave up on pretending. The air was dewy and cold, and Ollie lent Makani his hoodie for warmth. It comforted her to remain embraced by his scent. When they shuffled into the kitchen, Chris was already in uniform and making coffee. Neither party was surprised to find the other awake. Chris looked as unrested and shell-shocked as Makani felt. Her eyes darted to the cabinets and drawers. They were closed.

How many times had David broken into her house? Her sluggish thoughts tried to recall each separate invasion. It usually happened when they were asleep. Had it ever happened when they were awake? Which was worse?

Squidward looked up from licking his bowl. His tags jangled as he moseyed up beside Ollie and followed them to the sunshine-yellow breakfast table. The seat cushions were upholstered in matching yellow vinyl. Thankfully, Chris hadn't left behind any folders. Makani wasn't ready to see the blood spatter inside her own house.

"So," Chris said. "I got up in the middle of the night to pee."

Makani and Ollie stiffened.

Chris thunked down an empty mug in front of Ollie. "You're sleeping in my room tonight, bro." More gently, he placed a second mug in front of Makani. It was a similar shade of bright yellow, and it contained SpongeBob's goofy, bucktoothed face. "I refuse to ignite your grandma's wrath when she gets out of the hospital."

Their eyes affixed on the Formica tabletop. They nodded.

Chris opened his mouth to say something. He hesitated. "You guys *are* using protection of some kind, right?"

Ollie buried his fingers in his pink hair. "Jesusfuckingchrist."

"Answer the question, and we'll never speak of it again." Chris paused. "Unless, you need me to buy—"

"*Yes.*"

Chris held up his hands. "Good. We're done here."

Makani's cheeks burned. She was already thinking about the similar conversation that she'd be forced to have with her grandmother. Somehow, she doubted Grandma Young would keep it so brief.

The coffee finished brewing, and Chris filled their mugs. No one mentioned food, because no one had an appetite. They stared at the rising vapors.

"So," Makani said. "He's still out there."

Because Chris would have told them, otherwise. The table only had two chairs, so he was slumped against the counter. "Last night, a K-9 unit tracked him to the fields surrounding the school, but they lost the trail when it hit the river. Maybe if we were a bigger town—if we hadn't needed to call up the unit from Lincoln—we would have found him before he reached water." His head hung as if it weighed heavily upon his shoulders. "The team's still searching, though. They're trying to pick up his trail again somewhere along the banks."

Makani imagined the predator slinking through the fields in his cornstalk-colored camouflage. A lion in wait.

Chris's voice firmed. "We'll get him soon. He can't hide for much longer."

Outside the windows, the fields were hushed and still.

"I know you answered a million of our questions last night," he said, "and I know you don't really know the guy, but what did you think about him, before all this? What was your general impression?"

Makani was surprised when she couldn't think of a reply.

"Anything," Chris said. "It might be useful."

"I guess . . . nothing. He was just a *nothing* guy, you know? Kind of a redneck. Scrawny. I've never really noticed any defining or distinguishing features." Makani tried to picture David at school. She tried to picture the version of David that wasn't inside her house. "It's like . . . he's all one color. Sandy-blond hair, tannish skin. They blend together. I don't remember his eyes. Maybe he has a weak chin?"

"Okay. But appearance aside, what kind of person was he?"

"Quiet?" She shrugged and then glanced at Ollie with a laugh. "Not as quiet as him, though."

Ollie gave her a small but knowing smile.

His brother also cracked a smile. "What else?"

"We sat near each other in a few classes. Alphabetical order. Ware, Young. I never took much notice of him, but he seemed smart enough."

"Can you explain why he gave you that impression?"

It was another hard question. "I guess because he always had a quick response—to jokes or whatever. And he listened and watched. Paid attention. He had a large group of friends, and I figured Rodrigo was his *best* friend, but maybe that's only because they sat near me in physics, so sometimes I overheard their conversations."

"What'd they talk about?"

"Tech stuff. Boring. I didn't understand most of it." Her arms folded over her stomach. "I still can't believe that he killed his own friend. You guys are sure he's working alone?"

"An imprint of a boot was left behind at the Moraleses' house," Chris said, and she nodded as if Ollie hadn't already told her. "It's David's size, and his parents confirmed that he wears the brand. They're missing from his closet. Combined with everything else we know, it seems unlikely that he's working with a partner."

Ollie traced his finger along the handle of his mug. "How did Rodrigo's parents react when they learned that it was David?"

"Bev gave them the news last night." Chris shook his head. "Said they appeared to be genuinely shocked. They told her that David had always been polite and respectful—more so than some of Rodrigo's other friends—and that he seemed like a normal teenage boy. Hell, they've known him since Montessori preschool."

"What about David's parents?" Makani asked.

"Chief questioned them all night, and the sheriff's guys are helping us search their property just outside of town. But they seem decent. Hard working, churchgoing. Their families go way back in Sloane County on both sides, and all the grandparents and aunts and uncles and cousins still live here. Dad had a disorderly conduct charge for public urination, but that was almost twenty years ago. And, apparently, he took David deer hunting every November, which explains a few things. But it's not unusual."

Not unusual for here, Makani thought.

"From what I heard," he continued, "David's parents were blindsided."

Ollie's brows knitted together in doubt. He was still fiddling with the mug.

"I'm sure it's hard for you to believe," Chris said, a familiar wryness to his voice, "but parents don't always know what their kids are up to."

"Then they should ask," Ollie said.

"They should. But sometimes kids lie."

Ollie's index finger stopped.

"But . . . you're right." Chris looked away. It was an attempt to defuse the old tension of him being a stand-in parent. Makani had only heard hints about the fights that had occurred since Chris had moved back home, but she did know it had taken them a few years to adjust to their circumstances. "Sometimes, parents are just shitty."

"If they're hiding anything," Ollie said, lifting his head to extend his own peace offering, "you'll find it."

Arduous days required scrupulous planning. Chris announced that he would escort them to Makani's house so she could grab some clothes and toiletries. After that, he'd go to work, and Ollie would drive her to the hospital. In the afternoon, Ollie would go to work, and she'd remain behind with her grandmother. And then when Ollie's shift ended, he'd pick her up, and they would all converge again at the Larsson house.

The brothers offered her the first shower. She'd rinsed off her skin in the sink last night, so she declined with a secret shudder. There was no way these white boys had the right hair products. She could wait another hour until she was home.

While Ollie showered, Makani faced the reality of her phone. In addition to a slew of new texts from Darby and Alex, unexpected messages had arrived from the student-council president and from Haley's best friend. Being president had given Katie access to her number, and Brooke had gotten it through Darby. Their texts were supportive and kind, but Makani couldn't deal with trying to form any polite responses right now.

She listened to her voicemail instead. Her father said that he'd heard what had happened from her mother, and to give him a call sometime. There was no urgency to this request.

There was also no missed call from her mother.

Principal Stanton had left a voicemail, which was awkward, and there was another from Tamara Schuyler at the *Omaha World-Herald*, which was unsettling. Despite their claims, Makani knew the type of journalist who hounded a minor post-trauma wasn't interested in that minor's well-being.

They were only interested in the salacious story.

Chris flashed his lights—*whoop whoop*—so that their cars could maneuver through the crowd. Grandma Young's yard had become a staging area for the media. The local truck, Omaha trucks, and cable news trucks were parked side by side with *Dateline* and *48 Hours*. There'd been a mass shooting at a university in Florida with eleven dead and six injured. There'd been a suicide bomber at a shopping mall in Istanbul with thirteen dead and twenty-seven injured. Yesterday's headlines were terrifying, but they were also so terrifyingly commonplace that the eyes of the country had turned to Osborne.

Tendons knotted inside Makani's shoulders. It was bizarre to see all the lights on in the windows when neither she nor her grandmother were home. How many strangers had prowled through their house in the hours since the attack?

How many hours had *he* prowled through it?

Makani wondered if an element of sexual perversion coexisted with David's breaking and entering. Did he watch her—through the slats of her closet door, from underneath her bed—while she changed? Did it get him off?

They parked in the congested driveway behind three other police vehicles. It felt as if a spotlight were following them as they exited and jostled through the shouting mob. Makani was still wearing Ollie's hoodie, shrouded under its black hood. Thinking about the hood hurtled her mind back to David.

Where was he hiding *now*?

Makani stared at her house, and her legs suddenly grew rigid.

Ollie's fingers clasped through hers. It was the first time that they'd held hands for anyone to see. Tethered to his grip, she felt safe. They ran together.

Inside, the situation was quiet and grim. Hideous bloodstains soiled the living room carpet. Smeary red handprints glazed the front window and door. It felt chillingly empty without the tick of the grandfather clock. The heart of the house was dead.

Makani listened in as Sergeant Beemer, a stout man with a bulbous nose, updated Chris with the latest. Splinters of painted wood from where David had been jimmying open the downstairs bathroom window had been discovered on the ground outside. The bathroom was located directly below Makani's bedroom, and the overgrown viburnum, which blocked the window's view, showed signs of having been trampled.

"The bush is right beside the water spigot. David's foot probably got tangled in the garden hose during one of his exits." The sergeant sniffed his ruddy nose. "It'd explain all the snapped branches."

A shiver rattled down Makani's spine. She knew *exactly* when David had snagged his foot. It happened the day after Haley's murder, while she'd been waiting for Ollie to call. She'd thought it was the neighbor's cat.

Makani imagined a hooded figure climbing into her grandmother's bathroom. Hiding in her shower. Peering through her private things.

And it was impossible not to *keep* imagining him as she closed her bathroom door and stepped into her own shower. Behind the clear vinyl curtain, she became Janet Leigh in *Psycho*. The shampoo stung her eyes, because she was too afraid to close them. Even with her eyes wide-open, she still saw the silhouette of a young man with a knife.

Ollie is right there. Right outside the door.

But Ollie had also been nearby when David had attacked her.

There's an entire squadron of cops downstairs.

But downstairs was so far away.

CHAPTER EIGHTEEN

"**WOULDN'T THAT TIME** be better spent looking for him?" Grandma Young cut someone off. "I know. I know about the search parties. I just don't understand why we can't *all* focus on capturing him first."

Makani and Ollie paused outside her door. It was a phone call—and not a pleasant one. Makani's heart swelled to hear Grandma Young sounding like herself, but they decided to wait in the hallway until the call ended. They didn't have to wait long.

"I can't *believe* you would ask that of her. It hasn't even been *one day*."

They heard a handset fall against a hard plastic receiver and realized she'd been using the hospital's telephone, which made sense. Her cell was still in their bag.

Makani knocked twice and peeked inside.

Grandma Young's energy and skin tone had improved over the night, though her posture remained exhausted. But when she shifted her gaze and saw them, she perked up. "I thought you were another nurse. Come here! Let me see you."

"How are you feeling? Who was that?" Makani kissed her cheek and then reached for the phone to place it correctly onto the receiver. It was hanging slightly off.

"Leave it. I did that on purpose. Already been too many calls this morning."

"Reporters," Makani said. They wouldn't hesitate to harass someone who'd been hospitalized.

"Oh, no. Well. Yes." She huffed. "But that was just someone from church."

It wasn't how those calls usually sounded. Makani frowned. "Who?"

"Doesn't matter." Grandma Young motioned for her to sit. "Show me your arm. Did I see it last night? I can hardly remember your visit."

Makani snuggled in on the side without all the wires and tubes. She'd changed into a clean pair of jeans, a long-sleeved shirt, and her surfer-floral hoodie. Ollie had resumed custody of his black hoodie. She'd been disappointed to return it.

"I'm fine, see? It was only a scratch." She lifted her sleeve to reveal the bottom of the bandage, expecting her grandmother to demand to see the rest. But the painkillers must have been pretty hardcore, because she accepted the partial reveal as the whole truth. The call seemed important, so Makani tried again. "What did they want?"

Grandma Young squirmed. Adjusted her position. "The town is planning some sort of memorial for the victims."

Makani glanced at Ollie, who'd taken a seat in the recliner. He gave her a small shake of his head, equally in the dark.

"It's happening this afternoon on Main Street," Grandma Young said, withholding eye contact. "The idea is that people are tired of being afraid, and fear didn't prevent the previous attacks, so we might as well go outside and support one another."

"But that sounds like a good thing," Makani said. "That sounds . . ."

"Brave," Ollie said.

"Yeah. Like those Parisians who went back to the cafés after the terrorist attacks."

Grandma Young's gaze snapped up. "It *is* brave. But if everyone put this much effort into the search, he'd be handcuffed by sundown. And *then* we could celebrate."

Handcuffed by sundown sounded very John Wayne, but Makani was more concerned by that last word. "Celebrate?"

"No, that's not what I meant. I just think the memorial can wait." Grandma Young was talking faster, agitated. Something else about this was bothering her.

"I don't know. I think it'd be nice to honor Haley and Matt and Rodrigo—"

"They want *you* to speak," she said. "The town. They want you to stand up in front of all those people and cameras and be their mascot."

Makani shriveled with revulsion. Now she understood.

"It'll happen over my dead body," Grandma Young said. "And I'm hard to kill."

Ollie burst into unexpected laughter. He covered his mouth with a hand, but Makani and her grandmother finally broke into smiles. He gestured to a cloth tote bag. "Hey," he said. "We brought a few things to cheer you up."

"Oh, yeah!" Makani slid off the bed, and they withdrew each item one-by-one like gifts. Purse, robe, pajamas, blanket, toiletries, phone, books, puzzle. All the comforts of Grandma Young's home. None of the carnage.

•   •   •

Makani's other home called around noon. Her mother's first inquiry was, "Are you okay?" It was an encouraging start, but the follow-up was, "I just can't believe it. There's always *something* with you, isn't there?"

Makani had always been a fleck of sand in the eyes of this person who was supposed to love her unconditionally. She was an irritation, a nuisance.

"Now, I'll have to fly to the mainland to babysit you while your grandmother—"

"Where were you yesterday, Mom? The police and the hospital tried calling you for hours. *I* tried calling you."

"Your father and I were in court. I called everyone back the moment I got home, which is more than he did, by the way." She didn't seem to be aware that *everyone* had not included her daughter. Nor was she interested in hearing her daughter's version of events as she launched directly into her travel plans. She would be in Osborne next week, probably. She had an important presentation at work—or maybe it was something related to the divorce proceedings, Makani's hearing had dimmed—that couldn't be missed.

"And now, look. Look what you're doing to me."

"I'm sorry, Mom—"

"I can't deal with you right now."

Silence. Makani stared at the blinking number on her phone. *Three minutes and fourteen seconds.* She'd almost been killed, and her mother had given her three minutes and fourteen seconds. And she'd turned it into *her* problem.

Of course it was about her. It was always about her.

But Makani felt unexpectedly devastated. The phone trembled in her hand. She hadn't realized that her mother could still hurt her like this.

Ollie stared at her, unable to hide the empathetic sorrow from his usually reserved expression. Something about that was painful, too.

"Have you eaten today?" Grandma Young asked.

The question surprised Makani. As she struggled to focus, she touched her arm. The wound was sensitive and sore. "I don't think I've eaten anything in the last twenty-four hours."

"Oliver, would you get my purse? There should be a twenty in my wallet. I'd like for you to go to the cafeteria and pick up a few things. Something that would be easy for Makani to digest—soup or bread. And whatever looks good to you."

"Sure, Mrs. Young. I'd be happy to." He found the twenty and gave a low wave of goodbye to Makani as he disappeared.

"She's my daughter. And I love her," Grandma Young said quietly. "But she's a raging narcissist who married an asshole."

Makani had never heard her grandmother say the word *ass*. Under any other circumstance, it would have been hysterical. Right now, it only stung like the truth.

"None of this is your fault," Grandma Young said.

"*I know*," Makani whispered. A lie.

"Do you?"

Makani nodded. Another lie.

Grandma Young patted the space beside her, and Makani sat. She patted closer. Makani scooted, and her grandmother cradled her with a tilted head. They sat like this for several minutes. The affection felt painful. Makani's whole existence was a mess of secrets and lies and pretending. Her grandmother was the only person in Osborne who knew why she was really here, yet she still loved her. Makani wanted to be comforted, but she didn't deserve it.

Her grandmother released a weary sigh. "You lied to me."

Makani stiffened. Terrified by her own transparency.

"You lied to me yesterday, and we'll have to deal with that. I'm not sure how yet. This is all . . . a lot to process. But I love you, and I want you and Ollie to be safe—"

Oh God. Wait. Was this about staying safe from murderers or safe sex? Makani knew it was wrong, but she hoped her grandmother was talking about murder.

"—in *all the ways possible* for you to be safe."

She wriggled out from her grandmother's embrace.

"We'll talk about it more soon," Grandma Young said. "When I'm not in the hospital, and your boyfriend isn't down the hall."

A tiny particle of hope shot through Makani's distress. It did seem like maybe Ollie was her boyfriend now. Or that he would be soon.

Her grandmother continued, "But I wanted to mention it, so that I can also say: I trust you. And I trust that you'll be honest with me from now on."

I trust you.

It rattled her. Those three words made Makani *want* to be more open and honest. They made her want to be the person that her grandmother believed she was.

Just then, a loud exclamation trumpeted down the hallway of the ICU. "You!"

Makani knew that voice. Her pulse quickened.

"You saved her!" Alex said.

"She was saving herself," Ollie said. "Her grandma and I only helped."

Makani could almost hear Alex's grin. "Hell yeah, she was saving herself."

"We're just glad that you're all okay," Darby said.

They burst into the room, energetic bundles of joy and relief, and threw their arms around Makani in an enthusiastic group hug. She hadn't realized how badly she'd needed them until this moment. Their embrace rejuvenated her spirits.

"How did you know we were here?" she asked.

"We heard that your grandma was hurt," Darby said, balancing a box of gas station doughnuts. "Where else would you be?"

Alex leveled a saucy look at Makani. "No help from you, though. Next time, answer your damn"—she glanced at Grandma Young—"dang phone."

"No next time," Darby said.

"Amen to that," Grandma Young said, and they bounded over to hug her, too.

Alex's hair was woven into a strange and complicated configuration, and a loose braid flew into the air when she spun back around to Makani. "We brought treats." She opened the lid to show off the sugary rings. "Maple for you, chocolate frosting for Ollie."

Makani was touched they'd remembered his preference. Perhaps it was only penance for accusing him of being a serial killer behind his back, but she was happy to grant them atonement. Ollie stood near the door. He was holding a tower of Styrofoam cartons from the cafeteria, but he smiled, not in the least upset to be upstaged.

"Mrs. Young, this one is for you." Alex pointed to a doughnut with orange frosting and black sprinkles. It was a Halloween doughnut.

"Because your house is always so seasonal," Darby explained.

Grandma Young glowed with pleasure, even though it would be a few weeks before she could eat solid food. Everyone was talking at once, lively and loudly, when a nurse that Makani didn't recognize popped his head around the door.

"We understand these are special circumstances," he said, "but I'm sorry. Only two visitors at a time are allowed in ICU rooms."

"Oh," Makani said as the chatter halted. It was clear that none of them had considered this.

"That's all right," Grandma Young said. "Why don't you go to the waiting room to catch up? I'm feeling a nap coming on, anyway."

She did look tired, so Makani kissed her cheek. "Ollie and I will be back in a bit."

Grandma Young thanked Darby and Alex for coming, and then Makani and Ollie followed them out. They were able to find a different waiting room from the main room the previous night. It was smaller, but the seating was more comfortable. Even better, it was empty of other people. Makani and Ollie took separate chairs beside each other, and Darby and Alex squeezed together into a love seat. They exclaimed over Makani's arm.

"It's not that bad, really," she said.

"Not that bad?" Alex was aghast. "A berserk teenage boy broke into your house and tried to stab you to death. Get some fucking perspective!"

Everyone froze as Alex realized that Makani probably already had a decent grasp on the situation. And then she lost it. Alex's laughter was crazed and contagious, the kind only borne from dark situations. Like giggles at a funeral, it infected them all. Out of the four of them, she seemed the closest to the edge. But perhaps Alex sensed Makani intuiting this fragility, because she grabbed a doughnut and waved it around. Feigning an air of composure. "Looks like we're real cops today. Think we can crack the case?"

"Hey," Darby said, licking glaze from his thumb as he took a doughnut for himself. "Stereotype. Brother of a cop right there."

Alex rolled her eyes, but Ollie gave Darby a smile.

"Speaking of . . ." Darby was hesitant. "What *are* they saying? The cops?"

With occasional interjections from Ollie, Makani filled them in on the last twenty-four hours. But she tripped up when she reached the part about him being naked.

"Hold up." Alex's gaze whipped to Ollie. "A minute ago in this story, you were covered by only a blanket. Did you run downstairs in a *blanket toga*?"

"Yes," Makani lied, as Ollie said, "Not exactly."

Alex cackled. "Ohmygod!"

An inevitable blush spread across Ollie's face.

"Please confirm, yes or no," she said. "You, Ollie Larsson, chased after the Osborne Slayer in your bare essentials." When he nodded the affirmative, Darby and Alex erupted with a fresh round of riotous laughter.

Sorry, Makani mouthed.

Ollie shrugged helplessly. *You tried.*

Makani understood where her friends' laughter was coming from, so she wasn't offended. It was the necessary moment of levity that would get them through the rest of the story. By the time she finished filling them in, their expressions had sobered.

"The part I can't get over," Darby said, "is *David.*"

Alex shook her head in equal disbelief.

"He seemed so normal and boring," Darby continued. "Like one of those guys who'd fade into the landscape to live the same life as his dad—"

"And his dad before him," she said.

Ollie stared at nothing. The shock of what had happened to them was circuitous; it kept coming back. "I guess you never really know what's going on inside someone else's head. His external life seemed dull, but his interior life . . . must be a lot more complex."

"It must be angry," Alex said.

He nodded. "Hurt."

Makani hadn't planned on telling them, not ever. Certainly not now. But as their words stirred inside her, they melded with her grandmother's trust, and that powerful undertow of resistance— as familiar as it was formidable—suddenly released its grasp. Her mother didn't care about her, but her friends did. She wanted them to know.

"He must have been planning this for months, maybe years," Darby said. "What cracked? What makes a person go from fantasizing to actually doing?" And as he turned to Makani in bewilderment, she knew his next question—the big one—before he even asked. "And why did he go after *you*?"

Makani took a moment before answering, but her voice was steady. "Because I think he might have learned something about my past."

Their silence was weighted with curiosity and pressure.

"My name," she said, "wasn't always Makani Young."

CHAPTER NINETEEN

ALEX'S EYES WERE saucers. "Ohmygod. You killed someone."

"What?" Makani was taken aback. "No. God, *no*. If I'd killed someone, how could I even be here? Wouldn't I be sitting in prison somewhere?"

Ollie and Darby stared at Alex in disbelief.

"Okay," she said shamelessly. "Overreaction."

Ollie turned his body toward Makani to encourage her. "Go on."

Makani Kanekalau startled awake with a terrified gasp as Gabrielle Cruz and Kayla Lum burst into her bedroom. They yanked her to the floor. Makani's skin smelled like body odor and day-old suntan lotion, and her hair was an untamed 'fro. She was wearing a tank top without a bra, and her pink pajama shorts were an old pair, see-through with age.

The girls pointed at her striped panties and laughed.

Gabrielle's teeth flashed like razors through the darkness—the last image Makani saw before she was blindfolded. "Tonight's the night, rookie," Gabrielle taunted. The blindfold was too tight, but Gabrielle was the captain, so Makani didn't dare complain.

Kayla hissed in her ear. "You're coming with us."

"I'm sorry," Alex interrupted. "These girls *kidnapped* you? Were they your friends?"

"Teammates," Makani said. "Sometimes friends, sometimes rivals. But they were seniors, and I was a junior. This was last October. My first year on varsity."

Darby seemed startled that she'd been an athlete. "Varsity *what*?"

The swim team's hazing rituals were notorious, and they'd been growing worse every year. Escalating. Now their turn, the senior girls of Kailua-Kona High School were hungry for revenge. The power of authority coursed through Gabrielle and Kayla, no doubt blinding them in its own way, as they tugged and shoved Makani down the hall.

Makani stiffened as her mother's harsh laughter cut through the narrow space. "Sorry again about the locked door, girls." A familiarity on the word *girls* indicated that she was on their side—and she wasn't surprised that they were here. "Glad I was still awake to hear your knock."

It was well known that parents were informed of the initiation ahead of time so that they could leave the front door unlocked for the older girls to get in. It was understood that the parents would play along, but that they'd also give their daughters the heads-up. That way, the rookies could already be dressed in their cutest pajamas with swimsuits underneath. That's what parents were *supposed* to do.

Makani tensed in hopeful anticipation of another

apology, this time for her. Or, at least, an excuse. But as she was pushed outside, all she heard was the *click*—and lock—of the door behind her.

"Umm. Your mom sucks?" Alex was both stating it and asking for confirmation.

Darby looked too sad to berate her.

Makani didn't want to see Ollie's reaction, so she kept going.

Gabrielle and Kayla prodded Makani outside and wrestled her into an open-air Jeep. Makani knew it was the captain's car. Gabrielle swerved wildly, purposefully, down the street as Makani fumbled for a seat belt. The wind blasted her as she jostled from one side of the Jeep to the other, frightening her with the sensation that she was about to fall out. At last, she managed to strap herself in.

"Where are we going?" She tried to sound like she was fine, down for anything. But fear clouded her voice.

The girls just turned up the radio, and Makani's neighborhood was left behind in a thundering wake of Beyoncé. The air was thick with humidity. The breeze was scented like salt water and sweet plumeria. Recognizing that she was being ignored, Makani lifted her blindfold for a peek. The dashboard clock said it was almost midnight. On the Queen Ka'ahumanu Highway, skinny palm trees were silhouetted by the night sky, the tallest vegetation amid the scrubland that characterized this side of the Big Island.

Only a few minutes later, Gabrielle cut the engine. The music vanished. Ocean waves boomed. "Time to deplane, rookie," she said, and Kayla laughed at the dumb joke. Kayla was always trying to impress the captain. They grabbed

Makani by the upper arms, one on each side, and steered her, barefoot, over a beach of volcanic rocks. Something punctured the ball of her right foot, and Makani hissed in pain.

Their grips tightened around her arms.

A crackling bonfire strengthened into a roar as Makani's feet touched sand. Peals of girlish laughter swirled and eddied. She knew they were aimed at her.

"Are we the last to arrive?" Kayla called out, reveling in the attention.

Catcalls and whistles rose above the laughter. The blindfold was ripped from Makani's eyes, and she squinted, holding up a hand against the sparks from the fire.

The whole team was there. The other rookies' blindfolds had already been removed. They were laughing at her, too.

Even Jasmine was laughing. She and the other three rookies were dressed in bikini tops and board shorts. Their hair was done—Jasmine's straight hair was pulled back into a neat ponytail—and some of them were even wearing makeup.

Mortified, Makani crossed her arms over her chest. She felt ugly and exposed. She'd swum with most of these girls since childhood. They'd seen her thousands of times in swimsuits, but it didn't matter that her ratty tank top and pajamas covered more skin; she was the only one wearing the wrong thing. The *private* thing.

A rush of anger washed through her humiliation. Clearly, Mrs. Oshiro, Jasmine's perfect mother, had warned her. Why hadn't Jasmine said something? She was her best friend. They texted each other first thing in the morning and last thing before bed. They'd texted less than two hours ago, and Jasmine hadn't given any indication of anything unusual. And she *knew* Makani's mom couldn't be relied on for things like this.

Gabrielle gestured at Makani's pajama shorts. "Might as well take those off."

Makani didn't move.

"The captain said strip!" Kayla screamed into her ear. "Strip!"

"Strip! Strip! Strip! Strip!" the other girls chanted.

The intimacy of her underwear made Makani want to cry. Shivering, she pulled down her pajama shorts and folded them neatly on the sand.

The captain snatched them up and waved them triumphantly like a flag. "Let the games begin!"

Cheering broke out as the girls split into five teams, with two veterans to every rookie. The rookies' veteran teammates were the same as their kidnappers. In block-lettered Sharpie, the captain wrote SLUT, NYMPHO, WHORE, and CUNT on the other rookies' foreheads. The marker pressed against her skin, and Makani was informed that she was BITCH. If she responded to any other name, she'd have to take a shot.

Four vodka bottles were produced, two in each of Kayla's hands, and she waved them like pom-poms. Kayla swam freestyle. She had insane endurance, and her muscles rippled in the bonfire's light. "What's your name, Bitch?" she yelled.

"Bitch!" Makani said.

"I said, what's your name, Bitch?"

"BITCH!"

"Okay," Gabrielle said. "Makani, your spot is between Hannah and Jasmine."

Makani took off.

"Wrong! Who's Makani?"

She couldn't believe that she'd already forgotten. Divers were precise. They performed well in the spotlight. Makani did not make mistakes. Everyone cracked up again as she downed the first repugnant shot, trying not to gag. She'd never liked vodka. It reminded her of nail-polish remover.

Gabrielle's best stroke was butterfly. The captain had the team's strongest arms, so when she clapped Makani's back, it stung. "Take your place, Makani."

Makani stood her ground. Swallowed her tears.

"Hey! The rookie bitch has learned her lesson," she said.

"Great job, Bitch." Kayla ruffled her curls. Few things grated Makani more than someone touching her hair. "Now get your ass in line."

Makani jogged to the area between Hannah (SLUT) and Jasmine (CUNT). It pleased her that Jasmine had gotten the meanest name.

"Are you okay?" Jasmine asked, placing a pitying hand on Makani's arm.

Two days ago, they'd gotten matching gel manicures of alternating silver and blue. School colors. Now Makani wanted to shove Jasmine to the ground and cram her mouth with dry sand until she choked. Makani fixed her with a livid glare. Jasmine seemed surprised by the intensity, but she removed her hand in silent surrender.

They were not a team tonight. She would *not* lose to Jasmine.

The games involved running and performing their usual dry-land calisthenics—lunges, jumping jacks, push-ups, and sit-ups—only they had to do twice as many reps and with two veterans yelling in their ears, forcing them to repeat pledges of team loyalty and tricking them into responding to their real names. It was the veterans' job to make their rookie finish last in as many rounds as possible.

Between each round, the rookies had to drink a shot of vodka. The last rookie to finish had to drink two. The veterans could drink as little or as much as they wanted, and they all took swigs before stalking toward their rookies with brown-paper grocery sacks.

The first round began. Makani ran the beach with grim determination. The veterans removed egg cartons from the mysterious sacks and hurled their missiles from a distance. The eggs were rotten and sulfurous. Some of the girls dry-heaved. As Jasmine's ponytail bobbed ahead of her, resentment scorched through Makani's veins.

It must be nice to have someone who gives enough of a shit about you to warn you. Must be nice to have been given the opportunity to prepare.

Kayla wasted her carton early, but the captain saved hers for the final lap, when Makani was panting and light-headed. Gabrielle jogged beside her, chucking her own dozen *hard*. With each hit, Makani felt an accompanying shot of adrenaline. She pushed ahead of Jasmine, and Jasmine finished in fifth. Last place.

Makani took a single shot, and Jasmine took two. The veterans also took shots. Gabrielle and Kayla drank more than the others, Makani's non-loss adding fuel to their competitive and exploitative inclinations.

As the rookies lunged, the veterans squirted them with baby oil and shaving cream. As they did jumping jacks, they flung mayonnaise and Spam. In a blur of screaming and vodka and exhaustion and confusion, Makani soon grew ill, but she kept her eyes on Jasmine. Forced herself to keep beating her.

"We've got a tough one." Gabrielle grinned. "But don't worry. We'll break you."

"Looks like she's out for your job, Captain," Kayla said.

Even though it was a joke, it was the first time that anyone had ever mentioned the possibility of captain. Divers never got to be captain because so much of their training was separate. But Makani *desperately* wanted to be captain next year. She was good at what she did. None of her teammates got more elevation from their takeoff, executed their twists so gracefully, entered the water with so little splash.

Jasmine stumbled into Makani and toppled her to the sand. A vodka bottle emptied the rest of its contents onto Makani's underwear.

"God, keep your failure to yourself!" Makani said.

"Sorry, sorry," Jasmine slurred. She'd never been able to hold her liquor.

The older girls were rolling with laughter. "I take it back," Kayla said to Gabrielle. "That's job security right there."

Makani's insides strummed with fury. She imagined seizing Jasmine's hair and yanking until the flesh ripped from her scalp. Thrusting her lacerated head into the salty waves. Holding her in place. Drowning her.

"Shit," Gabrielle said, brandishing a can of something. Makani couldn't tell what. "These don't have pull tabs. Did anyone remember to bring a can opener?"

None of the other veterans had, but a girl named Sarah kept a knife in her car. While she ran to fetch it, another bottle was passed around. The vodka burned as it slid down Makani's throat. She licked her lips.

Sarah's knife turned out to be large, something made for hunting or survival, and it easily pierced the cans. The smell released was repellent.

As the rookies did push-ups, chunks of meaty dog food were lobbed onto their backs. Crouching in front of Makani, Kayla pushed a wet handful directly onto her face and up her nostrils. Makani blew her nose and spit, retching. And then something thick was cascading down her head. An entire jar of honey oozed over her neck and through her hair. It would take days to wash out.

With each push-up, her body encrusted itself with more and more sand. "What's your problem, Bitch?" Kayla screeched. "Can't handle a few push-ups, Bitch?"

"Makani!" Gabrielle said.

"Wha—?" Makani turned her head, and her veterans high-fived.

Kayla lowered a bottle to Makani's lips. "Drink up, Bitch."

Another shot was forced down her throat. It mixed with the dog food and sickly sweet honey. She vomited. The veterans exclaimed with disgusted glee, but Makani couldn't escape the stench. The honey clung the puke to her chin. As the other rookies finished their reps, Gabrielle and Kayla whooped and danced. Two more shots. Makani threw up again, but she refused to go down alone. "Hey, Jasmine."

Her best friend was doubled over in sickness and exhaustion, but she glanced up at her name. The word CUNT was smudged but still legible. "Yeah?"

Makani pointed her finger. "Ha!"

It was a direct violation of best friendship. Jasmine's jaw unhinged, hurt and upset, while the other girls laughed at the deception. They made her drink.

As the final round began, Makani had no idea who was losing. Her eyes scrunched closed as she did the sit-ups—just trying to breathe, just trying to keep everything from coming up again. Someone straddled her legs.

"Look at me," the captain said.

Makani opened her eyes, and a bottle was thrust toward her face. She screamed as something splashed onto her eyeballs. The liquid burned like an instant inferno. She tried to wipe it away and then shrieked like she'd been wounded again. Her hands were still covered in sand and honey and gloppy food droppings. Blinded and in agony, she scrambled to her feet. "What is it? What did you to do me?"

Bedlam erupted as the other rookies cried out all around her. Screaming and yelling. Laughing and cackling. The intensity of the pain reminded Makani of being stung by a jellyfish. Someone said habanero Tabasco. Someone else grabbed her.

"Tilt your head back," the girl said.

Thinned filth streamed in every direction across Makani's face, but she could make out—she could *see*—a bottle of water. She crumpled to the sand. The girl ran off to help someone else. Makani moaned and gnashed her teeth. Through her tears, she saw another plastic water bottle near the bonfire, only a few feet away beside the empty cans and knife.

As Makani reached for the water, Jasmine swooped in and grabbed it. Her ponytail, thick with honey, smacked Makani across the eyes.

Orange sparks flew into the star-strewn sky. Rage, white-hot. With a deep guttural growl, Makani snatched up the knife. The blade flashed in the firelight. It was long and sharp and vicious. She grabbed the ponytail and sliced upward into the night.

CHAPTER TWENTY

"**THE TENSION RELEASED,** and her hair gave way." In the waiting room, Makani could still see the limp ponytail in her grimy hand. "It was this . . . instant, overwhelming shame. The realization that I'd done something terrible that could never be undone.

"Jasmine was so drunk"—her voice choked—"that she almost drowned. A *swimmer*, and she almost drowned. And it was my fault."

Ollie's hand rested gently on Makani's back. He glanced at Darby and Alex, but they weren't following what she'd said, either. "What do you mean?"

"The other girls didn't see what had happened. Everything was so chaotic." Makani paused, experiencing the trauma again. "Jasmine freaked out, of course she freaked out, and ran toward the ocean. I guess she wanted to rinse off—the Tabasco was still blistering our eyes—and to get the hell away from me. She looked *afraid* of me. I knew that I should go in after her, she was so out of it, but I didn't."

Makani had watched her best friend weave and stumble into the ocean. And then she'd turned her head away in shame. It had been too painful to watch the aftermath.

She'd figured Jasmine wouldn't even want her help, which was probably true. But Jasmine had *needed* her help. And Makani had curled up in the sand. Eyes burning, tears streaming. The knife in her right hand, the ponytail in her left.

"The captain was the one who finally noticed and dove in after her. She worked as a lifeguard on a resort, so she immediately started CPR. Jasmine wasn't breathing."

Makani shouldn't have been able to hear the wind shaking the palms or the waves lapping the shore, but the bonfire had burned to smoke and embers, and the other girls had trembled in quiet hysteria. Sirens cut through the silence. Compression and a defibrillator and some kind of alarm, another wail. Or maybe the banshee was only screaming in her head. Petrified, Makani didn't move throughout the whole ordeal.

"The paramedics arrived and got her breathing again," she said, wiping her cheeks with her fingers, "and she was okay—suddenly, she was okay—but then she was rushed away to the hospital. And by now, everyone had seen her hair . . . and they'd all seen me with the knife. The police put me in handcuffs."

They'd ushered her into the back of their car, behind the metal grate, and driven her to the station. She'd taken a Breathalyzer test, and then she'd been photographed, fingerprinted, and questioned. *"You're in a lot of trouble,"* an officer said. *"We could charge you with public intoxication, and you're looking at a third-degree assault."*

Makani's heart had plummeted into the dark sea.

Assault. She'd committed *assault.* On her *best friend.*

Even as she confessed the charge now, she couldn't look anyone in the eye. "The magistrate set the bail, and my parents arrived separately. They were already doing everything separately. But their anger . . . it *suffused* the entire station."

"I'm so sorry," Darby said. "This is all so awful."

"What about the parents who provided the alcohol?" Ollie asked. It was a question his brother might pose.

"They were charged a while later," Makani said. "That October was hell in slow motion. The school suspended me for thirty days, and I was kicked off the swim team. I'd *always* been a part of a team. And then I wasn't. The guy I'd been dating for over half a year, Jason— he was a diver, too—stopped returning my texts and unfollowed me on every platform. Our breakup was unstated but immediate."

Alex asked with atypical delicacy, "And Jasmine?"

Makani's expression gave the answer. Their friendship had died on the beach.

"Around school, her butchered hair couldn't be ignored," Makani said. "It looked so cruel. It *was* so cruel. Because I was a minor, my name wasn't reported in the media, but that didn't stop anyone from talking online. It didn't stop anyone from learning that I have a mug shot with the word *bitch* on my forehead or that the word *cunt* was still visible when Jasmine arrived at the hospital. The whole team was shamed, but people saw me as the ringleader."

"Even though you had a word on your head, too?" Ollie asked.

"They thought mine spoke the truth." Makani lifted her face to look at him squarely. "I was the one who picked up the knife."

Thousands of messages from classmates, neighbors, and strangers had focused their outrage on her. There were threats of scalping. Threats of rape. Threats of murder.

Shame on you, the internet said. *Why don't you just kill yourself already? #SwimSluts #KonaGate #CommitSuicideSquad*

Makani slept long hours and stirred aimlessly through her house. The barrage was endless. Immeasurable. Sometimes it hurt because everyone had the wrong idea about her, but usually it hurt because it felt like they had it right. She didn't know what to do or where to be or who to talk to. She kept wanting to call Jasmine—the one person who'd always understood—except she was the exact person Makani had failed.

"I wrote Jasmine this long apology letter. Like, I actually wrote it on paper and mailed it. She never responded, but I wouldn't have responded to me, either. Meanwhile, my parents hired an attorney who told me that I should never contact Jasmine again. And then I was asked to pay restitution."

When Makani saw that her friends didn't know what that meant, she explained, "I was asked to give her money for a professional haircut." She shook her head. "As if that were anything close to enough." Makani would have paid any amount they'd asked for. She would have cut off her own hair—she would have cut it off for the rest of her life.

"So, what happened?" Ollie's hand wasn't on her back anymore, but his body was close. "Do you still have an assault on your record?"

"No. About a month later, my district attorney dropped the charge, and I got my record expunged."

"You must have been so relieved," Darby said.

"Not really. I felt like I deserved it. And then the DA made the mistake of telling a reporter that I was sorry for what I'd done, but *'one night of fun shouldn't ruin her life.'* She literally used the phrase *'kids will be kids.'*"

Everyone winced.

"Yep," she said. "Social media . . . did not like that."

The public wanted Makani to be punished. They became more furious, *more* incensed. The violent threats increased. The overreaction was catastrophic.

Ollie's countenance had taken on a perceptible weight, but it looked heavy with understanding—not judgment. At least, that's what Makani hoped she was seeing as he asked, "How'd you wind up here? When did your name change?"

"When my school suspension ended," Makani said, "my classmates . . . the *looks* they gave me. The things they said. I didn't even make it to lunch. My dad picked me up from the nurse's office, and on the ride home, that's when he told me that he'd filed for divorce. And later that night, that's when my mom told me they were sending me here."

Ollie and Darby seemed dumbfounded. Alex swore.

"The DA was the one who suggested that I might have an easier time adjusting if I changed my name to one that wasn't so easily traceable."

"Did you *want* to change it?" Ollie asked.

"I don't know." Makani had been so depressed that she'd just let it happen. And there *had* been some relief from having a new identity. Not much. But some.

Sharing her story now, however, had opened a valve of tremendous internal pressure. Her secret—this self-inflicted burden—had finally been released.

Darby set the doughnut box onto the floor, stood from the love seat, and pulled Makani into a determined bear hug. He wouldn't release her until she received it and returned it. "I'm sorry that you've lived alone with this for so long. I wish you would have told us."

"You're not afraid I'm a vicious sociopath? Someone who gets off on other people's pain?" Makani's jokes were only half jokes.

Darby pulled back, hands on her shoulders, to examine her. His nose and mouth screwed up in exaggerated concentration. "Nah."

"I don't know if you remember this," Ollie said, "but we've actually met a vicious sociopath. And he wasn't anything like you."

"Besides," Alex said, "we already know that *pain* doesn't get you off. Ollie does."

Makani buried her face in Darby's shoulder, but it made them all laugh.

"Honestly?" Alex continued. "I think it's rad that you have a mug shot with the word *bitch* on your forehead. I'm gonna be you for Halloween this year."

Makani's body uprighted as her emotions crashed back down. "It's not funny. I ruined my best friend's life. I will *never* forgive myself—"

"David is ruining lives. By taking them. You did a shitty thing, and, yeah, she'll probably hate you for the rest of her life—"

"Alex," Darby warned.

"—but she still *has* a life."

"That's beside the point," Makani said. "My actions weren't harmless. I didn't just snap a wet towel or shoot my goggles at her."

Darby stepped in front of Alex to block her from Makani's view. "You're right. But I know what it's like to be angry—to think that everyone has it easier than you. Or that everyone is against you. And if you don't deal with those feelings, they don't go away on their own. They keep building and building until they *force* their way out."

Tears pricked Makani's eyes again as she stared at her bandaged arm.

"You aren't a bad person," Alex said. "You just had a bad night."

Darby guided Makani onto the love seat, squishing her in between him and Alex to confront the real issue. "So," he said, "you think David found out what you did."

Her head hung even lower. "Yes."

"You think he chose you—"

"Like Harry Potter," Alex stage-whispered.

"Oh. My. God," Darby said. "Can't you hold it in for, like, one second?"

She gave a nonchalant toss of a braid as he turned back to Makani. "You think David chose you as some sort of act of . . . antihero or vigilante justice?" he asked.

"There's nothing else it *could* be," Makani said. "I don't have any connection to the other victims. I think he found out something about all of us, and he's punishing—"

"No," Ollie said.

They looked at him in surprise. He sat, unmoved, across from them, and his voice was resolute. "You aren't being punished. You've *already* been punished. You were publicly shamed, and you've spent the last year shaming yourself. How would he even know? I didn't know, and I've Googled the hell out of you."

The love seat froze in astonishment.

Ollie's face skewed with regret. "Not anything *creepy*. Normal Googling." He paused. "But, like, a lot of it."

Darby's and Alex's eyes popped.

Queasiness and curiosity mixed inside Makani. "What did you find?"

"Not much." Ollie seemed pained, perhaps because he only had himself to blame for this conversation. "Small things, funny stuff you said. Pictures on their Instagrams." He motioned toward Darby and Alex.

Makani blinked.

Ollie was growing smaller. "Please say you've Googled me, too."

"We've *all* Googled you," Alex said.

Heat slipped up Makani's neck as she nodded.

"Thanks for leaving me hanging." Ollie exhaled, shoving his hands into his pockets. But then he sidled her with a grin. "So, what'd you find out about me?"

Makani snorted. "Even less. Though, I *did* already know that you used to wrestle in middle school. I saw a picture of you in one of those weird blue leotards."

"It's called a singlet."

"It's a leotard."

He laughed. "Now, you *have* to show me that swim team photo. You owe me."

But Makani's mind had already circled back to her worries. She chewed her lip. "You never found anything about my past?"

"No, I swear . . ." But then his head cocked.

She recoiled. "You did."

"Okay. I did do a search for 'Makani and Hawaii,' and I think, now, that I might have found something on Reddit." He didn't notice her shudder, but he spoke faster, betraying his concern. "How could I have known what I was looking at? I barely even remember the thread. I discarded it so quickly. It wasn't your name."

Her blood drained. There it was. Proof that her past was available for anyone to discover. It wouldn't be a huge step to notice the dates of the incident, search for her old name, and then find her in the swim team photos on the school's website.

Ollie was following her train of thought. "No. It's too unlikely."

"Too unlikely that a serial killer with an elaborate plan would have the patience to discover that I'm actually someone else?"

"You aren't *someone else.*" This distinction seemed to bother him.

"But it's the only explanation that makes sense. I don't have a single connection to the other victims."

"That's not true," Alex said, jumping in. "He's clearly attacking one person from every clique. He's plucking out the shining stars for some macabre collection."

Makani glowered. "I'm not a member of a single club or team. I don't talk to anyone but you guys. And who says Rodrigo was a shining star?"

"*Me*," Alex said. "He was really freaking smart. Probably the smartest person in our whole class. Probably the whole school."

"So, what's my special talent? Having brown skin?"

Alex hesitated. "Well. You do stand out."

Makani stared at her for several long seconds. "Fuck," she said, looking away. She didn't know if she was angrier with Alex for pointing out something so stupidly obvious or for the idea that her skin color or being biracial or *whatever* might even be a *fraction* of David's motivation. Of course it could be.

Even smushed between Makani and the love seat's arm, Darby managed to tuck his thumbs under his suspenders. "Okay, let's pretend your theory is correct, and David was trying to punish you. What about the other victims? What did they do?"

"They were probably assholes, too," Makani said. "I mean, look at Matt."

Ollie frowned. "Some of his friends are worse."

"Yeah, but Matt was their leader. He set the example, and his friends followed."

"What about Rodrigo and Haley?" Alex asked.

"I don't know," Makani said. "But none of you knew what *I* did. Everyone has secrets." She couldn't help glancing at Ollie, but he was distracted, so he didn't notice.

"I don't know about Haley," he said. "But I do know something about Rodrigo."

Makani felt Alex's spine straighten beside her.

"It feels wrong to speak ill of the dead, but one of his friends gave the police a tip, which they checked out—and it was true. Rodrigo was a troll."

Darby frowned. "What kind? Like, a comments troll?"

"The kind who threatened women," Ollie said.

Makani's stomach dropped.

"Dozens of platforms," he continued. "Hundreds of aliases. Mainly against women in gaming. He stopped doing it a few months ago. The friend said Rodrigo realized it was wrong, but he wasn't sure what had happened to trigger his conscience."

Alex twitched sharply. This new information appeared to upset her more than Makani's confession.

"So . . . I'm right." Makani pressed her clenched fists against her forehead. Suddenly, everyone was taking her theory a lot more seriously.

Darby tugged on his suspenders. Their elasticity wouldn't last long under this much stress. "I don't know if you're *right*, exactly, but there is a strong pattern. And there *could* be something unknown about Haley."

"So, who else would David have on his list?" Ollie asked.

"But that's the thing," Makani said. "We don't know. Whatever they did, it's probably a secret."

"Unless . . ." He sagged with fatigue. "I mean, Zachary Loup. Right?"

The waiting room fell into a hush. This was the closest Makani had heard to Ollie admitting that he'd known the rumors about him and Zachary. He sighed. "Look, I know one of us was supposed to be the killer. And maybe I am a loner, but he's *definitely* an asshole. It's reasonable to assume that he'd be a target."

"Oh my God," Alex said. She didn't need to think about it.

"We have to warn him," Darby said. Instant agreement. "We can't take the chance."

Ollie called his brother. Chris sounded doubtful, but he promised to check in with Zachary. A minute later, a text arrived. It was the owner of Greeley's Foods: *Your shift has been canceled. Store closing early so employees can attend the memorial.*

"Shit!" Alex sprang from the love seat. "I'm supposed to be in the band room in five minutes."

Makani's fear reignited at the thought of anyone leaving her sight line. "What? Why? You can't go on campus!"

Alex tried to allay Makani's concern with a reassuring smile. It didn't work. "We're playing the memorial. They're just letting us in to pick up our uniforms."

"Don't worry," Darby said as he hustled Alex away, car keys already in hand. "I'll drop her off, and then we'll both be safe in the crowd."

When Makani and Ollie returned to Grandma Young's room, her bed was gone. The nurses informed them that she'd been wheeled away for a test. They sat on the floor and picked at the cold food that Ollie had brought earlier from the cafeteria. Now that they were alone, Makani wanted to talk more about her past—she wanted to be *comforted*—but Ollie was deep in contemplation about something else. The moment didn't seem right.

The vibration was faint, but they sat up like a shotgun blast.

"It's Chris," Ollie said, checking his phone.

Makani stood and walked to the mirror above the sink to give him the privacy of a few feet. Futzing with her shirt, she peeked at Ollie's reflection. His pale brows were pinched, which matched the frustrated tone of his conversation. The call was short.

"The police can't do much," he said. "They don't want to freak anyone out. But Chris did check in with Zachary, and he's safe. He's at home with his mom's boyfriend."

"So . . . that's it?"

Ollie's jawline was rigid. "Yep."

"I thought they might send a patrol car to watch over him or something."

"Maybe if they were a bigger department. Or if we had any shred of proof. But they're stretched thin, and now they have to work the memorial. Chris is already there."

Makani slumped. "I'll let Darby and Alex know."

Darby's response was immediate: *But we just saw him!*

Her breath caught. *z's at the memorial?*

Yeah we saw him walking toward main street. There are a TON of people here. I just dropped off Alex so I'll find him to make sure he understands how serious this is!

don't!!! what if david is stalking him?? we'll help you!! we'll be right there!

Ollie read the texts over her shoulder. "What about your grandma?"

Makani stopped, halfway to the door. She'd vowed to be more honest with her grandmother. What possible excuse could she give for leaving the hospital right now?

"We'll leave a message with the nurses," he said, decoding her troubled expression. "We'll say that we wanted to pay our respects, that we'll meet up with my brother, and that we'll be back as soon as it's over. None of that is a lie."

It wasn't a lie. But it didn't feel good.

CHAPTER
TWENTY-ONE

ZACHARY LOUP WAS stoned. He'd only come to the memorial because it was better than being at home, better than being alone with his mother's lecherous boyfriend. Zachary saw the hatred burning in Terry's eyes whenever Amber wasn't looking. What kind of man was jealous over his girlfriend's son? What kind of man felt *threatened* by that relationship? Zachary prayed that Amber had the sense not to marry Terry. Zachary's first stepfather had been bad enough. He was beating the shit out of some other family now.

Black satin ribbons were tied around every telephone pole on Main Street, and they fluttered in the crisp bite of the wind. The marching band was warming up in the grocery store parking lot. Brass instruments hummed and bass drums boomed. Cops were patrolling the two-lane street, which had been blocked off from traffic. The quaint thoroughfare was packed with county locals, vibrating with fury and injustice, as well as every news-media outlet that had raced to Nebraska to chronicle it.

The memorial was supposed to be a dignified remembrance of

the victims, but even Zachary could see that wasn't *exactly* what was happening. From the makeshift stage, a flatbed truck parked in front of the old bank, Principal Stanton shouted declarations to the masses: "This spring, the school fountain will be turned into a monument for the victims!"

Cheers.

"This weekend, our drama department will hold a fund-raiser for the victims' families!"

Cheers.

"And tomorrow night, our football team will take to the field in the playoffs!"

Losing-their-goddamn-minds cheers.

The principal was a balding man with a sturdy frame who wore his masculinity as if it were a badge of honor. Zachary detested him. Stanton was a son of a dick who punished Zachary for every fight, even the ones started by other students. Today, the principal sounded more defiant than respectful, and the spectators sounded more aggressive than supportive. The whole town was seething with outrage as their fear reached its boiling point.

Which came first, the outrage or the fear?

Ms. Clearwater, his favorite counselor, liked to give him Zen koans to keep his mind engaged. But koans were paradoxical riddles, which meant this wasn't actually a good example. Zachary knew from experience that fear always came first.

He drifted through the agitated flock. Every conversation was about David. A middle-aged woman spoke loudly to whoever was listening. "Did you see that picture where he was posing with that buck carcass?"

"Creepy smile," a guy with meth-mouth said. "Gave me the willies."

"His family goes to my church," a conspiratorial male voice said.

"The dad always seemed real shady. The mom's a prude, too. Never looks happy."

Zachary stopped wandering when he reached the fringes. He felt more comfortable on the outside of any crowd. Leaning against the brick storefront of Dream's Bridal, the outmoded boutique across from Greeley's Foods, he checked his messages to see if his friends were coming to watch the circus.

Damn. Drew and his brother were headed to an out-of-town wrestling match, and Brittani's mom had quarantined her until David was behind bars.

David Thurston Ware was born two days after Zachary. Zachary had been held back in eighth grade, so he was still only a junior, but they'd spent enough time together that he knew David wasn't what he seemed. Osborne was raring to cast ominous insights onto his character today, but just last night they'd been confused. *I can't believe it,* they'd said. *He seemed like such a normal teenage boy.*

Years ago, Zachary and David had lived next door to each other. Like most children who happen to be neighbors, that also made them friends. They watched cartoons, played Legos, went dirt biking. Zachary remembered David as a quiet kid prone to sudden outbursts. Unlike Zachary, who yelled at and threatened and terrorized the younger neighborhood boys, David held in his anger until he couldn't anymore. Until he snapped.

Admittedly, Zachary was no role model. But he still didn't think holding it in was healthy. He'd never forget the day when he'd borrowed David's new bike without asking, something he'd done a dozen times before, and David flew into the street and shoved him to the ground. The fall broke Zachary's arm, but that wasn't what had scared him.

It was the unbridled rage on David's face.

At the time, Zachary shook it off. Fair was fair. But deep down, it unsettled him that David had appeared from seemingly out of nowhere. He must have been hiding in the bushes. He'd been *waiting*.

But geography had been stronger than their friendship. When Zachary's mom remarried, his family moved into the trailer park, and things with David came to their natural end. The last time Zachary remembered talking to him was nearly two years ago, when they'd run into each other in the candy aisle of the drugstore. They'd debated the merits of chocolates versus gummies like they were kids again.

A new text vibrated in Zachary's hand: *BUSTED. ERIKA SAW U AT THE MEMORIAL!! GET UR ASS HOME RIGHT NOW!!!!!*

Not Drew, not Brittani.

Amber. *Mom*. Erika was Amber's coworker at Curlz & Cutz. She was only a few years older than him, and she was hot. Dark hair, sexy tattoo. Why had she ratted him out? Fuck that. Fuck them both. No way was he going home for some quality time with Terry. Amber picked the worst times to give a shit about him.

On the stage, Principal Stanton exited to make way for Pastor Greeley from Grace Lutheran, who introduced his son, Caleb. The Greeley family ran Osborne. The pastor's brother owned the grocery store and several of the buildings downtown. Their father founded the grocery store and had been mayor for a record-number of terms. They were the opposite of Zachary's family, and Zachary resented them for it.

Caleb was a senior, like David. Like Zachary was supposed to be. Caleb was round-eyed, square-faced, and as earnest as his khakis, but as he spoke about their classmates, it sounded like he hadn't really known them. He talked about Haley, Matt, and Rodrigo by using pull quotes that Zachary recognized from the news.

Zachary grew irritated. And then bored. His gaze roamed until it settled on a very pretty girl—a very pretty girl who was heading straight toward him.

Caleb Greeley hopped off the flatbed truck with as much dignity and respect for the dead as possible. He strolled to the edge of the crowd, and then, as his father raised his hands to address them, sprinted down the side alleys to the grocery store's parking lot.

Caleb played first trumpet. He didn't want to miss his second act.

After the sermon, his father would lead the crowd in a prayer, and then the band would march everybody up from Main Street to the memorial of flowers and cards in front of the high school. Everyone would be holding a candle. A cable-news program had donated them, though Caleb doubted the gesture was made out of goodwill. More likely, someone with a lot of money had recognized that it'd look better on television if the thousand crying marchers were also holding a thousand lit candles.

Caleb understood this, even if he didn't respect it. He was an overachiever, too. He'd been the youth leader for Grace Lutheran Church since he was fifteen and the trumpet section leader for the O.H.S. marching band since sixteen. Excelling in all his classes, he'd successfully campaigned to remove the word *evolution* from their textbooks, and he already had post–high school plans to do missionary work in Papua New Guinea. He would be the first Greeley to leave Nebraska in several generations.

His belongings were on the loading dock behind the store, where he'd left them. He hurried into the bibbed trousers and jacket—freshly dry-cleaned, that pungent uniform smell impossible to erase—and slid into the padded shoes. Slipped on the white gloves. Reaching for his hat, he realized it was missing its gold plume. Caleb grabbed his instrument and ran toward his section. "Alex! Have you seen my plume?"

Alex Shimerda's lip curled. "No one wants to see your plume, Caleb. Gross."

His face grew red with embarrassment. He hated jokes like that. They made him uncomfortable. "Has *anyone* seen my plume?"

The trumpeters who bothered to pay attention shrugged.

"Thanks for the help," Caleb muttered, jogging away.

"Ask the boosters," Alex called out.

But they hadn't seen it, either. A mother with a bobbed mom-hairdo scolded him. "It wasn't in your hat box? You'll have to pay to replace that, you know."

"I had it earlier. I must have left it in the store." Before the memorial, he'd been practicing his speech inside the employee break room.

"Better hurry," she said.

As he fumbled with the key to the back entrance, Alex dashed over to him. "We're lining up. It's just a stupid plume. Don't worry about it."

"Have you *seen* how many television crews are out there?"

Alex looked startled. And then her disgust returned. "Right. You wouldn't want to look bad on TV." She shook her head as she stalked away.

"I didn't mean it like that!" The key rattled inside the lock, but it wouldn't twist. *Dang it.* Caleb didn't care how *he* looked. He didn't want the band to look bad as a whole. It would be awful if they appeared sloppy—like they didn't care about the victims—because they all cared. They cared about their classmates a lot.

The key gave way, and Caleb burst through the door.

• • •

Zachary stared at the candle in his hand. It had a paper ring to catch the wax drippings, and it looked like the type that his church brought out when they all sang "Silent Night" on Christmas Eve. Amber only took him to church on Christmas Eve and Easter. He preferred the Christmas service. The world seemed more at peace.

Katie Kurtzman stood before him, talking about . . . something. She'd given him the candle for the walk. He tried to concentrate, but he was high, and she was pretty. Katie was tall and graceful with long hair that shimmered and changed colors in the light. Right now, caught by the rays of the sun, it looked like copper. Pretty copper.

She was different from the rest of the smart kids. Those other assholes acted like he was invisible, which was why he treated them like shit. Zachary *made* people look at him. But Katie was nice to everyone, and everyone liked her back. It's how she got to be student-council president. He'd tried to be rude to her once, and she'd called him on it. He respected that.

"Oh, no!" Katie dropped the cardboard box that held the candles. A man had spilled a blue slush on her arm.

Zachary sniffed the air for the signature Sonic drink flavor—Blue Coconut or Blue Raspberry. *Indeterminable.*

"Sorry!" The man was in his mid-twenties and wore tortoiseshell eyeglasses. "Oh my God. I'm so sorry."

Katie's cheeks flushed as she wiped the ice from her blouse. "It's okay."

The man tried to help her brush it off, but his touch made her wince, and he immediately backed off, looking even more chagrined.

Raspberry. For some reason, that was the wrong flavor. Zachary inhaled deeply and widened his chest. And he was already a big guy. "What the fuck, Glasses? Why don't you watch where you're going?"

"I—I was looking for my cousin in the band, and—"

"Really," Katie said. "It's okay."

"He should have to pay for your shirt," Zachary said.

The man went for his wallet, but Katie stopped him. "There's no need. These things happen." When Zachary puffed up again, she added, "I'm *fine*, Zach."

His father called him Zach. His real father. Zachary didn't let anyone else call him that, but with her coppery hair and leggy tall-ness . . . yes.

Zachary was tall and broad and fat. His ex-stepfather used to tease him about his weight. The bastard had known what he was doing—he'd known those jokes hurt boys as much as girls. Zachary had tried to deflect them, but the snide comments had landed any-way. He was perfectly aware that his thoughts were both corrupted and misguided, but tall girls made him feel like the right size. They made him feel like less of a freak.

His chest deflated. He let her *Zach* slide. The man with the glasses scurried away into the crowd.

Katie sighed. "I should go."

"Right. Gotta hand out the rest of those candles." But when Zach-ary peered into her cardboard box, it was empty.

She smiled. "You were my last stop. I just need to get home. My mom's leaving for work, and I have to watch my brother and sister."

"Do you need a ride?"

"Nah." She said it lightly, but she hugged the box against her chest. His question had made her uncomfortable. "I live nearby. I walked here."

"How old are your brother and sister?" Zachary had to keep the conversation going, if only to prove he wasn't that guy. He wasn't a threat.

"They're twins. Six. Do you have any siblings?"

"Nah," he said, echoing her earlier *nah*.

Katie smiled again, but this time it was tinged with something else. Sadness, perhaps. At least it wasn't pity. "Stay safe, okay? Find someone here to hang out with."

As she walked away, he changed his mind. It *had* been pity.

"Fuck you," he said. Louder than his normal voice.

Katie stopped. She looked over her shoulder and met his stare. "I don't think you mean that." And then she vanished in the crowd.

Maybe he'd been wrong about her.

Maybe he was just an asshole.

Zachary shoved the candle into his pocket. He leaned against the bridal shop and closed his eyes. His head swam. A drum began to beat, and his eyes popped back open, paranoid that he was about to see David—that David was about to attack Katie—when he caught a flash of camouflage in a window across the street.

"Oh, shit. Shit!" He glanced wildly around, but she was gone. He knew she was gone. He was really, really stoned. After all, he'd stolen Terry's good shit. He closed his eyes again. Opened them. Stared hard at the grocery store's dark windows.

Nothing. There was nothing there.

Caleb retraced his path to the dusty break room, but the plume wasn't there. The stupid feathery pipe cleaner wasn't *anywhere*. Had he missed it outside in his panic? Wherever it had fallen, it no longer mattered. The drum cadence had begun. The sharp *rap* of the snare reverberated off the thin walls of the empty store. The band was on the move.

As Caleb rushed into the back room, his face warmed with

premature humiliation. *Arriving late. Not properly dressed. Footage broadcast around the entire country, capturing my incompetence for all to see.*

Stop it, he forced himself. *This isn't about you.*

He hurried past the cardboard boxes and reached the exit.

And then, suddenly, it was exactly about him.

"Zachary! Zachary! Zachary!"

People were shouting his name, and an instant later—before he could figure out who or where or why—three figures bombarded him, buzzing with suppressed energy. His eyes widened before narrowing again, lazily. Suspiciously. Makani Young, Ollie Larsson, and . . . Darby. He just went by Darby now, he remembered. They were anxious and expecting something from him.

"What?" he said. Not politely.

"You shouldn't be here." Makani's face was partially concealed by the hood of her hoodie. "You shouldn't be standing by yourself."

He couldn't remember the new girl ever speaking to him before. When she'd transferred here last year, she'd seemed sullen and hurt, and her hips moved through the halls with a fuck-you energy that had intrigued him. He thought maybe she'd find her way to his group of friends, but she'd made Darby and Alex a trio instead.

Zachary pulled out his smokes and put a cigarette between his lips.

"Didn't you talk to my brother?" Ollie asked.

"Your brother, the cop?"

"He's the only brother I have."

Zachary lit the cigarette. He took a long drag. "No."

The three friends exchanged worried looks. "Chris said he spoke to you," Ollie said. "He told me he called your house."

"Maybe he called my house, but we sure as hell didn't talk. He probably talked to Terry."

Ollie frowned. "Who's Terry?"

"My mom's boyfriend." The shittiness of this person was implied in his tone. "What'd you do to your hair?"

"Dyed it," Ollie said with a straight face.

Ollie was good at that, at being expressionless. Zachary couldn't hide his emotions if his life depended on it. "I know *that*. Why?"

"Literally nothing could matter less right now," Makani said.

Ollie's mouth twitched unexpectedly with a smile. Something she'd said.

"You two," Zachary said, gesturing between them, "are fucking."

Makani flinched. Ollie's smile went cold.

Point, Zachary. And that's what you get for disturbing my solitude.

"You know," Darby said, "if you weren't maybe about to be killed, we'd walk away right now."

Zachary raised his eyebrows. "Fightin' words."

A few feet away stood a large family with several children. The dad glared at Zachary over his shoulder. They hadn't realized that the crowd had stopped talking to watch the band file down the street. But then an odd thing happened. The dad saw Makani and did a double take. He nudged his wife and whispered into her ear.

Zachary gave him the finger.

The dad turned away quickly. But then he glanced at them again, and Zachary had the craziest feeling that a murmur was traveling through the crowd.

Makani stepped closer. She was so focused on Zachary that it seemed like her eyes were avoiding someone else. That dad? "Listen," she said quietly, "we have reason to believe that you're David's next victim."

"Not likely," Zachary said. "Me and David go way back."

She looked surprised. Until she registered the smidge of doubt that he was unable to mask, and then her friends were pressing up against him, too, hissing about some lunatic theory that David was murdering everyone who'd been a bully.

Zachary stomped out his cigarette to push them away. "Well, if that's true, it won't be much longer until David kills himself. Problem's gonna sort itself out."

Makani grimaced—and he remembered. It explained why all these people were staring at them. It explained why the murmur was becoming a small furor.

"Oh, shit." Zachary finally lowered his voice. "You were the one attacked last night."

Her eyes widened with annoyance.

"So . . . wait. If your theory is correct, that makes *you* an asshole, too." He paused for a fiendish grin. "What'd you do, Young?"

"It doesn't matter." Makani rolled up her left sleeve. A bandage was wrapped around her arm, as high up as he could see. "All you need to know is that I earned this."

Her friends tried to protest, but she interrupted them. "We're worried for your safety. This Terry guy doesn't sound great, but can you trust him? When this is over, can you go home and stay with him?"

"No," Zachary said to the first question. He stared at her forearm, which she'd already covered back up. "But, yeah. I can stay with him."

"Good," she said.

Zachary didn't like the catch of fear in his chest. He side-eyed Ollie. Their classmates were always comparing them, lumping them together. "What about you? You've done some shit."

"Yeah," Ollie said. "But the only person I've ever hurt is myself."

"And your brother."

Ollie flinched. Not so stone-faced, after all. Makani glanced at him as if she were trying to figure something out.

Two points, Zachary.

"In the movies, it's always the kids who have sex and do drugs that are killed, right?" Zachary forced another grin. "I guess that means we're both gonna die."

"You aren't supposed to be here." It was the first coherent thought that Caleb could complete.

The hooded figure was blocking the exit. In one hand, he held a plume. In the other, a knife. "Where should I be?" David asked. His dull monotone matched his colorless appearance. The emptiness of humanity shook Caleb to the bones.

He took a trembling step backward. "In the fields. Or in somebody's barn."

David took a measured step forward. "I'm not."

"H-how did you get in here?"

"Why would I answer that?" David let go of the plume. "What if you escaped?"

The band started to play, but something about the music was strange and off-putting. They stopped bickering. Zachary frowned. "What *is* that? Why do I know that song?"

Darby looked stunned. "It's the graduation song. 'Pomp and Circumstance.'"

"Jesus," Makani said, as Ollie said, "Christ."

"I guess they didn't have a go-to funeral dirge in their repertoire," Darby said.

Zachary listened to the swell of rising pageantry. With each re-frain, the march grew more disturbing. "You know, this is the only time this song will ever be played for them."

"This is so messed up," Darby said.

"This is gonna get old," Ollie said.

"This might be worse than if they hadn't played at all," Makani said.

The crowd progressed forward. It felt like everyone was staring at them, waiting to see if Makani would join in. She seemed resigned by her despair. Like she didn't have a choice anymore. Even though there was still an hour before dusk, the townspeople lit their candles. Zachary wasn't sure why they didn't wait until they reached the me-morial. In the afternoon light, their flames looked weak and silly.

Makani, Ollie, and Darby removed candles from their pockets.

"Coming?" Darby asked.

Zachary pulled out his lighter and candle. "What the hell." He uncrumpled the candle's flimsy paper ring. He lit his wick first before touching it to Makani's.

It blackened. And then it sparked into flame.

Caleb tore out of the back room and into the store, knocking over glass jars, towers of canned goods, and racks of cheap clothing printed with the words LION PRIDE.

David dodged the mounting chaos with alarming ease. Caleb shot past the produce, battering down a carefully constructed pyra-mid of butternut squash, but David still reached him just before the entrance. David stabbed him in the back. Ripped the knife down-ward.

Caleb screamed, but no one could hear him over the sound of the band. He flattened against the cold floor. The drum line was poised in front of the doors—the last in line and the last to march away. Caleb pounded on the glass, stamping it with bloody fist prints.

David dragged him out of view.

"What are you gonna do?" Caleb was crying. *Haley's throat. Matt's brain. Rodrigo's ears.* "What are you gonna do to me?"

David straddled Caleb's body and stared down at him.

He didn't smile. He didn't scowl. He just finished his work while the people of Osborne marched to the school in their parade.

CHAPTER
TWENTY-TWO

MAKANI AND OLLIE walked back to Main Street. If the mood weren't so subdued, it might have even been called a stroll. The sun was setting, the candles had melted, and the memorial was over. Zachary had been escorted to his car, and Darby had been dropped off with Alex. They were meeting back up with Chris. Their brief time alone was dwindling to an end, and they were trying to make it last.

Makani didn't feel like Ollie was judging her, or even looking at her askance, but there was something new—faint but solid—wedged between them. They didn't hold hands. Their hands were tucked back into their pockets, unsure again.

As they turned onto Main Street, only a few short blocks away from Greeley's, where Ollie's and Chris's cars were both parked, she spoke out of last-ditch desperation. "Thanks for listening earlier. In the hospital. And for not judging me." She paused. "You *aren't* judging me, are you?"

Her directness loosened him up. He shook his head with a smile. "No."

The road had been reopened, and a tailgating stream of cars and trucks were heading home in both directions. Compelled to keep filling the space between her and Ollie, Makani kept talking. "It's just I never thought I could be that type of person. But I am."

Unexpectedly, her voice cracked like a mirror. Before the incident, she hadn't believed that she could be capable of cruelty. Now, she knew that she was.

Ollie stopped. His expression was serious. He waited to speak until she stopped, too. "Everybody has at least one moment they deeply regret, but that one moment . . . it doesn't define all of you."

"But it does. It ruined my life. And I deserved for it to be ruined."

"Makani. *Makani.*" Ollie repeated it, because she was walking away from him.

She halted. Kept her back to him.

"I'm not trying to absolve you from your sins," he said. "But the person I know? She's a good friend. And a good granddaughter."

Makani crossed her arms. Her uninjured arm pressed against her bandage, and she winced and uncrossed them. "I don't know. I'd like to think I'm a better person now, but for the rest of my life, I'll always have this question in my mind. I'll always have doubt. Something could trigger me, and I might snap or freak out again."

"Well, *I* know that our regrets change us, and that's how we grow—for either better or worse. And it seems to me, you're growing better."

Makani wasn't sure what to make of this.

"Hey." He gave her a small smile. "I'm still here, right?"

"Well, yeah, but—" She cut herself off.

The smile twisted into a knowing smirk. "Ah. But I'm a fuckup, too."

Makani looked away quickly. He shrugged like it didn't matter. But he wasn't looking at her, either. "I'm sorry," she said.

"It's fine." He started moving again. "It's not like this town can keep a secret."

She frowned. Stayed put. "I can't believe I'm saying this, but I disagree."

Ollie glanced back over his shoulder, a disbelieving eyebrow raised in her direction. But her expression made him falter.

"I mean, I've heard rumors," she said, "but not even real rumors. Like, *rumors* of rumors. And I have no idea what's true and what's not, so I assume most of it is not."

He grimaced. "Some of it's true."

"I wish you'd tell me."

There. Another confession. Now that she'd started, she couldn't stop.

Ollie's gaze fell to the sidewalk, and the hard exterior cracked, revealing some of the damage underneath. "I've *wanted* to say something, even more since you told us about what you've been through, but . . . I didn't want it to seem like I was comparing my situation to yours or like I thought mine was worse. Or even equal. But I don't mean to *not* talk about it. And I know everybody talks about me, anyway."

"I'd like to hear your version of the story," Makani said. "Whatever it is."

Ollie nodded, accepting her confidence. He gestured toward a neon sign behind them, at the opposite end of Main Street from Greeley's. "You know the Red Spot?"

She did. It was technically a greasy burger joint, but its regulars used it as a bar. And if you weren't a regular, you didn't go. The rumor was that you could buy anything there—as long as you were looking for illegal drugs or sex workers.

"After my parents died . . . it messed me up for a few years. When I turned sixteen and got my license, I started hanging out down there.

I should have driven somewhere better—somewhere out of town—but there was this girl who worked there. Dark hair, bleeding-heart tattoo. You know, those little pink flowers? Only these were actually dripping blood. I kinda had a thing for her."

Makani felt a sharp pang of jealousy.

"Everybody there knew who I was. They felt sorry for me, so most of them left me alone. I was like their depressed kid brother. It took weeks of relentless flirting, but I finally got her attention."

"How old was she?"

"Twenty-three."

Not as old as the rumors. But way too old for someone who was barely sixteen.

"I guess she pitied me, too." It seemed to hurt him to admit it. "We hung out at her trailer sometimes and got high."

"What happened?" Makani asked.

They started walking again. Dried leaves crunched under their shoes.

"Chris found out that we were sleeping together. He was *furious*. He wanted to arrest her, but . . . words were exchanged first." In his pause, Makani understood that Ollie's fight with his brother was still too raw to be spoken aloud. "It was just this whole big, stupid mess. He was still trying to figure out how to be a parent, and I was—I'm not sure what I was trying to figure out."

"Did he arrest her?"

"No," Ollie said.

"But I'm guessing you didn't see her anymore."

"He forbade me from seeing her, which wouldn't have worked, except it wasn't necessary. I think Erika was embarrassed." Ollie turned his face away from hers. "She didn't want anything to do with me after that."

Erika. The name pierced Makani's heart. "Does she still live here?"

"Yep. Comes into Greeley's a couple times a month. She's married now. Cuts hair. We don't speak," he added. There was something in his tone.

"You liked her a lot, didn't you?"

"I thought I loved her. I was an idiot, but that's what I thought."

The sadness expanded inside her, enough for the both of them.

"A few days later, I reached the genius and original conclusion that life was shit. I drank two forties and waded into the river. I was going to kill myself."

Makani sucked in her breath. She'd been severely depressed, but she'd never been suicidal. It was upsetting to learn that Ollie had stood so close to the edge.

"I stumbled and fell," he said, "and as I was flailing in the water, realizing that I *didn't* want to die, the manager of Sonic drove past. By some miracle, the guy saw me. He pulled over and dragged me out. The river was only a few feet deep—I was just scared and wasted." Ollie gave a regretful laugh. "It's probably the real reason I hate Sonic. Reminds me of my dumb-ass self."

An old pain distorted within Makani as she pictured Jasmine vanishing, also scared and wasted, into a different body of water. The situations were so different, yet eerily similar. She didn't have the strength to let her thoughts linger there. "Well, it makes *me* like Sonic more. I'm glad he saw you. I'm glad you're still here."

Ollie bit his lip ring. "I'm glad you're still here, too."

Recalling a rumor associated with the river, Makani blurted, "Were you naked?"

He glanced at her with surprise. "What? Do people say that?"

She nodded guiltily.

"No," he said. "In *that* particular brush with death, I had my clothes on."

It was so tragic and absurd that it made them both laugh. "I can't believe that happened," she said.

Ollie shook his head in amazement. "I know."

"You were *naked*."

"I *know*."

Her smile grew. And then faded. "What happened after the guy rescued you?"

"I wasn't arrested—thank you, nepotism—but I spent some time in a psychiatric unit. After that, Chris sent me to a therapist in Norfolk. But, by then, I wanted help. I stopped drinking and doing shit." He gave a loose shrug. "And that's it."

"Is that what Zachary meant when he said you'd hurt your brother?"

The lightness disappeared from his voice. "Yes."

Makani was relieved that nothing worse had happened. And Ollie hadn't even done anything truly awful; most of the disappointment was inside his own head. She could tell that, for Ollie, having worried his brother *was* the worst thing he could have done. Instead of pressing him, she backtracked. "When you said you got high . . ."

"Weed."

"You never did any harder drugs? Pills or opioids or anything?"

He shook his head.

"And you never sold them?"

Ollie sighed. "Cool. You heard that one, too." He shook his head again. "The only thing I've ever sold is produce."

"Did you sleep with anyone else?" *Please say no.*

"Only in my dreams," he said. "Only you."

It was cheesy—definitely a line—but Makani didn't mind right now. She smiled at him as they stood in front of Greeley's. "Hey, Ollie?" she asked softly.

"Yeah?"

"You know how you said that I'm a good granddaughter and friend?"

He smiled back. "Yeah."

"Do you think I could be a good girlfriend?"

Ollie's hands reached for hers through the dusk. Their fingertips touched, and the streetlights flickered on behind them. "I think you're *already* a good girlfriend."

They kissed while they waited for Chris. It felt absurd, kissing in public. Kissing after a memorial. Kissing when they'd been so close to being actual subjects of the memorial.

It also felt euphoric, rapturous, and profound.

Ollie's nose was cold, but his arms were warm as they slipped around her back. It was the thrill of summer, revived—making out beside the grocery store when they shouldn't be doing it. Except infinitely better, because the questions between them had been answered.

Their lips parted to catch their breath. Makani laughed, glancing aside. And that's when she noticed the blood.

Red handprints. Beaten fists. Dragged fingers. The fine lines of the skin that had touched the glass were shockingly clear and shockingly human.

Makani stiffened with fright.

Ollie followed her gaze, and they startled apart. They stared at the bottom left side of the store's automatic entry doors. The blood was on the inside.

Their limbs reached for each other again, clinging, as they

frantically checked their surroundings. Except for the cars, the parking lot was empty. The traffic had unclogged, and only a few people remained on foot. None of them were close by. None of them were Chris or any other officer. And none of them appeared to be David.

Makani's heart raced. Ollie cupped his hands to peer inside the dark store, while she kept her eyes on the street. "Is he in there?" she asked.

"I think somebody was dragged toward the checkout lanes. But I can't see them."

"Oh God." She ripped his phone from his pocket, bouncing anxiously on the balls of her feet. "I'm calling your brother."

"The whole place is ransacked."

"Shit! What's your password?"

"9999."

"What? Why would you do that? Somebody could guess that!"

"You didn't," he said. "Shit! Something just moved."

Makani lurched against the door. He pointed toward a shadowy area, a pile of . . . she couldn't tell what. "I think there's someone there," he said. "Someone on top of that."

It was impossible to tell. But there was definitely something that *might* be a person.

Chris's number rang emptily in her ear. The shadows shifted again, and Makani gasped. Before she realized what he was doing, Ollie unlocked the door. As a longtime and trusted employee, he had a key. "Someone's still alive!" he said.

The overhead sensor picked them up. The doors whooshed open. They rushed inside and then staggered backward, stunned by the true destruction. Overturned vegetables, boxes, cartons, bags, and cans were everywhere—an abundance of food, splattered like congealing fireworks across the linoleum.

Ollie yanked her aside so they wouldn't track through the blood, the streaks of a body hauled across the floor. They ran toward the shadows and then crashed into a halt. Makani clamped her hands over her mouth to mute her scream.

In front of the checkout registers was a permanent display of merchandise whose profits helped support the football team, something Makani had once found incredibly strange but she'd slowly grown used to. Now that she knew Osborne, it made sense. But tonight, it had been razed to the ground. And in the center of the debris of jumbled sweatshirts and flags and tchotchkes was Caleb Greeley.

The boy lay atop the heap like another item of garish memorabilia. His feet and knees were splayed outward. His face was on its side, and a swollen tongue protruded out from between his front teeth. The chest and stomach had been mutilated. Long incisions slashed through his blood-drenched band uniform, but, despite the clothing, the unnatural splaying of his limbs made him look more like one of those realistic sex dolls than a human being. It was his body's complete and utter lack of dignity.

But that still wasn't the worst part.

The worst part was the hands.

Caleb's fingers had been laced together, and then his hands had been severed. They rested over his heart in prayer position. Red gore and white bone.

But if Caleb was dead . . . someone else was the moving shadow.

Makani and Ollie backed into the cereal aisle, each placing a protective arm across the other person's chest. They pressed against the yellow Corn Pops and green Apple Jacks. Their hearts slammed against their rib cages.

The air was sharp. Acidic. It stung their nostrils and watered their eyes. Caleb must have been chased down the condiment aisle, one over. The vinegary fumes from the smashed jars of pickles and olives were ghastly. Makani covered her nose. She was still holding Ollie's phone, and Chris was shouting at them through the speaker.

The metallic thud of a push bar echoed throughout the building.

Their hearts stopped.

And then a heavy door settled closed.

Makani whispered into the phone, *"David Ware just went out the back exit."*

CHAPTER
TWENTY-THREE

THE CAN OF tuna fish had been bothering her all week.

Katie Kurtzman had discovered it last Friday as she was moving a load of whites from the washing machine into the dryer. The flat can was eye level and sitting on the sill of the basement's only window. The long, narrow window was closed, but its latch didn't work. It was just big enough for a slender body to squeeze through.

The tuna had been cheap. A discount brand. The lid's edges were sharp and crude, as if the tin had been cut with a hand-cranked opener, not the electric one that they had in the kitchen. The can was empty, but it was still damp inside. That's how she'd noticed it.

That faint underpinning of *fish* underneath the cloud of bleach and detergent.

She'd asked the twins, but they claimed not to know anything about it. She didn't think they were lying. They were afraid of the basement, so they never played there. Her mother didn't know about it, either. She supposed that it had fallen down from one of the ceiling beams—a trash relic left behind from the previous homeowners. But that didn't make sense to Katie. The can was far from its stamped expiration date, and they'd been in this house for five years now. Plus, there was the dampness.

And the smell.

Katie knew she was being paranoid. She hadn't known any of the victims, not really. She'd never had any personal connections to them, and she'd only ever been friendly to David. Still, as she applied stain stick to her sleeve where the blue drink had spilled, she eyed the window ledge. She couldn't shake the feeling that someone had been here, sitting on top of the dryer, listening to her family upstairs. Eating tuna fish.

She undid the first few buttons of her blouse but then, thoroughly spooked, decided against it. She could wash the shirt tomorrow. Hurrying toward the planks that served as stairs, Katie glanced over her shoulder for one last look. She stopped.

A quart of latex paint sat on the floor beside her mother's old treadmill. She picked it up and placed it on the ledge against the window. And then she felt foolish. How could *that* protect her from an intruder? But she was scared enough to leave it. Perhaps it would be the magic charm that warded off the evil spirit.

Upstairs, Leigh and Clark were spread out on the living room carpet, reading comics. Leigh noticed her first. "What's for dinner?"

"What's for dinner?" Clark parroted.

Katie hurried past them toward their shared bathroom on the second floor. Her arm felt gross and sticky, and her cramps were getting bad again. "Mac and cheese."

"With hot dogs?" the twins asked.

"Only in Leigh's half," she said, and the twins cheered. Clark hated hot dogs. He also hated hamburgers and pizza. For a child, his eating habits were baffling.

As Katie bolted up the stairs, her mom thumped down them. She worked the twelve-hour night shift at the hospital. Three days on, four days off. She was currently on, without the option to take off any shifts to watch over her children. The staff was doing mandatory training in preparation—anticipation—of further attacks. "Do you have everything you need? What happened to your shirt?"

"I'm fine, we're fine," Katie said.

"Keep your phone in your hand. Don't open the door for *any-body*."

"I know, Mom."

"I love you!" she called out.

"Love you, too." Katie didn't look back as she said it. Her mom kissed the twins goodbye as Katie grabbed a clean T-shirt and pajama pants and locked herself in the bathroom. She removed her blouse to scrub her arm with a warm washcloth and *Sesame Street*–branded soap, and then she swallowed an Advil and peed.

Leaning over to grab a new tampon from under the sink, Katie startled. All the toiletries were in the wrong place. The tampons and extra rolls of toilet paper were out of reach and had been rearranged entirely with her makeup caddy, flat iron, and hair products in the back of the cabinet, and the twins' old bath toys in the front.

Katie's first thought was scary and irrational: *David.*

She'd heard a rumor at the memorial that he liked to mess with his victims before he killed them. That he moved their stuff around to make them think they were losing their minds. The man she'd over-heard swore that he'd gotten the information from a county deputy, though there hadn't been any mention of it in the news.

Her second thought was much more realistic: *Mom's been guilt-cleaning again.*

Katie usually cleaned, because her mother worked nights and took care of the twins during the day. Her off-days were for catch-ing up on sleep. But as Katie pushed the toys onto the bath mat and stretched for the tampon box, she noticed dust inside the cabinet. *Mom cleaned, but she couldn't even do it right.* Katie groaned.

Her mom claimed that Katie had obsessive-compulsive disorder. As a nurse who'd spent her early years working in psychiatric units, she was always diagnosing everyone.

Outwardly, Katie denied it. Inwardly, she knew it was true.

Katie worked long hours, too. School and the twins' bedtime routine, in addition to college applications, student-loan applications, extracurriculars, and volunteering at the hospital—all the while worrying that she *still* wasn't doing enough to get out of Osborne. Ritualistic cleaning and straightening and checking and organizing made her feel calmer in a world that was out of her control. Six years ago, everything had blown up when her dad stormed out only a few weeks after the twins were born.

Antisocial personality disorder, her mom had diagnosed.

Katie refused to go back to the way things had been.

As she moved everything back to its correct location, her eyes snagged on a fresh droplet of blood. It was on the alligator-shaped bath mat, near the toilet—and it was her own. Katie swore under her breath. She blotted it with a tissue and scoured it with cold water. There was a *thunk* downstairs. "Hey," she yelled. "What was that?"

"We don't know!" the twins said.

"What'd you guys do?"

"Nothing!"

Katie sighed. *Sure.* She changed into her pajamas and hustled toward them. Ninety minutes later, she tucked their warm, sleepy bodies into bed. She turned on their matching night-lights, closed their door, and sighed again. Time was hers, at last.

She headed back downstairs to work on an essay for the University of Southern California. All the universities she was applying for required a flight—or, at least, a lengthy car trip—to get there. She loved her family, but she'd love them more with distance.

Night had spread its bat-like wings. Katie turned on the porch lights and the overhead light in the kitchen, where her work was laid out across the table. As she reflected on a time or incident when she'd experienced failure (tonight's essay topic), it took all her willpower not to check the news. She wished that she could have walked to the school with everybody else. Even Zachary—*Zachary*, who smelled like stale cigarettes and unwashed clothing, who'd never given a crap about his grades and pretended not to give a crap about anyone—was in attendance.

Katie suspected that he actually cared about other people a lot, but he hadn't had enough people in his life who cared about him. Despite Zachary's abrasiveness, she had a soft spot for him. He was smart, and, if he applied himself, he could go on to do great things. It was frustrating to know that he probably wouldn't. Most likely, he'd drop out and get a job on the floor at Nance, the town's only manufacturer. It built machinery for food-processing plants. Or maybe he'd become a day laborer, detasseling corn and castrating piglets. Either way, it was unlikely that he would ever leave Osborne.

There was a creak on the basement stairs.

Katie's heart juddered as she whirled around in her seat. Beside her, the refrigerator hummed and the dishwasher sloshed. Above her, the twins' white-noise machine whirred. But below her, the basement remained silent. She picked up her phone—ears pricked—but set it down after another minute.

It's just the house.

She tried to refocus on the essay. She read her last sentence five times, but she couldn't shake . . . a feeling. Katie stared at the basement door.

Another creak.

She jumped up, the wooden chair legs scraping against the floor. Her pulse beat violently as she grabbed her phone and dialed 911.

Connecting, her phone said. *Connecting. Connecting.*

Heavy footsteps pounded up the stairs. Katie's senses exploded with terror as she threw herself against the door, which could only be locked from the other side. At the same instant, another body landed against it full force—just enough to open it.

They struggled. Open, shut, open. An arm and shoulder wedged through, and a knife slashed toward her body.

Katie pushed the door against the arm with all her strength. The arm flailed. There was another weighty thrust, and her side gave way. She fell, and her phone slipped from her grasp. It skidded across the floor as David Thurston Ware burst into the kitchen.

He was wearing jeans and a LION PRIDE sweatshirt. They were splattered with turquoise paint—the same color that her mother had meant to repaint the kitchen chairs last spring. The same color that Katie had propped against the basement window that evening. She took all this in, in an instant, as she scrambled to her feet.

He lunged for her. She ran toward the butcher block, reaching for the biggest knife as he stabbed her in the shoulder. When he yanked it out, she kicked him. David shoved her against the cabinets. His hands smeared her skin with red and turquoise. She was five foot ten, and so was he. Their weight was similar, and the same amount of adrenaline coursed through their bodies. But he was the one with the weapon.

Katie kneed him in the balls as David stabbed her in the upper right abdomen. They both buckled over. The knife pushed deeper into her liver.

She collapsed, frightened and crying. But oddly hushed.

David peered over her. His question was curious, though his voice was dead. "Why aren't you screaming?"

Because I don't want to wake up my brother and sister.

When she didn't answer out loud, he finished her off. He didn't have time to wait.

He checked her phone, which was still trying to connect to the police. David ended the call. The cops already knew he was in the area, and he was angry. He didn't like having to rush. He sawed through the rib cage—stomping on the knife to help crack the bones faster—and ripped out the heart. He slammed it on top of the glossy college brochures that had been stacked on the table for months.

Because Katie's *heart* had been *set* on college.

He was funny. Nobody seemed to get that.

Lights flashed outside the kitchen window. Red and blue, one street over. He tugged off the sweatshirt. It wasn't camouflage, but it had acted as camouflage. Nearly everyone on the street today had been wearing school colors. He threw it as he ran, and it landed on Katie—the Katie-husk—crumpled on the floor, no longer of use.

CHAPTER
TWENTY-FOUR

MAKANI AND OLLIE had waited, terrified, in the cereal aisle until Officer Bev had escorted them out. Chris had tried to chase after David, but he'd already disappeared.

Makani and Ollie were interviewed and gave statements. Again. Now it was late, and they were back at the Larsson house, decompressing at the kitchen table and attempting to excise the horrendous image of Caleb's grotesque prayer from their minds. Chris was on the phone in the next room.

Ollie stared vacantly at the oven. "Maybe we should have chased him," he said. "Maybe we could have caught him."

Makani's knees were up in the chair. Her non-bandaged arm was wrapped around them, and her head was tucked down. She felt too broken to lift it.

"He killed *Caleb*," he said. "Not Zachary."

His words hung limply in the air between them. Out in the fields, the nighttime insects whirred and buzzed. The wind chimes on the front porch sang three notes.

"I don't think this is about bullying," he said.

She shook her head, but it was in agreement.

"So, what the hell *is* it about?"

It scared her to admit that she had no idea. She hadn't realized that she'd taken a measure of comfort in at least knowing *why* she'd been attacked. There'd been a *reason*. Not knowing David's motivation felt like everybody she knew was in danger again.

A shadow fell over them as Chris stepped back into the light of the room. His face was white with disbelief. "There's been another one."

The midnight sky wept in an unexpected drizzle. Chris moved his laptop, binders, metal ticketing notebooks, and food containers into the trunk of his car. Makani darted into the emptied passenger's seat, and Ollie slid into the back. In the rearview mirror, his face was printed with diamond-shaped shadows from the metal dividing grate.

They'd been at the house for less than thirty minutes. Chris had to return to work, so he was driving them to the hospital to stay with Grandma Young. He refused to leave them alone.

Makani felt so exhausted that she wanted to cry, but she didn't want to be left alone, either. As the endless rows of cornstalks rolled past her window—long corridors into murky blackness—she shivered with the unshakable feeling that David could be anywhere. Her lower legs pressed against the bulletproof vest resting on the floorboards.

Chris noticed her shivering and turned up the heat. The windshield wipers swiped at a slow and steady pace.

"She texted me this morning," Makani said, remembering.

He glanced at her sharply. "Katie contacted you? About what?"

"She said she was sorry to hear what had happened to me, and she was there if I wanted to talk." Another deadening inside Makani. "I didn't text her back."

"Did you talk to her often? Was she a close friend?"

"We weren't friends at all. We were friend*ly*. Sometimes we talked in class, but we never texted or hung out or anything."

Chris frowned. "So, why start texting you this morning?"

"That's just Katie being Katie." From the backseat, Ollie dismissed the notion of there being anything odd or sinister behind it. "She was nice to everyone."

"Who found her?" Makani asked. They already knew *how* she'd been found.

"Her mom." It seemed hard for Chris to say it. "Apparently, she works the late shift at the hospital, and Katie wasn't answering her phone, so she came home on her break to check in. Katie's younger brother and sister were still asleep upstairs."

Makani used to shave her arms for diving. Now, her arm hair stood on end as she remembered a laminated ID badge. *Kurtzman.* The kindhearted nurse who'd given her blueberry yogurt and watched over her was Katie's mother.

"She couldn't have known." Chris sounded shaken. Maybe he was picturing himself in her place. "I doubt that she actually expected to find something wrong."

The rain ticked staccato against the roof of the car. Perhaps sensing that his brother needed to think about something else, Ollie asked him to repeat his knowledge of David's whereabouts.

After attacking them yesterday at Makani's house, David had traveled upriver instead of down, which the police hadn't predicted. Under the cover of night, he'd crept back into town and hidden inside the back room at Greeley's, correctly guessing that everyone would be searching for him out in the countryside.

He'd been right under their noses the whole time.

At first, the police were flummoxed as to how he'd broken in, because none of the doors or windows had been damaged. But then Caleb's uncle, the owner, recalled having to cut a new key for Caleb a few months back. His uncle had found this odd, because Caleb wasn't usually forgetful or careless. The police speculated that David had stolen the key and entered the store as if he belonged there. It probably wasn't the first time that he'd broken in. And the key probably wasn't the only thing he'd stolen.

Several members of the marching band, including Alex, reported that Caleb had practiced his speech inside the store, and then when he returned from delivering it to the crowd, he'd claimed that his hat plume was missing. It seemed possible that David had stolen it while Caleb was practicing and then used it to lure him back.

"It's still not clear why he didn't kill Caleb *before* the memorial," Chris said, keeping his eyes on the two-lane road. "Maybe because people would have looked for Caleb sooner? And we also don't know—" But he cut himself off, with a glance in the rearview mirror at his brother.

"Know what?" Ollie asked.

Chris looked like he didn't want to answer. "We also don't know if David had more than one target inside the store."

Ollie's tense expression showed Makani that the thought had already crossed his mind.

"We *do* know that he stole a sweatshirt," Chris said, trying to hurry past it, "which he left behind at Katie's before jacking her 2011 Ford Fiesta. The sweatshirt was covered in blood and paint from her basement. We don't know what he's wearing now. We still haven't found his hoodie, and no one noticed him leave her neighborhood. Everyone was looking for someone on foot."

"So, he's leaving town." Makani wasn't sure if she believed it. And even if it were true, it wasn't what she wanted. She wanted to know *exactly* where David was. Until he was captured, she would never feel at ease again.

A pair of headlights loomed through the rain in the distance.

"What color was the car?" Ollie asked.

"Blue," Chris said quietly.

The headlights grew closer. Makani's heartbeat spiked, and Chris's grip tightened on the steering wheel. It was impossible to tell anything about the car, except that it was small. Everyone held their breath until the car passed.

Red. A Ford Focus.

They exhaled. A minute later, there was a new pair of headlights, and their lungs tightened again. And then released. Tightened. Released.

It was like that for the remainder of the drive.

Grandma Young was asleep, heavily sedated. Makani and Ollie tried to sleep, too, taking turns on the comfortable recliner, but their brains were wired. As the night droned on, they watched the cars in the parking lot below and stared at the flickering television screen. It wasn't a heavy storm, but it was enough to mess with the signal.

The TV was set on the lowest volume above mute. For hours, CNN cycled between an airstrike in Syria, a group of missing hikers in North Carolina, and the latest murders in Osborne.

Caleb Randolph Greeley Jr.

Katie Teresa Kurtzman.

Their full names were spoken aloud by strangers. The same atrocious clips of the same panicked citizens were replayed. The victims were turning into numbers, statistics that were being used to compare David with other notable serial killers. He'd obliterated two people within a three-hour gap *and* with a crowd nearby. It wasn't just Makani; the entire Midwest had the crawling sensation that he was standing right behind them.

But here, inside the hospital, it was even worse. Katie and her mom were the subject of every low-spoken conversation. It was impossible not to overhear the muffled crying coming from the nurses' station. The choked sobs. The noses blowing into tissues.

It was nearly daybreak before the talking heads had something to report. "Breaking news in the hunt for the Osborne Slayer," a woman's voice said.

Makani's and Ollie's bleary eyes sprang open as the Latina news anchor continued, "You're looking at footage from a truck stop near Boys Town, Nebraska, just outside of Omaha, at eleven o'clock last night. An unidentified driver called 911 after spotting a blue Ford Fiesta ditched on an embankment near the truck stop. When the police pulled the surveillance video, this is what they discovered."

Black-and-white footage showed a figure in a long coat walk up to a semi and speak to the driver through the window. Even though the outdated cameras made his movements jerky and pixelated, Makani could tell that the grainy figure was David. A nauseated chill washed over her. David climbed inside the truck, and it drove away.

"As you can see," the news anchor said, "the truck makes a right turn before traveling out of frame. It looks like the driver is headed *back* toward Osborne."

Makani glanced at Ollie. His face was a perfect reflection of her fear.

"At this time, the police have not revealed the driver's name, only that his tags were from Indiana. It is not yet known if he was aware of the hitchhiker's identity."

That was it. The news rehashed the story from the top. David kept climbing into the truck, and it kept making a right turn.

The killer kept going home.

CHAPTER
TWENTY-FIVE

IT WAS THE eve of All Hallows' Eve. The rain had stopped, but the asphalt was still slick with water and oil. A lurid sunrise—worthy of Hawaii—illuminated the sky. It was such an obscene contrast to the overhanging dread that it felt like they were being mocked.

Makani and Ollie had slipped away from Grandma Young before she'd even known that they were there. Chris drove them back to the Larsson house. This time, Makani sat beside Ollie in the backseat. Their fingers were icicles as they grasped each other with all four hands. Despite the ideal opportunity to escape, David had chosen to come home. He'd tried to kill her and failed. What if he was returning to finish the job?

"The truck driver was stopped just past Norfolk at twelve forty-five a.m.," Chris said, filling in some of the blanks. "Must've been the only person in America who hadn't heard about the manhunt. He claimed that he only listens to Christian talk radio, and they've been yammering about the new Supreme Court justice all week. He told the deputy that David was quiet and polite. He also said it looked like he was wearing a woman's coat."

Despite seeing it in the surveillance footage, this last detail startled Makani.

"My guess," Chris said, "is that he's still wearing the same bloodstained jeans and hoodie, and he needed something to cover them up. The coat probably belongs to Katie's mom. The driver said he dropped him off in front of a farm near Troy."

Troy was only one town over. Alex lived on a ranch just outside it.

"David told him it was his parents' farm. We've already interviewed the farmers, but they were asleep. They didn't see or hear anything unusual. The other neighbors are being interviewed now, and there's a team searching the surrounding fields."

Makani and Ollie tightened their icy grips.

There was nothing else they could do.

The cold autumn air crackled throughout the countryside, electric with anticipation.

Makani and Ollie were bundled inside sleeping bags on Chris's hardwood floor. Heat whirred out from the registers. With the daylight, locked door, and armed police officer, Makani's body finally succumbed to rest. Her dreams began heavy and empty, but, over the course of the afternoon, they struggled into existence. *A sharp knife in one hand, a severed ponytail in the other. A hooded figure lurching out from behind a grandfather clock.* She would fight these nightmares for the rest of her life.

While the trio slept, strangers streamed in from out of town. Even more media, but also armchair detectives—online sleuths, some well-meaning and some not, jumping into ambitious action—as well as morbid gawkers, deceitful psychics, and drunk college kids, who thought it'd be a hoot to visit the famous corn maze. The displaced *Sweeney Todd* cast and crew had turned it into a *haunted* corn maze, and the Martin family would donate the weekend's profits to the victims' families.

"Knowing he's still out there just makes the maze a lot scarier," a student wearing a scarlet ball cap with a cream *N* said, speaking to a field reporter. His fraternity brothers whooped behind him on camera. "Plus, you know. Charity."

Even the National Guard rolled in. They were to stand watch over the football game so that the townspeople would feel brave enough to attend. There were no parking spaces left at the school. The tailgate party had started early. The playoffs didn't stop for tornado sirens, and they weren't about to stop for a serial killer.

And through it all, Makani, Ollie, and Chris slept.

Chris's phone rang when the sun was low on the horizon. Makani scrambled up to a sitting position against his bed, her bulging eyes on the door. It was still closed.

"Yeah," Chris said into the phone.

Ollie scootched out from his sleeping bag to hunker down with Makani. He was careful not to sit on the side of her injured arm.

"Shit." Chris sighed. "Okay, yeah. See you soon."

Makani burrowed into the shelter of Ollie's body as the phone thumped onto the bed above them. Chris released another sigh. "What is it?" Ollie asked.

"Nothing. Nothing new," Chris clarified. "Just . . . shouldn't have slept so late."

"You need to go in?"

"Yeah." His feet swung over the edge of the bed beside Ollie. "So, I've gotta head toward Troy, which is in the opposite direction of where you need to go. We'll take separate cars, but we'll leave at the same time. You guys are to drive *straight* to the hospital, okay? And you're to stay there until I tell you to leave."

Makani and Ollie nodded.

"I'm gonna check the house, just to be safe." Chris stood, picking up his gun from the nightstand. "I'll be right back. Wait here." In the doorway, he glanced back at them. "Do you have your phones?"

Their phones were already in their hands. They held them up.

Chris vanished down the hall. Ollie's under-eye circles were so dark that it looked like he'd been punched. Makani wished that she could touch his skin and heal it.

"You okay?" he asked.

"No. Are you?"

"No." But he smiled, which made her exhale a faint laugh.

Chris's bedroom was as disheveled as Ollie's. Bags from Sonic and the gas station were scattered everywhere, and heaps of clothing were piled in front of the closet. The clothes looked clean, though permanently unfolded. The only vestiges of his youth appeared to be the three dusty guitars hanging on the wall—one acoustic, two electric. Beneath them was an amp covered in coffee cups and mail.

The upstairs floorboards creaked as Chris moved from room to room. Makani's gaze snapped back to the door. "This is so messed up."

"The *most* messed up," Ollie said.

She held her breath as the footsteps continued toward the bathroom.

"I mean," he said, "I slept beside you all day and didn't think about sex once."

Her head remained locked, but her eyes swiveled toward him.

He grinned. "That was a lie."

The wooden stairs groaned as Chris crept down them. Makani shook her head, but she was smiling slightly. Their ears strained.

They waited.

Suddenly, a yell rang out, followed by a loud crash. Makani gasped and shrank as Ollie clung to her in horror. There was the indistinct sound of things settling to the floor.

"*Squidward!*" Chris said. "Fuck! You scared me."

Ollie pried his body off hers, embarrassed, though she sensed he'd been more scared for his brother than himself. She wondered if he was afraid every time Chris left for work. That must be tough.

A few seconds later, Chris returned. "Sorry about that." He seemed embarrassed, too. "We're good. We leave in fifteen minutes, okay?"

Fifteen. The number surprised Makani. Clearly, they weren't used to having a girl around. She hurried to wash her face and change clothes, and realized—as the brothers were both ready in under ten—that the number had actually been inflated for her sake.

Ollie handed her a steaming Pop-Tart as she slid into his car. She practically swallowed it whole. When they hit the highway, they parted from Chris.

"What the—?" Ollie said under his breath.

Makani looked up from checking her texts. The opposite lane of traffic was at a standstill. Dirty cars and trucks and RVs were backed up as far as she could see as a lone, redheaded employee with a flag waved them into the parking lot for the corn maze.

"Is it always this busy on a Friday night?" she asked.

"Never," Ollie said.

Vehicle after vehicle was packed with college-aged kids—voices hollering, music thumping, windows rolled down despite the frigid temperature. Makani stared at them with open displeasure, though not with disbelief. She'd lived through too much to feel disbelief. "People are sick. They think this is all a game."

On the other side of the maze, one of Ollie's neighbors was trying to turn out of their driveway. "That's gonna take a while," he said.

Makani texted her friends with an update and told them where she was going. It was important to know where everyone was right now. Darby was at home, and Alex was at school with the band. But as soon as Makani's message disappeared, her phone vibrated with a response from Alex: *I'm freaking out.*

Makani frowned as she texted: *???*

Too many people here. Too crowded. Can't breathe.

can your parents come back and pick you up?

They think it's safer in a crowd! I reminded them about Caleb and the memorial, but they weren't having it. I'm freaking out. I'm totally freaking out!!

Ollie watched her from the corner of his eye. "What's going on?"

"Alex. I think she's having panic attack."

He was a QUARTER MILE from my house last night. Now it feels like he's here. I can't do this. I SERIOUSLY CANNOT DO THIS!!!

"Does she need us to come get her?" Ollie asked as another text appeared from Alex: *Could you come get me?*

on our way, Makani said. Emoji heart.

Hurry, Alex said. Emoji scream.

The stadium was packed, and the wind carried the cheers and marching band and commotion all the way to downtown Osborne. As their car raced past Walnut Street, Makani looked toward her grandmother's house. It was just out of sight.

The bright lights of the football field pierced through the dusk. Alex was waiting for them at the front gate. The whole area was packed, but she stood alone.

Ollie unlocked the doors, rolled down his window, and waved to her. The aroma of cheap chocolate invaded the car. Tomorrow's trick-or-treating had been canceled, and word had spread to bring candy to the game. Costumed children dashed through the madness, collecting treats in their pillowcases and plastic orange pumpkins. Teenagers and adults had been banned from wearing costumes—in fear that David might hide among them—so they were decked out in scarlet and gold instead.

The home crowd was so huge that it had spilled onto the visitors' side. The cheerleaders were leading them in the "Lion Roar," a school-spirit chant, and a powerful stampede of feet pounded and rumbled against the metal bleachers.

Two members of the National Guard were visible just behind the main chain-link fence. They were dressed in fatigues and carrying assault rifles. They were supposed to make everyone feel protected, but Makani felt a nervous, unpleasant shudder.

Alex flew into the backseat with her trumpet. Her plume caught on the doorframe and knocked the hat sideways. "*Ow.*" She undid the chin strap and ripped off the hat. She glared at the plume. Or maybe she was scared of it.

"Are you okay?" Makani asked. It was a dumb question.

Alex slammed the door closed. "Go!"

"Won't you get in trouble for leaving?" Ollie asked.

"Fuck that," Alex said. "Fuck all this. I can't play a peppy fight song and pretend that you guys weren't almost murdered. I can't pretend that my crush and my section leader and three of my other classmates weren't *actually* murdered. And I can't pretend that the loser who did it isn't still out there!"

That was enough for Ollie. He pulled away from the curb. Makani unbuckled her seat belt and crawled over the console into the backseat, where Alex was fumbling to unzip her red uniform. Makani helped her with the hidden buttons, which Alex had forgotten about, and then out of the jacket. Alex shook it away on the verge of tears.

As Makani dug through her pockets for tissues, her phone rang. Darby had skipped straight past texting. "Is everything okay?" Makani asked.

"Put him on speakerphone," Alex said.

"I'm fine," Darby said. Makani pressed the button, and his voice filled the car. "I'm only calling because I'm driving."

"That's still unsafe," Ollie said. And then he winced for being the square.

Makani wondered if his reaction was triggered by too many car-crash stories from Chris. Or maybe any type of accident reminded him of his parents. She still wasn't wearing a seat belt, so she strapped in and motioned for Alex to do the same.

"I know, but I just got your texts," Darby said. "My signal was on the fritz from all these damn tourists. Is Alex with you?"

"I'm here!" Alex said. "Where are you?"

"I was coming to get you. I'm passing the Dollar General right now."

"We're almost to the hospital," Makani said. "Meet us in the parking lot?"

Darby's hatchback pulled up beside them less than five minutes later. Darby's and Alex's doors flew open, and they ran into each other's arms. They hugged for days.

Makani crawled back into the passenger's seat and rubbed her hands in front of the vents. Ollie turned up the temperature.

Darby and Alex popped into the vacated backseat. Darby was

dressed in an old-man tweed sport coat with actual elbow patches, and he was wearing a button-up and sweater underneath it for warmth. He snapped the suspenders of Alex's uniform. "Did you guys see this? She's trying to steal my look."

"Did you lock your car?" Ollie asked.

The question instantly brought the mood back down.

Darby assured him. "It's locked."

They fell into silence as they surveilled their surroundings. The parking lot was nearly empty. After several tense seconds Makani said, "We're running out of time."

No one challenged her. The apprehension in the car was suffocating.

"I can't just *sit* here," she said. *He might be looking for me.*

Alex agreed. "He's killing faster and faster, and since everyone's looking for him—everyone not at the football game," she added darkly, "he probably feels like he has to finish his stupid plan, whatever it is, *now*. Before he gets caught."

"I wish we knew who else he's been gaslighting," Makani said.

Ollie stared, unblinking, through the windshield. "Haley, Matt, Rodrigo, you, Caleb, Katie. What's the real connection?"

"Cliques?" Darby was hesitant. "None of you hung out together, but you all had a unique social group. Maybe David felt alone. Like he didn't belong to any group."

"Except he did," Alex said.

Darby shrugged. "I know, but . . . I *don't* know. It seems like there's something there. So far, he's singled out one person from every group."

"I still think he's targeting the most talented students," Alex said. "Or ambitious. Or maybe even just the people who stand out. Maybe you all make him feel inferior and invisible, and this is his way of becoming *more* visible."

When no one disagreed, Alex pressed on. "Who else seems exceptional? Who else is out there standing in front of crowds or making headlines or winning competitions?"

"*Shit,*" Ollie said quietly. His expression turned grave. "Do you remember the day when there was hardly anyone at school but us?"

He was still staring ahead, but Makani knew the question was for her. "You mean, Wednesday? Two days ago? The day we were attacked?"

This realization seemed to stun him. During periods of trauma, time could be funny like that. He tried to shake it off. "Right. But do you remember that bad joke I made? Stanton told us over the announcements that Rosemarie Holt had won a barrel race, and then *I* said that she should watch out."

Makani touched her lips in fear at the memory: *Clapping with the other students. So grateful for any small piece of good news.*

Darby shifted uneasily. "Rosemarie's been winning those events for a long time."

"Years," Ollie said.

"Oh God." Alex looked like she might throw up. "What do we do?"

Chris answered after the first ring. Ollie repeated their theory but was quickly cut off. His brow furrowed as he listened. "Yeah, we're fine," he said. "Yeah, okay—"

Ollie stared at his phone. "He hung up."

"What is it?" Makani asked. *What is it* now?

"They received a call from another trucker who picked up David. The guy just saw him on the news and recognized him. This new driver said he must have picked up David not long after the first driver dropped him off, and Chris said he knew the exact location. It was just stupid, random luck that neither driver knew who he was."

Makani's heart plunged. What were the chances?

"This guy claims to have dropped off David on the *other* side of Osborne. The police are headed there now. They think he's been snaking his way back to town through the fields. They think he might be headed to the stadium for a blitz attack."

Alex grabbed Makani's seat and shook it roughly. "I knew it!"

Makani fixed a hand over Alex's to stop her. "That doesn't sound like his MO"

"Are you kidding? What would shake up this town more than an attack during the first game of the playoffs?"

"What did Chris say about Rosemarie?" Darby asked.

Ollie frowned. "I think when Zachary wasn't a target, we lost any small sway we might have had."

"But someone needs to warn her!" Darby said.

Ollie was already scrolling through his contacts. He caught Makani's look and explained, "Neighbor. Her family lives on the other side of the corn maze."

Of course. Everyone was connected to everyone in Osborne. Makani tamped down her ill-timed jealousy as the call went straight to voicemail.

"Hey, it's Ollie Larsson. Call me as soon as you get this. It's an emergency. Everyone's okay, just . . . call me back."

Makani stared at him, her eyes wide and frightened. "What now?"

His voice hardened. "Seat belts, everyone." And then he turned the key in the ignition and pushed the pedal to the floor.

CHAPTER
TWENTY-SIX

MOONLIGHT GAVE A high-pitched whinny and pawed the fresh shavings.

"*Shh.*" Rosemarie Holt stroked the brush in calming sweeps down the horse's sorrel neck. "They're just a bunch of dumb rubberneckers. Nothing to be afraid of."

Lights strobed and music howled. Screams of rowdy laughter erupted from the cornstalks, carrying to the stable at the edge of the Holts' property. Normally, it was a minor annoyance to live beside the tourist attraction. Tonight, however, the land was teeming with drunken rednecks, frat guys, and sorority girls all out for a good scare. It was as if David Thurston Ware were a campfire urban legend and not an actual murderer-at-large.

In the next stall, Cash stomped his feet with nervous agitation. The maze had never had lights or music at night before. "I don't love it, either, buddy," she grumbled, feeling a fresh flush of anger at Emmet for leaving her with the chores.

When they were children, they'd each been given an American Quarter Horse. Emmet had chosen one with a black coat, so he'd named him after the Man in Black. This turned out to be prophetic as it reflected the way he treated Cash—like an accessory to look cooler. Rosemarie and their parents did most of the caretaking.

Rosemarie had always wanted a horse. When she was little, she'd never been interested in a book or movie unless it contained at least one. Moonlight had been named after her favorite fictional horse. Even though hers wasn't golden (she was a light brownish-red), nor did she have a white mane or tail (hers were flaxen), Rosemarie believed that she was just as loyal a friend as Alanna's Moonlight had been to the Lioness herself. Over the years, admittedly, Rosemarie had outgrown the name. But she still remembered why it had mattered. What it had meant to her.

"All right, girl." She touched the horse's rump as she walked around, so she'd know Rosemarie was there, and then tossed the brush into a plastic bucket of grooming tools. "Almost done. I'll get your hay."

Rosemarie took down the cross ties and picked up the bucket. She closed the sliding door behind her and left the bucket to grab the pitchfork, which was inside one of the empty stalls.

The stable smelled wonderfully familiar: wood shavings, sweet feed, and old leather, though it also held a pungent underpinning of ammonia. The urine scent was always stronger after mucking out the stalls, but it would fade within the hour. Her waterproof boots tread quietly over the rubber floor pavers.

Rosemarie and Moonlight were a good team. They started barrel racing when she was eight and competing when she was nine. The Sloane County Championship Rodeo used a traditional, three-barrel cloverleaf pattern. The event was timed, and if the racer knocked over a barrel, there was a five-second penalty. Some rodeos had hat fines, too, where they'd charge the racer twenty-five dollars if her hat fell off.

Moonlight rarely bumped a barrel. And Rosemarie never lost her hat.

Rosemarie wasn't without injury, though. A year ago, she'd broken her right arm when she slipped off while riding bareback. And only two months ago, her strap had broken when she was hanging upside down at a full-blown gallop while trick riding. It was the strangest thing. The strap wasn't even that old. She'd almost broken her neck.

The accident shook her up, but it didn't stop her. She was competitive, headstrong, and faster than the other racers. She was ready to go national.

As she strode into the dark stall, an earsplitting scream from next door startled her. Rosemarie waited.

Yep. Laughter.

Her jaw clenched as she imagined Emmet as one of the laughing imbeciles. *Hope you're having a good time,* she thought bitterly. He'd come home from UNL for the weekend. He was supposed to be *here*, helping her, but when he'd learned that some of his school friends had also driven into town, he'd ditched her to join them. Their parents were at the football game, supporting her cousin on the team.

Rosemarie reached for the pitchfork through the black shadow, but her hand only greeted air. Patting the rough, planked wall farther and farther into the stall, she finally fumbled against the handle in the far corner.

She grabbed it and turned back toward the light.

The bucket was gone.

A confused moment—a dreadful heartbeat—and then her nostrils filled with an unfamiliar and unwelcome odor. It was the unwashed scent of another human being.

• • •

The former cruiser tore out of Osborne, but as it hit the connecting highway, the car speeding ahead of them unexpectedly and drastically slowed down.

Makani glanced at the speedometer. It was five under the posted limit. "What the hell?" she yelled at the other car. "Go!"

Ollie's knuckles tightened on the steering wheel. "This happens all the time. People look in their rearview mirrors, and they think I'm a cop."

In the backseat, Darby tried to reach Rosemarie, but the cell towers were still overloaded. The calls either went straight to voicemail, or they wouldn't connect at all.

Ollie swerved into the oncoming lane and stepped on it. They raced past the car, and he zipped back into the right lane. With every mile, his adherence to safety regulations was going increasingly out the window.

Less than a minute later, it happened again. Makani and Alex moaned.

"All. The. Time," Ollie said, gritting his teeth and passing the second car.

Another speedometer check. Thirty over the limit. He caught Makani eyeing it. "No one's pulling me over tonight. They're all on the other side of town."

Makani liked that Ollie was a careful driver. She respected it. But she was grateful that he felt the urgency of their current situation.

She gave the road a grim smile. "I'm not complaining."

Rosemarie knew that scents could be comforting, but this was the first time she'd ever smelled a scent that was frightening. The stench of rancid body odor was close, and it was male.

And it didn't belong to her brother.

A slender figure stepped out in front of her stall. His gait was calm and measured. He was dressed in a strange coat, and he was holding the grooming bucket.

Rosemarie's knees began to quake.

David Thurston Ware set down the bucket. He didn't need it. He'd only brought it to show her that *he* was the one who'd moved it. He shrugged off the coat, which fell to the ground in a woolen puddle. He was wearing the hoodie that she'd heard about on the news. The camouflage was covered with splotchy brown stains that were darker than the fabric's pattern. Dried blood.

The reveal was both unnecessary and terrifying.

He removed his knife from a sheath on his belt. The blade glinted. Staring into the darkness of her stall, he kicked the plastic bucket, and the tools clanged together.

"They wouldn't have helped you much." He took a step forward. "But they would have been better than nothing."

Rosemarie tightened her grip on the pitchfork and lunged.

Traffic deadened into a complete stop. Hawaii was notorious for its impassable, two-lane roads, and it wasn't uncommon to get stuck behind a sightseer driving fifteen-under. Yet Makani had never felt road rage more intensely than she did right now.

"Her house is *right there*." Ollie gestured angrily at a plain one-story just before the corn maze. The house was set back some distance off the road.

Darby and Alex reached for their seat belts. "We'll make a run for it," Alex said.

"No!" Makani's rage turned into panic. "No splitting up. We stay together."

"I agree," Ollie said as the cruiser inched forward.

"But we can't just *sit* here," Alex said. "David could already be there!"

Darby attempted to soothe her. "Most likely, he's in town. It's probably okay."

Alex fumed. "Whose side are you on?"

Ollie craned his neck to see around the gridlock. A pickup passed, and then he sharply turned the wheel and accelerated into the oncoming lane.

A semi was coming straight toward them.

They screamed. The truck blew its horn. Ollie drove straight into the ditch beside the road and kept driving. The truck flew by, and the other drivers laid on their horns, shouting obscenities, as the cruiser hurtled down the length of the ditch, kicking up dust clouds into the night sky. The car bumped and rattled and thumped and shook.

"Oh my God, oh my God, oh my God," Makani and Darby said together as Alex shrieked, somewhere between pleasure and fear.

They hit the Holts' driveway, which was a dirt road. The car settled into a quieter grind, roughening as they picked up speed. Makani pointed at a small building away from the main house. Its lights were on. "There!" she said.

"Hold on," Ollie said, an instructional warning as he veered into the pasture.

Makani, Darby, and Alex screamed again.

"There was a fucking road up there!" Makani said.

"Sorry!" Ollie said as the car barreled through the grass toward the stable. "I got caught up in the moment!"

"What are we doing?" Darby yelled.

Alex shouted with the entire force of her lungs. "We'd better not be wrong about this!"

•   •   •

Rosemarie didn't grow up in rodeos for nothing. She was tough. A farm girl. And she wasn't about to be killed by a pathetic boy with a stupid knife.

David looked astonished by the pitchfork coming at him. He dodged, but he wasn't quick enough. The far tine gouged into his side. He cried out with shock and pain.

Startled that she'd made contact—that her weapon had slid through a living human being—she pulled it out. His body squelched as it released its hold.

He staggered backward.

"That's right!" Rosemarie said. She kept shouting at him, but she didn't know what she was saying. It didn't feel like any of this was actually happening.

David ran from the stable, clutching his bleeding left side.

The horses were upset. They neighed and kicked the walls as she raced through her options: She could wait for a signal and call the police. Or she could make sure that David wouldn't come back to kill her first.

Rosemarie gripped the pitchfork's handle so tightly that she felt bruises forming. She took a cautious step forward. Another. And another.

As she reached the stable door, a hand shot out and grabbed the pitchfork—right above her hand. She cried out as she struggled to regain control.

David pulled her toward the ground. For some reason, he'd set down his knife to seize the pitchfork, and now he was trying to pick it back up.

Like hell he would.

Rosemarie wrenched the pitchfork from his grasp. And that's when she became aware of a pair of headlights and a car thundering straight toward them.

They were both stunned, but David recovered first. He snatched up the knife and swiped. The blade sliced into the flesh of her right thigh. She whacked him on the back with the pitchfork. She saw him double over, and then there was a blinding white light.

And then she couldn't see anything.

CHAPTER
TWENTY-SEVEN

THE SPOTLIGHT FROM Ollie's cruiser sliced a blazing hole through the black landscape. Only a few feet in front of them, Rosemarie and David were hunched over. Their frames were locked together, knotted in a struggle.

"I changed my mind, I changed my mind," Alex said. "I wish we'd been wrong!"

Makani threw open her door and bolted through the icy air and muddy grass. The other three doors flung open behind her.

David twisted his body behind Rosemarie's, securing an arm around her neck. His knife aimed for her throat. It was coated with a liquid shadow of fresh blood.

Rosemarie's round face looked pinched and paralyzed. Makani saw the whites of her eyes like a spooked horse. Her long, straight hair leaned to one side as she held all her weight on a single leg. She clutched at the other.

Everything happened in an instant.

Alex screamed toward David. He turned in the direction of her caterwaul, angling Rosemarie toward her and leaving his back to

Makani. Makani jumped on him. Everyone toppled to the ground, and Rosemarie cried out. Arms and legs and torsos tangled, and other hands were prying them apart, but Makani couldn't tell whose hands were friendly and whose were *his*. Another cry shredded the night.

David wriggled out from the pile. His head turned back to them, and his eyes flashed as he recognized Makani. She was trapped, and he was right there.

But he was outnumbered. So he ran.

Rosemarie was curled up like a fallen leaf. Makani touched an unmoving shoulder, bracing for the worst. And then the girl looked up.

"Oh my God. Oh, thank God." Makani began to weep. "Are you okay?"

"Just this leg. It hurts to move." Rosemarie seemed a little dazed, but she gestured to the gash in her thigh. "How did you know—"

Darby dropped to his knees with a strangled sound. At first, Makani thought he'd been injured. But he was looking at Alex. Makani crawled forward.

No. Please. No.

It was starting to snow. Or maybe it had been snowing this whole time. Makani suddenly felt the cold wetness against her cheeks. She glanced up as David vanished into the maze. Plump flakes tumbled behind him through the car's spotlight and headlights.

Ollie stood frozen above them. Maybe he was back inside the cereal aisle at Greeley's, trying to decide whether to stay or give chase. The world felt locked in suspended animation. The only thing alive was the snow.

And then Darby released a gut-wrenching wail, and Makani knew. They all knew.

As Makani reached for Darby, Ollie shot toward the maze. Darby shuddered, hysterical, stretching to touch Alex but then pulling back his hand, afraid. The bumpy white vertebrae of her spine were exposed. Her neck had been slashed so deeply and so far across that she'd nearly been decapitated.

Makani's skin went clammy. Bile rose in her throat.

Rosemarie pulled herself toward them but then turned away in shock.

"Call the police," Makani said, clambering upright to face the enormous maze. The wind gusted, and the stalks swayed and rippled outward. Ollie dove into the current. So many people were in there. She couldn't leave him to face the massacre alone. The cops were on the other side of Osborne; it would take them too long to arrive.

Rosemarie made a noise of surprise, no doubt discovering the missed calls on her phone. "It's searching for a signal," she said with frustration.

Makani nodded at Rosemarie and Darby. "Stay together."

"No way." Darby scurried to his feet, wiping tears and snot onto his sleeve. "I'm coming with you."

Makani didn't protest. They ran, full throttle.

Snapped cornstalks revealed David and Ollie's entrance. The outer wall was at least a dozen stalks thick, and the brittle leaf blades scratched and tore Makani's skin. Snow that had landed on the plants flew back into the air. Strobes burst erratically. A sinister soundtrack blared. Screams chorused nearby, and Makani's chest seized, but the screams were followed by laughter. Just a couple of friends, stumbling across a costumed ghoul.

She exploded out from the stalks. Three guys shrieked, completely losing their shit. One of them was wearing a camouflage hoodie. Makani fell backward, but Darby caught her as he crashed through. The hoodie guy screamed again, but the other two were already cracking up. Thinking they were in on the haunted maze's joke.

Makani took a second look.

It was a David Ware *costume*. The guy was also holding a plastic knife. She held back her fury to warn them. "You have to get out of here. It's not safe!" She pointed toward the crushed cornstalks. "There are two girls out there who need your help!"

The hoodie guy grinned. "Ooooh."

"You don't understand," Darby said. "David is *inside* the maze. He just *slaughtered* my best friend."

"*Ooooh,*" the trio said together, louder. They shook their hands with the universal sign for spooky.

Makani couldn't afford to give them any more time. "Which way did they go?"

Darby had the sense to look at the ground. Brace roots reached out from the soil like swollen fingers. Ears of fallen corn looked like blackened teeth and shrunken heads, their silks dangling like stringy hair. It was less muddy along the path—straw had been sprinkled over the whole thing—but it was muddy enough, and the indentations caused by two sets of running footprints were clear.

He pointed. "Here!"

The tracks led away from the point where Makani and Darby had entered the maze. "Go look! You'll see them," Makani shouted to the trio as she and Darby took off. As they rounded the corner, out of sight, Makani heard one of them ask, "Why weren't they dressed up like the others?"

They traced over the doubled footprints, turn after turn. Every time someone screamed, Makani jumped. A sharp right, and teenage boy covered in blood and wielding straight razor leaped out at them. Makani and Darby shrieked and recoiled. But he was in Victorian costume, and the razor wasn't real.

"So, you've found old Sweeney," the boy said in a rough accent, somewhere between cockney and Australian. "But will you discover his secret?"

Darby's brow rose with recognition. "Jonathan?"

"Ain't nobody here who goes by that name, mate. The name's Todd, Sweeney Todd, and—"

"Jonathan." Makani didn't know who Jonathan was, other than clearly he was from the drama club. "Did you see them? Did you see Ollie or David?"

Immediately, Jonathan dropped the act. Even in the violent strobe light, even underneath his pancake makeup, she saw belief—and then horror—register on his face. "He's here? David Ware is *here?*"

"You have to warn them! You have to get everyone out of here!" Makani said.

"Go," Darby said. "Go!"

Jonathan skittered away as Makani and Darby raced back down the trail. "Get out of the maze," they shouted to everyone. "Get out of here, now! David is here!"

Nobody took them seriously. They either thought Makani and Darby were actors or that they were acting like obnoxious, insensitive teenagers.

It was snowing harder. Flakes swirled down and around them. Makani hunched as she ran so that she could still see the footprints through the white. Just as she feared they were chasing the wrong tracks, they busted through another wall. And there they were. Wrestling, like the days of middle school gone by.

David was on top, but Ollie had somehow managed to pin David's dominant wrist. The knife shook in David's hand, but he wasn't letting go.

Makani screamed again and rushed them. David made eye contact with her just as she kicked him in the forehead. His muscles loosened. The bodies shifted. David rolled over, and Ollie scrambled away through the straw. They were both coated in mud.

Makani planted herself between them. Darby shouted, another voice called out, and Makani was knocked to the ground. The wind sucked out from her lungs.

David was above her. His *knife* was above her.

She closed her eyes as it came down for her heart.

A wave of blood crashed against David's head and showered down onto her face. They gasped, and the pressure of his body released from her. Someone pulled her to her feet and held her securely, their arms wrapped around her waist and chest.

"I didn't know what to do!" a panicked voice said.

Makani wiped the blood from her eyes. A tall girl in rectangular glasses and Victorian dress was holding a bucket. *Brooke. Haley's best friend.* The blood trickled between Makani's lips, and she tasted something sweet. *Corn syrup.*

A heart was beating against her back. *Ollie.*

She squeezed his arms. He hugged her tighter.

Darby positioned himself between them and David. Brooke was backing against the far cornstalks as David wiped the fake blood from his face. He flicked it to the ground in disgust, sneering at Darby. "It was almost you."

"W-what?" Darby said.

"Before *she* moved here"—David pointed his knife at Makani—"I'd considered you."

Darby was already in tears. "I don't understand."

David had more emotion in his voice than usual. He sounded angry. "You want out, but your roots are too strong. She's the one who will leave."

"You don't want us to leave?" Darby said it like a plea. "We won't. We'll stay. We can help you. How can we help—"

David lashed forward, and Darby went down.

Makani screamed. Darby was on the ground, clutching the wound in his chest, which was gushing blood. Ollie pivoted to shield Makani—to place his body in front of hers—before releasing her to rush David. But David rushed Ollie first.

Ollie cried out near her ear. The blade sucked out. Squelched back in. Ollie's breath was hot on her neck. Back out. She was still screaming as Ollie crumpled limply to the earth.

Another chest wound. Gaping. Their hearts, or maybe their lungs.

Her screams turned into hyperventilating gasps. A group of tweens appeared from around the bend and shrieked. David spun to attack, but Brooke was right there, and she shoved them, hustling them back through the maze.

Makani trembled between the bodies of her last remaining friends. David stared at her, predator to prey. His face was long and homely, but his entire head was dripping red as the coagulating theater blood mixed with the real blood. He swished his knife and more blood flew off and through the air. Blood was everywhere.

The terror was finally spreading outward. If the corn were an ocean, the cries were its waves. Manic, frenzied people tore through the dry vegetation.

But Ollie and Darby had stopped twitching.

Ollie and Darby were dead.

"What . . . what the fuck?" Makani said it quietly, exhausted. She was crying. Her question was rhetorical and not one she expected David to answer. But he did.

"The *fuck* is," he said, "you were supposed to die two days ago, and I was supposed to have another week. But I pushed through. I made it work. And now we're here, and soon the cops will be here, and it's fitting that you'll be my last."

He stalked toward her. Backed her against an arrangement of hay bales and pumpkins and a life-size skeleton wearing a frilly Victorian corset.

"You'll be here forever," he said. "And I get to leave."

"To prison," she said.

"I was looking forward to turning myself in. But this gets me there, too."

He actually *wanted* to be caught. "So, it's about fame?" she asked. "You wanted a high body count so that you could be another Gacy? Another Dahmer?"

"Those assholes killed for sexual pleasure."

"And you're killing for the fun of it?"

"This isn't fun," David said as he lifted the knife above his head. "This is just something I have to do."

CHAPTER TWENTY-EIGHT

MAKANI DUCKED AS the knife thunked into the pumpkin behind her head.

She ran for her life.

She fled down the path blazed by the terrified people before her—a straight line through the cornstalks. Her sneakers slapped against the churned mud as David crashed through thick stalks that hadn't yet toppled.

She burst out from the maze into a huge thoroughfare. It looked and smelled like an abandoned traveling carnival. Plastic soda bottles, hot dogs, funnel cakes, roasted corn on the cob—everything discarded and trampled in the rush to escape. Fried food blended into a manure stench as she raced past the live enclosures. Pygmy goats. A hunched zebra. Scraggly coyotes. The animals paced and howled.

Behind her, the footfalls grew louder. She glanced back just as David was close enough to swipe. She dodged and swerved, and then careened toward the vast corn pit. The parking lot was visible on the other side of it.

A split-second decision, and she hurdled herself over the edge. Corn sprayed over the rim like a pool. She hit the kernels hard. Stitches snapped in her injured arm, and her swimming muscles were weak from disuse, but her adrenaline was pumping. Makani stood, and the kernels were nearly pelvis deep. She slog-ran toward help.

Cars and trucks jammed the parking lot with everyone trying to exit at once. She yelled at them, waving her good arm, but their shouting and honking drowned her out.

She looked over her shoulder to find David hovering at the pit's edge. He was waiting to see what she would do, determining how he should respond. He climbed onto the rim and prepared to jump.

But he didn't see what Makani saw behind him.

David keeled forward, knocked into the pit by a blow to the head from an iron folk-art skeleton. He face-planted into the corn. His body didn't move.

Relief shocked Makani. "You aren't dead!"

"No," Darby said. "I'm not."

Mud and snow and blood spattered his tweed sport coat. He clutched the decorative skeleton by its spinal cord. He used it to gesture at David. "But is *he*?"

They bent toward the body. Afraid to get closer.

"I don't know," Makani said from the center of the pit. "I don't think so."

Darby hesitantly stepped forward and then rapidly backed away. "Screw this," he said, dropping the skeleton. "Meet you on the other side!" And he took off, sprinting around the perimeter.

Makani's mind shouted at her to run.

Her gut hissed that David was alive.

She saw her grandmother lying in the hospital. Heard Alex crying out into the night. Felt Ollie crumpling against her to the ground.

A hooded figure lurched out from behind a grandfather clock. A hooded figure lurched out, a hooded figure lurched out, a hooded figure lurched out—

"What are you doing?" Darby's voice sounded muted. "No!"

The parking lot was still packed with people, and the highway was clogged. Makani couldn't hear any sirens. If she ran, David could kill someone else.

David *would* kill someone else.

Makani waded toward his prostrate body. His hands were empty. Desperately, she foraged until she spotted it: a nub of black rubber poking out of the yellow corn.

She lunged for the handle. It slipped out as David rolled onto his back. His eyes were groggy and unfocused. She towered over him. Her hand was sweating. It was heavier than she'd expected, heavier than the knife in her memories.

David began to blink as his awareness returned. He gazed up at her. The blade flashed in the light of a distant strobe. It was long and sharp and vicious.

"You don't have it in you," he said.

"You don't know me," she said.

David didn't know her, but Makani knew herself. And neither of them was a monster. She was a human who had made a terrible mistake. He was a human who had planned his terrible actions.

You'll be here forever, he'd said. *And I get to leave.*

Standing above him, she realized it was about Osborne. Everyone on David's checklist had been destined to move away—whether it was because they were bound for greater things, or, like herself, they had never belonged there to begin with.

Growing up in a town like Osborne made it difficult to leave. It

was easy to get tied down to family or the land or the community. Everybody depended on one another to survive. It took a person with extraordinary drive and ambition to break from the pattern.

Haley, Matt, Rodrigo, Caleb, Katie, and Rosemarie—they were ambitious. They rose above their peers. Makani *used* to be ambitious, but David didn't know that. He just viewed her as temporary.

It's why he'd chosen her over Darby, or even Ollie. They dreamed of other places, but to someone who didn't know them well, perhaps they seemed destined to become stuck here, too. Perhaps they seemed too passive. But it was impossible to know what was *inside* a person, or how they might change over time.

Years ago, Makani's mother had been ambitious enough to get out of Osborne, but as quickly as she'd left, she'd gotten tied down to a new place. She hadn't changed at all. Maybe that's why she resented Makani. When she looked at her, she saw the loss of her freedom, and she was too selfish to notice what she'd gained.

David had planned to turn himself in. He knew that he'd be sent to the Tecumseh State Correctional Institution, the same maximum-security prison Chris had visited a few days ago for work. Ollie had told her that it was only two and a half hours away.

For an instant—all this burned through her mind in an instant—Makani felt sad for David. His big, ambitious dream . . . it was so small.

Running away from home didn't change the fact that a person still had to live with themselves. Makani had learned this, though perhaps her mother never had. Change came from within, over a long period of time, and with a lot of help from people who loved you. Osborne wasn't David's problem. For Makani, Osborne had even been restorative. Being a psychopath was David's problem.

David was David's problem.

Maybe there had been more people on his list, or maybe she and Rosemarie were the only ones left. Maybe he had a bad childhood, maybe he was born this way, or maybe he just felt trapped. Whatever his plans, whatever his reasons—they didn't matter anymore. He'd made his decision. And now she had made hers.

As David dove at her legs to knock her down, Makani stabbed him in the middle of his back. The blade went in up to its hilt. His body collapsed into the corn.

She tugged out the knife and struggled toward Darby's voice.

Slowly, David crawled. A vile trail of blood slathered across the kernels behind him as Darby hefted her over the edge. Makani was shuddering in his arms, still grasping the knife, when she became aware of the crowd. They were circling the pit. Surrounding it. She didn't know if David was dying, but he wasn't getting away.

Osborne wouldn't let him.

He had underestimated them all. He had terrorized the community, but instead of tearing them apart, the townspeople had grown closer. As the sirens broke through the silent, snowy night, his body stopped crawling. And then it stopped moving altogether.

David Thurston Ware died knowing that he would never leave Osborne.

David Thurston Ware died knowing that he would be buried there forever.

CHAPTER
TWENTY-NINE

THE POLICE RUSHED toward them. When Chris saw Makani's wretched face, his body seemed to shatter. Officer Bev grabbed his arms to keep him from falling.

"Where is he?" Chris asked.

Makani could only point. He shook off Bev's grip and ran.

She approached Makani and Darby with caution. "May I take that?"

It took a few seconds for Makani to realize that Bev was asking about the knife. Bev removed an evidence bag from her jacket, and Makani dropped it in.

"Rosemarie," Makani said, remembering as the paramedics swarmed them.

"She's all right. Three college kids found her and stayed with her. One of them was wearing a David Ware costume," she added wryly. "The media's gonna love that."

At least it meant the kids had also stayed with Alex.

Darby lost control, sobbing, and Makani knew he was thinking about her, too. He'd been holding Makani, but now she held him as they were hurried into an ambulance. Bev stayed with them. Makani checked to see if her phone's signal was strong enough for a call. She needed to hear her grandmother's voice, or she'd lose her mind completely. The clock turned to midnight. It was officially Halloween.

Bev's shoulder radio fuzzed: "—alive! Do you copy? My brother is alive!"

All the atoms in the universe became motionless.

And then Darby whispered to Makani, *"Go."*

As the paramedics reached to close the doors, Makani burst back out of the ambulance. She tore through the fairgrounds and down the path of demolished cornstalks, officers and medics racing behind her.

Please, please, please.

Gasping and panting, she ran straight to him. He was still lying on the ground. Chris was holding his hand, and his police coat was bundled under his head as a pillow.

"Ollie," she said, falling to her knees beside him.

His eyes lit up when he saw her. Snow dusted his lashes. "Makani."

"I thought . . . I would have *never* left . . ."

He broke into a smile, but his voice was weak. "Darby?"

"He's okay. We're both okay. How are you?"

His smile widened. "Nothing your grandma's doctors can't fix."

Makani laughed, wiping the tears from her cheeks, and put on a brave smile of her own. She kissed his forehead. His skin was warmer than she'd expected. He tilted his head, and she moved to his lips. Softly, she kissed them.

A faint but reassuring pressure answered back.

Chris was still holding one of Ollie's hands. With his other hand, Ollie fumbled for hers. She grasped it, and the autumn moon shone brighter—rendering the night soft and cold and safe.

ACKNOWLEDGMENTS

I WANTED TO read this book, but my dear friend Kiersten White suggested that I should write it instead. This book exists because of her. She's also read it more times than anyone else. She's read *all* of my books more times than anyone else. She is a saint and a beautiful magic rainbow unicorn. Thank you, Kiersten. I love you.

Thank you to my fantastic agent, Kate Testerman, who made it happen, and to my brilliant editor, Julie Strauss-Gabel, who worked and worked and worked and worked to turn it into a fully functioning novel. I'm so grateful that they both took a chance on it.

Thank you to Lindsey Andrews, Lindsay Boggs, Anna Booth, Melissa Faulner, Rosanne Lauer, Bri Lockhart, Natalie Vielkind, and everyone else at the Penguin Young Reader's Group. Additional thanks and hugs to Sean Freeman, Eve Steben, and their team for creating such a gloriously eerie cover.

Writing this book required six years of research, critique partners, and in-depth discussions. Humble thanks to Leigh Bardugo, Luce Beagle, Lauren Biehl, Holly Black, Emily Brock, Cassandra Clare, Brandy Colbert, Alexandra Duncan, Shannon Fang, Leslie

Golden, Manning Krull, Myra McEntire, Marjorie Mesnis, Chris Prahler, Rainbow Rowell, Jon Skovron, Amy Spalding, Robin Wasserman, Jeff Zentner, Heidi Zweifel, and all the readers who answered my questions on Twitter and my surveys over email. And to David Levithan: I'm sorry. Ha! That happened before we became friends.

To the real Katie Kurtzman: Thank you for being more excited than *anyone*. Your enthusiasm gave me courage and strength.

So much love and endless thanks to my family: Mom, Dad, Kara, Chris, Beckham, JD, Fay, and Roger.

And thank you to Jarrod Perkins. My family-family. My partner in horror movies, life, and everything in between. Thank you for the laughter and for cleaning the mud off my boots in that cold Nebraskan cornfield. I love you the most of all.

THE
WOODS
ARE
ALWAYS
WATCHING

NEW YORK TIMES BESTSELLING AUTHOR
STEPHANIE PERKINS

For Jarrod, best friend & true love

TOGETHER

NEENA CUT THE engine, and the speakers went silent. Mid-lyric. The trail was straight ahead, but her gaze could only follow it to its first bend. The overhanging forest, a drab and washed-out green that presaged the end of summer, obscured the rest of the path.

"How many days do you think we'll last?" she asked.

"How many hours," Josie said.

"If I die out there? I'd be honored if you ate my body."

"I would *never* let a bear get to your body first."

"Oh my God." Incredulity tainted Neena's laughter. "Would you please stop it with the bears?"

"Only if you promise not to mention their existence for the next seventy-two hours."

"I didn't! *You* brought them up. Again."

Josie shuddered, darkening. "I'm serious. I don't know if I can do this."

"Just think of them as big Winnie-the-Poohs."

"Shut your hole."

"Paddingtons. Baloos. Fozzies."

It was a joke—it was always a joke—but Josie jerked open the passenger-side door and got out. It slammed shut behind her. Neena grabbed her phone off the charger and followed her best friend into the parking lot.

"Berenstains," she said, digging in. Neena always dug in.

Her hiking boots crunched against the wet gravel. The rain had just stopped. In these mountains, it rained most afternoons during the summer—violent downpours in the early season, irksome drizzles in the late—but cleared quickly. It was the third week of August. The Little South Chickadee River burbled and sang nearby. Insects hummed and clicked their wings. The lazy breeze smelled of sun-warmed pine.

Josie pivoted with sudden interest. "Ooh, did you ever have a thing for Brother Bear? I mean, before you realized they were über-Christian hillbillies."

"What are you talking about?" Neena asked, confused.

"Brother Bear. With the red shirt and blue pants."

"I know who Brother Bear is. The Berenstain Bears were Christian?"

"There were numerous books with the word 'God' in the title."

"Huh," Neena said. "I guess my parents didn't check those out from the library." She popped the Subaru's hatch. Everyone in Asheville drove a Subaru, the preferred mode of transportation for modern hippies and outdoorsmen, among which the girls were neither. Neena's parents had purchased the Impreza because it had a high safety rating. Their backpacks crowded its hatch like monstrous, bloated caterpillars. Very hungry caterpillars. Neena realized her thoughts might be stuck on picture books.

She moaned. "I don't wanna."

Josie copied Neena's moan. "I don't wanna, either."

The packs didn't budge, refusing to help. These were not their school backpacks, retired from service and recently replaced by more stylish backpacks for college. Josie's brother and his girlfriend had loaned them a pair of backpacking packs: a boggling assemblage of padded straps, hip belts, bungee cords, mesh pockets, and bulging compartments. Neena prickled with renewed trepidation. Not only were these packs borrowed, but so was the equipment inside them. Even her boots—an outmoded pair, heavy and ugly—were borrowed from Josie's mom, who wore the same size.

Unfortunately, they had no one to blame but themselves. The trip had been concocted only two days ago during their morning shift at Kmart, a pre-Amazon relic where customers often exclaimed in astonishment, "I thought you went under years ago!"

Alas. The chain clung on for its meager life. Their particular location had a whopping 1.5-star rating on Yelp. Its shelves were largely empty and in permanent disarray. Clothing hung askew on broken racks, dented cans lingered past expiration dates, sports equipment was shellacked in off-putting colors, and the book selection was a smattering of religious overstock and failed themed-mystery series. *The Thanksgiving Murders. The Body on the Badminton Court. 'Til Death Do Us Sudoku.* The store looked like a former roommate had never returned to pick up the last of his boxes.

That Saturday shift had been Neena's last. In one week, she would be moving to California for college. Josie was staying in North Carolina.

"We should do something," Neena had said.

"We are doing something," Josie had replied flatly. "We're restocking the shampoo aisle."

"Something significant. Something just the two of us."

"It's always just the two of us."

Though her gaze had remained detached, Josie's eyelids twitched at her own slip. It wouldn't *always* be just the two of them. The impending separation pressed against them like a loaded shotgun.

Josie was acting glum and bitter, as she had been all summer. Neena longed for the old Josie, who was lively and game. She needed the old Josie. She'd tried again. "Something big, I mean. Maybe we could drive to Dollywood."

"Roller coasters give you migraines."

"We could go camping. Like Galen and Kyle."

"We hate Galen and Kyle," Josie had said. They hated everybody; it was one of the things that had sealed their friendship. But their teenage redneck coworkers were particularly loathsome. They spat watery brown dip onto the break-room floor, ignored calls to the registers for backup, and viewed feminism as a threat to their masculinity. "And we don't know shit about camping. Nature is for . . . other people."

Their classmates had all taken advantage of the mountain lifestyle. They had always been off tubing and kayaking down the French Broad River, hiking and camping along the Blue Ridge Parkway. A lot of beer, weed, and sex had been involved. It was a local rite of passage. Neena and Josie had never been interested in any of that, excepting the sex. But, regrettably, neither of them had ever had a boyfriend.

"Yeah," Neena had said, "but if they can do it, so can we. Didn't you used to go camping with your family?"

"When I was a kid. And my dad and Win did all the work."

Josie's father had died when she was in the eighth grade. Win was Winston, Josie's older brother. It was unnecessary to point out that Neena had never been camping. Everyone in her family was strictly an indoor type. Despite this, Neena unexpectedly latched onto the idea. "Okay, but Win goes all the time. We could borrow his gear." Her reasoning crumbled into pleading. "I mean, haven't you ever wondered if *maybe* we missed out on a vital high school experience?"

Josie had snorted with disdain. But she'd stopped restocking.

"Soon I won't even have the option to do things like this anymore," Neena had said. "Not in the city. This is my last chance."

Neena wasn't sure why Josie had eventually come around. Maybe because Neena had continued to monologue, hyping the excursion with notions of enlightenment. Being in the woods would be freeing! A technology detox! A chance to commune with Mother Earth, Mother Nature . . . whatever her name was! But by the time Neena had clocked out for the last time from the not-so-superstore, Josie had switched enough shifts so they could do it. Of course, they still needed permission. They had wanted to leave the next morning, but it took longer than that just to convince Neena's parents.

I won't see Josie again until Thanksgiving.

You will not see us until Thanksgiving, either.

I'm an adult.

You are eighteen.

I've never gotten into trouble.

You have never been given the chance, because we keep you safe.

Neena's father had relented first. Maybe it was because he'd spent more time with Josie, driving the girls around before Neena had gotten her license. Fixing them hot dogs and jhal muri after school. Watching every season of endless sitcoms with them. As the primary witness to their friendship, perhaps he held deeper compassion for their situation.

Our daughter is right, Baba had said, wearily rubbing his brow. Neena had been surprised to be right. *She is responsible and trustworthy. She has earned this.*

The trip would last three days, and the girls had decided to go backpacking, which, best they could tell, meant "hiking with camping." Camping-only sounded boring. Josie's brother had helped them select a trail, and, ever the diligent students, they crammed their research—reading articles, watching videos, scouring message boards. They'd organized an itinerary and printed out copies for their families. They'd downloaded trail-map apps onto their phones and marked the waypoints.

But Neena's parents still wouldn't give their final blessing until the girls proved they could use the equipment. Earlier that morning, all three parents had stood in Josie's overgrown backyard, scrutinizing them as they pitched the tent, lit the stove, and filtered water under Win's tutelage. The girls were unskilled and clumsy, and everyone had a good chuckle at their expense, but they'd passed the test. They excelled at passing tests.

And now they were here. And so were their enormous backpacks.

"Do you remember how we're supposed to put them on?" Neena tried to recall Win's backpack demonstration, but it blurred with all his other demonstrations and instructions.

Josie frowned. "Something to do with the knees. Or a knee? There's definitely some kind of knee-to-shoulder transfer. I think."

They glanced at each other. The absurdity of not even knowing the very first step broke them into nervous, hysterical giggles.

Neena reached for her pack. "Here goes nothing."

Literally nothing went. The pack was leaden.

"Well," Neena said. "Shit."

They cracked up harder. Using all four hands, together the girls scooted and grunted the behemoth forward, until Neena's pack was half on the car, half off. They were in tears from laughing.

"Was it this heavy when we put it in here?" Josie asked.

"I think it birthed a baby hippopotamus." Neena unzipped the pack's hip-belt pocket and squeezed her phone inside. Service didn't exist out here, but they'd packed a charging device so they could still use their cameras and GPS. They had been surprised to learn that

GPS would still work. Win had explained that it connected to satellites, not cell towers. The girls' last texts had been sent from a remote highway on the outskirts of Canton, just past a guzzling old paper mill. The cell signals had vanished soon after. Their families did not expect to hear from them again until they returned.

Josie pointed at the pack's straps, which were dangling above the ground. "Can you get underneath, maybe? Could you try to slip those on?"

Neena glanced around to ensure that no one else was watching. But it was a Monday, a weekday, and this wasn't a popular trail. Another Subaru was parked at the east end of the lot, because of course it was, and two pickups were parked at the west. The rest of the lot was empty—the weekend hikers and campers had already gone home.

Crouching below her target, Neena turtled it onto her body. Her arms threaded through the straps, her right foot took a labored step, the pack dislodged . . . and then slowly, steadily pushed her straight into the ground.

Josie lost her mind. She buckled over again, clutching her abdomen.

The crush was so alarming that Neena laughed, too, out of shock. Her clothes sponged up the sodden earth. "I don't recommend this method."

"I've never seen actual slow motion in real life."

"Hey. Help a gal out?"

It took a full minute for Josie to roll Neena over, and then for Neena to rock back and forth to gain some momentum. But, finally, Neena heaved upward.

Josie grabbed Neena's flailing hands. Their matching rings caught in the sunlight, glittering like miniature galaxies. The rings were all stone, no metal—carved ultramarine with clouds of white calcite and flecks of gold pyrite. Last winter, the girls had purchased them at a mineral shop downtown because the sign had claimed that lapis lazuli was a symbol of friendship. The rings had adorned their right index fingers ever since.

Josie lifted Neena to her feet and didn't let go until Neena was steady. "You look fantastic," she said. "Like you're ready to summit Everest."

Dampness muddied Neena's clothing. Gravel stuck to her cheek. "Ugh, this thing weighs a thousand pounds. People do this for fun?" She brushed the grit from her jeans.

Josie was wearing jeans, too, to shield her legs from ticks, which were abundant here and carried Lyme disease. "Cotton kills," Win had warned, a favorite refrain of the outdoor community. But he wasn't talking about protection from bloodsucking arachnids. Cotton was dangerous because it absorbed moisture and lacked insulation. Unfortunately, their choices were either jeans or leggings—the girls didn't own any other types of pants—and leggings weren't warm enough. Because he'd also said it got cold out here at night, even in August, even though they were only fifty-five minutes from home.

Neena snapped her hip belt together. "Your turn."

Josie wished it weren't. She had only agreed to this trip because Neena had begged, and because their days together were at an end. The trip almost hadn't even happened. Josie had allowed Neena to believe that Neena's parents were the holdup, but the truth was that Josie's mother had been equally resistant. She'd only relented after Win had intervened. Josie had overheard his muffled appeal from the other side of her bedroom wall. *Her best friend is moving away. Just let her have this.* It stung to hear her circumstances described so plainly.

Everything about this summer stung because Neena was leaving, and Josie was staying.

Neena was going to attend the University of Southern California, and Josie was going to attend the University of North Carolina Asheville.

Neena was going to live in a dormitory, and Josie was going to keep living at home with her mother.

Neena was going to have new friends and new experiences, and Josie was going to be surrounded by all the same people and places.

It wasn't that Josie didn't love their hometown. Asheville was beautiful and open-minded and had multiple concert venues, independent cinemas, and organic farmers' markets. It had Arts and Crafts neighborhoods and an Art Deco downtown. It had character and history and integrity. But it was also small—the kind of city that adults chose to live in *after* they'd explored the rest of the world. Neena was about to see the world without her. Josie was about to become a human Kmart. Abandoned and forgotten, but still here.

"Sorry I can't help you anymore," Neena said, shuffling toward her.

Josie startled. "What?"

"With your pack. We should have moved yours, too, before I put on mine."

Sometimes Josie believed, sincerely, that Neena could read her mind. She was glad this wasn't one of the occasions. Putting on a show of false enthusiasm and roaring with exaggerated strength, Josie hefted her pack to the edge of the hatch.

Neena blinked at her. Mystified. "How'd you do that?"

"You've got the food. I've got the tent. The food weighs more."

"Fuck that. You're taking the food tomorrow."

Josie grinned, for real. "After we've already eaten some? No problem."

"You devious, devious wench."

"That was the deal. You got the lady backpack, so you got the extra pounds." Josie shoved her pack into an upright position. It took several attempts before it stayed.

"I got the lady backpack because I'm shorter than you. And I still think the lady backpack should necessitate fewer pounds."

"The lady backpack distributes the weight more evenly across the lady's body."

Neena waddled in a circle. Her hands were posed like she was modeling. "Now, tell me. Is it this luscious shade of purple that makes it a lady backpack?"

"Luscious lavender."

"*Ladies in Lavender* . . . wasn't that a movie with Judi Dench?"

"And Maggie Smith. They nurse a sexy, young violinist back to health."

"When we're old," Neena said, "I want us to be surrounded by sexy, young violinists."

"I'd settle for us just being Dames," Josie said. Her pack was navy blue and stained from years of rugged use. Win had started solo backpacking after their father's death. Their father had loved the outdoors, and, in his grief, her brother had found refuge there. He'd been seventeen then, only a few months younger than Josie was now. It was a surprising realization. Now Win was twenty-two, but it seemed like he'd been an adult forever.

Meegan, owner of the lavender pack, had only taken up backpacking when she and Win started dating. Josie hoped she would never stoop to something like that. But if a guy ever showed any interest in her, maybe she'd take up a dumb hobby to impress him, too.

"Obviously we'll be Dames," Neena said.

Josie loved talking with Neena like this. Like their future was certain. Like they would always be friends. She backed up neatly into her upright pack, slipped the straps over her shoulders, snapped it all together, and stood.

"Aw," Neena said. "That's not fair."

Compared to Neena, Josie was tall. Practically brawny. She had the type of body that could have real, natural strength if she put forth even a modicum of effort. But she never had, so it didn't. The burden on her back—the sheer resistance to her effort—was staggering. She balked. "Oh my God. People do this for fun?"

"That's what I said!"

Panic flooded through Josie. It hadn't occurred to her that they might not be physically capable of this trip. "How are we supposed to carry these for three days?"

Neena shook her head. "I have no idea."

"How?"

"I don't know," Neena said. But the joking had stopped. Whenever one of them freaked out—and, admittedly, it was usually Josie—the other went calm. "We just will."

Josie was sure that if Neena could have shrugged right now, she would have shrugged. Not condescendingly. The gesture would have been comforting. Josie's panic dulled back into an uneasy, unidentifiable dread. "Right. People do this all the time."

"Yeah. And we're people," Neena said. "Surely we can do this, too."

"Did you see us in gym class?"

Neena slammed the hatch closed. Birds squawked and took to the humid air. "I kept my eyes closed in gym class."

"That explains a lot."

After double-checking that they had everything, Josie stuffed the car keys into the top of Neena's pack.

"Oh, jeez," Neena said. "Don't look."

Moving to investigate, Josie whacked Neena with her pack. "What?"

Neena oofed.

"Sorry. What? I don't see any— Oh."

"I told you not to look."

A plywood notice board stood beside the trail. In large type on a sheet of copy paper protected by plastic, a faded sign read: BEAR CANISTERS REQUIRED.

"It's okay," Neena said. "We've got one."

A second notice with smaller type was tacked beside it, and Josie toddled over to read it. The unwelcome words raked across her skin so viciously that she felt marked. "It says if we don't have a canister we can get fined. Or even get jail time."

"Again. We have a canister."

"It's from the Forest Service. 'Emergency requirement to use bear-resistant canisters in . . .' And great. It lists Frazier Mountain, Deep Fork, Misty Rock Wilderness, and Burnt Balsam Knob. That's our whole itinerary."

Neena sidled up to her and pointed. "What are those?" Several different sets of handwriting were scrawled directly onto the splintered plywood.

5/20 *bear walked through Misty Rock campsite at 9:40* PM

6/2 *Meadow Ridge Cove 2x bears*

6-9 *saw one bear cross Misty Rock Creek*

6/17 *meadow ridge cove 1 bear 6 pm*

6/29 *one bear in Misty Rock Wilderness*

7-7 *Burnt Balsam 2 bears*

Josie's head wrenched away, trying to avoid absorbing the information. Primal anxiety swelled within. In her mind, a lumbering beast snuffled outside their flimsy tent. The hackles of its shadow rose. A ferocious claw slashed through the defenseless nylon, attacking with frenzied black eyes and snarling white teeth.

"No activity since July," Neena said. "See? They're already hibernating."

"We're so getting *Revenant*-ed."

"That was a movie."

"Based on a true story!"

"Okay, but it happened, like, two hundred years ago in Canada or Alaska or whatever. And he was attacked by a grizzly bear. No one gets hurt by black bears."

Actually, in this decade alone, ten people had been killed by black bears in North America. Josie had looked it up. None of them had been on this part of the continent, but still. In recent years, black bear traffic had increased significantly throughout Asheville. Heavy rains due to climate change meant it took longer for nuts and berries to ripen, which meant that bears were emerging from the woods in search of other food. Trash cans were gashed with claw marks. People were hospitalized after accidentally interrupting feasts. And then there was the man who had weaponized his own mountain bike to fend off an aggressive mama bear. That had happened here, inside this very forest. Where there were no cars or houses or buildings to provide protective shelter.

"Oh, shit." Neena punched Josie's arm. "Smokey Bear. How did we forget him? He's a park ranger. He saves lives. Think of them as helpful Smokeys."

But Josie didn't want to think about bears at all. She desperately wanted to *stop* thinking about them. She couldn't admit, not even to Neena, that *The Wizard of Oz* had frightened her as a child—not because of the Wicked Witch or her squadron of flying monkeys, but when Dorothy and her friends had chanted, "Lions and tigers and bears! Oh my!" as they'd skipped into the dark wood, they had introduced Josie to the concept of being eaten alive. Flesh ripping. Teeth gnashing. Watching your own meaty chunks be swallowed down the throat of another carnivorous mammal.

Lions . . .

Black panthers had long been part of state folklore, but they were as likely to be discovered as Bigfoot. Bobcats did live here, though they only attacked humans if they were sick or rabid. However, once upon a time, mountain lions had also lived here—and some believed they still did. Sightings of long-tailed cats with tawny-colored fur remained rampant among hunters, though experts claimed if they did exist, they were simply exotic pets that had been released. This didn't make Josie feel any better. A pet mountain lion was still a mountain lion.

. . . and tigers . . .

At least there weren't any tigers. Although Josie had once read that there were more tigers in captivity in the United States than in the wilds of Asia, a fact that distressed her on multiple counts.

. . . and bears!

But bears. There were definitely bears out here. *Oh my.*

Josie shifted to her mental checklist: *Keep the campsite clean. Make noise. Place everything that smells out of reach. Watch out for scat and tracks and rubbed tree bark. Urinate far away from the tent.* Her palms were clammy. She didn't want to do this. Why were they doing this?

"Where's your phone?" Neena asked. "We need to commemorate the moment." She nodded toward the other sign, the one beside the notice board. It was large and proud and distinctly American with its National Forest typeface and specific shade of brown.

WADE HARTE TRAILHEAD, it said. PISGAH NATIONAL FOREST.

Josie tugged the phone out from her jeans—her hip belt didn't have a handy pocket like Neena's—and they took dozens of selfies in front of the sign, hoping that at least one would make them look good. Giant smiles. Sunglasses on, sunglasses off. The screen blurred because Josie's glasses were prescription. To conserve the battery, she switched the phone to airplane mode, and then Neena stowed it in the top of Josie's pack so that it wouldn't dig into her thigh. It barely fit. Josie wondered if the weight would lighten as they consumed the food or if it would grow heavier with their exhaustion.

"Nothing to it but to do it," Neena said, quoting their least-favorite teacher because they liked reminding each other how awful he was.

"Keep calm and carry on," Josie said as they set off down the trail.

"Too blessed to be stressed."

"Oh God. Why do they all have to rhyme?"

Their banter continued as they rounded the first bend. Josie glanced back. The burbling river softened and then silenced. Neena's car disappeared.

The woods swallowed them whole.

ROBUST EVERGREENS TOWERED overhead and deciduous hardwoods preened, dappling the midday light. Rhododendrons spiraled with leathery leaves. Wildflowers dipped their heads in greeting. *Those*, smooth and red. *These*, frilly and white. A weedy vine tangled to form a wall of electric-orange blooms. It was a dramatic contrast from the tired vegetation that had edged the parking lot, yellowed by car exhaust and human presence. The inner forest was lush and vigorously alive. Even the air smelled better here, pristine with fresh oxygen and perfumed by rainy loam.

Neena would have been awed . . . if only her backpack wasn't trying to murder her.

The Wade Harte Trail had been challenging from the start. It began with a climb and then continued to a steeper climb. The ascent was unrelenting. Roots, rocks, and downed trees were scattered everywhere across the path, treacherous obstacles lying in wait to roll their ankles. It was exactly what Neena had expected but also somehow worse. Hunching and huffing beneath her pack, its straps dug nastily into her shoulders. No amount of adjusting them or cinching the belt helped. Her limbs dragged with unparalleled fatigue. They had been walking for eight minutes.

"Fuuuuuuuuuck," Neena said, for the fifth time.

"At least we're only doing half the trail. Can you imagine?"

"Who is Wade Harte, anyway?"

"No idea, but I read somewhere"—though neither girl had much life experience, they'd always read something, somewhere—"that hikers call this a mini-AT."

"A mini-what?"

"Appalachian Trail." Josie pronounced it correctly, like a Southerner. *Latch-un*, not *lay-shun*.

"Oh. Doesn't that run nearby? Or am I thinking of the Mountains-to-Sea Trail?"

"Both, I think."

Neena bragged. "Look at us, knowing stuff about hiking."

"We're hiking geniuses."

The girls were traipsing up Frazier Mountain, the tallest of several mountains that crested six thousand feet in these woods, but they weren't hiking to its peak. Thank God. They planned to ascend two-thirds of the way up the mountain before descending into a clearing called Deep Fork, where they would set up camp and spend the night. Measured from the parking lot, the elevation gain was over two thousand feet.

Due to the ascent, today's hike would be more physically challenging, but tomorrow's mileage would be more than double. In the morning, they would head into the Misty Rock Wilderness, which sounded like a location on a Tolkien map, and then eat lunch at Burnt Balsam Knob, which sounded like a penis that had been caught in a forest fire. After that, they'd turn around and come back, looping onto a different trail for scenic variation. Tomorrow night, they'd sleep somewhere back in the Misty Rock Wilderness before returning to the trailhead on Wednesday afternoon.

Round trip, the journey was nearly twenty miles. A through-hike on the Wade Harte was just over thirty—stretching from Frazier Mountain in the north to the town of Brevard in the south—but Neena and Josie had wanted this trip to be theirs, completely. They didn't want another person dropping them off at one end and picking them up at the other.

The trail would eventually cross through a protected wilderness area where signs and trail markers weren't allowed, but, so far, the path had been well-worn and easy to follow. Neena prided herself on a strong internal compass. Her parents, however, had also made them pack an actual compass, a printed trail map, and further printouts about the trail sections and water sources.

But mainly they were relying on technology. Their phones already had compass apps, and GPS was even easier.

Neena wobbled over another supine tree decomposing across the trail. Behind her, Josie's footsteps halted. "Did you look?" Josie asked.

"At what?"

"You should always look before stepping over a log. In case of snakes."

Neena shuffled around to face her, wielding a deadly stare.

"I know." Josie blushed as she peered over the log. "But seriously, timber rattlesnakes and copperheads. You need to be careful."

Neena wondered if their entire trip would be peppered with these lists of lethal fauna. She changed the subject to something far more pressing. "I need to pee."

Josie's response was exuberant. "Yes! I'm dying, but I was afraid to say something. I mean, if it weren't for the trees, we'd still be able to see your car."

The girls had "pre-hydrated"—they despised this word, cudgeled into the English language by coaches and jocks—by consuming a liter of water each on the road. Supposedly, this would give them a head start on fluid loss. Win had advised them to drink slowly, because chugging would make the liquid pass faster, but that didn't seem to have mattered. Their bladders were already bursting.

Neena unsnapped the sternum strap and hip belt, slid out, and gasped as the pack almost ripped her arms from their sockets. The pack thudded straight to the ground. She teetered with the drastic shift in her center of gravity.

Josie made a similar gasp and teeter.

"Okay," Neena said, massaging her shoulders. "We'll find a better way to do that." But the freedom was rapturous. They were like a sagging mule team lugging supplies into the Grand Canyon. Two liters of water per day, per person, was required, so they'd secured one-liter bottles to both sides of each pack, which they planned to refill along the way. Only luck had kept the bottles from cracking in the fall.

"Do you need the shovel?" Josie asked.

"Thankfully"—Neena shuddered—"not yet." Win had been remarkably unperturbed as he'd given them the instructions about defecating in the woods.

"Toilet paper or are you gonna air-dry?"

"We have to bury it if we use it, right?"

Josie scratched behind an ear. "Probably?"

They decided to air-dry.

Neena climbed uphill, off the path, and ducked behind a boulder—but not before first checking for venomous snakes. *Damn you, Josie.* Positioning herself so that the stream would travel downhill, Neena tugged her jeans and underwear down to her knees.

The forest canopy swayed overhead. The wind chilled her exposed flesh.

Josie piped up from behind a nearby conifer. "I read that this land used to be part of the Biltmore Estate, and the Vanderbilts were the ones who sold it to the Forest Service." The Biltmore was the largest privately owned house in the United States, and, at the time of its construction, the Vanderbilts were the country's wealthiest family thanks to the fortune they'd made in shipping and railroads. Now their house was Asheville's main tourist attraction. It looked like the *Downton Abbey* house on steroids. "Apparently, Pisgah was one of the first national forests in the east."

"How was this even theirs to sell? Surely, it belonged to the Cherokees." Neena's parents were Indian, but strangers often mistook this for American Indian, which, around here, meant Cherokee. Unless they presumed her family was Mexican. Which also happened to a ludicrous degree.

"Surely."

"What does 'Pisgah' even mean? It sounds so ugly. I used to think it was *Pig*-sah."

"I did, too," Josie said. "I think it's biblical."

Neena's squat was careful. Her legs trembled. Nature finally overtook performance anxiety, and she sighed with relief as the trickle turned into a gush. But when she waved her hips to shake off, a watery red droplet splashed onto her thigh. "Shit," she whispered.

"What?" Josie called out.

"When you're done, I need the toilet paper."

"Oh, you *have to shit*. I thought you saw something."

"No," Neena said. "I'm spotting."

"Oh! Shit."

Neena's period wasn't supposed to start for another week. Hopefully, this was as heavy as her flow would get. Foliage rustled, footsteps scuffled, and a pack unzipped. Josie hustled up the bank. "I have something better," she said. An arm materialized around the boulder holding out a puffy object in a rosy pink wrapper.

The sight instantly soothed Neena. "You're a gem."

"Be prepared," Josie said. "The Boy Scouts were talking about menstruation, right? I'm not looking," she added, shuffling backward until Neena could grab it.

Neena was grateful they subscribed to the same philosophy regarding privacy. While they didn't mind peeing beside each other in public stalls, neither wanted to be seen with her pants down. Their philosophies split, however, when it came to products. Though a real pad was far superior to folded toilet paper, Neena still felt as if she were wearing an adult diaper. But Josie's periods were lighter, and Neena knew tampons were uncomfortable for her—Josie said it was like hard-packing her vagina with dry cotton balls.

It was a lot to know about another girl, but Neena Chandrasekhar and Josie Gordon were as familiar with each other's cycles as they were with their own, having been best friends since freshman year.

They'd attended the same middle school but had only known each other by name. That changed one day when their Honors Biology teacher had removed his scuffed dress shoes to display an eleventh toe. While the other students scrambled from their lab chairs in a mad rush to gawk, Neena and Josie's disbelieving eyes had met across the room as if to say, *What does this have to do with dissecting fetal pigs?*

The funny and bizarre often kick-started great friendships.

Before they found each other, they'd had different best friends, but those attachments had fallen apart around the same time. As their exes rose into bigger crowds—Neena's to the cross-county team, Josie's to a group of girls who didn't *do* anything, but who were moderately more attractive—Neena and Josie became a new twosome. To this day, they still talked about Grace and Sarah the way others might pore over a painful romantic breakup. Because that's what it had felt like to lose the person who had once been each girl's *most important person*. The losses were devastating.

Though their bond had strengthened over being dumped, it was solidified by a shared sense of humor and passion for the same TV shows. Josie was the first classmate Neena had met who not only watched all the best current sitcoms, but all the old ones, too. They were willing to try anything from any country or decade. They loved good comedy with the fervor of televangelists. Josie didn't even mind whenever Neena insisted on listening to the commentary features, and it was within these tracks that Neena had begun to realize *people* were making these shows—*writers*, not just the actors and comedians in front of the camera. Neena wanted to be one of those people.

Her plan was to major in economics at USC, but to study film and television production on the side. Maybe, eventually, she could even convince her parents to let her double major. Because what she wanted more than anything was to be a showrunner someday—to write and sell a pilot and have her hand in every aspect of its production. And she was willing to work twice as hard as the other students, pursuing two careers at once, if it kept her parents happy.

They didn't hide that they would have rather she attend MIT, like her brother, Darshan, or at least—*at least*—one of the Ivy Leagues. It embarrassed Neena that her parents fell into this cliché. Briefly, she had even considered disguising her intentions, but she wasn't the type of teenager who lied to her parents. And, perhaps because of this honesty, they had reluctantly given their support.

Her father had instilled a love of comedy in Neena, but this time it was her mother who had argued on Neena's behalf. *What did you expect, filling her head with Mindy Kaling and that* Fleabag *woman, day after day?* Ma had said to him, her stacked bangles jangling with each emotional finger jab. And Neena had been granted permission to study film production as long as it didn't interfere with her economics classes.

Despite this, she was afraid. Soon she would be dropped off in America's second-most-populous city, and she would be alone. No Ma and Baba. No Josie. She was scared to move somewhere so unfamiliar, and she was scared of not being able to make any new friends. People in LA were undeniably more sophisticated and worldly, and she worried that she would appear plain and backwoods by comparison. That the other students would all have better clothes than her, better skin, better hair.

But, most of all, Neena was afraid of failure. Of not being good enough and getting stuck in the economics department forever. Or maybe being *just* good enough to find employment someday as a writer's assistant, but never good enough to climb any higher.

She also feared that if she admitted any of this to her parents, they would change their minds about letting her go. And whenever she broached the topic with Josie, Josie quickly shut it down with tight-lipped petulance. Because even though everything felt scary, she knew it was also exciting. One day, it would even feel normal.

Meanwhile, Josie would still be living in this version of normal. The depressed mother, the filthy house. It was why Neena kept trying—to buoy Josie's mood, to keep her active and *doing*. Not only had this trip been Neena's idea, but she'd also had to reach for her pack first. Step onto the trail first. Hell, she'd even had to announce her intention to pee first.

As Neena zipped up her pants, Josie's gaze remained tactfully averted. They trudged back down the bank, and then Neena tucked the empty pink wrapper into her top pouch. All trash had to be carried out of the forest.

Neither girl wanted to struggle into her pack again.

"Do we really need food? Or water? Or shelter?" Neena asked.

Josie squinched her nose in concentration. "There's a correct way to do this. I know it. We just have to remember."

Neena stood aside, idle and useless, while Josie grunted through several flawed attempts. But then, miraculously, she hoisted her pack onto a knee, turned her upper body sideways, slipped the pack onto one shoulder and then efficiently onto the other.

"How'd you do that?" Neena asked, despite witnessing the marvel.

Josie beamed. The thirty-something pounds of discomfort only mildly tarnished her smile. "Told you it had something to do with the knees."

She guided Neena into the lavender pack, and they basked in newfound confidence. Their endorphins were finally kicking in. The righteous pleasure of their hard work was certain to propel them up the rest of the mountainside.

It wasn't to be. Once again, the trail was instantly grueling. Nonstop switchbacks kept the incline constant and demanding. Twenty feet up from their resting place, Neena gasped—bug-eyed and wretchedly out of shape. Her clothes, muddied from earlier in the parking lot, were drenched with sweat. No doubt this trip would be a disaster, but, even so, Neena was still hoping for a *lighthearted* disaster. At the very least, this would make a funny story she could tell at parties. Assuming she ever started going to parties. Her borrowed boots slipped on a tottering rock. Her heart catapulted in panic.

"Are you okay?" Josie asked behind her.

Neena steadied herself and held up a hand that meant, *Yes, too breathless to speak.*

As her best friend literally walked her first mile in somebody else's shoes, Josie tromped forward in her own. Her sturdy hiking shoes, more like sneakers than boots, had only been worn twice, including today. They had been preserved in closet dust ever since her mother, in one of her sporadic attempts to *be* a mother, decided they needed to get out of the house. She had surprised Josie with a name-brand pair, purchased off the clearance rack at DSW. They had driven out of the city to hike, but, after only a few steps toward Looking Glass Rock, her mother had crumpled into the dirt. Inconsolable. Win had to pick them up because Josie was afraid to drive. Later, she learned the trail had been one of her father's regular haunts. Now these mountains felt haunted in a different way.

The untested shoes pinched her toes and rubbed her heels. Josie comforted herself by remembering the Band-Aids. If necessary, they could be slapped over any blisters later tonight. She had packed more than enough for three days.

The girls were returning home on Wednesday because Thursday was Josie's freshman orientation. Unlike Neena, Josie had no idea what she wanted to study. She wasn't excited about college. It felt like being sentenced to four more years of high school. Though her situation wasn't uncommon—most teenagers didn't know what they wanted to do with their lives—it was impossible not to compare herself to her best friend, and it was inevitable that she had interpreted this uncertainty as a personal shortcoming.

But, secretly, Josie wondered if this trip was about to change everything. This wasn't as outlandish as it sounded. It wasn't unreasonable to hope that her passion might turn out to be the same one as the rest of her family. Surely the outdoors coursed through her blood, too; she'd only been denied the opportunity to discover it. Josie imagined these mountains becoming her sanctuary. Envisioned herself as such a natural that she would be mystically compelled to through-hike the Appalachian Trail, like in *A Walk in the Woods*, or the Pacific Crest Trail, like in *Wild*. Would this trip be the turning point when she stopped envying everyone else's adventures and started having her own?

The trail dipped unexpectedly. Josie fell.

Neena spun around at the sharp cry. "Oh my God. Are you okay?"

The pack was so huge that the spill didn't hurt. Josie landed on padding. But the drop had startled her, and unwanted tears sprung to her eyes. "I'm fine. I'm fine." She laughed to disguise her embarrassment. *Of course I'm the one who can't catch herself*, she thought, conveniently forgetting Neena's incident in the parking lot. Her mind was skilled at self-sabotage. "Uh, remind me again why we're here?"

"Because we're becoming one with nature. We're soaking in Gaia's bounty! And tonight, we'll sleep beneath the stars like . . . sumptuous pagan goddesses."

"This backpack," Josie said as Neena helped her stand, "does make me feel mega Zen."

Neena burst into laughter. Her outrageous cackle had been the soundtrack to their entire friendship. Normally, it was Josie's favorite music. But in her humiliation, it grated.

The path worn into the mountain was only one person wide, and, as always, Josie fell in line behind Neena. An ancient oak surveilled them from the woodsy depths. The unusual tree was stripped bare—struck by lightning or disease, Josie couldn't tell. A single arthritic branch remained, pointing like a crooked arm and knobby forefinger back the way they came. A strange revulsion drifted over her.

"Maybe it's just because hiking is terrible," she said, "but doesn't it look like that tree is telling us to go back?"

"That tree is an asshole," Neena said.

The forest returned to tranquility. Strenuous, laborious tranquility. Panting and puffing and chattering like wheezy songbirds, the girls crossed through a velveteen outcrop of mossy green boulders. Ferns carpeted the shady groves. Tumbling cascades of a nearby stream, present but unseen, were amplified throughout the canopy.

The combination of sublime beauty and severe exhaustion began to soften Josie's fatalism. A tenuous but arresting sense of empowerment manifested in its place, and, although she didn't realize it, the same sensation was happening inside Neena. It was their first taste of adulthood. A preview of what was to be forever. They were here without parents, teachers, or supervisors. They were going to feed themselves and build their own shelter, and no one could tell them where to go or what to do.

Gnawing disquiet gradually slowed Josie's pace. Her instincts perceived the subtle shifts in the trees before her ears understood: shuffling leaves and crunching dead wood.

She stopped. Stiffened.

The faint noises grew more distinct. Neena halted. She glanced back at Josie, and the girls exchanged mirrored expressions of wide-eyed alarm.

Josie's nerves pulsated. *Bear.*

A man's timbre rumbled down the mountainside. But as Josie slackened with relief, Neena compressed with fear. The voice was heading toward them, broadening and becoming cavernous. The southern half of the trail was often used for day hikes because it was easily accessible from the parkway, but the northern half, their half, was less traveled. More isolated. It wasn't that Neena hadn't expected to run into anybody out here, but the sudden approach of an unknown man cowed her. She felt disarmed in the most literal sense—like his presence stripped away any weapons she thought she'd had.

The voice grew louder.

Neena couldn't pick out any of his words, only his tone. The boom was commanding and confident. Almost sardonic. It reduced her back into a child.

"I'm sure it's fine," Josie said, although doubt had already crept in. "He's probably someone like Win."

Immobilized by dread, Neena didn't respond. Humans were far more dangerous than bears. She knew plenty of stories about hikers who had disappeared, plucked off the earth by their own careless mishaps . . . or by other hikers.

"I used to think that if I said hello to somebody," the voice said, "and they didn't respond . . ."

Josie gestured toward the trees. Neena nodded but then shook her head. It's what they *should* have done—hidden—but the voice was too close now. They were out of time. Neena strained to listen for the sounds of a woman, hoping he wasn't talking to another man. Or worse, himself. But *was* that worse? Would she rather run into two men or one possibly deranged man?

". . . it meant I was a ghost," the voice finished.

He emerged into view. Neena shuddered from the release of tension. His companion was a girl, and he wasn't even a man. They were teenagers, maybe twenty at the oldest. The atmosphere brightened. The trees shook out their nervous leaves.

"I'd love to see a ghost," the girl said.

"But that's the problem," the boy said. "Nobody *could* see me."

The two jumped as they rounded the switchback, startled to discover Neena and Josie on the other side. "Oh! We didn't see you," the girl said, which made her laugh. An accidental callback. They both looked at ease, the type of people who hiked difficult trails and made their own gorp. Neither wore a backpacking pack, but the boy had an enviably small daypack. He was white, and the girl's features were East Asian. Her hair was pinned up in a thick crown braid. A Heidi milkmaid braid.

"I like your hair," Josie said. Her own strawberry blonde locks were in two long plaits—a much more simple style. Josie usually wore her hair loose or in a ponytail, and Neena suspected she'd done the braids to look outdoorsy. It was cute, though. Sweet. Neena's black hair was snipped into a blunt bob, too short to do anything but hang.

Heidi's smile grew. "Thanks."

Normally, this was when the two parties would nod and move along, but a conversation had already been started. It seemed polite to talk a little bit longer.

"Are you headed to the summit?" the boy asked. He was tall and strapping, and his irises sparkled in a warm chestnut brown. The whole package reminded Neena of Win. A long time ago, she'd had a crush on Win. If she was being honest, she still did, though not in any serious way. Just in the way that when he was around, he was pleasing to look at. Perhaps for this reason, Neena felt tongue-tied.

"No," Josie said. "We're doing the Wade Harte."

Neena was glad when Josie didn't clarify they were only doing part of the Wade Harte, and equally glad that the couple didn't comment about how defeated they already looked. These two must have arrived at the crack of dawn to have already summited and be on their way back down. Neena felt envious that their torture was almost over.

Concern flickered across the boy's face. "You aren't staying in Deep Fork tonight, are you?"

"Yeah." Josie frowned. "Why?"

"Oh man. You haven't heard?" When the girls gave him a puzzled look, he glanced at Heidi. Her eyes flashed a warning at him.

"Heard what?" Josie asked.

"No, nothing. It's fine. It's just . . ." The boy appeared torn between regret at bringing it up and a pressing need to continue.

Unconsciously, Neena leaned in. "Weird stuff happens there," he finished. "Be careful, is all I'm saying."

"What kind of weird stuff?" she asked. Voice rediscovered.

"Unexplained noises in the night. Items stolen from tents."

Neena's pulse thumped.

"A buddy of mine once swore that someone took a picture of him while he was sleeping." As the boy gripped the straps of his backpack, his eyes darted into the woods behind them. "He'd been out here hiking solo, and he didn't find it on his phone until he got home. I would have thought he was messing with me, except his hands were shaking when he showed me the picture. He looked dead asleep in it . . . I don't know." His cadence was changing, dropping into a redneck lilt. "Some folks say when the mist creeps in after midnight, there's a man who likes to play tricks on campers—"

Heidi thwacked him across the chest. "He's joking," she said as he collapsed into laughter. "I'm sorry. My boyfriend has a horrible sense of humor." And then to him, "God, you almost had me, too. You're such a dick." But she grinned as she scolded him.

"Sorry," he said to Neena. "I couldn't resist."

The hot shame of gullibility flared inside her. But then she was laughing, too. She admired his boldness and showmanship. Josie glanced at her, less amused, as their bodies all shifted and resumed walking—interaction complete.

"Safe travels," Heidi called from behind them.

"Lock your tent flaps," the boy said.

As soon as they were out of earshot, Josie muttered, "That was odd."

"I liked him. I thought it was funny."

"Really?" Josie's brow wrinkled. "He reminded me of my brother."

Neena was grateful that her dark brown skin could hide a blush. "Speaking of photos," she said, backpedaling, and they took another series of selfies to mark their progress. This time, their screened reflections were disheveled. Distant. And when Neena tucked her phone away again, her hand felt naked. Even in a relaxed state, her fingers were still gripped as if they were holding a rectangle. Nurture overtaking nature. The compulsion arose to Google if other people had this problem, too, but she knew she couldn't.

For a moment, Neena wished they could turn around and follow the couple out. She wanted to slump in her car and lose herself in the comfort of her phone. But Josie was behind her, as always, and the thought of abandoning this trip that she herself had insisted on made her feel guilty. And then resentful for feeling guilty.

The girls slogged deeper into the lonesome infinity of forest.

THEY KEPT PLODDING, kept resting. The humid air became moist rather than fresh, and the water they drank evaporated into sweat that attracted hovering clouds of gnats. Stagnant pockets of the unseen stream bred and released mosquitos. Their arms itched with round, angry bites. Despite their being on a mountainside, there were no views. No sweeping vistas. The trees and rhododendrons enclosed them in a cramped realm.

Uneasiness settled underneath Josie's skin. It was as if something was watching them from behind the trees, always ducking out of sight before she could name it. When the stream finally did reveal itself, the girls crossed it, and then they crossed it again a half hour later. Sometime after, a small—almost trivial—grassy clearing appeared, which Josie guessed was an empty campsite . . . which made her realize she wasn't even positive what a campsite was *supposed* to look like.

Neena didn't seem concerned. "I'm sure it'll be obvious later."

They trekked beside a third prong of the stream, one that was wider and prettier, and declared themselves overdue for their first real break with sitting. Glorious, glorious sitting. Proud of their cleverness, the girls shed their packs by backing up and releasing them onto waist-high boulders.

Neena inhaled with pleasure. The water warbled in an agreeable manner. "Is a creek the same thing as a stream? Or do you think there's a scientific difference?"

"I don't know." Josie removed her phone from its zippered prison. A comforting rush swept over her hand, which had been tingling with emptiness since the trailhead. "I'll look it up— Oh."

Neena laughed once through her nose. "I keep doing that, too."

"How did anyone know anything before the internet?"

"Our parents were idiots."

"Or," Josie said, "were they smarter because they actually had to retain information?"

"No."

"Your parents, maybe."

"No," Neena repeated. "We're smarter because we figured out a way where we don't *have* to."

"We are so smart to have figured that out."

"We should figure out," Neena said, "where we packed the snacks."

The snacks were near the top of Josie's pack, where she had carefully separated out this afternoon's allocation—two single-serving bags of chips and a sandwich-size Ziploc of dried apricots—from the rest of their food. The chips were Cheetos and Nacho Cheese Doritos because the girls believed in chips that stained their fingertips orange. It was only a coincidence that the fruit was orange, too.

Josie had been in charge of snacks because she had the snack house. Neena had the meal house. When Josie's father was alive, her parents had bought from bulk bins and had cooked giant pots of organic comfort food. Naturally, Josie had developed a taste for junk. Now she missed the rice and beans. Her mother shopped only sporadically, and the groceries were haphazard, as if she'd forgotten the purpose of shopping. Though she still patronized the same stores as before, everything became convenient to consume. Josie's kitchen cabinets were scattered with nuts and bananas and granola—squirrel food—while an under-the-bed tub in her bedroom was stuffed with Frito-Lay variety packs and Campbell's soup and Top Ramen, purchased with her Kmart employee discount.

The girls washed their hands with globs of sanitizer and settled onto a flat boulder that touched the stream. Unlike the other rocks, which wore fuzzy sweaters of verdant moss, this rock was bare and had perfect indentations for two human bottoms. Trees dipped their exposed roots into the water as it flowed and bubbled past. The girls' matching blue stones of lapis lazuli shimmered in the refracted light, but Josie's swollen finger throbbed around her ring. Her aching feet groaned in her shoes.

"This part, I understand," Neena said. "This part where I'm sitting."

"The whole thing should be this part."

"Remember when we thought camping—staying in *one place* for *three whole days*—would be boring?"

Josie loosened her laces. "We were so naive. Staying in one place is the best."

They divvied up the bounty by mixing the chips half-and-half. The apricots were placed between them. To Josie, dried fruit tasted like sadness and neglect, but today it was as delicious as candy because it gave her another reason not to move.

Her first bottle of water was already a third empty, so she took prudent sips, luxuriating as it swelled and replenished her cells. She and Neena would refill their bottles at a spring near the campsite tonight. Neither wanted to refill now because they didn't want to carry the extra weight. Neena downed the rest of her first bottle. Recklessly, she unscrewed the lid off her second and began to chug.

"Hey!" Josie stopped her. "Save some for later."

"I am."

"I know, but . . . save some *extra*. For *in case*."

"In case of what?"

"Anything," Josie said.

"You are such a mom," Neena said, thinking of her own mother and realizing belatedly that she'd made the slam worse. She cringed but didn't apologize. She was embarrassed, but she also worried that acknowledging the subject might hurt Josie further. Unlike Josie's mom, Neena's was constantly butting in with her concerns, thoughts, and opinions. It was maddening, but Neena knew enough to be grateful.

Ma was the only person besides Josie who texted her regularly. Though she worked considerable hours as a neurologist, she was always available by phone. This afternoon was already the longest they'd gone without talking in . . . who knew how many years. Forever. This trip was a trial run for their upcoming separation. Except, even then, they would still be texting and FaceTiming.

Neena glossed over her blunder by stretching out on the rock. "Oh my God." Her tormented muscles whimpered in relief. "Lying down is even better. You have to try this."

"I'll never get up if I lie down," Josie said as she lowered herself.

They ate on their backs like otters, orange crumbs littering their bellies and chests, pacified by the babbling stream and its soft, cooling aroma. Neena sniffed the breeze. The scent was rich with minerals. Compared to Josie, Neena was always more aware of her breath.

Her asthma required two puffs in the morning and two at night on a steroid inhaler, and she had a rescue inhaler for when she was sick or before exercise. She'd used the rescue inhaler on the drive here, so her lungs were okay. Of greater concern were the bruises she felt blossoming below her shoulder blades.

Her head turned toward Josie. "Oh no. Are you a little pink?"

Josie bolted upright, pressing her thumb into her forearm. A white print was left behind. Swearing, she scuttled off the rock and fumbled through her pack. Her skin was fair and freckled and already slathered in SPF.

"Maybe it's just warm from the exercise," Neena said.

"No," Josie said, reapplying. "I'm definitely burning."

The chemical tang of sunscreen mixed into the air. Neena examined the bottle without picking it up because she didn't want to get her hands greasy. "A *hundred*?"

Josie snorted. "SPF 100+. Don't forget the 'plus'—it's important."

Neena shook her head when Josie offered the bottle. She was also already wearing some, and the whole trail had been in the shade. She was fine. Josie packed up the sunscreen along with their empty food bags. The sight made Neena flinch. "My hips hurt," she said. "And my back." *We don't have to leave now, do we?*

"Mine too," Josie said. "And my feet." *Hell no.*

They watched the water. After a few minutes, Josie began to wander and collect stones. Neena observed as Josie stacked the pile, biggest to littlest, into a satisfying decorative cairn. She croaked to her feet and joined in. Selecting, balancing. The process was both meditative and addictive, like solving a puzzle. Soon the girls had constructed an entire village out of stacked stone—a hamlet overlooking the sea. They took dozens of photographs from every angle. Neena admired their sprawling creation with pride.

"Godzilla time." Josie reached out to topple the stacks.

Neena thrust out both hands to stop her. "What are you doing?"

"Leave No Trace." When Neena didn't respond, Josie went on. "Leave No Trace? It's a thing. Like, an ethical code of honor. You've really never heard of it?"

Neena had not.

"It means that whatever you bring into nature, you carry out. It doesn't only apply to garbage. You're supposed to leave everything the way you found it. So, if we let these stones stand, we'd be leaving behind proof of human impact. It'd be like carving our names into a tree. Or throwing the Doritos bag into the ferns."

"But . . ." Neena hesitated. Wondering if this made her a lesser person. "What if I *like* the idea of leaving something behind?"

"Then you'd be ruining the view for the next people who sat here."

Josie's pronouncement felt harsh—that their pretty stone towers could ruin anybody's view.

"Imagine if everybody who sat here left one of these," she continued. "This place would be nothing *but* stacked stones. It'd be the same as a crowd of people."

"Okay," Neena said, "so the next hiker who sits here gets peeved and knocks them down. Who cares? Just . . . let's not do it ourselves."

"We're not leaving them."

"Why not?"

"Because I just said!"

There was a burst of irritated silence. Once again, it was like being trapped in a loop with her mother. Neena hated feeling like a child.

"Fine," Neena said. Childishly. "Whatever."

Resisting the urge to add that moving rocks around could also contribute to erosion, Josie tried to spin the ring on her index finger, a nervous habit. The ring didn't budge. Her fingers had fattened into sausages, swollen from hanging at her sides during the hike.

"How about we leave one?" she finally said. "This one." She

pointed to Neena's tallest cairn. "I like the round stone on top. It seems like it should roll away, but it doesn't."

Neena shrugged.

Josie sighed. But correctly interpreting the ennui as acceptance, she dismantled the nearest tower. The rocks tumbled to the earth and splooshed into the water.

Neena joined in the demolition until they were all gone except the one. "You sure?" she asked, rearing back to kick it.

"Don't," Josie said.

"I wasn't going to," Neena lied. She glanced at her phone, which was still in her hand. "*Shit*. It's a quarter till five."

Josie was equally startled. "What?"

The girls had read that the average backpacker could hike two miles per hour, including breaks, so they'd lowered their own estimation to one and a half. This meant that with three hours of hiking—plenty of padding for their 4.2-mile day—they would arrive at their destination around 5:45 p.m., which would give them three additional hours to set up camp, make dinner, and hang out before it got dark. Sunset was at 8:15, but Win said they'd have light on the mountain for at least an additional half hour.

Neena flushed with stress. "I knew we were behind schedule, but . . . How many miles have we hiked so far?"

"Almost two," Josie said.

Neena erupted. "Not even half?" She did the math, calculating from the time they'd left the trailhead. "We're traveling less than a mile per hour." Panic made her turn on Josie again. "You've had your phone out since we stopped here. Why didn't you notice how slowly we were traveling?"

"So have you! Why didn't *you* notice?"

Neena didn't like the accusation directed back onto her. It was neither of their faults. Or they were both at fault. Whatever. "Okay," she said, trying to convince herself as much as Josie. "We're okay. We'll be fine." True, they would no longer have any time to relax at the campsite, but they could still easily make it there before dark. Neena squirmed at the thought of *not* making it before dark.

"Yeah." Josie sounded even less assured as they strapped into their packs. "We'll just walk a little faster."

Their spirits picked up in earnest as, at long last, the elevation took a dip. Unfortunately, this downhill respite was only a blink before the trail resumed its murderous ascent. The girls tunneled upward through a dense tract of mountain laurel. Branches on either side of the path interlocked overhead, creating a human-size passageway that canopied them in flora. Green sunlight strained through the leaves.

Time marched forward as their pace slowed down. The tunnel was endless and claustrophobic. Out of breath, they had no choice but to take frequent breaks. After an hour—around the time they had originally planned to reach their campsite—the climb intensified. The incline grew hellishly steep. The terrain became rockier.

It felt more precarious, which forced their steps to be more cautious.

Another hour passed. Despite the perspiration and heat and suffering, Neena felt the temperature begin to drop. A warning of the night to come. They'd planned for three hours at camp before nightfall, but now they were looking at half that.

Their salvation would arrive in the form of a spring, which would also be their water source for the night. Shortly after the spring, the path would fork—the trail to Frazier Mountain's summit on one side, the Wade Harte Trail on the other. Their instructions were to take a right, and then the Deep Fork campsite would be immediately ahead. But as Neena peeked through a rare break in the tangled thicket, the only thing above them was more trail.

Josie's phone had been lodged permanently in hand since the stream, monitoring their movements, a single dot blinking eastbound across a digitized landscape. Neena had pretended not to notice how often Josie checked their progress, despite the path being well trod. Now she wondered if they had both missed something. What if they'd already passed the spring and the fork? The spring was supposed to be small but reliable. But what if it had dried up? Or what if the fork wasn't an obvious split? Even more troubling, if the spring *had* dried up, did that mean they would have to trek all the way back down to the stream to refill? Or could they keep hiking until the next source tomorrow?

Restlessly, they fiddled with the stays and sternum straps—open, closed, up, down—shifting to distribute the weight to their hips and elsewhere—but any relief was temporary.

"Try this," Neena said. With deliberate and mindful footfalls, the earth lent support from beneath. "Walking with a slow roll helps. A little," she added.

"I'm. Already. Doing that."

Neena circled around at the unexpected growl in Josie's throat.

Josie's cheeks were crimson. "Sorry," she grumbled. "These shoes. I don't know how I'm supposed to wear them for two more days."

"We've gotta be close. What does your phone say?"

"I don't know. It says we're in *green*."

Neena grabbed the map. The dot showed them in the correct area of forest, yet . . . how could they be in the right place, on a straightforward trail, and still feel lost?

Josie swore.

"Calm down," Neena said, instantly regretting it. She handed back the phone. "I'm sure the spring is just ahead."

Calm down? Josie could throttle Neena. The gnarled laurel branches twisted all around them. Her skin was filthy and disgusting,

and her braids had frizzed loose. She wasn't even walking anymore—
she was hobbling in singular steps. One hobble. Then another. Each
brutal motion was a betrayal, her blisters begging her to stop.

"God, I'm starving," Neena whined.

Hunger clawed at Josie, too. A faerie feast shimmered ahead of
her, an absurdly long table piled high with silver platters of golden-
cooked geese, fruits and breads and butters, cheeses and cakes, tu-
reens of soup and goblets of wine.

Suddenly, Neena stumbled backward to a halt. "Oh, holy—"

Josie almost smashed into her, ripped from dreamland into reality: tufts of mottled fur and blood and viscera, festering black flies
and squiggling yellow maggots.

"Ugh." This was muffled by Neena's arm, which covered her
mouth and nose.

The smell was horrendous. Josie shielded her airways but couldn't
pry away her gaze. A white-tailed deer lay a few feet off trail, its unmoving frame crushing the thick brush. Its eye sockets had been
pecked clean, and its muscles were skinny and emaciated. It looked
as if it had died of starvation. Scavengers had ripped open the meager carcass, plundering it to expose a grotesque pinwheel of color.
Pinks and purples and browns, everything tinged with gray death.
Brushed with venous scarlet.

The girls moved along, shaken, but the repulsive stench lingered.
Exhaustion plummeted their tanks back to empty. They straggled
onward until, at last, Neena crested another slope. "The spring," she
said. "I see it! This has to be it."

Water was trickling out of a white PVC pipe that jutted from the
earth. Josie had no idea how the system worked, and the spring was
minimal and low-flowing, but the water was clear. And it existed. She
wanted to weep.

The girls gave feeble hurrahs and exchanged a weak high five.

"Do we refill now?" Neena asked.

Josie's thoughts unclouded enough to form a plan. "Let's find the campsite first, so we can shed our packs."

"Good call. Yes." Neena mumbled it like a zombie. "Shed first. Then filter."

The ground leveled out after the next switchback, and the path forked. The girls released another wilted whoop. Ninety minutes of light remained. Setting up camp would be a hustle—and they were in no condition to hustle—but they were here. They could do it.

Following the Wade Harte to the right, the girls expected to find the Deep Fork clearing after the turn. Instead, they stared into an abyss of more tunnel.

"I guess the clearing isn't *immediately* after the fork?" Neena said.

Josie bit her lip and glanced back behind them. Unsure.

"It's probably just up here." Neena plodded forward with a drained sigh. "I'll keep going, if you want to stay."

But Josie followed. "We're not separating."

Secretly, Neena was relieved. As daylight sank into twilight, she didn't want to be alone, either. The darkness itself didn't frighten her; it was what the darkness concealed. Her brain liked to play tricks. Create specters. She didn't believe in the supernatural, but she did believe in hidden men. Murderers peering in through windows, rapists waiting underneath beds, kidnappers crouched behind closet doors.

When she was young, her brother had turned off the lights while she was fetching a hula hoop from the basement. He'd locked the door and ignored her cries for help, finding her terror to be hilarious. Ma had discovered her an hour later, catatonic on the top step. Darshan wasn't a monster anymore—he was kind and thoughtful, as far from monstrous as possible—but his joke had done permanent damage.

The girls hiked in silence on flat but uneven ground. As the distance from the fork grew, so did Neena's apprehension. "Should we turn around? Try the other path?"

"Win definitely said it was the right fork," Josie said. But she pulled out the printed instructions from Neena's top pouch to confirm. "Yeah. It says right."

"Maybe he remembered wrong. We should have seen the clearing by now."

"He's not wrong," Josie snapped.

The girls stewed in frustrated nervousness. From the forested depths, an owl hooted at the encroaching night.

"Well?" Neena said. "What do you want to do?"

Retracing their steps, they tried the left fork but encountered another compact tunnel. The path was steep and craggy, and, after a few minutes of arduous upward trekking, there was still no clearing. No space anywhere for a tent. The pitch rose in Josie's voice. "Where are we supposed to sleep? We only have an hour of light left."

"I guess we could stretch out our sleeping bags on the trail?"

"On the *trail*? Without a tent?"

"I don't know! I don't want to do that, either." Neena gestured, harassed, in the direction they'd come from, signaling for Josie to turn around.

"You don't think we should look any further up here?" Josie asked.

"I don't know." Neena repeated it, because it was the only true thing. She would have screamed it, if she had the energy. "Do you?"

Josie stared up the trail. Her gaze darkened with unseeing. "Shit," she whispered and then stomped back down.

Neena followed close behind, bumping and dragging her body. She nearly crashed into Josie when Josie stopped abruptly at the fork.

"Now what?" Josie asked.

"Now what *what*?"

"Should we try the other way again? Maybe we didn't walk far enough."

"I still think we should set up camp here at the fork, where there's the most room." Neena imagined them trapped, unprepared, on the trail—pointy black treetops silhouetting themselves against an obsidian sky. "We're running out of time."

"I *know* we're running out of time." Josie shed her pack and scurried up the right path without a goodbye, no longer concerned about being alone. The excruciating rub of inflexible shoes against inflamed flesh fueled her indignation. Neena didn't understand how serious this was. She never took anything seriously.

"Josie," Neena shouted. "Josie!"

"What?"

"Josie!"

As Josie skittered down the mountain, her glasses slid down her nose. She shoved them back up. *"What?"* The question shook with a fury that dissolved the instant she saw.

Neena was holding aside a willowy vine as if it were a theater curtain. The new growth had concealed a third path.

NARROW AND FOOTWORN, the path opened up to a clearing, which was secluded from the main trail inside a dense grove of pine trees. Empty campsites dotted the forest floor. Josie had imagined that Deep Fork would unfurl to reveal a panorama of wide sky and azure mountains. But the clearing remained enclosed. The gap was pretty, at least. Cozy. She stumbled across a blanket of spongy pine needles, her swollen feet already shutting down in anticipation of rest.

"So, the right turn should have been immediately at the fork," Neena was saying. "Instead of taking the right fork and *then* seeing the clearing."

Both girls felt less dumb. Anyone could have made the mistake. The sky hovered on the rim of darkness. Across the gentle slope, seven or eight possibilities spread out before them—flat pockets of uninhabited space, each containing a telltale circle of charred rocks. At the top of the embankment, like a beacon or warning for ships, perched a bright yellow-gold tent. The girls stared at it. The campsite was silent and motionless.

"They're probably still out day hiking," Josie said.

"Or already asleep."

Josie fake-sobbed. "Sleep."

"You know"—Neena glanced again at the yellow-gold disturbance—"if we stay here, we can stop walking."

Josie intuited the rest: *And we can keep our distance from the strangers.* Her pack hit the ground with the weight of a corpse. "Sold."

Neena's pack followed. "Thank God, I don't have to carry that beast again until tomorrow."

Neither girl made an effort to move. Their arms hung flaccid at their sides.

"Refill our water now," Neena asked, "or wait until morning? I'm thinking . . . wait."

Josie's expression hardened into a discouraged scowl. "We *should* do it now, but it's already so dark. And there's so much left to do."

"Try taking off your sunglasses," Neena said.

The sky eased from an ominous dusk into a manageable twilight. Normally, Josie would have laughed, but she was cranky and didn't want to give Neena the satisfaction of being right. "I still think we should wait," she said, wincing onto her knees to rifle through her pack. Travel-size toiletries hurtled to the ground like missiles. "We have less than an hour, and we still have to pitch the tent, start the fire, cook dinner—"

"I wanted to wait, too. I'm not arguing with you." Neena dodged a flattened roll of toilet paper. "Careful."

Locating the case, Josie made the exchange for her regular glasses. The case snapped its impatient jaws shut. As the world sharpened into focus, her anxieties continued in a pile-on. "Hey, did we ever figure out if we're even allowed to have a fire here?" she asked. A campfire would be forbidden the following night in the Misty Rock

Wilderness, but Josie hadn't been able to find any rules about Frazier Mountain.

Neena pointed at the nearby circle of rocks. "All the sites have one of these."

"Yeah, but they aren't using theirs." Josie gestured to the tent uphill. "Just because campers have done it before, doesn't make it legal."

"Come on, I've never made a fire. It'll complete the experience."

Josie hesitated. Weakened. Caved. "Fine. But if they yell at us, you're the one who has to apologize."

"They're not going to *yell* at us."

Unlike her best friend, Josie was always worried about making other people mad or upset or disappointed. She suppressed it now for the semblance of peace. "Well, if we're building a fire, then there's definitely not enough time for the water—"

"Do you have enough for dinner? For both of us, I mean. I'm pretty low."

Josie still had a full liter of water left. Examining Neena's bottles, she was dismayed to discover that Neena only had a quarter of a liter. She couldn't hold back a sigh. "That's why I told you to go easy earlier."

"Yeah, but we were supposed to have three hours to hang out tonight."

"Well." Josie sighed again. "As long as you're careful, I probably have enough for the both of us."

A moment of testy silence swept over the woods. Then Neena stalked away.

"Where are you going?"

Neena called out without turning around. "To collect sticks for the fire."

"We need to set up the tent first!"

Neena stamped back, grumbling under her breath.

"We've only done it once before." Josie was exasperated. "It would be really hard to put together in the dark."

"Fine. Where is it?"

"It's in my pack, remember?" Josie unzipped her main compartment and yanked out more supplies—first-aid kit, clothing, cook kit, camp chair. The tent was near the bottom, on top of her sleeping bag. Fifteen disgruntled minutes later, they had interlocked the poles and raised the tent, but the process went faster than expected. The girls stared at their red dome, awash with achievement. And then Neena started to wander away.

"We're not done," Josie called after her.

"What?"

"The rainfly." At Neena's blank response, she added, "The part that goes on top of the tent."

Neena appraised the clouds through the pines. "It's not going to rain."

"The weather can change rapidly. All of our shit would get wet."

Neena stomped back, which nettled Josie. It implied that Josie was being a nag, and she was sick of being treated like one. Rained-out gear would ruin their entire trip. And who gave Neena exclusive rights to being miserable? All Josie wanted was to take off her shoes and surrender to the night, but there was work to be done.

The girls pieced together the extra poles and joints and fabric and attached the rainfly over the main dome. Before Neena could think about disappearing again, Josie reminded her that they needed to put together the chairs, too.

"Can't we do that later?" Neena asked.

"No. Let's get it over with."

Josie dumped her chair parts from their pouch as Neena rooted through her pack for her own. Win's girlfriend, Meegan, had purchased the matching pair for his last birthday, but Win had discouraged the girls from bringing both because of the added weight. "One of you can sit on the bear canister," he'd argued. The plastic barrel was approximately the same height as a chair.

Neither girl viewed this as acceptable.

The canister flew out of Neena's pack, along with socks and shirts, a compact stove and fuel, and another sleeping bag. The second pouch was discovered, and then more poles and fabric were flung onto the ground. She jabbed them at each other with livid abandon. Quick to frustration, she threw down the mess. "Fuck you!"

This time, Josie didn't take it personally. It was outrageous how heavy *ultralight* was when you were exhausted. They hadn't practiced putting the chairs together because it had seemed like it would be obvious. Through trial and error, Josie figured out hers while Neena watched and stewed. Then, together, they assembled Neena's.

Josie blinked at their modest creations. "That felt like a microcosm of this whole trip."

"At least we got it right the second time?" Neena framed it as a question. *We* got it wrong the first time. *We* figured it out.

Josie prickled but let it slide, because this three-day trip was about them, plural, together. "Sticks," she instructed. "As many as we can gather."

Neena brightened—somewhat—and hastened into the surrounding woods.

Josie moved with a grimace. Pain bedeviled every step, each one a howling confirmation of the blisters on her heels. On the balls of her feet. On the bony knobs that protruded beside her big toes. They'd been worried about Neena with her borrowed boots, but at least those had already been broken in. Josie shambled around near the campsite, depositing twigs into a pile beside their rock circle. She stole a moment to rest and tidied the rocks, tightening the circle, while Neena dropped off a substantial load of large branches. Fearing a scolding retaliation, Josie limped away for more.

"Did you twist an ankle?" Neena asked. She sounded concerned.

"Blisters."

"Uh-oh."

Josie dismissed it, despite wanting the sympathy. "I'll be fine." Continuing to hobble and gather, she scanned the ground for tracks and scat. She didn't even like bears when they were jailed behind bars in a zoo. The thought of one roving past their tent . . . She tried to recall the scrawled handwriting on the plywood notice board. Had any of those hikers spotted a bear at Deep Fork? She couldn't remember, but surely it would have jumped out at her at the time.

Neena dropped another armful onto the pile. It landed with a satisfying clatter. It seemed like enough to start the fire, so they tossed the heftiest branches into the pit.

Josie packed some of the smaller sticks in between. "Kindling, I think?"

Neena shrugged. "That sounds right."

Searching and collecting had eased the tension between them. Josie found the matches, and they took turns trying to light the kindling. A few twigs singed, but none would burn. Their frustration rose again. Now that they'd stopped moving, the chill from the lofty elevation crawled under Josie's skin. It settled into her bones.

She shivered. "I'm gonna get my hoodie. Would you like yours?"

Glowering at the matches, Neena shook her head. She still looked warm and flush. Her body temperature was always higher than Josie's. Josie located her own hoodie on the ground beside her pack and brushed off a stray pine needle, faintly tacky with sap. Zipping up, she spotted a new hole in the stitching where the left sleeve met the left shoulder. Holes tattered the elbows, too, in a way that seemed cool and purposeful. Like she didn't give a damn.

Josie did give a damn, and she would have preferred a new hoodie, but it never felt okay to buy one when there were other things she needed more.

Something else on the ground caught her eye. She carried it over.

Neena was confused. "You want to burn your journal?"

"Only a few sheets," Josie said. "The paper will catch fire, and maybe that'll be enough to get the rest going."

Win had said it was a bad idea to bring their journals—again, the unnecessary weight—*Write on the backs of the printouts, if you're that desperate*—but the girls couldn't imagine not having the option. Finally, they felt vindicated to have ignored his advice. Josie tore out two sheets, crumpled them up, and tucked them into the kindling. The paper lit. The burn was quick, but the paper slid the fire onto a skinny twig.

Josie sucked in her breath. "Come on," she begged the other sticks.

The fire went out.

"Try it again," Neena said, growing excited. They tore and tucked another sheet. "Do you think we're supposed to blow on it?" she asked. "To give it more oxygen?"

"We breathe in oxygen. We breathe out carbon dioxide."

"But doesn't fire need air or whatever? Isn't that a thing?"

"Yeah, but it's too small. We'd blow it out."

Neena leaned into the circle and started puffing anyway.

"You're going to blow it out!" Josie said.

Another puff. "No, it's like a bellows."

"A what?"

"Those old-timey, squeezey accordion things. Like in Victorian times— Aha!"

Orange flames spread across a second stick and then licked onto a third. Above the kindling, a stout branch sputtered, thinking of catching fire. As more sticks were thrust at the blaze, the girls learned that dry sticks worked better than damp, and, at last, the campfire roared into life. They were as proud as cavewomen.

They were also paranoid about it dying again. "You watch the fire and start dinner," Neena said. "I'll collect more wood, so you don't have to walk."

It felt generous. As if Josie had expected Neena to have either forgotten about her feet or to not care, even though Neena wasn't that type of person. Neena had never been either absentminded or malicious. Guilt rumbled inside Josie.

The sun had set, and the light was dying. They strapped on their headlamps before separating. If their emotions hadn't been stretched so thin, they might have laughed at the sight—the white spot in the center of their foreheads like a blinding third eye. Josie used hers to spelunk inside the bear canister. The barrel had a tight screw-on lid and notches around the sides, a design that prevented bears from unscrewing it and getting the goodies inside. It held all their food. And, hopefully, it also held all of the enticing, food-related smells.

Tonight's dinner was lamb curry with rice, courtesy of Dr. Chandrasekhar. All Josie had to do was reheat it. She was surprised to locate it inside a bulky glass mason jar. Unlike Win, Neena's mom had forgotten they'd be carrying everything on their backs. Josie dumped the contents into a tiny pot before realizing the stove wasn't ready. As she threaded the collapsible stove onto its fuel canister, the campfire dimmed. Inside her vault of fading memories, the shadow of her father poked expertly at a fire with a stick. Beside the woodpile was a long, sturdy branch they'd rejected for being too damp. Josie picked it up and poked. A gratifying shower of sparks exploded into the night sky.

From the depths of the forest, Neena whooped.

Josie smiled. She developed a routine—darting back and forth between preparing the curry and tending to the fire. It was nerve-wracking how quickly the flames wanted to die out, and it seemed silly to use the stove when they already had a fire. But to use the fire, they would have also needed a grill to lay across the rocks.

It was ridiculous how much gear was required for roughing it.

The sensation of falling light barely lingered on the fringes of Deep Fork, just beyond their shelter of pines. Neena's headlamp bobbed like a lantern through the dark and quiet trees. Periodically she would stop to unload another bundle of sticks.

"That smells good," she said on her final deposit.

Josie glowed in agreement. The little stove hissed, sending up threads of rising smoke. After dividing their dinner between two bowls, she lowered herself into a chair, closed her eyes, and groaned. Neena chorused beside her.

"I am never getting up," Josie said.

"Mmm," Neena said in agreement.

The girls ate ravenously, teeth and tongues and fingers and sporks. Every scrap was devoured. Neena's parents were from Kolkata, and her mother's Bengali cooking had been keeping Josie fed for years. She loved it. The pleasurable tear of tender meat, the nutty tang from the mustard seeds, the warming heat from the green chilis. Normally, she would have killed for a side of chapati, but she was so famished that flatbread didn't matter. Lamb curry had never tasted so delectable.

The remaining water was wedged between their chairs, and Josie reached down for a sip. Neena was already glugging from the bottle.

"Hey," Josie said.

Neena's body slunk like guilty dog. She handed it over. "I know, I know."

The water was tepid but refreshing. Josie drank mindfully. They needed enough to wash the dishes and brush their teeth—with an emergency ration still left over at bedtime.

Neena's headlamp vanished with a faint tick. Feeling for the rubber button, Josie clicked hers off, too. Absolute night cloaked the forest. The cool mountain air smelled like woodsmoke and evergreens. Josie inhaled deeply. Her body grew heavy and relaxed. Her gaze zoned out, inert, at the fire. The flames crackled, hot and hypnotic. Smoke billowed in phantasmagoric shrouds.

"We did it," Neena said after several minutes. Her voice was thick and slow.

"Yep. We did."

"One day down. Two to go."

Josie managed to laugh. So did Neena. They lacked the energy to set their empty bowls on the ground. The insects chirred, the fire spit.

Josie bit her lip. "Are you worried about tomorrow?"

"Nah. We've got this." Neena hoped she sounded reassuring, but undercut her own confidence a few beats later. "At least it's not uphill. That was the worst part."

"Definitely."

"And our return on Wednesday will be downhill."

"*Wednesday.*"

The word enveloped Neena in the same melancholia. Wednesday meant the end. "Hump Day," she trilled, because it was such an odious phrase.

But Josie didn't laugh. The mood didn't lighten.

"It sucks that we're so close to the summit, but we won't even get to see it," Josie said. The top of Frazier Mountain was only a mile and a half away, but the trail to reach it was separate from the Wade Harte.

Neena frowned into the snickering fire. Still wanting to help. "Maybe we could hit it on the way back. We could stash our packs here so the climb wouldn't be so bad."

"Maybe that's what the other campers did."

Though they hadn't discussed them since arriving at the camp-site, Neena and Josie remained keenly aware of their neighbors. Neighbor? Simultaneously, the girls wondered if the other tent be-longed to one person or two. They glanced up the slope, but the pitch black had long since swallowed the yellow gold.

An earsplitting crack exploded across the clearing.

The girls jumped and shrieked, but it was only the fire. They glanced at each other and finally started laughing again, punchy and shaken and tired. Their former classmates would have been party-ing by now, swapping ghost stories and urban legends. Or was that only kids' stuff? Josie supposed they'd be drinking beer and smoking weed, but she had a better idea. She revealed a small Ziploc packed with something else entirely.

Neena perked up. "Marshmallows! I thought—"

"I refuse to let you move away without tasting a proper s'more."

The ingredients were yet another thing Win had told them not to bring, which Josie had ignored to the detriment of her own back. But it was criminal that Neena had only ever made s'mores in a mi-crowave. She tossed the bag to Neena and followed it with a bar of dark chocolate. The graham crackers had been padded inside a shirt to prevent breakage. Josie selected two sticks of scrubby underbrush from the reject pile, lounged back into her seat, and held a skewered marshmallow toward the fire.

"I like mine nearly burnt," she said.

"You're the best," Neena said. "I thought we were going without dessert tonight."

"Bite your tongue."

After a leisurely minute toasting the sugary pillows, Neena's fore-head creased. "So . . . remind me. How does the chocolate melt?"

Josie's brow folded into an identical frown. Years had passed since she'd made a s'more, and it had been with her parents' help. "Huh."

"Do we cook it on a separate stick?"

That didn't seem right, but Josie couldn't think of another way. She held Neena's stick while Neena procured two more, pronged this time. Balancing the graham crackers on the pronged ends, the girls topped each with a square of chocolate. Immediately, Josie's dropped into the fire. They erupted with more laughter, and she tried again, concentrating on steadying her exhausted arms.

Again into the fire. Their laughter grew loose and giggly.

Neena examined her chocolate, which had scarcely melted, and her marshmallow, which was golden brown. "Screw it. I'm going in." She made a sandwich and took a bite. Her eyes closed with hedonistic delight. "Yes," she said through a stuffed, sticky mouth. *Yeth.* "Oh!" Her eyes leapt open in surprise. "The chocolate is melting from the heat of the marshmallow."

Tears of laughter pricked Josie's eyes as she motioned toward the pronged stick. "I knew this was too hard."

"I bet milk chocolate would melt even faster."

"I actually remembered my dad using milk chocolate, but I brought dark—"

"Because dark is better."

"Exactly. Sorry."

"Don't be. I love it. My first proper s'more!" Neena's shout reverberated throughout the forest, and Josie admonished her, still giggling. Like the boy earlier on the trail, Neena adopted the voice of a hackneyed redneck. "Quit yer worrying, girl. Ain't nobody gonna hear us, not all the way out—"

She cut herself off. Her eyes darted to the woods.

Josie's spine froze along its full length. The fire popped. Insects rattled. Josie glanced at Neena—overly stiff and riveted to the tree

line—and then flopped back into her seat. Flush with embarrassment, she tried to hide her anger. "Ha ha."

Without detaching her gaze, Neena lowered her voice. "Something is out there."

"Smokey, right? Ooh, or is it Brother Bear?"

"Shh!"

The shush was piercing. Josie's sinews tightened. Neena nodded
toward the darkness ahead of them. "What is it?" Josie whispered.

"I don't know. Something . . . large."

They listened. Waited. With a thumping chest, Josie silently set
down her twig. The burning marshmallow sank into the pine needles. Her hands gripped onto each other, her knuckles whitened. She
twisted her stone ring.

Neena's eyes widened with terror. "There!"

"Where?" Josie hissed.

"You didn't hear that?"

Josie turned frantic. "Hear what? What is it?"

"There. There it is again!" Neena bolted up. Her chair tipped
backward and clashed to the forest floor. "Oh my God! Oh my God!"

Josie vaulted to her feet, hands clawing for Neena. She screamed.

"*OW,*" NEENA SAID, prying Josie's fingers from her arm.

Confusion flickered within Josie's dilated pupils as Neena burst into cackling laughter. Stunned, Josie was forced to reorient herself. Outrage swiftly replaced fright. "I knew it. I knew it!" Humiliation scorched Josie's cheeks. "God, you're such a bitch. Why do you always do that? When are you gonna learn shit like that isn't funny?"

"Oh, come on. That was pretty funny."

"No. It wasn't. There *really are* things out there, and we're alone. In the middle of nowhere."

Neena's tone corroded with derision. "Not the bears again."

"I'm not making them up! They fucking live out here!"

"Yeah, and your yelling is scaring them all away." The instant it left her mouth, Neena wished she could take it back. She knew she shouldn't have tricked Josie even before she'd done it. But now she was already caught in the loop. "I don't know why you're so scared of them, anyway, when it's people you should be worried about."

"Do you see any other people around here?"

"Do you see any bears?"

Tears sprung to Josie's eyes. She fought them. "Fuck you."

"I'm just saying—"

"Maybe I *should* be afraid of people. Maybe I should be afraid of *you*. It's not like mass shooters hang out in the woods." Josie spread her arms in a wide and fuming gesture. "No masses."

Neena shoved the barb aside. "I'm not talking about mass shooters. I'm talking about serial killers."

"Please." Josie stomped toward her pack. "Son of Sam, Zodiac, the Osborne Slayer—yeah, they're all hiding out there, waiting to get us. Should I also be worried about the Slender Man or some other creepypasta bullshit? What about that guy with the hook?"

"Actually . . ." Neena said, her inner voice battling with itself, pleading that she didn't have to prove her point. Shouting that it would be cruel to force any more horrific stories into Josie's head. "Tons of crimes have been committed in national forests. Cary Stayner in Yosemite. David Carpenter, the Trailside Killer." The examples burst forth, unwanted, like pop-up ads. Neena's father was a lawyer who investigated claims of innocence for wrongful conviction cases. Neena knew a lot about the worst humanity had to offer. "Israel Keyes. That guy was really messed up. He hid kill kits in rural areas all across the country—"

"I don't want to know—"

"Gary Michael Hilton! They literally called him the National Forest Serial Killer. When we were kids, he killed a man and woman right here in Pisgah, right in this area—"

"Why would you tell me this?"

"He's in prison now, but do you remember that group of hikers who went missing a couple of years ago near Hot Springs? Two girls and a guy. They were found murdered only a week later." Hot Springs was a rural town located in a distant area of Pisgah. It wasn't close enough to be a concern, but it was close enough for Neena to make her point. "The guy's body was untouched, but the girls had rope burns around their wrists and ankles."

Josie looked up from digging through her pack. The shovel was clenched in her hand. "*Four* hikers went missing." Win and his friends had volunteered in the massive search party. "The other boyfriend was never found, and they think he's still on the run. The crime was personal. Not random. And I don't want to talk about this anymore."

"I'm just saying—"

"Fine. Enough." Josie was crying as she fled away, gait limping, with the shovel and a handful of toilet paper. "Are you happy now?"

No, Neena wasn't happy.

The moon was sliced neatly down the center, half in darkness, half in light. It was close, and it blotted out any additional starlight that she had been expecting. No more glimmered here than what she might have seen in her own backyard. Perhaps they were still too close to Asheville's electric glow. But this place didn't look like home as Josie's headlamp switched on and teetered between the skeletal shadows of pines.

Neena shuddered. Maybe it had been easier to attack Josie's weaknesses than to face her own. But just because Neena didn't like the darkness didn't mean she couldn't handle it. She grabbed a sanitary pad and some toilet paper from the smushed roll and then shuffled off in the opposite direction. Not wanting another scolding, she made sure to walk far enough away from their tent. According to Josie, the scent of urine appealed to bears because it carried the smell of whatever food the human had recently eaten.

The ground crunched underneath her boots. Neena's lamp only illuminated enough to see one step at a time. The unlit woods meant that the summer fireflies—the only cheerful denizens of the night—were already gone for the season. But, away from the campfire, the mosquitos thickened. She swatted them sightlessly into her bare arms.

The missing and murderous boyfriend lurched into her mind. Until Josie had mentioned him, Neena had forgotten that he was a part of the story, but now it was easy to imagine him hiking south into these woods. She had to remind herself how unlikely that actually was. No doubt he'd hitched a ride somewhere or was hiding out at a friend's house. Or was still hiding up near Hot Springs. Why hadn't she been able to stop herself from trying to scare Josie? She had only angered Josie, and she had scared herself, instead. Her muscles ached as badly as her conscience.

At least she still didn't need the shovel. Not yet.

After finishing, Neena returned to the fire. It had already weakened in the short time since they'd stopped feeding it. She burned the toilet paper and debated tossing the bloodied pad into the low flames with it, but the material was probably plastic or something awful like that, so she stuffed it into the trash bag inside the bear canister.

The cold night slithered over her. She rubbed her itchy, bitten arms and leaned toward the waning heat. The pit belched out a caustic cloud. Eyes stinging, she gasped soundlessly, determined not to alert Josie to her mistake. Josie would know better than to stick her face into the smoke. Neena blinked through the rush of tears.

Where *was* Josie? She strained to hear the shovel against earth.

The fire crackled and snapped.

"Josie?" she called out.

She waited a few seconds.

"Josie?" Her voice rose. "Is everything okay?"

Neena dabbed at her burning eyes with her shirtsleeve, which was salty and stiff from dried sweat. Fear gnawed. She couldn't see Josie's headlamp. What if, in her anger, Josie had walked too far? What if she was lost? All Neena knew about getting lost in the woods was that you were supposed to stay put until someone found you. Her parents had told her that when she was a child. But did the same strategy apply to adults? They had packed an emergency whistle, but Neena doubted Josie had taken it with her. Should she rouse the strangers in the yellow-gold tent to help her search? What if the murderous boyfriend was out there? What if he was in the tent?

She yelled Josie's name again.

"Yeah?" a distant voice called back.

Neena's arms curled around her stomach. She felt embarrassed at how quick she'd been to panic. A lamp bobbed into view. It approached slowly, bumpily, through the dark forest. Like being blinded by an oncoming car's brights, she couldn't see Josie herself until she finally stepped into the firelight. She looked broken. Depleted.

"I thought you were lost," Neena said.

Josie tossed the shovel to the ground. "No."

Worried that it might have sounded like she was suggesting a flaw in Josie's navigational skills, Neena lied. "I got turned around out there, too. How are your feet doing?"

Josie gave a morose shrug but then sharpened with an accusatory thought. "Did you remember to bury—"

"I burned it. And I put the pad in the trash."

"Ugh, that reminds me. We need to get rid of the canister."

"No problem," Neena said. But as she tried to add their empty bowls to the canister, Josie harped again.

"You have to wash them off first."

"I thought we were running low on water."

"Yeah, but we still have to wash them off. They'll get gross. That's one of the reasons why I wanted you to be careful with the water."

Neena swallowed her irritation because she was still paying penance. They poured a splash of water into each bowl and scrubbed them with their sporks. When Josie grew agitated that hers wasn't spotless, Neena physically removed it from her hands. "It's fine,"

Neena said, packing away the dishes and screwing the lid shut. "Good enough."

Expecting Josie to snap back, Neena felt even worse when Josie remained silent. On the ground between them lay the remnants of Josie's s'more. The shame sunk in deeper. With a timid voice, Neena asked, "Would you like a new one?"

Josie broke off the stick ends that had touched the food and tossed them into the fire. "No," she said. The graham cracker, chocolate square, and marshmallow followed.

The flames burned and swallowed them.

Neena slunk away with the canister, which had to be placed far from their tent for safety. At least it wasn't a bear bag, which she would have had to hoist into a tree. She had no idea how she would have managed that alone.

"Wait!" Josie said. "Our toiletries."

Everything that smelled had to be stored away. The girls brushed their teeth and then spit into the final dregs of the fire. Only embers remained, pulsing lumps of orange and red. Neena wished she could rinse out her mouth, but she didn't dare touch the water.

The girls rifled through their belongings for any remaining scented items—sunscreen, baby wipes. "Lip balm?" Josie asked, uncapping it to sniff.

Neena shrugged.

It all went in.

"Make sure you take it far from the tent," Josie reminded her.

Neena lugged away the unwieldy canister. Though she didn't have any blisters, her feet were still killing her. Her body was still freezing. Without the campfire, the temperature had taken another significant drop.

A jagged tree root snagged her boot. She nearly face-planted, and the canister thudded to the ground. Struggling up, she brushed the grit from her palms. The woods were as black as crow wings. Feathery shadows shifted. Sentient trees concealed. Her imagination began to spin wild and nightmarish tales, and she ditched the canister.

Back at the campsite, Josie was unfurling her sleeping bag inside the tent. "Everything go okay?"

"Fine," Neena said icily.

"I didn't know what to do with our packs, so I brought them in. I don't know. It seemed . . . vulnerable to leave them out there."

"That's fine," Neena said again, ducking to enter. The backpacks overcrowded the cramped space, but she agreed that it felt safer to keep them close.

The wind whistled across the netting. Josie poked her head through the flaps and made an ugly noise. Neena didn't ask. She waited to be told. As Josie turned toward her, their white headlamps bore directly into each other's eyes. They both hissed as if being attacked and winced away.

"The embers are still smoldering," Josie said.

"Is that a problem?"

"We have to put them out completely. Something could spark and catch fire."

"So put them out."

"I already took off my shoes."

Neena wanted to take off *her* shoes, too. She wanted to burrow into Win's stupid girlfriend's stupid sleeping bag and not speak to Josie again until morning—until their emotions had chilled and their bodies were in less pain. She huffed outside, back into the cold. The fire had been threatening to die out the entire time, but now it was impossible to fully extinguish. She was too afraid to stomp on it, blowing made it worse, and spitting wasn't enough. The embers clung on for dear life. Her teeth chattered. Stretching her upper half back into the tent, she searched for, and nabbed, the water bottle.

"Hey," Josie said as she realized what was happening.

The embers extinguished with a satisfying sizzle.

"What the fuck!" Josie shouted.

"I put the fire out."

"You don't use *water*."

"What do you mean, you don't use *water*?" Neena emphasized it in the same snotty way. "I'm pretty sure firemen aren't shooting Cheerwine from their hoses."

Josie's tone clenched. "I meant that everybody knows you smother a campfire with dirt to save water. And that was the last of what I'd saved."

"*Everybody knows?* Jesus, Josie." Reentering, Neena jerkily zipped up the solid flap behind her, then the netting flap. Woodsmoke choked the tent. It permeated their clothing, hair, skin, lips. They tasted it on their tongues.

They didn't speak as Neena wrestled with her sleeping bag. Their headlamps shone on opposite corners of the tent. Backs to each other, they removed their bras through the armholes of their shirts. Neena unlaced her boots and stifled a moan. The unwanted brutes were discarded at the end of her sleeping bag, away from her head so that she wouldn't have to smell them. Her feet had never felt so sore—or so blissfully free. She exchanged her soiled socks for clean ones and put on her hoodie.

Josie, who was cold-natured, removed her jeans to add a pair of long johns and then wriggled back into the jeans. She also added a second pair of socks and a knitted hat, as well as a long-sleeved shirt between her T-shirt and hoodie.

You are going to boil, Neena thought with exhilarating meanness.

The girls both stormed into their downy sleeping bags—as best they could storm in an overstuffed, two-person tent—and turned off their lamps. Darkness engulfed them.

"Shit," Neena mumbled. Realizing she didn't have a pillow.

Josie did not respond.

They had planned to use their clothing for pillows, but the only thing Neena could locate in the dark was a clean T-shirt. She tucked it underneath her head. The comfort was flat and unsatisfying. Knowing Josie, she probably had an amazing pillow. She'd probably made it while Neena was snuffing out the fire.

"All I meant," Josie said, her voice slicing through the dark, "was that you never know what might happen, and water is kinda important. The *most* important, actually."

Neena closed her eyes and hoped that Josie would choke on her self-righteousness.

"Like, what if we try the water filter at the spring tomorrow, and it doesn't work?" Josie pressed.

"Then I suppose we'll have a shitty morning as we walk back to my car."

"Or what if one of us gets thirsty in the middle of the night?"

"I told you I'm sorry." She had not. "Okay? It won't happen again."

Silence. Twenty seconds, maybe.

"It's just . . . sometimes I think you don't take me seriously. It's not outlandish to want to save a little water in case of an emergency."

"Oh my God, Josie. How many times do you want me to apologize?"

"*Once* would be nice, but I'm not asking for that. I'm tired of you making me feel like shit all the time over totally rational things."

Neena was blindsided. "Excuse me?"

"It's not unreasonable for me to want water, or to want the tent set up before sundown, or to be afraid of animals that can eat me. It's common. Fucking. Sense."

"Okay." Neena inhaled. Her lungs filled to capacity. "You want to play this game, let's play it. How about how shitty you've made *me* feel today? 'It's common fucking sense.' Well, I'm sorry I've never been in the goddamn fucking woods before. And it's not common sense. Somebody told you once, too, so you don't have to condescend to me like I'm an idiot every time I do something wrong—"

"*Me?* You're the one—"

"I'm the one holding your hand." Neena unleashed her resentment. She snarled it. "Without me, you wouldn't even be here. You'd still be at home, feeling sorry for yourself like always."

Josie's voice glinted into a blade. "Without *me*, we wouldn't be here. I'm the one who found the trail, I'm the one who had the gear—"

"Your brother found the trail, and your brother had the gear. And you lean on him like you lean on me. God, I'm so sick of it! Always having to make the decisions for both of us. Always having to watch what I say around you."

"Are you serious? This is you watching what you say around me?"

"Oh, please. The moment I mention Los Angeles—"

There was a sharp intake from Josie.

"—or college anymore, you freak out. I'm moving in five days, and I'm terrified, and I can't even talk about it with my best friend because she gets mad at me. Because, somehow, her feelings on the subject are more valid than mine. Her feelings always win."

"Well, I'm sorry that it's hard for me to pity someone who's going to an awesome school in an awesome city." Josie pronounced the word "awesome" as if it tasted like dung. "I'm sorry that it's hard to have two supportive parents and that your life is so perfect and easy."

"That's not fair—"

"What's not fair is that we made the same fucking As, and you get to follow your dreams, and I get to keep working at Kmart. So, yeah." Josie spat it. "Maybe I'm testy."

"All I'm saying is that I wish you could separate the two things and be happy for me. Or at least accept that I might be scared right now, too. But instead, you keep dragging me down—"

"Dragging you down?"

"Yes!" Neena hated how shrill her tone had become.

"How can I drag you down when nothing can stop you? You never stop needling. You *never* know when to quit."

"Because if I didn't push you, you'd never do anything! You'd be just like your mom."

There was a ghastly beat. The tent thickened with malevolence, and Josie's voice shaped into a damning and unrecognizable form. "You're selfish, you're reckless, and you have no idea what you're talking about."

Both girls burst into tears.

DEEP DOWN SOUTH in the Appalachian Mountain system, in the Blue Ridge province, in the Pisgah National Forest, in the narrow gap between Frazier Mountain and the Misty Rock Wilderness, sat a tent. Tucked inside its fragile shell, two teenage girls were crying in the dark. Their tears streamed hot and quiet, punctuated by sniffles. Blubbery snot was gulped and choked. The girls lay side by side. Back to back. Their sleeping bags touched, but they had never been farther apart.

Me, me, me.

You, you, you.

Their unspoken, unscreamed grievances had finally exploded, and neither girl understood why she hadn't been able to back down. Or laugh it off. Or attempt to salvage whatever was left. But perhaps it was easier to attack and sever ties now than to watch their friendship disintegrate over time as they grew into their new and separate adulthoods. Perhaps it was easier to kill something than to save it.

The tent bottom was nothing more than a tarp. They'd been

advised to bring sleeping pads, which would have provided an additional barrier of insulation and cushioning from the ground, but they had decided not to. They'd needed the room for their chocolate and marshmallows, for their chairs and journals. Cold dampness seeped up through the crinkly fabric. Brittle pine needles stabbed and hard rocks wedged, agitating and deepening their bruises. Ironically, journaling might have provided some comfort.

Neither girl was willing to turn on a light.

Outside the tent, a lone bird called in the night.

Nothing responded.

Hours passed.

Every speck and seedling that landed against the nylon, every leaf and stick that tumbled over the earth, was thunderous and abrasive. To Neena, the wind blowing through the trees sounded like rushing vehicles. It reminded her of walking across an overpass in a big city. It made her anxious, like the guardrail was broken and she was about to fall.

To Josie, the wind sounded like the ocean. It reminded her of her father's arms, strong and hairy and tanned. Every August, her family used to rent a house on Folly Beach, where they would spend a whole week gorging on shrimp burgers and basking in the sun. In an alternate timeline, she would have been there right now—or maybe returning home, asleep in the back seat with Win, sand on their flip-flops. But the tradition had died with her father.

Grief was peculiar. Enough time had passed that she was okay, mostly. Days or even weeks could go by without incident. But then something unexpected would happen, and the pain would come roaring back. The something could be good or bad. The response was simply triggered by being caught *unaware*. Her hurt was still instantly accessible. Her membranes were still thin and defenseless.

She was roasting in her sleeping bag. Silently, she stripped off her hat and the extra pair of socks. Her arms throbbed with the prickling heat of sunburnt skin. She imagined her father surrounded by nothing. She imagined herself, on the other side of nothing, surrounded by too much and not enough.

Josie was sweating.

Suffocating.

Neena was freezing. Shivering and shaking, she hated herself for not bringing more layers, and she hated Josie even more for bringing plenty. How could summer feel so much like winter? She had a headache from crying and a mounting pressure in her intestines. She tried to ignore it. All she wanted was to sleep soundly and without dreams.

It was so cold outside. So dark.

Neena had glow-in-the-dark stars on her bedroom ceiling. Her family—and even Josie—believed they were decorative, but they actually functioned as nightlights. Their soft green luminescence comforted and lulled her to sleep. There would be no such solace here. Rustling leaves gave the impression of a black bear trundling through the woods. Had she dropped the canister far enough away? The question made her molars grind.

Her stomach gurgled. Unable to wait a second longer, Neena squirmed out of her sleeping bag. Any last vestiges of warmth vanished. Her eyes had adjusted enough that she could see her boots, but her hands were so numb that it was difficult to tie the laces.

Beside her, Josie was stiff with alertness.

Neena grabbed a few squares of toilet paper and shoved them into a pocket, but she couldn't find the shovel and didn't want to ask. She groped for the exit. The zippers shrieked. She winced, even though Josie was already awake. Even though she wanted to propel Josie off the side of the mountain.

Josie's sleeping bag swished as she lifted her head. An inquiry.

"I have to pee," Neena whispered in annoyance, and as the flaps fell back behind her, she turned on her headlamp.

Mist had spread across the entirety of Deep Fork. The air shimmered in the lamplight. A screech owl called out to her solitary beam, its strange hoot like the whinny of a horse. With a shudder, Neena stumbled forward into the misty pines. Water steeped through the threads of her clothing. It dampened her nose and cheeks. Cautiously, she trod, aiming for the same area that she had used earlier, trying to fight the sensation of being watched by someone or something lurking just out of sight.

Her lamp ran into a thicket.

She didn't remember one being here. Deciding that she'd steered too far to the left, she retraced her steps, back and diagonally to the right, but then hit another thicket.

Too far to the right or not enough?

Her light scanned the thickening mist. It was impossible to see more than a few feet ahead. She didn't know where she was, but she had to go. Scouring the ground, she located a rock to use for digging. It was glacial to the touch. Neena tugged her sleeves down over her hands and clumsily held on to it through her hoodie. When the hole seemed deep enough, she undid her jeans. The air was an icy slap against her skin.

For as long as I live, she vowed, *I will never go camping again.*

Business done and wiped, she reached for her pants. A faint crack rang out from beyond the thicket—the sound of a twig snapping.

Neena froze.

It's nothing, she thought.

But then another twig snapped.

Her chest seized. Frantically, she hunted for the source, but the mist had swollen into a fog. Everything was the same color of wet darkness.

Something was moving. The forest was disturbed. Though the movements felt predatory, Neena didn't think the something was an animal. She fumbled to switch off her headlamp. Anybody out there might see her light, panning back and forth, and know she was lost. A mosquito whined in her ear. Startled, she crushed it, smearing her lobe with her own blood.

She waited.

Listened.

The rustling and crunching grew louder. Closer. It wasn't her imagination. Still in a crouch, Neena's legs began to shake. Goose bumps dimpled her bottom and lower back. Never before had her flesh been so vulnerable or exposed.

The noises honed into distinctly human footsteps.

Fear thumped through her. The footsteps moved heavily, steadily through the underbrush. Her vision strained. They were only a few feet away, but she couldn't see anything through the veil of fog. She prayed her light hadn't been noticed.

On the other side of the thicket, they stopped.

She covered her mouth. Positive her breathing was audible.

Solid and immovable as a boulder, the presence felt menacing. A darkness darker than the surrounding forest, a mass as obliterating as a black hole. Every fear she had ever had of the night, compacted and concentrated into a single, unseen form.

But then, just as unexpectedly, the footsteps moved on. Heavily, steadily. Fainter and fainter, until they faded away altogether. The woods held their secret in silence.

Neena's limbs weakened into jelly, and she sank toward the forest floor. She hastily rose to avoid falling into her own excrement. Fumbling, she pulled up her jeans, used her boot to swipe the dirt back over the hole, and reexamined her surroundings.

She had no idea where the tent was. Her mind hurtled through the options. She'd left the emergency whistle in the tent—*stupid, stupid*—but if she cried out, Josie would come. Probably. But who *else* might come? Though Neena couldn't hear the footsteps anymore, surely their owner was still close enough to hear if she called for help.

The tent had to be nearby. She hadn't walked that far. Had she?

Why didn't she bring a compass? She could have navigated by the stars or some shit! Okay, no. That wasn't true. But she couldn't stay here, and she couldn't risk using her headlamp, either.

Neena hunched over and crept along the thicket line. Her best guess was that when the bushes ended, the tent would be at about forty-five degrees.

If she was remembering the correct thicket.

If she was oriented in the correct direction.

How easy it would be to wander in the *wrong* direction.

With each step, she tested the ground with a toe before putting down the entire boot. The pine-needle carpet crackled softly—still too loudly—beneath her feet. Her fingers felt the thicket's end before she saw it. She took a frightened and hesitant step away from the vegetation, her hand dislodged . . . and she was unmoored.

Fog rolled around the pines like a current as Neena waded into the dark sea. She swam between the trees, arms outstretched, hands grasping at nothing. She shuffled forward in meek increments. Each time she moved, the other footsteps moved, too. The sound was in her head. It wasn't real. Was she alone or had they returned?

Panic screamed at her to run, but she fought it, afraid of alerting the stranger to her location, afraid of running in the wrong direction, afraid, afraid, afraid—

Her toe tapped against a low stone. The rest of her boot came down with confidence, but another stone was touching it, and the rocks clattered together. Startled, Neena tripped over a third rock, kicking it, only to realize she was standing inside the campfire circle. She shot off and sprinted several feet, expecting to crash into the tent.

All she found was more fog.

"Neena?"

Neena darted toward the familiar voice. Her outstretched hands smacked into nylon. Scrabbling for the door flaps, she lunged inside and feverishly zipped them closed behind her. "Somebody is out there," she hissed.

Josie didn't respond.

"There were footsteps."

"Yeah," Josie said at a regular volume. She was fuming. "Yours. That's why I called out."

"Shh!"

"Seriously?" The question wasn't, *Are you being serious?* But, *Are you seriously kidding me with this same fucking joke?* Neena wrapped a hand over Josie's mouth, and Josie let out a muffled cry. The force of Neena's pounding heart against Josie's back made Josie stiffen in alarm. She fell quiet. Neena released her.

The girls sat—almost touching—in petrified silence.

Their ears strained. *Wind. Insects. Leaves.* As the seconds ticked into a minute, Josie shoved Neena away, incensed.

"I swear," Neena said, still whispering, "somebody was out there."

Josie flumped noisily back into bed. "It's not even warm anymore," she grouched, meaning her sleeping bag.

"I *swear*," Neena said.

Perhaps it was the note of desperation that gave Josie pause. Finally, she lowered her voice to match. "Are you sure it wasn't a deer?"

"No. It was a person."

Josie remained skeptical. "I bet it was a deer."

"It wasn't . . ." Neena said through clenched teeth, ". . . a deer." Now that the threat had seemingly passed, anger rushed back in. She yanked off her boots and crawled into her sleeping bag. "And it wasn't a bear, either."

The silence was hostile but brief.

"Okay, then you probably heard the person from the other tent." Even though Josie was humoring the idea, her tone was frosty. "And you probably freaked them out as much as they freaked you out."

Neena seethed because the explanation made sense. Hell, maybe Josie's first guess was correct, and it was a stupid deer, and her imagination had gotten carried away in the fog. What did a deer sound like, anyway? Or maybe it was an elk. What *was* an elk? Was it just a larger kind of deer? She hated how ignorant this trip made her feel.

The temperature continued to drop, and Neena shivered in her wet clothing. Fog had saturated the cotton, refusing to let it dry. Until now, she'd never understood the purpose of wicking fabrics. It seemed against common sense that a synthetic would dry faster than a natural fiber, but, clearly, she was wrong again.

A rock underneath the tarp jammed into her hips. Her useless T-shirt pillow made her neck crooked with knots. Her head still throbbed from the crying headache.

It wasn't a deer.

Two faces materialized in her mind: the young teenage girls who had been found murdered on a hiking trail a few years ago in

Indiana. One of the girls had managed to use her phone to secretly record audio and video of the man that police believed to be their killer. The news story had been chilling—the idea that you could be out with your best friend, doing something as basic as taking a stroll through the woods, with no idea of what was waiting for you on the other side of the bend.

The fog curled around the tent like the tail of a sleeping wolf.

Her thoughts drifted to the fourth hiker here in Pisgah, the one suspected of murdering his friends in Hot Springs. The one still on the lam. Earlier that day, the boy on the trail who had reminded her of Win had teased them about a man who raided these campsites at night, but . . . sometimes jokes were based on rumors. And sometimes rumors were based on truth.

Nobody is out to get me.

The fog nudged and bumped against the tent.

Nature isn't out to get me.

The fog was merely a low-lying cloud that had rolled in. This was a normal meteorological phenomenon that happened in the mountains. *I'm falling asleep on a cloud,* she tried to convince herself, *and it's idyllic.*

I'm falling asleep on a cloud.

I'm falling asleep on a cloud.

Trembling, Neena repeated it until she believed it. Until she fell asleep.

THE HISTORY OF American forestry was rooted in Pisgah. The Cradle of Forestry, located twenty miles south of Deep Fork, was the country's first forestry school, and it still existed to this day. Josie had gone there on a field trip in the third grade, where they had sifted through decaying leaf mold to search for creepy crawlies. Her favorite sneakers with the rainbow heart shoelaces had gotten muddy.

Josie hadn't felt cradled by the forest then, and she didn't feel cradled by it now as the first rays of light pierced through the canopy. She had managed two, maybe three, hours of restless sleep, hounded by stressful dreams and intrusive thoughts. She wasn't an early riser. On the rare day without school or work, she slept well into the afternoon, unlike Neena, whose parents always guilted her out of bed by eight o'clock.

Josie checked her phone, which was still attached to the charger.

5:51 a.m. How obscene.

Like a reflex, her fingers opened the weather app, forgetting that it wouldn't be able to connect to a cell tower. The blue light of her screen froze and then blackened—but not before she noticed the battery indicator.

"Shit," she said.

Neena stirred at the muttering. "What is it?" She sounded groggy but coherent. Her body was curled into a tight ball, and Josie suspected that she'd had even less sleep.

"My phone. It was at thirty-one percent, but it died. Just like that." Josie checked the charger's cord, but both ends were firmly attached. She pressed the charger's buttons. None of its lights came on. "The charger's dead, too."

"What?" An arm reached out from the confines of Neena's sleeping bag. It snatched up her phone. "Mine won't even turn on," she said a moment later.

"Shit. *Shit.*"

"They were fine last night."

Josie put on her glasses to inspect the situation more clearly. "Maybe the cold killed the batteries? I've heard that can happen."

"The charger's dead, too?"

"That's what I said."

"But . . . how is that possible?"

"I guess it also lost its charge in the cold. Or, I don't know. Maybe we forgot to charge it before we left."

"You *forgot* to charge the charger?"

"No! I remember doing it." Josie's thoughts swam. Yesterday morning had been a blur of preparations. "I'm just saying . . . I don't know. No. I'm sure it was the cold."

"So, what?" Neena lifted her head. "That's it?"

Josie threw up her hands. *Do you see a charged phone anywhere?*

"Oh my God. Just when I thought this trip couldn't get any worse."

Even though Josie felt the same way, it still smarted to hear Neena say it. "So, what do you want to do?"

"What do you mean? They're dead. There's nothing we *can* do."

"I meant, today. Do you want to keep hiking? Or do you want to go home?"

Neena sighed. Her fingers templed against her forehead. "I don't know."

Neither of them spoke. The silence was tense.

"Well," Josie said. "We still have a map. And the trail has been pretty obvious, so far."

"Except for this campsite."

"Yeah, but we'd be staying in an open area tonight. We could put the tent anywhere."

"Look at you, suddenly the optimist."

Josie reddened. "I'm just saying, if you want to keep going, we can keep going. We still have the printouts. The only things we've actually lost are our cameras. But if you want to head back—"

"Do *you* want to head back?"

"I don't know. I don't care! That's why I was asking you."

"Well, I don't care, either," Neena snapped.

And that was the moment Josie realized she'd been hoping to salvage the trip. She'd wanted *Neena* to salvage the trip. She'd wanted Neena to beg and fight for it, but Neena wasn't going to push Josie to do anything anymore.

At an impasse, the girls forced themselves from bed. The atmosphere was sulky and dismal. Smoke still smothered the air. Josie peeled back her socks to examine her feet in the low light. They were swollen and ripe with tender blisters that would have to be popped.

After locating a safety pin inside the first-aid kit, she cleaned it with a baby wipe. Her skin, too. Neena remained silent but observed the surgery with attentive eyes. Josie refused to be seen as weak. With a hiss and a wince, she stabbed the ball of her right foot. Clear fluid spurted onto her sleeping bag. Neena grunted in nonjudgmental disgust as Josie coaxed out the rest of the liquid, then jabbed the other sacs in quick succession. Gingerly, she cleaned and bandaged each wound. When she pretended that it didn't hurt, it hurt a little less.

Wishing she had room in her hiking shoes to wear both pairs of socks, Josie pulled only the thickest back on. She loosened the shoelaces and wriggled her feet inside the shoes. It would have to do. The temperature seemed to be above freezing, but barely. Maybe the low forties. If so, it was almost ten degrees lower than what had been forecast. Josie caught Neena eyeing the extra clothing layers that Josie had stripped off in the middle of the night, as well as Josie's backpack, which had been plumped for pillow usage. Josie shoved her hat back on for protection against the morning chill.

Neena turned away with a tiny shake of her head.

"What?" Josie said.

"Nothing." But Neena was shivering, and her lips were tinged violet.

It's not my fault you didn't listen when Win said it would be cold. On any other day, Josie would have felt bad for Neena. She would have apologized for being unaware that Neena was freezing and would have offered her the extra clothes.

Today, she would do neither.

Josie unzipped the tent and stepped outside into the early light. Though the fog had rolled along to other mountains, it had left behind a glistening sheen. High in the treetops, the elaborate weavings of the fall webworm moth sparkled in the dew. Down on the ground, the marshmallow remnants of her uneaten s'more had glommed onto the pine needles. An army of industrious ants teemed over the unsavory memory. She shuddered, grateful that insects were all it had attracted.

The girls plodded away to relieve themselves. When Josie

returned, she dug out the filtration system and gathered their water bottles.

Neena materialized a few minutes later. "Breakfast?"

Josie held up the equipment.

"Great." Neena slumped, dejected. "This'll be fun."

Josie headed for the spring, but, after a few seconds, Neena still wasn't following. She paused to find Neena staring at their campsite.

"It just feels weird to leave all our stuff," Neena said.

"Who's going to take it?"

The girls glanced up the slope. The yellow-gold tent appeared undisturbed from the previous night. The structure was soundless. Lifeless. It made Josie uneasy, although she couldn't pinpoint why. Neena was also staring at the campsite with an unsettled furrow in her brow. Eager to get the filtering over with, Josie limped on.

Eventually, Neena trudged along behind her.

They hiked the five minutes to the spring without a word, reacquainting themselves with every ache, chafe, and bruise that had worsened overnight. Their task required filling a liter-size bag and then squeezing the water through a small filtration device directly into their bottles. Josie unrolled the bag and began to collect water.

"So . . . we didn't decide. Are we staying or going home?" The "we" left a bitter flavor on Josie's tongue. An off note.

Neena shrugged.

"That's not an answer," Josie said, exasperated.

"Why is it up to *me* to make the decision?"

The accusations from their fight were still raw. Josie angled her face so that Neena wouldn't see the tears pricking her eyes. "Fine. I think we should keep hiking."

"Fine," Neena said. "We'll keep hiking."

"Fine," Josie said, embarrassed at her own childishness. Aware that she'd made the wrong choice for the wrong reason.

•   •   •

The spring was only a few inches deep, and it was taking forever for Josie to fill the bag. The trickle out of the PVC pipe had created a shallow pool. Or maybe it was a stream. It was impossible to tell where the water ended—or if it even did. Neena couldn't fathom why Win had recommended this for their water source. The only reasonable explanation was that the flow had diminished since the last time he'd seen it, which begged the question: What else had changed out here?

The air resonated with the monotonous din of mosquitos and stinging yellow insects. Her head buzzed, fatigued and headachy, on the same frequency. Already she regretted the decision to keep hiking. She'd only agreed because she didn't want to be the one who backed down. What were they doing out here, wasting time by pretending that their friendship was still functional? She should be packing boxes at home. Savoring this final week with her family. Drinking water from a tap.

Her gaze hadn't left the bag. "Oh my God," she said, thrusting a large leaf at Josie. "Use this to help scoop, or we'll be here all day."

Josie seemed hurt and taken aback, but Neena didn't care, because her idea worked. The bag filled faster, and they were able to filter their first liter. In a resentful and protracted silence, the girls swapped turns and then lugged the bottles back uphill to the campsite. When Josie inquired about the bear canister, Neena pointed in its direction. *Get it yourself.* She plopped into a camp chair, shook her inhaler, and puffed.

"Really?" Josie didn't even have to raise her voice. "*This* was your idea of far away?"

Neena swiveled, startled. Under the spell of night, it had seemed far away, yet the canister was nestled beneath a pine that was twenty feet away, at most. Shame washed over her. Holding in her medicinal breath, she struggled for an excuse but failed.

Josie shook her head with disgust, as if Neena weren't speaking because she was unwilling. Neena exhaled slowly. She sipped her water, swished out the inhaler taste, and spit. *Now* she was unwilling.

Though neither girl was a coffee drinker, the chilly morning campsite felt like the right time and place for a cup of instant. Unfortunately, they hadn't thought to bring any. Breakfast was a protein bar each. Tuesday was supposed to have been oatmeal day—the protein bars had been rationed for tomorrow—and the warm meal would have been nice. But Neena didn't want to remind Josie or ask for any favors. And she certainly didn't want to keep hiking. But if Josie could keep going, she sure as hell could, too.

Taking turns inside the tent, they bathed with more baby wipes and a shared stick of deodorant. Win had warned them that bringing it would be pointless—it added weight, and the scent wouldn't last long, anyway. Judging from yesterday's odors, he was right.

Neena's hips were bruised like rotting plums. Shivering and goose-bumped, she exchanged her T-shirt for the flattened pillow T-shirt. A sweater would have been a better option, preferably one of those thick Icelandic woolly ones. But at least this shirt was dry. Between the puddles and sweat and fog, Neena had been moist since their arrival. She zipped her hoodie back up and hoped the sun would dry it out.

Josie shed her hat and underlayers and changed shirts, too. Both girls wore the same jeans as yesterday, although Josie's weren't damp. Her skin was blotched and ruddy from a slight burn. They both applied sunscreen and gallons of bug spray.

Tent and chairs were returned to their waterproof sleeves. It was harder to pack without helping each other, harder to stuff the sleeves with everything unfurled back to its full size. But the girls each worked alone. Once again, the food was loaded into Neena's pack. Josie had promised to carry it today. Neena wondered if Josie had forgotten, or if she was deliberately choosing to keep Neena's pack heavier.

They were ready to leave sooner than expected. It had taken a lot longer to set up the camp than to take it down. Neena glanced upward through the pines. The yellow-gold tent was still without any signs of life, but it was early. And if the tent's owner had been the person in the fog, then they'd returned late. It made sense that they would still be sleeping.

And yet. There was *quiet*, and there was *empty*.

"Where are you going?" Josie asked.

Neena climbed the slope softly, not wanting to disturb the mysterious camper. As she drew closer, and the campsite seemed more and more unoccupied, her curious steps grew confident. Two chairs similar to their own sat neatly around a similar rock circle. The seats were dusted with pollen and leaves. The stones and ash were cold.

She turned toward the tent. A sickening, eerie feeling overtook her.

"Don't," a voice said behind her.

Neena jumped, despite knowing it was Josie. "I wasn't going to," Neena insisted. But Josie was right to warn her not to touch anything. An hour earlier, Neena had even been concerned about strangers pawing through her own unguarded possessions.

Josie's hands settled on her hips. "I guess they're still out back-packing."

Neena assumed this, too, despite the fact that the campsite felt abandoned. But perhaps every dwelling felt this way as soon as humans left it behind. Perhaps nature reclaimed its territory faster than she gave it credit for.

The frightened sensation dissipated . . . and yet, the memory of the footsteps bothered her. She could still hear them disturbing the underbrush. Heavily. Steadily. Maybe it had been a deer, after all—an imposing buck stacked with antlers. In the tenuous light of dawn, the grass at the edge of the pines looked as bright as spring. It seemed possible now that the grass was always greener on the other side of night.

The girls returned to their own belongings. In their absence, a few pine needles had fallen upon Neena's pack.

ONLY A SHORT hike beyond where they'd traveled the previous evening, the Wade Harte Trail was finally freed from its claustrophobic tunnel and opened to the sky. At last, the surrounding mountains revealed themselves, layered and endless in every direction. Low clouds lent the impression of a distant mountain lake. Water trickled down a craggy rock face. Josie marveled, once again, at how the Blue Ridge Mountains were *actually* blue.

Pale blue, dark blue, purple blue. Her father had taught her that these colors were created by isoprene exhaled from the breathing trees. How peculiar that the same spectrum that made her surroundings so thrilling and wondrous had also warped her mind into such a vast and sucking hole. Her outlook had been blue for a long time.

She already knew how the rest of this trip would go: They were stuck, and they were stubborn, so they would be polite. When Neena dropped her off at home, they would lie stiffly about having had a nice time. A handful of bland texts would be exchanged before Neena moved away, and another would be exchanged during the first month of school. And then they would never speak again. Josie had been through this before with Sarah, her best friend before Neena. Finality loomed. Their friendship was heaving its last breath.

The elevation remained steady, and the atmosphere strained, as the girls trekked southward along the stony ridgeline. They were in the Misty Rock Wilderness now. Neither of them fully understood what was meant by this particular definition of "wilderness," but it had something to do with a federally preserved area of land. The Misty Rock Wilderness was still inside the Pisgah National Forest.

It did feel different, though. The temperature rose along with the sun, but the exposed high ridges were cooler and windier than the humid woods below. The terrain was sparser. The shrubbery had grown dense, but the deciduous trees had thinned. Everything looked a little thirstier.

Josie's blisters pulsated, and her heels were as raw as ground beef. What if she was creating permanent damage? Would trekking poles have helped? How did those even work? They made people look as if they were trying to ski across dry land. Vaguely, she cast about the trail for a big stick like a wizard's staff. Or a crutch.

The gentle but persistent up-and-down felt like walking across the spine of a dinosaur. The girls traversed the glistering-white, quartz-crusted summit of Misty Rock Mountain without celebration. The intense exercise had tempered their emotions. Rests were fleeting, and silence kept them moving. Moving was better than talking.

After another brief dip, the elevation increased more significantly as the ridgeline trail headed toward its next peak. By the time they entered into the treeless balds, exhaustion forced the girls to take a real break. They perched atop a rocky outcrop and ate pre-packaged trail mix with an unusually high percentage of M&M's. Rolling mountaintops extended beyond them in every direction. The Appalachians were one of the world's oldest mountain chains. Once soaring to majestically Himalayan heights, they had been gradually sinking for millions of years. In time, they would vanish completely.

"Good trail mix," Neena said.

"Yeah," Josie said.

"How are you doing on water?"

"Good." Josie checked her bottles. "I have about a liter and a half left."

"Me too."

"That's good."

Good, good, good. What an empty word.

The girls unshouldered their packs at Burnt Balsam Knob around eleven. They guessed. They couldn't check their phones. Despite their aches and pains, the long hike to the turnaround point had been far less grueling than the previous day's shorter, steeper hike. Six hundred feet of altitude had been gained since the campsite this morning, but it had been across a distance of about five miles. The gradual incline made a difference. They were making better time. Somehow, this only made Neena feel more despondent. This summit was the literal high point of their trip, and it felt anything but.

They ate turkey jerky on an expansive grassy bald with yet another sweeping view.

"Do you think there was a forest fire?" Neena asked, wishing Josie would make the effort to start one of these stilted conversations herself. The bees were loud, droning and swarming from wildflower to wildflower. With a wrong move, she might get stung.

"Hmm?"

"*Burnt* balsam."

"Oh. Maybe." Josie ripped into a hunk of leathery jerky. She chewed slowly. Swallowed. "Or maybe it's because that stand of trees looks kind of black." She pointed toward the dark swath of forest beneath them.

Supposedly, this was the most popular section of the Wade Harte because it was the trail's highest point, and because the knob connected to several shorter, busier trails. But nobody joined them. Neena would have killed for a noisy family with a spunky labradoodle sporting a bandana. Anything to disrupt the depressing silence.

Her heart panged for home. Her family wasn't loud, but at least they would talk to her. At least they didn't think she was a selfish idiot. All morning long, Neena had toggled between hurt and anger, her mind incessantly repeating the unrepeatable accusations that she and Josie had hurled at each other. Now she was too tired to launch a defense. Stretching her muscles, she searched for an area to relieve herself. Despite the vacant crest, the whole area felt exposed.

A brass gleam caught her eye.

"Hey," she called out. "Come see this."

Josie ambled over with a wary gait.

WADE CECIL HARTE

1894–1962

CAPITALIST AND CONSERVATIONIST

WHO DEEPLY LOVED THESE MOUNTAINS

The plaque was affixed to a stone. "The man of the hour," Neena said. "You don't see 'capitalist' and 'conservationist' in the same sentence very often, do you?"

Josie hmphed. "Not anymore."

"Well, if entitled white men don't kill us first, climate change will." Neena paused as the wind shifted. The sweet scent of the balsam firs below rose to greet them on the breeze. It smelled like something precious that was about to be lost forever. "Nature always exacts its revenge."

After packing up their lunch, the girls headed back the same way they came in. They were halfway done, and Neena's gut twinged. Because the trip was a failure? Or because she was afraid of what came after the trip?

"It's all downhill from here," Josie said.

Neena wanted to believe that she was talking about the trail.

"Do you still want to take a different loop back?" Josie asked, about an hour later. She was standing beside a scrawny, overgrown path that branched to the right off the main trail. "We have a few options. I think this is the one that Win said was his favorite."

The sun was high in the sky. A choir of cicadas rose and fell in waves. Their winged undulations vibrated and thrummed, infusing the expanse with unsettled energy. This was the first time that Josie had been in the lead, and she waited for Neena to catch up.

For their return, they could either continue retracing their steps on the Wade Harte, or they could take one of these lesser-known side trails, created by hikers who frequented the area. The trails weren't marked on traditional maps, but they did have blazes that could be followed. Next to this side trail, nailed into the gaunt trunk of a lone evergreen, was a triangle made out of three beer-bottle caps—one cap above two.

"Win said it drops down off the ridgeline and wanders beside a creek," Josie said. "It'll spit us out near Deep Fork. There might even be some places to camp down there." The girls hadn't decided yet where they were stopping for the night. The plan was to unload their gear wherever looked okay, whenever they were tired. It wasn't like the previous night; there were plenty of places to camp inside the Misty Rock Wilderness.

"If we hike down," Neena said, "we'll have to hike back up."

"Not like yesterday. It only goes down a little."

Neena gestured at the bottle caps. "That's a blaze?"

After explaining the concept, Win had quizzed them about blazes. The girls had done well, but they'd already forgotten everything. Anticipating this, he had printed out a chart so they wouldn't get lost trying to decipher them.

"Yeah," Josie said. "It might be fun to play follow-the-bottle-caps." When Neena didn't respond, heat rose up Josie's neck. "It would give us something to do, at least."

Neena gave a deflated shrug.

Forced to defend a suggestion she barely cared about, Josie turned so that Neena could unzip her pack. "The chart's in here."

Your brother found the trail, and your brother had the gear. And you lean on him like you lean on me.

Shame and foolishness reverberated inside Josie, but she held her body rigid while Neena sorted through their papers. It was the closest they'd stood all day—the position no longer natural, but invasive. The chart confirmed that the pointy-side-up triangle indicated the start of a trail.

"If it sucks, we'll turn back," Josie said to no one.

Neena clumped ahead, leaving Josie behind yet again.

At times, the bottle-cap trail was obvious. Other times, not so much. But the blazes were generally within sight of each other, and the girls didn't venture far until they were able to locate the next.

One bottle cap meant *continue straight.*

Two vertical bottle caps—the top one just to the left—meant *left turn.*

Two vertical bottle caps—the top one just to the right—meant *right turn.*

It did feel like a game, and Neena begrudgingly admitted to herself that the distraction of the hunt was welcome. Though the trail wasn't official—and the bottle caps, which definitely left a trace, weren't permitted in this designated wilderness area—she assumed the forest rangers looked the other way because, without the markers, it would be easy for hikers to get lost down here, off the ridgeline and off the beaten path.

The girls had been back inside the woods for about an hour. Hidden birdsong accompanied them from blaze to blaze. Leafy trees and mountain laurel and ruffled ferns encased them once more in green. Though their view had disappeared, they still had the sky. If only they had looked up, they would have noticed it was no longer clear.

The trail didn't follow beside a creek, like Josie's brother had described, but instead crisscrossed over numerous slivered tributaries. Wild blueberries flourished under the canopy in unripened clusters. The berries should have darkened and sweetened in July, but the changing climate meant they were still pale and sour. Surreptitiously, Neena tried to eat one. She spit it back out. It needed at least another week to ripen.

She touched the nail in the center of a blaze. *Continue straight.*

The nail was rusty, the bottle cap faded. They were all Cataloochee Light, a cheap regional brand with a distinctive logo—red with tiny white stars inside a blue X. Neena considered the type of person who proudly drank Confederate-flag beer, and perhaps her shudder was visible, because Josie gave the tree a second look. Josie's eyes bugged, but she wasn't looking at the bottle cap. She had zeroed in on the trunk. Claw marks gouged its rough bark. Tufts of black fur had snagged in the stubs of missing branches.

Neena tasted the blueberry, still sour on her tongue. She thought about hungry bears.

A thunderclap rolled and shook the mountains. The girls jolted as if struck by lightning. They had been so absorbed with their task that the graying light had escaped them. Though it was early afternoon, it looked like dusk. The sky was ominous with heavy clouds.

"What do we do?" Neena asked as they scurried to the next bottle cap.

"I don't know," Josie said, equally helpless.

The sky opened. The rain poured. They were drenched by the time they reached the next blazed tree, and the rain still pummeled them even underneath its boughs. The roar was loud and all-encompassing. Their hair was plastered against their cheeks. Neena squinted to keep the water out of her eyes, and Josie's sunglasses fogged. They hunched together, gloomy and immobile, as the minutes dragged by—the sky dark, the rain unabated.

"Fuck it." Neena had to shout to be heard. "We're already soaked. Wanna keep going?"

Josie rotated, shoving her wet pack into Neena's stomach. "Get my glasses first."

Neena grimaced. Reflexively, she pushed the bag away, and Josie tottered.

"Hey!" Josie said.

"I couldn't reach them." Neena's peevishness increased as she dug. Her entire arm disappeared. "Where the hell . . . Why'd you shove them all the way down here?"

With a glare, Josie whipped around and snatched them up. The lenses fogged instantly, but at least they weren't tinted. She stomped toward the next bottle cap.

"Hold on!" Neena stumbled behind her, arm still attached. "I have to zip you up."

Locating the blazes no longer felt like a game. Progress was slow and arduous. The bottle caps were harder to see in the storm, and they had to travel farther to find them. The distance between blazes seemed to be growing. Josie was limping again.

"Blisters?" Neena finally asked.

"Blisters and regret." Perhaps yesterday this might have been funny, but Josie was churlish as she wiped her glasses again. "Where the fuck is the fucking blaze?"

Neena pointed ahead toward a circular nodule. But when they reached it, it was only a knot of bark. The blaze was nowhere in sight.

"We should backtrack," Josie said. "I think we've gone too far."

Hoping their mistake would soon become obvious, they returned to the previous blaze before searching in another direction. This pattern continued for what felt like ten minutes . . . twenty . . . thirty. They still had no phones and no real sense of time. The rainfall was relentless. Their shoes stamped the muddy forest floor with zigzag treads.

"I still think it's the orange plastic ribbon," Neena said, referring to an earlier discovery on a nearby trunk.

"I told you that just means the tree needs to be cut down."

"Yeah, but who'd bother with that out here?"

"The rangers, if the tree is diseased and they don't want it to spread. What else could it mean?"

"I don't know. To keep going straight, I guess."

"We're not following a *ribbon*."

"Okay. Fine." Neena seethed. "What do you suggest?"

"Ten more minutes. If we don't find it, we turn around."

"Turn around?"

"Do you have a better idea?"

"Yeah, we follow the orange ribbon!"

"That's not a better idea!"

They were shouting again, but not because the downpour, finally weakening into a drizzle, made it difficult to hear. The cease-fire had ended. Neena clutched at the sides of her head. "We should have gone home," she said. "I wanted to go home."

"So this is my fault?"

"I didn't say that."

"Well," Josie spat, "I'd rather be home, too."

"Then why are we here?"

"Because you made me! You wouldn't shut up about it until I agreed to come."

"Because you've been miserable all summer! What are you gonna do when I'm gone? You have no other friends, no interests. You won't even drive. Just because your dad died in a freak accident doesn't mean that you will, too."

A cold wall slammed between them.

Josie turned away and started walking. Neena watched her recede for several seconds, furious that they were still dependent on each other. "Where are you going?"

"I'm going home," Josie said. She didn't stop.

"You're going the wrong way."

"We *can't* go your way. We have to turn back."

"You're the one who wanted to take this stupid detour! I'm not turning around now."

"We don't know where we're going."

"We've been down here for, what, two hours? That'd be so much backtracking."

Josie spun to face Neena. Her expression was dark and impenetrable.

"Let's just go a little farther and see what we find," Neena said.

"In what direction?"

Neena pointed at the biggest gap between the trees, a natural pathway that seemed like a logical place for the trail to continue. "That direction."

"Why?"

"Because it looks right."

Josie gritted her teeth. "We have *no reason*—"

The drizzle stopped. Neena stared down the line of her own finger.

"—to believe that *that's* the right way—"

Neena sidled forward to inspect a towering red spruce. The rain clouds cleared, and the sky brightened. The sunshine felt discordant with the way Josie was still berating her. She cut her off. "Josie!"

Josie bristled with outrage—but then slackened as her gaze landed upon the spruce. On its trunk, at eye level, were two indentations the size of bottle caps.

Neena examined the ground, expecting to find the missing bottle caps resting in the moss. "They must have fallen off."

"Fine," Josie said, though her voice was tight with resistance. Obeying the missing instructions, she veered course to the left. "But we're still going home. If you think I'm spending one more night with you out here—"

"Or . . ." Neena peered closer at the holes. "It almost looks as if they were pried—"

A crash of sticks and branches and debris exploded through the woods.

Josie screamed as she fell into the earth.

CRACK. JOSIE'S LEFT fibula snapped as her left tibia punctured through skin. The fracture was heard before it was felt. Josie's vision blurred as she thunked to a splashy halt. Her heartbeat flailed erratically, and her face flushed blazing hot.

Even here, her first emotion was humiliation.

Even now, her first thought was, *Of course it was me.*

"Josie! Oh my God. Josie!"

Stunned, Josie blinked at her left foot, which was mangled around a gnarled root. Something was wrong. *More* wrong. She squinted. A thick hunk of bone was bulging out from within. Her shoed foot hung limply from her ankle, held on by torn muscle and bloody flesh. Pain and terror rocketed through her. She screamed again.

"Josie!" Neena was shouting, sobbing from above. "Oh my God. Answer me. Answer me, please!"

Josie gasped. "Something's wrong with my foot."

"I know." Neena's tone changed abruptly. She sounded peculiar, gentle, shaky. "You're okay. It's gonna be okay."

Josie glanced at it again. Sour nausea rolled through her. She whimpered.

"You fell into a hole," Neena said.

"I didn't see it."

"I didn't, either. It must have been covered with debris. You slipped in the mud and then slid right in."

"My foot."

"I know. Can you move?"

Fear, dark and glassy, descended over Josie. Neena was asking her if she was paralyzed. Observing Josie's expression, Neena quickly adjusted the question. "No, I mean, can you move your right foot? Is it still okay?"

Unsure—petrified—Josie attempted to wiggle it. It wiggled. The girls exhaled their collectively held breaths. Josie moved one arm and then the other. Everything . . . everything else—*oh God, the left foot was barely attached*—seemed to be working.

"Can you get out of your pack?" Neena asked.

Josie was lying on her back at bottom of the hole. It appeared to be eight or nine feet deep and only a few inches wider than she was tall—maybe six feet. Roots jutted out from the earth like grabbing, snatching fingers. Her left leg was ensnared a couple feet above the rest of her body. Her pack was underneath her. With a grimacing twist, she slid out from the straps. Fiery pain bolted up her leg, spinal cord, brain. She gasped in shock. Her arms freed, and she fell back against the cushioning pack. Tears stung her eyes.

Neena's voice cracked. "That's good."

"It *hurts.*"

"I know."

A sludgy pool of water stagnated beneath Josie's buttocks. She looked up and discovered that Neena was a remote blur. She panicked. "My glasses!"

"I think they fell off when you fell down."

Josie squirmed, patting around until she located them in the muddy slush underneath her pack. But when she put them on, the frames were bent and sat wildly askew. Her final shred of composure vanished. She began to wail.

"It's okay," Neena said. "You can wear your sunglasses."

"I can't reach them."

"You can. I know you can. Come on, Josie."

"I can't move. It hurts too much."

"It's okay. Those are only a little crooked, right?" Neena disappeared above her. "Shit. Shit, shit, shit!" She was yelling now. "Help!" Her vocal cords strained to their breaking point. "Help!"

The forest didn't respond. Trees dripped softly as rain shed from their boughs. The surrounding emptiness was total and immense.

Neena dropped onto her stomach on the squelching ground at the edge of the hole. She stretched an arm toward Josie. Testing. Already knowing she couldn't reach. "It's okay. We're going to get you out." She sniffled.

"You aren't allowed to cry," Josie said. Snot oozed down her chin as she tried to unbend her glasses. They resisted. "You're not the one stuck in a hole."

Neena laughed through a sob. She sniffled harder and swallowed her mucus. She didn't know what to do. Feet weren't supposed to *dangle*. "Can you reach me?"

Josie lifted an arm.

Their straining fingers were nearly three feet apart. But, even if they could have reached, Neena wasn't strong enough to haul her up. She didn't even know if moving Josie was the right thing to do. Unless they made a brace? Out of what? Frenzied and distraught, she considered anything in her pack that might be retooled before realizing there was still the basic problem of getting Josie out. Her brain scanned for information gleaned from movies and TV shows. "We need to bandage the wound to stop the bleeding—I think," she said. "Is there anything like that in your first-aid kit?"

Josie put her glasses back on. Her breathing was short. "Band-Aids."

"Anything bigger? More, uh, bandagey?"

Josie suddenly cried out, and Neena lunged back into her pack with an inspired recollection of T-shirts in action movies. Tomorrow's clean shirt proclaimed in bold type that she was a PAWNEE GODDESS. She ripped it. *Tried* to rip it. As she bit down, the fabric squeaked unpleasantly against her teeth. With more precision, she bit again and rubbed with her canines until a hole formed. "Aha!" It sounded maniacal—she felt maniacal—as she wriggled a finger inside the hole and ripped.

"Pads," Josie said.

Neena tore the shirt into a strip. "What?"

"Pads. In your bag."

"Oh my God. You're a genius." Four menstrual pads were left—clean, sanitary, and absorbent. Neena laid them out before attending to her patient. Her patient that she still couldn't reach. The ankle gaped open like the slit of a lewd mouth. A knob of bloody bone and pink muscle protruded from the skin. The dangling foot rocked in the air.

Neena's throat convulsed, and she retched, nearly vomiting. *Pull yourself together.* She had a vision of long white casts in hospital beds. Legs raised in spidery contraptions. "I need you to be brave, Josie. I need your help. You're the one who has to do this."

Josie's eyes spilled over with fresh tears. "No."

"Tap into that adrenaline, okay? We're gonna untangle your foot, and then we'll use that same root to elevate it." Neena prayed this was the right thing to do, but at least keeping it elevated would prevent more blood loss. Maybe? "One step at a time. First, I need you to scoot your butt forward so you can reach the root."

"I can't."

"You have to."

"I can't."

"On the count of three," Neena said harshly. "One. Two. *Three!*"

Josie scooted and screamed. Her vision spotted and fuzzed in electric bursts, fuses burning, as Neena handed down the supplies and barked the orders. The pain sizzled. Her ankle and foot became a singular *it*, separate from the rest of her body, as she complied with Neena's sadistic demands. She unsnagged it. Cradled it. Supported it with pads. *Support the gap, not too tightly. Wrap it, wrap it!* Wrapped the whole thing in cloth. Woozy with agony, Josie blacked out. Only for a second. She was screaming again.

Lie back, Neena was shouting.

Breathe, Josie. Deep breaths. You did so well.

Breathe with me.

Josie found her breath and clung onto it. Her pulse was going haywire. She goggled at her ankle, fatly wrapped in feminine hygiene products and bandaged with the T-shirt, her mind blank with trauma.

"Can you hear me?" Neena said. "I'm going to get help."

Josie's pupils widened in fright. "No."

"I can't get you out on my own. I'm sorry."

"You can't leave me. Please don't leave me."

Their eyes locked through Josie's lopsided glasses.

Neena's heart shattered into spiky fragments. "I'm leaving my stuff here so I can run faster. It'll still take a few hours, but at least it's mostly downhill. I'll plug my phone into my car's charger, drive until I get a signal, and then I'll call emergency services and bring them back with me. I'll only be gone for a few hours—I promise."

"It'll be dark."

"Only for a few hours. I'll be back so soon."

Josie's complexion blanched. "I don't want to be alone."

"I know, sweetie. It'll be okay." Hurriedly, Neena rummaged through her belongings. *Hoodie.* She put it on. *Headlamp.* She hung it around her neck. *Water.* She'd have to carry the bottle. What else? "Car keys," she said, stuffing them into a hoodie pocket. "What else? What else?"

"Phone?" Josie asked.

"Oh my God." It seemed unbelievable to Neena that she'd almost forgotten the one thing she never forgot. She snugged the phone into her back jeans pocket, where it felt safer because she'd be able to feel it the whole time. Paranoid, she moved the keys to her other back pocket.

"Food?"

"It'd weigh me down. You should have it." As Neena searched for the safest place in the hole to drop the hefty canister, the shiny metallic wrapping of a protein bar winked at her from behind the clear plastic. Changing her mind—*don't be stupid, you might need the energy*—Neena grabbed and pocketed it. Then she crawled onto her belly and lowered the canister so that it wouldn't have as far to fall.

The canister reached Josie without incident. She hugged it like a teddy bear for comfort. "Which way are you going?"

"The way we came in. Maybe it's faster the other way, but I'm afraid I might run into more missing blazes and get lost."

"Okay."

"Don't move your leg. And drink lots of water. You can reach it, right? I'll be back soon, so don't dehydrate yourself. And eat."

Josie lifted a trembling arm. "Be careful."

Neena reached toward the tips of Josie's grubby, outstretched fingers, hoping that she could reach them this time. She couldn't. Instead, she mimed squeezing them tightly. And then she was gone.

APART

JOSIE

THE LEAVES WERE still clinging, hopeful and green. They didn't realize that their time was almost up. That soon they would yellow and wither and brown, and fall to the forest floor. Their skeletons would grow brittle and crumble. Rubbery worms would swallow them up and shit them out. Their bodily remains would enrich the soil, feeding and fortifying new life, but their true forms would never be seen again. They would be ghosts.

With her glasses askew, Josie's world had split. Her depth perception was gone, and neither eye could see in perfect focus. The leaves above were an Impressionistic blur. The sky seemed weak and anemic, and the storm had left behind wisps of streaky clouds.

Among all of her meticulously rationalized disaster scenarios, she had never imagined breaking her bones and being left alone. Being left *behind*. But how fitting that it was her—not Neena—trapped in the middle of the woods. It would have been downright poetic if it weren't so goddamn typical. What kind of hapless loser fell into a hole? It was like a cartoon, if Bugs Bunny had ever been stupid enough to be tricked by one of Elmer Fudd's traps.

Too deep to have been dug by hand and too remote to have been dug by machine, Josie had concluded that it must be a sinkhole. It was roundish in shape, all earth and roots, apart from a skinny rhododendron that grew out from the side near the top. Branches poked underneath her body, too. They had probably been covering the hole and had come down with her in the fall. This was the most comforting narrative—that she hadn't noticed the hole because nature had hidden it. It wasn't her fault.

Sinkholes were common around here, but the only one she'd ever seen was in the parking lot of a vacant building on Merrimon Avenue last year. She and Neena had taken a special trip just to peer down into the newly ruptured asphalt. At the time, she had been unimpressed. The darkness had been vague and bottomless.

Josie cried softly. The pain was as lonely as it was agonizing. Hovering gnats whined around her face. When she waved them away, they pestered double. Her skin was pink and warm. A warm body temperature was good, though, right? At least her breathing had stabilized. And her blisters weren't bothering her anymore. Ha.

Having never broken a bone before, she hadn't expected it to be so revoltingly *auditory*. That snap. How many months had it taken for Win's arm to heal after he had attempted to slide over the hood of their dad's sedan like a cool detective in a B-movie? "Action cop," he'd called the move. He'd had that dumb bowl haircut back then, and her little-kid, chicken-scratch signature had taken up most of the space on his cast. He'd gotten so mad at her for that.

A few years later, her father's car was the scene of a second accident when a refrigerator slipped from the back of a pickup truck driving in front of him on I-240. The driver hadn't wanted to pay Best Buy to deliver it. Instead, he was charged with manslaughter for not securing it properly, and he went to prison.

He was out now. Josie's father was still dead.

The brute power of vehicles terrified her, but equally frightening was the idea that one careless slip could cost somebody their life. Josie began to collect stories about mistakes and tragic accidents. People who fell off cliffs while taking selfies. People who were killed by foul balls while watching baseball games. People who choked while eating competitively, were sucked into jet engines while repairing them, were impaled by fence posts while playing tag. People who fell into sinkholes while backpacking in the woods.

In the ninth grade—only a year after her father died—she'd had a panic attack during the behind-the-wheel training of her driver's ed course. The teacher had passed her anyway, out of pity, but Josie was still too afraid to apply for her limited learner's permit. She had leaned heavily on Neena's father to drive her around and then, later, on Neena. She felt safe with them. They were responsible. She didn't feel as safe with her mother or even Win, who drove too fast and didn't always signal. With Neena leaving, Win had been urging Josie all summer to get back behind the wheel, but he didn't realize that time hadn't lessened her fears. It had expanded them.

Proving her point that the world was dangerous, however, was not a satisfying victory.

How long would it take for Neena to return? And who would arrive with her? Josie imagined a team of medics sliding down the ropes of a helicopter, racing down the Wade Harte with a stretcher. The ring of uniformed adults would scrutinize her from above and scold her for being careless. How much did a rescue and evacuation cost? Her mom would be in debt for years to come. The gulf of shame widened.

Josie would have to start college in a wheelchair. At bare minimum, in one of those clunky Velcro-strapped boots. What if it took so long for help to arrive that her foot became infected? What if she lost it altogether thanks to sepsis or gangrene or any of those other conditions she'd heard about but couldn't actually define? She visualized coming to in a sterile room and groping down the side of her leg—only to discover the lower half was missing. The doctor would be harsh and ill-mannered. The nurses, stern but sympathetic. Her sobbing mother would cradle her, assuring Josie that she could still lead a full and fulfilling life.

It would be true, of course. It would also be devastating.

It's only a foot.

But it was *her* foot. How long would it take to learn how to walk again? Was a prosthesis hard and smooth like a mannequin, or did the plastic have some softness and give? Or were they all metal these days? Those good prosthetic blades, the ones athletes wore, had to be expensive. *Oscar Pistorius.* She'd nearly forgotten the man on the cover of the glossy magazines from her childhood. He was a Paralympic athlete, the first double-leg amputee to participate in the Olympics. He had been so cool, until he murdered his girlfriend. Then he was on even more magazines.

Josie continued to catastrophize. She began to think of her injured leg as already gone, a phantom limb, and it twitched in self-pitying outrage. Perhaps the rescue team would *never* find her, and she would starve to death like the deer they'd seen the previous afternoon. The same carrion birds would claw into her flesh and peck out her eyeballs.

Or maybe an internal injury, something unknown, would kill her first. How many people would attend her funeral? The turnout would be poor, she decided, which felt irresistibly worse. And Neena would be destroyed. This felt both terrible and gratifying.

The rainwater evaporated, but Josie's ass remained submerged in the dormant puddle. The afternoon sun baked the mud onto her skin. The light forced her eyes into a squint. Maybe she *could* reach her sunglasses. Delicately, her arm stretched behind her head, and she fumbled to unzip her pack. The top pouch opened tooth by tooth. As her fingertips groped, something small fell out. She shifted for a better angle, and pain shot through her. It ripped and blinded. She gasped and hissed. The pain was a chasm, and, as she strained to touch every item, she plummeted all the way down.

Best she could tell, the sunglasses weren't there. Maybe they had dropped out during the shuffle in the storm.

Her hand dropped and clenched, digging into the branches and mud. Josie screamed. Wept. Tore at the earth until, unexpectedly, she grasped the small object that had fallen from her pack. Recognizing it, she yanked it free and drew it to her lips.

The sound pierced the woods. Birds scattered from the treetops.

Josie squeezed the emergency whistle so tightly that the orange plastic bit into her fingers. She whistled without knowing or caring who she was trying to call.

NEENA

NEENA WAS HALFWAY back to the Wade Harte Trail before realizing that she'd forgotten her inhaler. The journey had been so much lighter without her pack. She'd run. She'd *flown*.

And then she'd jogged.

"Jogged" was a bullshit way of saying that she was running slowly because she didn't have the strength to run fully. Her adrenaline had vanished at the first indication of tightness prickling her chest, but that prickle was merely a caution. Not even a warning. She stopped before the coughing could begin, checked in with her lungs, and sipped her water. Her asthma wasn't mild, but she dutifully puffed her steroid inhaler every morning and night, so the medicine was already built up in her system. And she'd used the rescue inhaler— the fast-acting, emergency inhaler—this morning, too. She would be fine.

She would have felt *better* if she had remembered to grab the rescue inhaler, but there had been the foot. Josie's mangled foot. The foot had been distracting.

An estimated six or seven miles stretched between her and the car. Returning for the inhaler would mean an additional hour of jogging—the last thing she wanted—so Neena continued to retrace their prints through the mud. With her sharpened gaze, she felt like a hunter stalking its prey, except . . . by following her own tracks, didn't that mean she was *also* the prey?

The path grew difficult to make out once Neena reached the pre-storm tracks. The footfalls weren't as deeply imprinted, and many had washed away. Supplementing with the bottle caps, which took longer to find, her progress further slowed.

She would be fine. Josie would be fine.

They'd both be fine, and everything was fine.

The rainfall evaporated, but her clothing remained soaked with sweat. She yearned for dryness. *Fluffy bath towels and ionic hair dryers.* Would she have to run back with the emergency responders, or would they fly out in a helicopter? *Shea butter lotion and freshly laundered pajamas.* Did you have to actually be missing—or near dead—to get a helicopter? *A mattressed bed and cool summer linens.* What level of emergency was a teenage girl with a broken foot stuck inside of a hole?

But it wasn't just a broken foot. The graphic injury was most likely a compound ankle dislocation. Again and again, Neena rehearsed the plan in her mind: Get to the car and call 911. Then, call her parents. Then, Josie's mom. A mixture of premature anxiety and humiliation surged through Neena. Their parents would be frantic, but, even worse, they would be disappointed. She and Josie had failed their first test at being self-reliant adults.

As the bottle-cap trail left the forest floor and headed steeply upward to meet the ridgeline, Neena cursed herself and Josie for deciding to leave the main trail in the first place. She hadn't even reached it yet. The mileage technically hadn't even started.

An unknown noise pierced the forest chatter.

The fine hairs on her neck stood alert. Quiet rippled out as every woodland creature strained to place the sound. It seemed far in the distance, though she couldn't tell in which direction. But the noise was human-made, and it was insistent.

The answer crashed into her like an avalanche. *The whistle.*

Had Josie's condition worsened? Was she asking for Neena to return, or was she calling out for help from somebody else? Why hadn't they thought to teach themselves any whistle signals or codes?

Neena booked it toward Josie. Seconds later, she stomped back toward the ridgeline. The whistling stopped. She spun around again. A growl of frustration escaped, snowballing into a yell, and she screamed Josie's name.

Her heart floundered. The scream was futile. Josie wasn't close enough to hear it, and Neena wasn't close enough to turn around. But what if Josie's condition had worsened, and she needed immediate assistance? Or, what if another hiker had found her, and they were signaling for Neena to return? Then again, what if Neena did return, but then found Josie in the exact same condition? Or, what if her condition *had* worsened, but Neena still couldn't help? Either way, Neena would only be prolonging the agony.

Even though it felt deeply wrong to ignore Josie's cries for help, Neena chose to jog away.

JOSIE

WAS IT UNSAFE to fall asleep, or was that only for concussions? With a shot of disoriented panic, Josie touched her forehead, expecting blood.

Her head was fine.

She settled back against her pack. Everything hurt, though it was tolerable if she didn't move. The hole was muggy, and her eyelids were heavy. Mud caked on her skin in reptilian flakes. Hazily, she flicked off the scales. Here, there. Wherever the crust peeled up. Her body smelled of the warm woods—of dank verdure, crumbling soil, and rotting vegetation. How fitting if the sinkhole collapsed and the earth swallowed her whole.

After her father died, nature overtook their house. Yellow pollen floated in through the window screens and nestled into the cracks of the furniture. Dust thickened and transformed into grime. Greasy dishes crusted in tottering stacks, and abandoned saucepans molded with woolly spores. Rodents appeared, drawn by the glazy smears and scattered crumbs, and shit their droppings along the baseboards and into the open drawers. Photographs faded on the fridge and weren't replaced. Appliances broke and weren't fixed. Tree limbs fell and weren't hauled away. Weeds decimated the flower beds and annihilated the unmown lawn. Josie and Win taught themselves how to do laundry, but even their clean clothes were heaped in piles like discarded corpses.

When Josie became friends with Neena, she tried to block her from knowing or seeing, but Mr. and Dr. Chandrasekhar had insisted on meeting her mother. Shortly after, their house had magically opened to Josie after school. She was absorbed into their afternoon and evening routines. She did homework and ate meals at their table, watched TV and played Xbox on their sofa. The space was safe and sacred, and even after the counters in her own home were eventually scrubbed and sterilized, it remained her safe space.

Only yesterday, she'd wondered if nature might become her new haven. She had imagined spending months out here, trekking all two thousand miles of the Appalachian Trail from Georgia to Maine. Now, she'd either never leave or never return.

Had Neena reached the Wade Harte yet? Josie dreamed of it like a GPS map from above, following the moving dot along the ridgeline.

Go, she urged the dot. *Run, run.*

NEENA

NEENA BENT OVER in a coughing fit. Her chest was taut. The ridgeline was just ahead, but she couldn't continue to climb until her breathing had calmed. Steadying herself against a stalwart birch, she sipped more water. It was unrefreshingly warm and tasted like the woods. If only she had one of those ridiculous-looking pouches with the tube straws that people carried on their backs. Her arms were already sore from taking turns holding the bottle.

Spongy mushrooms with ribbed gills scaled the birch's trunk. Did the mushrooms harm the tree as they fed? It seemed sinister how fungus concealed itself—just out of sight—before erupting from the earth overnight, everything suddenly covered in mold and decay. Did it grow as quickly as it appeared? Or did it fester below the surface for weeks, months, even years before being pushed to its breaching point?

Josie was always future tripping; Neena had never known anybody more afraid of things going wrong. But maybe if they'd been friends before her father's accident, Josie would have been a different person. This idea made Neena uneasy, too. Would she have still fit into Josie's life if her father's absence hadn't carved out a void?

Somehow, the sinkhole felt to Neena like it was her fault. Like she had willed the danger into existence by denying its possibility. By not listening to Josie. Neena had said awful things, unforgivable things, but Josie had said true things. Neena *was* selfish.

When her parents had immigrated from Kolkata to Charlotte, her mother had to do her residency all over again. Her father had to pass the local bar. Later, when Neena was in elementary school, her mother had accepted a prestigious job at Mission Hospital, and they had moved to Asheville. Every day, her parents woke up at four a.m.—Ma to cook their meals, and Baba to commute the two hours back to his job in Charlotte. Ma would drive Neena and Darshan to school and then drive herself to work. Baba would drive home in time to pick them up from school. Yet they never complained. Neena had *never* heard them grouse about being too tired or stressed or busy.

They had sacrificed their own comfort to give their children access to greater opportunities. Every choice they made was for the people they loved, never for themselves. Darshan had followed in their mother's footsteps and was currently premed. Neena had rebelled and chosen a path that served herself. Not only was she turning her back on her parents' wishes, she was also abandoning her best friend—the one person who completely understood her and was always by her side.

Even now, leaving to get help . . . Neena was still leaving. Should she have tried harder to get Josie out of the hole? Her instinct had been to *go* and to *go fast*. It was the right decision, but it was also an uncomfortably close parallel to what was about to happen. Because even if Josie did find something or someone that she loved in college, she would still have to take care of her mother. By being healthy and successful, Neena's parents had given her the freedom to leave. Guilt chewed Neena up. She felt the dull, hot press of her phone in her pocket and wished she could text her ma.

Stop wasting time, Ma would text back. *This situation is not about you.*

Neena's selfishness burned everything it touched.

She pushed away from the birch and, a few minutes later, finally reached the Wade Harte. The daunting miles spread out, before her and behind her.

JOSIE

THE MOLD WAS spreading. Josie noticed it first in the bottom corner of a wall, an indistinct greenish-black spot, and scrubbed it away with a scouring pad. The wall dried, and the spot reemerged. As she scrubbed again, her eyes caught on another area, about the size of a quarter. She scrubbed this, too, before discovering even more. The spores grew fast, impossibly fast, like spilled ink or soured milk. She stumbled backward as they swallowed the wall and then shot off across the mopped floors and sterilized surfaces.

Chaos reclaimed her house in splatters of grimy, fungal watercolors. Josie glanced down at the yellow scouring pad in her hand, now blackened and rank, and discovered the darkness wriggling up onto her fingers. She dropped the pad, but the stain was already smothering her wrists, overtaking her arms. She ran to the sink, but the faucet was dry. She ran to the door, but the knob wouldn't turn. She ran to the windows, but the sashes were sealed shut. The mold crawled over her skin, alive and devouring—

Josie woke with a racing heart. An insect horde was swarming inside the sinkhole. Mosquitos, gnats, and flies vied for her immobilized body, attacking her exposed skin. Their host cried out. Flapping and waving her arms, she forced them off, but they careened straight back. Josie swatted them against her bitten flesh. She fumbled for the bug spray and bombed them. Her tormenters hurtled away.

Alone in the poisonous mist, she coughed and gagged. She leaned her head back to try and gulp at the fresh air, but it was too high to reach. Though the clouds had moved along, the wan color of the late-afternoon sky had barely changed. It was impossible to tell how long she'd been asleep. Her body spasmed. The buzzing wings haunted.

Slowly, then rapidly, her sunburn reintroduced itself. Her skin was angry pink and screaming hot, inflamed in the areas where she'd flicked off the dried mud. If only she'd remained covered in it like an adorable baby elephant. If only she'd remembered to reapply sunscreen at lunch. If only she hadn't fallen into this hole.

If only they'd never gone on this trip.

Her mind retraced the minutes before her fall. Getting lost, fighting. What were the chances of both bottle caps falling off the tree, anyway? What kind of rotten luck was that? Unless it hadn't been luck at all. She considered the rubbed-away bark on the other tree. The handwritten log of bear sightings scrawled across the plywood notice board at the trailhead.

She spun the stone ring around her finger in her usual nervous habit. It moved with resistance, tight from the heat. Less than a week after they'd bought the rings, she'd dropped hers into a cast-iron sink. It had shattered on impact. She'd had to borrow money from Win to replace it but had never told Neena, because she didn't want her to believe that this new ring meant anything less. Josie was careful with it now, always touching its smooth finish to ensure that it was safe.

She thought she'd been safe with Sarah. They'd been best friends since the first grade. But less than a year after Josie's father died,

Sarah had inexplicably abandoned her for a group of girls who had boyfriends and vaped scented clouds of cotton candy in the school bathrooms. Was it because Josie wasn't fun anymore? Because she worried too much? Because she was depressed? Maybe she put too much pressure on her friends to keep her happy. Maybe that's why they always left—the job was too big.

The bandaged mass on the other side of the hole was crusted red, but Josie's thoughts remained as detached from her ankle as it was from her. Her skin burned. Her bites itched. She fantasized about bathing, naked and clean, in a pool filled with clear aloe vera. The cold gel would hold her body aloft like gelatin. Protect her like a cocoon.

I could wait like that.

She placed herself inside the cocoon.

I can wait like this.

Something rustled in the woods. Her eyes popped back open.

"Neena?" Gently, she twisted, looking upward through her crooked frames. Her head throbbed with muzzy euphoria. She called out louder, "Neena?"

The rustling stopped.

No. It was impossible for Neena to have returned before dark. Unless she'd found help along the way?

"Neena? Is that you?"

Long seconds passed, and the noises resumed. As the shrubs shifted and resettled, her thoughts again sprang to bears. Her stomach plunged. The sounds grew close enough to become distinct—and then sharpened into footsteps. With unshakeable certainty, Josie knew the gait was human. And she knew Neena would have called back.

"Hello? Can you hear me?"

The footsteps continued toward her. Heavily, steadily.

"Help! Please help me." Her cries turned hysterical. "I'm in a hole! I'm down here!"

The footsteps stopped—just out of view. She was sobbing again, begging for a response. Something weighty and substantial was lowered onto the ground above her.

And then a man peered over the edge.

NEENA

THE JOGGING HAD ceased. Neena was speed-walking now, her formidable boots clomping low dust clouds along the balds. The hottest hours of the day were over, but the sun still persisted in the sky. She hoped to reach Deep Fork before dusk and to be down as much of Frazier Mountain as possible before nightfall.

Before this trip, Neena had never imagined that her upcoming separation with Josie would be anything more than locational. Their friendship was too strong. It could survive anything. Now, she wondered if she had been lying to herself the whole time.

She already knew she had been lying to Josie.

Freshman year, Neena's then best friend had joined the cross-country team. Physically unable to participate, when Neena had seen Grace running around the track with her new teammates—matching cardinal-red tank tops, ponytails bouncing behind them—she had felt targeted. Spurned. It felt like she'd been rejected for an entire girl gang. But the awful truth was that Grace had never rejected Neena.

Neena had rejected Grace.

Cutting the ties first became Neena's way of winning. Except the cold shoulder and ignored texts had only left Grace hurt and con-fused. Remorse had overwhelmed Neena, but, instead of apologizing, she averted her gaze. Instead of apologizing, she clung to cowardice.

Later, when Josie inferred that Grace had instigated the dump-ing, Neena had never corrected her. Partly because she felt sorry for Josie, but mostly because she still felt ashamed for how she had treated Grace.

It was shocking how quickly angry words—just like silence—could alter a shared history into insignificance. Neena knew Josie's order at Waffle House (patty melt with extra pickles, hash browns covered and capped). Where she kept her favorite lip gloss (Burt's Bees in Sunny Day, the back pocket inside her purse). How she couldn't roll her tongue (and rolled it using her fingers as a joke). Who her first crush was (Hiccup from *How to Train Your Dragon*). Neena was an encyclopedia of Josie knowledge, and now that book threatened to become as useless as the volume on Grace.

The surrounding panorama was lonely and foreboding. The sun-light was interrogational and oppressive. The clamor of insects shook the air like the tail end of a rattlesnake. Neena stumbled and gasped, overcome. It felt like someone was squeezing away her breath.

JOSIE

THE MAN WAS white. He wore a ball cap low over his eyes, and his body was broad and thickset. His beard was thick, too. He appeared to be somewhere in his thirties, maybe, and, though it was difficult for her to see his expression clearly, the energy behind his stare was intense. It sucked up all the air. He didn't speak.

Josie shrank, unnerved by his lack of reaction. Her sobbing ended in a wet hiccup.

"Well, I'll be," he finally said. "What're you doing down there?" His Appalachian accent was strong. It was the voice of the rural counties that surrounded Asheville, and the tone held a measure of accusation. Josie felt like she'd done something wrong as she tried to explain to him about the fall and subsequent injury.

His manner remained odd. Preoccupied. He was still standing, not crouching, as though he might take off at any second.

"I need help." She shouldn't have to state the obvious, except . . . it seemed that she did. Something wasn't connecting. "Can you get me out of here?"

The man glanced at the woods. "Where's your friend?"

Apprehension trickled through her veins. How did he know about Neena? How long had he been watching them? Was he the one Neena thought she heard in the fog last night?

He kicked at Neena's abandoned pack.

Oh. Though reluctant to admit she was alone, Josie couldn't see a way around it. "My friend left to get help," she said. *My friend knows where I am.*

"There ain't help for miles. How long has he—she?—been gone?"

It was only a one-word question, smuggled inside another question, but it turned Josie's stomach. Alarm bells clanged louder. She wanted to tell him that her friend was male and then later slip into the conversation that he was also a linebacker the size of a baby orca. But she was at this stranger's mercy. Facts were required.

"I'm not sure," she said. "A few hours. You didn't see her on the trail?"

"Which way'd she go?"

Josie hesitated—and then gave him Neena's location.

"She's your age? A teenager?"

Hesitated again. Confirmed.

"Naw," he said. "I ain't seen nobody. I came thataway."

Josie couldn't tell which direction he was pointing, and she didn't understand why he wasn't more concerned. If she had run into somebody in trouble, she'd be freaking out, trying to help. She would have at least asked the person if they were okay—even if it was clear that they weren't. But the man seemed calm and detached.

"Can you help me?" she asked again.

His demeanor changed so abruptly that she startled. With an interested step forward, he squatted to examine her. His eyes were dark and wide-set. His work boots poked over the rim. "You're in a mess, girl."

A whiff of sour breath struck her—an infected reek that hinted of diseased gums—but his countenance had lightened into a tease that expressed worry. Perhaps he'd only been in shock. Relieved at the change of character, she managed to choke out a laugh. For some reason, she was trying to make *him* comfortable.

"Can you move that?" he asked, referring to her foot.

"Not really."

"You shouldn't try."

"No," she agreed.

He shook his head. The gesture meant bad news.

Fear caught in her voice. "What is it?"

"Well, I sure hate to tell you this. I could probably get you out, but we might bungle that more on the way up. And if that gets worse—or if you lose more blood—there's a good chance you'd also lose that foot."

Faintness swallowed her. Distortion buzzed her frequencies.

"No," he said. "Best you don't move. Let them medics come to you."

"Do you have a phone?"

"Not one that works out here. Same as yours, I reckon."

"Ours died. Not that they had a signal."

The man thought for several seconds. He adjusted his ball cap. "How often do you girls come out here?"

"First time." She mumbled it because she was embarrassed. "Beginner's luck, right?"

"And your friend knows where she's going? She got a map?"

"Yeah, of course . . ." Josie cut herself off. "No. Shit. They're still in our bags. She knows where she's going, though. She's headed back the way we came in."

The man made an indeterminable noise. Turning away from her, he proceeded to rummage through Neena's pack.

"What are you doing?" Her heart battered against her rib cage. She felt protective over Neena's belongings. She didn't want this strange man touching them.

He held something up, and his concern grew more audible. "She okay without these?"

Josie squinted to make it out. It was the Ziploc with Neena's inhalers. The man's head cocked slightly—enough for her to understand he was processing the information that her bent frames had impaired her vision. Josie didn't want him to know that, either. The pain became vibrant and nauseating. She bit her lip, clenching to hold everything in.

"All right, now. Take a deep breath. You're turning purple."

"I think she's okay." The sinkhole whorled in dizzying spirals. "I'm not sure."

The man straightened. His stocky frame overshadowed her. "Right, then."

Her attention shot upward in distress. "You're leaving?"

"You ain't going nowhere, but your friend could get lost." His "get" sounded like "git." In one hand, he held the printout maps. In the other, he rattled the inhalers in their bag. "And she might need these."

"No!" Josie didn't like his company, but the thought of being alone again was harrowing. He needed to stay and protect her. In all likelihood, Neena was fine.

His dark eyes warned. "Don't try to move."

But if Neena *wasn't* fine, her situation could get dire. Which increased the direness of Josie's situation, as well.

"You'd only make it worse," he said, disappearing from view.

Josie's face pinched to avoid erupting in tears. She didn't want him to hear how upset she was to be left behind for a second time.

She heard him pick up the item that he had set down upon his arrival. From the bottom of the hole, she caught a glimpse—a flash—of the top of it. She couldn't be sure, but it looked like the barrel of a shotgun.

NEENA

NEENA WAS BEING hunted. For the last mile, she could swear that something had been tracking her from the forest below the ridgeline. A creeping awareness of movement had coupled with a visceral sensation of watchfulness. She tried to reason herself out of it. Being alone in the backcountry was unnerving, period, so her imagination was in overdrive. She was being irrational.

But then . . . a twig would snap. Or a branch would rustle.

And paranoia triumphed again over logic.

She reintroduced bursts of jogging back into her speed-walking. Her sporadic coughs were dry and hacking. Though she was well out of the balds, it was unclear how close she was to Deep Fork. She recognized enough landmarks to verify that she was on the correct trail, but not enough to gauge any real sense of time. The sooner she passed Deep Fork, the better. Her sweat chilled at the thought of navigating the dense tunnel of laurel in the dark with only the beam of her headlamp.

Shadows lengthened. Bees hushed. She raced the sun as it sank lower in the sky.

I'm sorry, Josie. I'm trying. I'm going as fast as I can.

A crack lacerated the silence. Neena shot out from her skin. Ahead in a nearby stand of trees, something had stepped on a stick. The foliage swished and splintered without wind. She hastened backward, pulse hammering, eyes scanning for beasts.

A man emerged from the cover.

He was an adult, maybe in his late twenties. He was white, lean and rawboned, with wispy patches of blond facial hair. His ball cap, rugged pants, and work boots didn't seem to belong to a hiking enthusiast, instead calling to mind the deer hunters who stocked up on Mossy Oak camouflage and discount Mountain Dew at Kmart. Though perhaps the gun enhanced this impression—visually jarring and slung so casually over his slim shoulders.

This was a different man. A second man. But Neena did not even know there was a first.

A certain pressure arose in her bladder. She glanced behind herself, suddenly terrified that she might be surrounded. She wasn't. She was alone with this man and his gun, and now that prospect seemed even more frightening.

"Shit, girl." The man drew a hand to his chest. "You nearly gave me a heart attack."

She was glad to hear that he'd been startled, too. And yet.

Yesterday, she had relaxed the instant the manly tenor was revealed to be the boy hiking with his girlfriend. The vibe here was different. Her muscles remained taut, her senses heightened. She didn't move to approach him.

"You must be the one I heard coughing," he said. "I was on the trail down there, but I couldn't see nothing. Thought I was going crazy."

His voice matched his appearance. It was the mountain accent that her future classmates in Los Angeles might think of unfavorably as hillbilly, or even basic Southern, but she recognized specifically as Appalachian. The South had a wide variety of dialects. Neena had met plenty of friendly and intelligent people with this particular drawl—those who dropped their gs and doubled their negatives—but she was ashamed to admit that she still felt nervous around the white people who had it. Or maybe it wasn't shame. Maybe it was something more practical.

Neena spoke cautiously. "Yeah. I kept hearing things, too."

Her gaze flickered back to the gun. Shotgun? Rifle? She only vaguely understood the difference, but its barrel was long, and it looked snug with its owner.

The man grew abashed and defensive. "It ain't for hunting. This rifle's strictly emergency use only. A few years ago, me and a buddy were chased by a mama bear protecting her cubs. We didn't get hurt or nothing, but I always come prepared." He adjusted the dingy shoulder strap and gave her a squirrelly grin. "Hey. Don't you go reporting me to the rangers."

She didn't believe him—he'd brought up the subject himself and then denied it too readily—but it reassured her that he was probably stalking something illegal or out of season as opposed to lone female hikers. Still. It seemed best to agree with whatever he said.

"Your secret's safe with me," she said.

The man turned expectant. Like he was waiting for her to join him. Like he assumed they would hike together for a while and shoot the breeze.

Neena wanted him to either start hiking in the opposite direction or to hike so far ahead of her that she couldn't see him anymore—that he would no longer exist in her visible universe. Except, of course, if he went ahead of her, he could hide and wait and then lurch out at her from behind another copse of trees. And if he went behind her, she would never be able to stop looking over her shoulder.

She was trapped.

Reluctantly, she approached the stranger. A putrid stench reached her first. Her own body didn't smell like lilacs, but the odor emanating from the man was an assault. Angling her head aside to prevent gagging—hoping the gesture didn't look rude—her gaze snagged on the brush where he had exited onto the Wade Harte. The vegetation was thick and barely trampled. There didn't appear to be a path there at all.

"Listen, uh." She coughed again. "I'm kind of in a hurry."

His hands lifted in surrender. "Hand to Jesus, I won't slow you down."

Shit. *Shit.*

She began to walk at a brisk pace. "You said you were on a trail down there?"

"There's a bunch of them." He moved in step beside her, and she noticed a large hunting knife strapped to his belt. "I know my way around these parts better than anybody. Hell, I blaze my own trails."

His eyes glinted. They were small and close together, a washed-out shade of blue. His whole body was vibrating with a peculiar, jittery energy like he was tamping down some sort of excitement. Everything inside Neena shouted at her to run, but he hadn't actually threatened her or done anything wrong.

Also, there was the rifle. And the knife. She tried to stay a few feet ahead of him, but he kept closing the gap.

"By any chance," he said, "that wasn't you who blew that whistle a while back, was it? I called out and searched around, but I couldn't find anyone."

His casual tone rang false. Unless she was projecting it? Sweat beaded her armpits. She didn't want to tell him about Josie, but . . .

what if he could help? What if she was being racist against white guys with hick accents and ugly clothes? She hedged her response with a question. "You don't happen to have one of those satellite phones that works in the middle of nowhere, do you?" But then a deluge of coughing defied her attempt at nonchalance. She choked down some water but kept moving.

"Asthma?" he asked.

It almost stopped her in her tracks. Wheezing, she snuck a sideways look at him as she wiped the dripping water from her chin.

His expression lit up. "I knew it. My wife—my ex-wife, we got married in high school—she had asthma, too. You should slow down, not speed up."

Neena didn't know what else to do but confess. "I didn't blow the whistle. It was my friend, who's hurt."

The man's footsteps faltered. "Your friend? What happened to her?" His eyes darted to the tree line. "Where is she?"

The feminine pronouns unsettled Neena. Was he assuming? Hoping? Yet the full, gruesome story tipped out of her in a torrent.

"Whoa, whoa, whoa. Your friend's foot's gonna fall off, and you're taking the long way back?"

Neena's lungs cinched another notch. "What do you mean?"

"You're headed for the parking lot on the other side of Frazier Mountain?"

She nodded.

"The Wade Harte ain't the *fastest* route. It's the *scenic* route."

"There's a faster route?"

"About a quarter mile ahead. Cuts straight down through the valley. I reckon you'd save an hour, at least."

Hope took a vast and fateful breath. "Could you show me where it is?"

"Hell," he said, "that's the way I was headed."

The man's pale eyes blinked too much when he spoke. His fetid stink curdled her stomach, and his gun was probably loaded. But perhaps he was a godsend, after all.

JOSIE

SHE COULDN'T STOP thinking about the gun. The man must be an illegal hunter, which explained why his initial approach had been so cautious—he didn't know who he was about to find. It also seemed possible that he'd hidden the shotgun because he thought it might scare her. Which made the gesture kind. Shivering in the dusk, Josie tried to convince herself that the man had only been trying to make her feel safe.

The trees above the sinkhole began to smudge like charcoal. The forest noises reshaped. Entire species of insects fell asleep as others awakened. The air didn't just feel colder. It smelled colder, too.

Josie put on her hat and draped her hoodie over her torso like a blanket. The puddle was still damp on her ass, and she couldn't contort her body into any angle that might allow her to reach her sleeping bag. She should have asked the man to toss down Neena's sleeping bag to her. He should have offered.

Her foot was still elevated on top of the roots. Her back and hips trembled with rippling aches that no amount of shifting could alleviate and that only disappeared whenever she accidentally jostled the horrific bundle at the end of her leg.

How long was it until nightfall?

She hadn't thought to give the man her name, nor ask for his. Why hadn't she armed him with more information? Her mother's phone number, at the very least. He'd reminded her, in a way, of her uncle Kevin, her father's older brother who still lived in Madison County, where they'd grown up.

Madison was only one county over, but the lines made a difference. Politics and attitudes changed. Income and education dropped. While her father had lost his childhood accent, her uncle had retained it. He was quiet and reserved and gave plenty of side-eye to the liberals in Asheville. But he was also big-hearted and dependable and the only relative who regularly visited her and Win.

He was a hunter, too. A few years ago, he'd taken her out onto his property and taught her gun safety and how to shoot. But, despite the lesson, Josie would never feel safe around guns. Because there was no arguing with a gun. When going up against one, the person without one always lost.

However, if Uncle Kevin—who owned a successful contracting business, as well as a small arsenal—were to ever discover somebody in distress, he would do everything in his power to help them. And he wouldn't be flashy about it. He would get the job done, and he wouldn't need thanks or praise. Maybe this man was the same.

She imagined her uncle's burly figure creaking in the rocking chair beside hers on his porch, teasing her about this "little mishap in the woods." Or her "little foot injury." Except it wouldn't be actual belittling. He'd be trying to make her laugh. And then her father would appear in the wrinkles around his sly, twinkling eyes, and he would live again for those few seconds.

The pain was unbearable. Time meandered and dwelled into oblivion. Hopefully Neena would reach the car soon.

Josie's appetite was weak, but keeping up her strength became motivation to eat. Tonight's scheduled dinner was chili macaroni with beef. A gift from Win, and she and Neena had been laughingly eager to try it. Not because the prepackaged backpacking food would taste *good*, but because it would be an *experience*.

Making the meal required boiling water. Josie poured tepid water into the pouch and waited as long as she could stand. In diminutive bites, she gagged and choked on the crunchy moistened shells and soggy compressed meat. She gave up quickly. Forcing down the last protein bar instead, she dreamed of hot mozzarella stretching away from a slice of pepperoni pizza. Sipping some water, she despaired for cold condensation slipping down a bottle of Mexican Coke.

These liquids reminded her of other necessities. With extreme difficulty, she maneuvered to urinate into the empty mason jar from the previous night's dinner. Some of it ran over her hands and slopped onto her jeans. *I should have just peed myself.* The thought wasn't funny. It was as honest as a deserved punishment.

A commercial airplane whined across the darkening sky. The sound magnified Josie's loneliness. She could see civilization, but it couldn't see her. She had no flares, no SOS spelled out in rocks. The passengers on board would never hear her cries for help. She watched the red blinking lights in silence.

The wind picked up with brusque and forceful gusts. Dead leaves swept across the ground and showered into the sinkhole. She gripped her hoodie tightly against her chest. *This*, she thought. *This* was the most sorry that she had ever felt for herself.

And then something unexpected blew into the hole.

It started with one piece of paper, then another. Then several more tumbled in behind. At first, Josie didn't understand because her mind didn't want to process what they meant—maps and directions and instructions, each sheet a memory from her mother's inkjet printer. The man had said he would bring them to help Neena. But he had left them behind.

Numbing dread sank over Josie. Her ears sharpened to the surrounding forest.

Night descended.

NEENA

THEY DESCENDED ON a narrow side trail off the Wade Harte. The man led the way. Neena didn't like how he kept glancing over his shoulder as if checking to make sure she was still behind him. As if her wheezing breath and crunching boots weren't enough reassurance. As if, at any instant, she might bolt.

The sun sank below the mountains. The final rays of daylight barely illuminated the trail. A nagging haze of gnats followed her. Visually and physically compromised, she swatted and stumbled down the slope with one hand clamped on the headlamp around her neck. It would be there when she needed it.

The man maintained a steady but incomprehensible monologue about digitally altered videos, trout fishing, his ex-wife, the judges on a network singing competition, pygmy salamanders, and phone addiction. She got lost in the connections and transitions.

Like the bottle-cap trail, eventually the path opened up, and the foot-worn rut vanished into the forest floor. Unlike the bottle-cap trail, the way to continue was unmarked. Neena's reliable internal compass—confirmed by the setting sun—was needling her northeasterly, so she was relieved when the man didn't break stride as he headed in the direction of the parking lot. It wasn't that she was worried he might get them lost. Clearly, he was familiar with the terrain. It was that she didn't trust him.

The man wasn't just a stranger. He was *strange*.

Something ferrety curbed his friendliness. His movements were scattered but quick, with purpose. It felt as if she were being shown one thing only to be distracted from another. Like that old man when she was in elementary school who waved her over to his car to ask if she'd seen his lost dachshund but then wasn't wearing any pants. She'd run away, hot with shame, feeling like *she'd* done something wrong. This felt like her fault, too. She never should have left the main trail. She began to pray to bump into another hiker, pray to reach the parking lot before dark.

They hustled deeper and deeper into the unknown woods. Somewhere nearby, water slipped and rushed over stones. The wind gusted up and shook the trees. And the whole time, the man never stopped talking. He swerved left around an ash with fibrous tumors of moss, and, expecting him to correct right and continue straight, Neena was surprised when he kept left—changing direction completely.

She hesitated.

Twenty seconds. That's how long she'd give him to start heading in the correct direction. Following behind him, she counted in her head. Upon reaching twenty, she decided she'd counted too fast and allotted for twenty more. Then it was only right to add another twenty because that rounded it to a full minute.

She wanted him to fix this. Now. Her panic spread like a virus. As one minute tipped into two, instinct overrode doubt. To prevent her from traveling a single step farther, her legs stiffened into a stop.

The man reacted like a trigger. His pale eyes bugged through the sooty black shadows. "What's the matter?"

"Why are we turning around?"

"We ain't."

"No." Something powerfully terrified detonated inside Neena. "We're headed back the way we came."

The man pointed behind her. "We came thataway."

"You know what I mean. We're walking back toward Burnt Balsam."

His pointing arm shifted. "Burnt Balsam is *that* way."

A blink of doubt. "No."

The story changed. "Well, hell. Yeah. But we have to go this way first. The trail's gonna loop back around." He took a few steps, attempting to shepherd her forward.

The problem was that no perceptible geological impediments existed that might require them to walk in this direction. This part of the woods looked exactly like the rest of the woods. Even the tumorous ash appeared to be random, as if he were following a blaze she couldn't see. She couldn't see much of anything anymore. Darkness had invaded the forest, and only one thing was clear: This man was not here to help her.

An unspoken transaction occurred between them.

The air congested with a toxic pall. In one swift motion, his mask of helpfulness vanished as the rifle slipped down from his shoulder and into his hands.

Perhaps he hadn't anticipated it—that she would anticipate him—because she had just enough time to bolt before the first shot exploded out. The boom quaked the earth.

Frantically, she zigzagged through the dark trees. Josie's voice screamed inside her skull as she tripped and bumbled: *Zigzag! Zigzag!* Branches slashed her face and snagged her hoodie. Brambles tore her jeans.

Another shot ripped through the woods. Bark exploded from the closest tree. The arboreal shrapnel stung her cheeks as the bang echoed against the mountains. *Zigzag! Zigzag!* Her airways narrowed acutely. The man tore through the bracken behind her.

She was choking, running, coughing, fleeing. She'd lost all sense of direction. Another shot, and she fell, but she'd only tripped over a root. Her wrists took the brunt of the impact, and as she swiveled to get back onto her feet, a slender gap revealed itself under the massive boulder beside her. A natural hollow. Flattening her body, she wriggled underneath. Too late, she realized that she'd entered the incorrect way, and her head was facing the wrong direction to see out. The squeeze crushed her breasts and lungs. She buried her mouth into her shoulder to muffle her coughs.

Inhale. She could hear Josie coaching her.

She used the muscles of her rib cage to breathe in.

Exhale, Josie said.

She couldn't exhale all the way. Every act was purposeful rather than automatic. Huge gulps of air felt like teensy puffs. Her eyes choked with tears as her neck tightened.

The man careened past the boulder—and then halted. No doubt, he'd realized he couldn't hear her anymore. How far away was he? A few yards? A few feet? She ceased trying to breathe. Her features twisted into a dimly rasping, openmouthed scream.

His footsteps trod back slowly through the undergrowth. Sinking into the ground beside her head, they stopped again. One way or another, she was about to die.

Please don't hear me.

Please don't look down.

Please don't hear me.

Please don't look down.

This was her final refrain. His boots shifted in the soft ferns, and she envisioned his stance following his eye line as it scanned the forest. Her abdomen quivered. She couldn't hold for much longer. The taste of ancient granitic bedrock, damp black loam, and milky green lichen infused her open mouth. Death had arrived at her tomb.

A bird made a startled caw as it flew from bushy cover.

The man shot again, and her coughing erupted as he thrust mistakenly toward whatever creature had frightened the bird instead of the creature hiding beneath the rock.

JOSIE

THE HOLE WAS black and clammy. Josie imagined the plastic bag of inhalers discarded in the fermenting leaves above. The printouts lay beside her in the mud. Night seeped in through the threads of her clothing and her sanity.

It had been dark for at least an hour, which meant that, any minute now, Neena should be reaching the car. If she'd made good time, perhaps she'd already done it. Help might already be on its way. Though it was unlike Josie to latch onto optimism, she placed a protective cage around these last glowing embers. Her ears strained for the distant notes of a helicopter or a team of emergency responders crashing through the forest. Sometimes she did hear them, only for the sound to persist unchanged and for her to realize that she was hallucinating in her exhausted delirium.

She heard four gunshots. They sounded like thunder. Perhaps they *were* thunder. But surely these were all delusions, too. The best-case scenario was that the man was only concerned with himself—and whatever animal he was hunting—and that he'd flat-out left the woods. Because if he *was* looking for Neena, what would he do to her? And if Neena couldn't get help, what would become of Josie? Would the man return for her, or would he leave her here to starve and rot? Which was worse?

Josie shivered. Her ears were cold shells, and her nostrils had hardened with the rusty scent of her own blood. The pain was so livid and fluctuating that it was almost redundant. Her only comfort was her backpack, the bulky presence hugging her from behind, the sole barrier between her and the surrounding dirt.

Night spiraled around her in lonely loops.

Two girls walk into the woods, she thought. But the story wasn't a fairy tale. They hadn't dropped a trail of bread crumbs, discovered a gingerbread cottage with sugar-paned windows, or shoved an old witch into a flaming stove. Nor was it a ghost story, traded in whispers around smoky campfires. It wasn't even an urban legend. Their story was flesh and bone. Urgent and real.

A firm crunch fractured the cloistered silence. The sound of an approaching human was definitive in its reality. "Neena?" Josie's voice surfaced as a croak. "Neena. Neena!" Each call grew louder and more unhinged. "Can you hear me?"

Neena would have called back. A medic would have responded, too.

"Help! Please help me!"

Heavily, steadily, the footsteps advanced.

"Oh God." Josie whimpered. "Please, no."

The steps were deliberate and unhurried. The man had returned, and intuition told her that he hadn't brought help. He stopped beside the sinkhole. Squinting upward through the inky nothingness, she tried to make out his figure, but he held himself just far enough back that she couldn't see him. Could he see her?

"Is that you?" she asked. "Are you the man who helped me earlier? I didn't catch your name. I'm Josie."

The man exhaled in the darkness. The sound was hushed, channeled through a robust and sturdy chest.

"Did you find my friend? Did you call for help?"

Each question swung ominously unanswered. Her denial took its final push in the form of honesty. "I wish you'd say something. You're scaring me." She managed a rough laugh to keep it conversational. "Is my friend okay?"

The man walked away.

But then he turned again, walked toward her—and kept going. As he passed the sinkhole, his large, shadowy frame materialized briefly before slipping back into black.

Fear stunned Josie like a captive animal.

The man retreated. Turned. Advanced. He was pacing, prowling, threatening her with glimpses of his presence. The hole grew deeper and darker. Hostility strangled the oxygen from the air. Intense anger radiated out from him, as well as something even more dangerous but stifled. A tangible manifestation of evil.

"Please," she begged. "Please stop. Say something."

He lapped back and forth.

With each predatory pass, her terror amplified. The man was enjoying himself. He was reveling in her fear. As his pacing drew closer, the outline of his shotgun became as clear as moonlight. Wishing for a weapon, she gripped the mason jar instead. Fright ignited into fury. "What do you want from me? Go away! Get the fuck away from me!"

In a flash, he was crouched beside the rim. She shrank back. The man stared, dark eyes unblinking, across the vulnerable length of her body.

She strained to see him better, to see him at all. "Wh-where's my friend?"

His shadow hardened. "No need to concern yourself about her."

A leaden weight dropped through her gut. "What did you do? Where is she?"

"I didn't do nothing."

Josie cried in soundless anguish. "Where is she?"

"I have plans for you."

"No. Please."

"I bet you love to party with the boys at school." His words vibrated with tightly bridled rage.

She cringed and recoiled. "Please," she said again. "Please leave. I won't tell anybody I saw you hunting. I won't say anything, I promise."

"Now, what makes you think I'm hunting, all the way out here?" The man paused to lift the gun. "This?" He laughed, but the utterance was low and malicious. "Yeah. I reckon you could say I'm hunting."

"Neena's getting help."

"Neena." His crude tongue tasted the name. "No. She can't help you."

An image appeared of her best friend crumpled on the forest floor, a vicious shot to the head, her gaze vacant. "Our parents know where we are. They're expecting us tonight. When we don't show up, they'll send help."

"They won't know you girls is gone for a while."

"They will. They're *really* strict. If we're late—even five minutes—they'll call the cops. My dad called them last year when—"

"Shut the fuck up," he snapped, dropping low to the ground. "I can smell a liar."

His halitosis stench blasted her olfactory organs, so abhorrent and animalistic that she believed him. Abruptly, he stood back up and stormed into the woods.

The crashing in the underbrush stopped with similar curtness.

Her heartbeat drummed. Seconds drained into minutes. She

concentrated for any noise that might betray his location, but the void had consumed him.

Her bones chattered and shook, and the jar of urine slipped from her grasp. She reached for it blindly before remembering the headlamp. Her pulse leapt. As she shifted to reach into her pack, the fragile skin around her ankle—barely holding on to her foot—jounced with shockwaves of pain. One hand clenched into her jeans for strength, while the other patted through the pack's top pouch. Her fingers snatched up the headlamp.

She listened, vigilant, holding the headlamp dark against her chest, not wanting to waste the battery until the light was needed. The elastic strap snugged around her fingers. The plastic indented her palms. The woods retained their secrets.

If the man was gone, did that mean Neena was alive? Did he leave to check on her? Torture her? Was he playing sick games with her, too?

I'm sorry I told him you were out there. Josie clutched the headlamp even tighter, hoping that Neena could read her mind, hoping the connection between them was real. *I didn't mean to give him your name. It just slipped out. I'm sorry that I didn't listen to you, that I yelled and called you selfish. You've never been selfish. I'm sorry. I'm so sorry.* Time crawled until she was positive the man was gone.

He wasn't gone. At first, it was a sensation. A prickle, a tingle, a feeling that something had changed. Her heart rate, having finally slowed, began to accelerate. Her ears perked but did not detect. But then . . . an inhalation.

Ice crystallized down her spine.

Exhale.

He was close. It didn't make sense that she hadn't heard his approach, unless he'd never walked away at all. Unless he'd been standing right above her the entire time.

Inhale.

Exhale.

Inhale. Exhale.

Each breath grew incrementally faster.

Inhale, exhale, inhale, exhale.

Josie struggled to operate her shaking fingers. They felt separate from the rest of her, a tool she'd never mastered. She pressed the headlamp's button, and the monster grunted away from the bleaching spotlight. It took a moment to process what was in his hand, pink and fat and wormlike. Repulsion quickly replaced confusion.

She seized the mason jar and hurled it. Glass shattered against the side of his head. His dripping face glinted, slick with blood and urine. He was stunned. And then he unraveled with fury. In swift retaliation, he picked up his shotgun and aimed. Her hand raised in defense as he fired into the hole. The explosion was the loudest sound she had ever heard. Debris and fluids blasted into a mass around her.

The man stormed into the trees. "Now try and get out," he called back.

She sputtered and choked in the aftermath. Her body was in shock. Warm liquid gushed down her arm. Her left hand fumbled for the headlamp and held it up. Floating specks of dirt glistered in the beam as she squinted through the settling cloud. She saw her right arm, which was still lifted in defense. But she did not see her right hand.

NEENA

AS HER HAND grazed the rock above, her ring scraped but did not crack. It wasn't the original. Neena had purchased it for a second time last spring, after the first had shattered when she'd banged it against her bathroom countertop at the wrong angle. She had replaced it straightaway with money from her savings, previously reserved for college textbooks, but she had never told Josie. Neena didn't want her to worry that the broken lapis lazuli was an omen— that it represented anything other than Neena's own carelessness.

The tight hollow under the rock was claustrophobically, suffocatingly black. It smelled of cold minerals and damp soil. Beetles and ants and grubs scuttled over her body, investigating the trespasser. Other invertebrates lay crushed beneath her, the same way that this stone—boulder, outcrop, whatever—was crushing her. Her rib-cage muscles hurt from having to force the act of breathing. Air was trapped in her lungs, unable to escape. She puffed out the old breaths. Gulped in the new. Through her pinpricked airways, it was like trying to suck up the oxygen through a plastic coffee stirrer.

After shooting at nothing, the man had erupted into an enraged frenzy. Bellowing and smashing through the vegetation, he would have been even more furious had he known that this outburst had concealed her coughing.

She had been hiding for a long time. The fear was endless and grinding. The man had been combing the area with greater stealth, in and out, on and off. She hadn't heard him in a while.

She needed to move.

She was terrified to move.

Was he still here or had he abandoned his search to look for Josie, instead? The idea was unendurable. If he found Josie, it would be Neena's fault. *I'm sorry, Josie. I didn't mean to tell him about you. I didn't want to. I don't know how he got it out of me.* Inside her mind, she saw her fingers unable to reach Josie's outstretched hand. *I'm sorry for everything I said, I didn't mean any of it. If you can just hold on . . .*

Dawn was still a long way away. Their families wouldn't recognize that anything was amiss until the afternoon, when the girls didn't come home, but they probably wouldn't start panicking until the evening. Help wouldn't arrive until nightfall at the earliest. She was the only one who could save them. Summoning a nugget of courage that she did not actually feel, Neena wriggled out from under the rock.

The cool whoosh of air was exhilarating. Unbound, she rolled onto her back, puffing and gulping in the wide-open night. She let herself breathe, exposed on the ground like an injured rabbit. Cloud cover had eliminated the starlight, but the dimmed quarter moon slowly began to illuminate the dark shapes of the forest.

It's not safe here, Josie said. *You need to move.*

Neena hoisted herself onto her trembling legs and took a tentative step. The noise was so loud that she froze. Where was she? Her internal compass was screwed, the compass app was on her dead phone, and the actual compass was still inside Josie's backpack.

A sound that had always been present separated itself from the din. Water warbled and flowed like indistinct white noise. It could be in any direction—all directions—but if she could locate the creek and follow beside it, the sound of the water might cover her movements. It might even cross paths with a trail.

The plan was terrible, but it was the only one she had.

Fearing the headlamp would alert the man to her location, she shuffled through the tactile darkness one leg at a time, tapping each like a cane. The ground was soft with rotting leaves and slippery roots. Perhaps she might trip over a rock, tumble down a ridge. Fall into a sinkhole. Her sodden clothes were freezing. Double- and triple-checking that her pockets still contained her car keys and phone, she rediscovered the protein bar and devoured it. The stale peanut-butter flavor parched her mouth, but her water bottle was gone, dropped somewhere in the fray. She crammed the wrapper back into her pocket. Seconds later, she changed her mind. After licking the silver lining, she dropped it to the forest floor. Maybe someday the litter might need to be tested for her DNA.

The man could be anywhere. He was in every hushed crunch, every splintered crack.

She listened for the coursing water in incremental tests. *Cold.* The rush softened. *Colder.* Darshan's giggly, high-pitched voice whispered to her from the trees, guiding her in a game they played when they were children. *Warm. Warmer. Hot. Hot! Burning hot. Fire hot. Lava hot. It's melting your feet, Neena! Don't you see it?*

The creek glistened before her with reflected moonlight. But it also contained its own source of mysterious light, slippery and quicksilver. The air shivered with the scent of undulating water particles. The sound was like a faucet filling a claw-foot tub, water agitating water, splashing and plopping.

Walking along the bank turned out to be impossible. The uneven terrain was too hazardous. A bullfrog croaked in a rumbling baritone, and Neena heeded its warning and retreated to slightly higher ground.

She followed the water downstream, traveling in the same snaking direction, hoping the flow would strengthen and lead someplace where she was more likely to encounter civilization. Of course, the flow might lead her *away* from civilization. Or over the ledge of a waterfall. But her parents' advice for lost children—stay put until somebody finds you—didn't apply tonight. The wrong somebody was already looking for her. She had to find somebody else.

A few feet away, something disturbed the brush.

She flinched and ducked. Her hands locked over her mouth. The noise was a low, whispered scurry. Were there mice in these woods? Voles? Moles? The stirrings were rodenty. She straightened, wobbly with respite. Arms extended and hands grasping, she fumbled deeper into the unknown. The shadows of the shadows tracked behind her.

On the Wade Harte, she had pushed aside her instincts about following the man off trail, believing that she was being paranoid, believing that he hadn't done anything wrong. But he had. He had made her *uncomfortable*. That was enough. She didn't have to apologize or make excuses. She didn't owe him—or any man, or any person—anything. She'd sensed what he was immediately but invalidated her own intuition.

Tears welled, salty, hot, and enraged. She felt ashamed for being gullible. She thought she had known better. It wasn't as if he was the first ill-intentioned creep that she'd ever met. Girls ran into men like this everywhere.

Her progress was slow and plagued with cowering doubt. Every step felt wrong. She was still stumbling and shivering when the eerie glow appeared through the trees. In English folklore, it was called the will-o'-the-wisp, but in North Carolina it was foxfire. Sometimes it was caused by the combustion of natural gases, but here it was from the bioluminescence of fungi and insects. She had never seen it before, only read about it. The mesmerizing pull of atmospheric light drew her in. Leaving the safety of the stream, she headed into the trees, but it was like chasing a ghost. The phosphorescent shapes kept changing and disappearing. Frustrated, she was about to turn around—the gurgling water was only barely audible anymore—when the lights reshaped again.

It wasn't foxfire. It was a campfire.

Neena saw it clearly now, so clearly that she wondered why she hadn't sooner. Dread warred with hope. Did the campsite belong to the man or to somebody else? Without knowing, she couldn't risk calling out for help. She was almost positive that she was still in the Misty Rock Wilderness, where fires were illegal. But sometimes even good people broke rules when nobody was looking. Right?

She slinked closer, conscious of every faintly booted crunch against topsoil as she moved from the cover of tree to tree. Stinging vines with three leaves brushed against her outstretched fingers. Coarse bark grated the tender pads. Heady woodsmoke reached her nose first, and then something else, something burnt.

The flames were lethargic and low. A shelter appeared through the wavering light. Constructed out of tree trunks and interwoven branches, the shelter was rectangular, almost tall enough for an adult to stand up in, and open on the side that faced the fire. Dark bulges inside gave the impression of camping equipment and gear. It was impossible to tell if any of those shapes were people, but the structure was large enough to hold two or three.

Nobody was tending to the dying fire.

If the campsite belonged to the man, it meant he had returned here after shooting at her. Otherwise, the fire would be dead by now. Nervously, furtively, she stole to the campsite's edge. Searching for life, she discovered none.

The scene was confounding. Something felt off, and it wasn't merely the absence of people. Perhaps it was the amount of work that had gone into the brush shelter; its permanent impermanence suggested that the same person frequented this remote site. Her confidence grew that the campsite was empty, but it wasn't comforting. Why would the camper—campers?—leave in the middle of the night? The only good reason she could think of was to go to the bathroom. Thinking of a bad reason was much easier.

The gear was mounded tantalizingly inside the shelter's cavernous black opening, perhaps containing a working phone or GPS device. But Neena remained still. The trees provided safety, and the moment she stepped into the clearing, she would be visible.

The campfire crackled. The insects chirred. Her surroundings gave nothing away.

She crept into the light.

The eyes of the woods turned upon her, boring into her from all directions. She broke into a scutter and ducked beside the fire. An unexpected warmth teased her body, a reminder that flames bestowed more than light. She crouched in to absorb their remaining heat, and her teeth began to chatter.

From this angle, two stumps or upright logs were suddenly perceptible. They weren't rooted into the earth but had been rolled here and positioned beside the fire like chairs. *Two chairs.* Hope flickered. A sauce pot rested on the ground near her feet. Hardened lumps in the bottom seemed to be a mixture of charred meat and baked beans, as well as the source of the lingering burnt smell. An eating utensil lay abandoned inside the pot, and a grill was still suspended over the fire. The cook had been either distracted or in a hurry. She poked at the dark lumps with a finger. The beans were cold.

A crack detonated across the clearing.

Her arms flew protectively over her head, but it was only the popping fire. Her hands lowered to clutch at her thudding chest—and that's when she saw it.

It lay on the ground in front of the trees, to the right of the structure and fifteen feet or so back from the fire.

It was a *still* thing. A terrible thing.

Her body straightened. Her heart thundered in her ears. She didn't want to go near it—she desperately wanted to run away from it—but this time, purpose overrode instinct. Forcing one shaking step and then another, Neena sidled toward it.

The whorling night kept it shrouded. *Run! Run!* She took off the headlamp from around her neck. *Breathe. Breathe.* Holding it like a flashlight, she clicked the button on. Its beam revealed the expected form, but that didn't make it any less shocking. The headlamp fumbled from her hands, hitting the ground and illuminating the bare purpled feet in appalling white light.

Both feet were still attached.

The body wasn't Josie. But it was definitely dead.

JOSIE

JOSIE'S HEADLAMP REVEALED a jarring dagger of bone and sagging strips of flesh. Everything past the wrist was gone. *Smithereens*, she thought. The man had blown her right hand to smithereens. She collapsed—but caught herself, mid-faint. Jerked upward with a stab of disoriented alertness. A fine mist of bloody bones, fingernails, and tendons had been sprayed across her body. She trembled and convulsed. Something hard tumbled inside her mouth. Without inspecting or touching it, she spit it out.

Her mind tweaked with shock. Inexplicable seconds passed in slow motion before the truth registered and a searing, transcendent pain shot up her arm. Josie cried out in astonished agony. How could something like this happen twice in one day? What were the odds? It was as if she'd been so deeply asleep that the first tragedy hadn't been enough to wake her, and the universe had been forced to double down.

Now, at last, she understood. Years ago, when she had fallen, the world had kept rotating without her. She hadn't known that it was her responsibility to get back up. No one could do it for her. But this pain screamed that she wasn't dead yet. This was her last chance. Did she want to live or did she want to die?

Josie wanted to live.

A determined focus washed over her. Vaguely, she was aware that the man had stomped away, but she didn't know if he had left or if he was hiding like the last time.

It doesn't matter.

If she were religious, she would say the voice was God or Jesus or a guardian angel. But this voice sounded like her father and Neena and Win and Uncle Kevin and her mother. It was everyone who loved her. It was the clear, convincing, empowering voice of survival. *Stay present*, it urged. *Take care of yourself first.*

She needed to tie off her stump—now. The hoodie was still blanketed over her torso. Locating the hole where the left sleeve met the left shoulder, she brought it to her teeth and ripped. The hole, once an embarrassment, was a lifesaver. The cumbersome fabric tore easily along the shoulder seam, giving little resistance until she reached the fabric overlap where it was sewn together. Her incisors gnashed, tugged, yanked. The sleeve ripped away. She laid it across her legs and centered the stump on top. When her skin touched the fabric, she bellowed. Every nerve ending was an excruciating live wire. With her left, nondominant hand, she wrapped the fabric quickly and tightly and then used her teeth to help knot it.

She fell back against her pack, gasping and panting. In shocked disbelief, she blinked at her bandaged arm. Her bandaged foot. Panic resurged, and she chugged half the remaining water supply before turning aghast at her blunder.

The voice returned to quell the cycle of hysteria. *Breathe.*

"Okay," she said. Anxiety would only jeopardize her condition.

Put on the hoodie. You need to stay warm.

"Okay." It was the only word she had left because she had to believe that everything *was* okay. She had to remain clearheaded. The left side was easy enough—her good hand, the missing sleeve—but the right side was a challenge. Her left hand held open the armhole and guided her right side through it. She bit her cheeks. Huffed to keep breathing. *Keep going. You're almost there.* Her right arm shoved through the hole, and the sleeve covered most of the injured bundle. *Zip it up.* Another difficult one-handed task, but it was comforting to have guidance.

Josie didn't speak out loud anymore. *Now what?*

Shh, it replied.

Wind chilled the woods. Her hearing strained through the turbulent tumble of foliage. She shivered in a cold sweat and cradled her right arm. Her right elbow remained cocked to keep the injury raised. Now she had *two* raised injuries. Blood was sopping through both layers of hoodie fabric. Hopefully, her grogginess was only due to exhaustion and stress. How much blood had she lost today? How much more could she lose? The new, makeshift bandage was unsanitary. If blood loss—or the man with the gun—didn't take her, surely infection would. She needed to get out of here.

Just because she couldn't hear him didn't mean he wasn't there. He might be messing with her again—or with himself. Revulsion triggered at the memory of the vile pink worm. It was the first time that she'd seen a man masturbate outside of pornography. It was the first penis that she had seen in person, period. How unfair that a violent man had gotten to choose the moment. It should have been her choice, but he had snatched it away from her, replacing what should have been a positive experience with a future boyfriend with a traumatic ordeal.

If only he had blown off the rest of her foot instead of her hand.

The thought was morbid, but at least she would have been able to move faster because she wouldn't have to drag the injured foot behind her. She was still in danger of losing her left foot, but she definitely didn't have a right hand anymore.

A fearsome vortex tore open—showering, eating, writing, cooking, tying shoelaces, making a bed, working a cash register— relearning how to live her entire life—but then, just as suddenly, it stoppered up. The protective act kept her focused on the current task.

Josie scooted forward on her butt. *Do it quickly.* Barely touching the lopsided boot, she released a ghastly cry. *Quickly.* The voice was stern. Hissing through clenched teeth, she grasped the injured foot and lowered it to the ground. A howl exploded out from her, screeching all the way up from her toes.

The night insects blinked, startled, and then resumed their trill.

If that fucker was still watching, he was relishing her pain more than ever. She felt like James Franco in *127 Hours* when he amputated his own hand after it got crushed underneath a boulder. But James Franco had been accused of sexual harassment, too. Was there any man left on the planet who wasn't a swine? She listed them to distract herself: Her brother. Her uncle. Neena's father. Neena's brother. Briskly, she inhaled and exhaled through her teeth, psyching herself up. With all her weight on her right side, she pushed herself up from the bottom of the sinkhole.

Josie stood.

Her right leg trembled and so did her heart. Grabbing the thick root that had snapped her ankle, she tried to pull herself out of the sinkhole with her left hand. Her right elbow dug into and scraped against the dirt wall, attempting to give lift. Her good foot scrabbled and pushed. Her efforts were as fruitless as they were monumental.

Depleted after mere seconds, she dropped back into the hole. Her swaying foot shuddered, the sinews ready to snap. She tried again and again, but each frenzied attempt was shorter than the last. Yelling, she cursed the man with every expletive and some that weren't words at all. Her frustrated gaze landed on the backpack. With the length of her bad arm resting against the wall for balance, her jawbone gritted, and she dragged the pack underneath the large root. She didn't know how she was dragging it one-handed. It had been almost impossible with two hands yesterday. *Super-fucking-human strength*, she thought, imagining adrenaline-fueled mothers lifting cars off their children.

She stepped on the pack, and this time when she reached upward, her hand touched the ground. But she still didn't have the strength to lift herself out with one hand—her weakest hand. Her good foot scrambled for additional leverage, but she fell back into the hole. Her bad foot cried out with an anguished wet pop.

Tears infuriated her eyes. She could touch freedom. She just couldn't get to it.

"I hope you're fucking happy," she screamed, before amending it. "Except I don't, because you're an asshole. And you're miserable, and you always will be, and that's your fucking problem, not mine!"

Her ears strained again, but the forest didn't give anything away. Where was he? What had he done to Neena? What would he do with her? She shrieked into the echoing night.

Preserve your energy, the voice said.

Josie was short of breath again. Her rash actions were undermining her efforts.

One thing at a time. Always do the most important thing first.

Grimacing, she twisted her body to root through her pack. The best that she could find was Win's Swiss Army knife. The longest blade was only three inches of feeble steel. She gripped the weapon with her remaining hand and awaited the man's return, her animal heart beating with vengeance.

NEENA

NEENA PICKED UP her headlamp and shone it onto the body. She covered her mouth in horror. A strong wind swept through the trees, and a gust of bodily odors assaulted her: oniony perspiration, blood like iron nails, the pungent stench of ammoniacal piss.

It was a young woman. She was splayed out on the forest floor, faceup and eyes open, wearing a long-sleeved button-down and nothing else. The shirt was undone. Her white skin was dirty and dehumanized, scraped with heinous scratches, obliterated with pounding bruises. Ragged red marks ringed her ankles and wrists. Her hair was plastered lankly to her neck, where brutalizing, fingerlike blotches still grasped her throat. She looked older than Neena and Josie but only by a few years. Maybe the age of their brothers. And she was dead. She *had* to be dead, but Neena also had to be sure.

She didn't whisper the words. She breathed them. "Are you okay?"

The young woman did not respond.

"Shit," Neena said quietly, crying as her voice rose. "Oh my God."

Bending over, her arm reached outward for inspection but then retracted. She forced the arm back out. With one trembling finger, she touched the skin. It was warm, barely. Though the muscles were still soft, it was clear that the person who had once lived inside this vessel was gone. Neena released a wretched moan. How long did it take for rigor mortis to set in? How long had this body—this *woman*—been dead?

She turned off her light, petrified, as her mind raced through possible scenarios: The man and woman were camping here together, and he'd murdered her. Or, this was the woman's campsite, and the man had stumbled across it, and then he'd murdered her. Or, maybe he had brought her here from someplace else as his captive. The two chairs and significant amount of equipment suggested they'd come here together willingly, but the only thing Neena knew for certain was that the man was responsible for this depravity. And she didn't doubt that he would return.

Total darkness eclipsed the campsite. Fear swallowed her. The flames had died, but the fire smoldered. Coils of acrid smoke wrapped around her throat in strangling, choking eddies. The eyes of the forest fixed on her again as she began to run.

JOSIE

HER STAMINA HAD succumbed, and Josie was back on her ass. Her bad foot was propped up on the pack. Goose bumps barbed her bare left arm. The damp sinkhole was cold and static, but her headlamp was at the ready, draped around her like a necklace.

The knife was still in her hand.

Another unforgiving object, hard and insistent, jabbed into the back of her thigh. When she mustered the energy, an oddly shaped pebble dislodged from the mud. Its surface was slippery-smooth. Tracing the C-shaped curve, she recognized it as a shard from her friendship ring. The shotgun blast had destroyed this, too. Had Neena made it out of the woods? Josie would give her bad foot to be in Neena's living room right now, snuggled together on the squashy couch and watching videos on their warm phones. She rubbed the sawtoothed edge before tucking the shard protectively into her pocket.

In a prolonged state of stress and fatigue, she drifted in and out of consciousness. Leaves shuffled in auditory hallucinations. Branches snapped. Once, she smelled his rancid breath. But whenever she startled awake with a fiercely pounding heart, it was always nothing.

• • •

Until it wasn't.

She didn't know when the man reappeared. It was the dead of night. In her mind, the hour was exactly halfway between sunset and sunrise.

The first twig was sharp, its dry crack unmistakable. It jolted her into alertness. The man walked straight toward her. No games. His stride was so purposeful that she knew some sort of decision had been made. She clambered onto her good foot. This time, she wouldn't greet him lying down. The small blade trembled in her clenched fist. The heavy footsteps stopped at the sinkhole's edge. Before she could make out his figure, a blinding light fractured against her crooked glasses and seared into her eyes.

"You're up," he said. A touch of surprise.

She squinted, refusing to block the light with her good arm. She brandished the knife like a sword.

"What's that?" He snorted. "You gonna stick me with a toothpick?"

Yes. And then she would drag his body down here and use it as another stepping-stone to get out.

"Put that down," he said.

"Come closer," she hissed.

In one fluid but unhurried motion, he tossed the flashlight to the ground and lifted the shotgun. His lower body revealed itself in ghostly, blurry form. The metal barrel winked in the light. Unlike the man, the barrel was sharply in focus, inches away from her forehead.

Ashamed, she dropped the knife. It landed with a dull thump. She felt young and frightened again. The gun had stripped away any last trace of bravery.

"It's time to join the others," he said.

Her heart constricted. "The others? Do you have Neena?"

He grunted and set down the gun.

"Where is she? What have you done with her?"

The man slithered onto his belly, and the smell of rotting teeth and diseased gums poured into the hole. She coughed and retched as he extended a meaty hand. Grime lined the creases of his skin. His fingernails were thick and ridged and plugged with dirty crescent moons. Maybe he was homeless. Or maybe these woods were his home. He seized one of her braids and yanked so hard that rooted follicles ripped from her scalp.

She made a sound between a gasp and a yell.

He let go and offered his hand again. "Take it."

Josie knew it was one of the golden rules of survival: Never go to a second location. Fight with everything you have from getting into a stranger's car, house, territory.

But this stranger had a gun. And she was powerless inside the hole.

The intensity of his voice changed very little. "Take it, or I'll blow you away right now."

He'd already proven that he would. "What are you gonna do to me?" Her left arm trembled as she reached up. "Where's Neena? Where are the others?"

"The others ain't alive anymore."

He grasped onto her with sandpapery hands and pulled. She screamed. Her good foot scrambled against the dirt wall for purchase, frantic to prevent her arm from being ripped from its socket. Her bad foot fizzed with bolts of lightning pain. Winded, he panted for breath, blasting her with the full brunt of his halitosis and the reek of her own dried urine as her body lifted over the edge. She rolled and toppled away. Her legs accidentally swept into his, and his footing slipped. Her eyes widened with the unforeseen opportunity.

Her good leg reared back like a horse. She kicked his buckling frame with purpose, and the man yelled in surprise as he toppled into the sinkhole.

Everything had happened so fast. Her senses reeled and stuttered. *The others ain't alive anymore.*

Her glasses were gone, lost in the transaction. Her gums were bleeding as she spit out the dried leaves from her mouth. She didn't know how they had gotten there. Missing a hand and deficient a foot, she had no chance of escape if he could climb out and follow her. He seemed tall enough and strong enough to be able to lift himself out.

She scanned for the gun and located it within reach. Belly down, she scooted and dragged herself into place, positioning the double-barreled shotgun against the ground at the edge of the hole. The stock was heavy and bulky and clumsy in her nondominant hand. Assuming he had reloaded, it contained two shots.

Grunting movements issued from below. A dark figure rose.

Josie pulled the front trigger. The shot was deafening, and she was no match for the recoil. Because she was unable to balance the gun against her body, it kicked straight back and jolted from her hand. Her eardrums rang in the furious silence.

Grabbing arms reached upward through the billowing clouds of dirt. The man was still upright and unharmed. She hustled the gun back into place. Channeling the training on her uncle's rural acres, she took a deep breath—just like he'd taught her—and exhaled as she squeezed the trigger.

It clicked. Nothing happened.

Panic fogged her. It appeared that the man hadn't reloaded, until her finger found the rear trigger. The shotgun kicked and blasted back out of her hand.

She scrabbled forward to peer down. It was too dark and dusty to see anything. His flashlight lay on the ground nearby, turned on and pointed at nothing. Its aluminum body was heavier than she'd expected as she picked it up and aimed the trembling beam.

This time, she hadn't missed. The man was sprawled at the bottom of the hole. Her pack was still under his feet as if he'd been standing on top of it when he'd been blown backward. It was impossible to tell where she'd hit him or how badly he was injured, but the mounded heap of his body was motionless.

Josie searched for something to throw at him, to test him. No other objects or stones were within reach, but her headlamp was still around her neck, and she would need the full use of her hand to get out of the woods. She threw the flashlight, hard. The tumbling light captured a flinch in his eyelids before making contact with a squelching thwack. The hit wasn't square, but it struck the side of his head. The white beam streamed upward into the sky. The light was unearthly, reminiscent of alien encounters and hostile spaceships. But the man was only human. And he wasn't moving.

She had no time to feel relief. She had no time to waste.

The effort to stand was tremendous, but adrenaline gave her strength, a staggering mixture of fear and euphoria. She collected the shotgun and tucked it underneath her left armpit as a crutch. Balancing and hopping and lurching away, the mangled foot dragged behind her. It bumped and popped across the earth as it caught on rocks and sticks, but she hardly felt the pain. Black spots kaleidoscoped her already hazy vision.

The others ain't alive anymore.

She fled from the light, back into darkness.

NEENA

SHE RAN UNTIL the campfire was a distant orange smudge. Her skull was swollen with shock. Terror pulsed through her bloodstream. Even without a closer look, she sensed that the woman had been tortured for a long time, perhaps days.

Dark terrain hurtled underfoot. Sweat soaked Neena's underwear, and her jeans chafed her thighs. The forest entangled her in a thicket of tendrils and saplings, prickles and briars. She cleaved through them in a splintering crash. Blackberry thorns zipped and stung her hands, snagged and tore her clothing, but she was already deep inside the brambles with no choice but to push through. Her lungs pumped, sucking the moist and bestial air. Gulping it. She wheezed in puffs that intensified into hacking coughs.

Her foot struck something hard, and she smashed to the ground.

The indifferent trees gazed down at her. The moon continued on its slow nightly path. Feeling for the object, she discovered a trifling nub of root. Tears spilled over her burning cheeks. She had run away without thinking, without a plan, and now she couldn't even hear the stream. She was lost. She had to find her bearings. The man was still out here, somewhere, hunting her. Hunting Josie.

Her mind thrummed with hectic calculations. Assuming that earlier he had been trying to lead her to his campsite, she could re-orient herself by coupling this information with the position of the westerly moving moon. It was only a guess, but a decent one.

She waited for her breath to regulate. When it was as good as it was going to get, she got back up. Her knees yowled in protest. Her thighs ached with stiffness. She turned on her headlamp but clutched the light to dampen it. Her glowing fist lit the way.

Steadily, Neena trekked northeast toward the Wade Harte. To have any hope of getting out, she needed to locate familiar territory. Fear churned her bowels as she slogged past the musty toadstools and stagnant pools, the dusky groves and pockets of absolute silence. Had she picked the wrong direction?

Unseen critters tussled with the fallen leaves. Bats swooped like startling apparitions. Every minuscule sound jackknifed her heart. Her ears were exhausted from listening so hard. Freezing and trau-matized, she shivered uncontrollably. Time plodded by, but, no matter how long or how far she traveled, she was always still in the woods.

Until—

A yellow-gold dome rose over the horizon. Elation swelled inside her as warm as daylight, but the beacon wasn't the sun. It was the tent they'd camped beside the previous night. No sight had ever filled her with such hope.

Opening her palm, Neena allowed the headlamp to fully illumi-nate her path. She scrambled up the slope and through the under-brush. Branches grabbed, but she no longer felt their claws. Rocks scraped, but she no longer felt their abrasions. She burst into the campsite and shone her light onto the tent. And then she gasped and staggered back.

A single, violating gash had lacerated the rear, creating a new door from the outside. The nylon had been split into two gaping flaps. The distressed fibers rippled in the breeze. Though the intrusion didn't appear to be recent, she spun in an anxious circle. But her shaking light revealed nothing more than the surrounding pines.

The hair rose on her neck.

This was the dead woman's tent. It had to be. If only she and Josie had inspected it more carefully that morning, none of this would have happened. They would have gone home and reported the crime, and Josie wouldn't have fallen into the hole. Neena wouldn't have been chased. The woman might even still be alive. The imprint of her screams from the moment when she had been wrenched from slumber and safety resonated throughout the mountains.

Uneasily, cautiously, Neena peered between the flaps. A hideous face leered back at her.

JOSIE

AS NEENA WAS still stumbling away from the first dead body, long before she found the second, Josie was staring at the woods ahead. They were as black as a cast-iron skillet. Propping her body against the closest tree, Josie wrestled the headlamp from around her neck, yanked it to her forehead, and turned it on. She did not look behind at the light issuing from the sinkhole. Squinting, she swept her lamp back and forth, back and forth—*there*.

She staggered toward a pair of bottle caps, untethered. Her face felt naked where her glasses used to sit. Her eyesight had smudged into a terrifying blur, but her other senses seemed heightened, sharpened, as if her pain sensors had shut off to provide strength for other operations. Had she killed the man? Injured him? She did not feel conflicted about having shot him. His actions had empowered her to protect herself.

The others ain't alive anymore.

He hadn't been talking about Neena. She couldn't let herself believe that. A great dam of grief quaked, threatening to crack and rupture.

There. Her desperate squint managed to locate the next pair of bottle caps.

Josie was traveling forward—not backward, the way Neena had gone—because she couldn't risk the additional time and mileage. She prayed the remainder of the blazes would be there. If even one blaze was missing, she was done for. Had the man pried off the bottle caps from the tree beside the sinkhole? It seemed plausible that he might have set a trap, but it didn't actually matter. Putting distance between herself and the man was all that mattered now. She hoped his wounds were severe enough to prevent him from giving chase, because otherwise her bloody, dragging trail would be easy to track.

She hobbled toward Frazier Mountain. Her injuries thumped hot. Blood weltered inside her shoes. Every step was an endurance test, a toddling balancing act between her good foot and the shotgun. The terrain was uneven, and her awkward grip on the gun was sweaty, tight, and strained. The stock dug an abusive trench into her armpit.

With agonizing slowness and feverish determination, the light from the sinkhole grew fainter. But even when it disappeared completely, she still saw it. Her heart pounded helter-skelter, deranged, and she was in danger of passing out.

She tripped over a bulging rock and smacked into the ground. Her bad foot screamed with the onslaught of pain. Gasping, tears flooding, she was unable to think. Several minutes passed before she recovered enough energy to push up against her remaining knuckles. With another cry, she struggled back into a standing position, purposefully not looking at her missing hand.

The gun crutch wobbled. Her chest spiked with the panic of falling again.

One step at a time, the voice said. *Just take it one step at a time.*

Was it the voice of the living or the dead—or something else entirely? From blaze to blaze, Josie clumped and tottered. The work was taxing, and she was at the mercy of the bottle caps. It wasn't clear which way was north or south or east or west. The forest isolated her in confused turmoil. Whenever she couldn't find a blaze, she shambled in dwindling circles, knowing this was the end. *This* was the dark place where she would bleed out and die. But then the blaze would manifest, and she would be saved.

The shotgun clinked, clinked, clinked with each step. Shivery and numb and delirious with tedium, she wished her bare arm had a sleeve. The mosquitos chewed her up. Her ligaments stiffened and groaned. A creek trickled a siren song, and her tongue bleated with thirst, but she knew the water wasn't safe to drink.

Not long after, she flagellated herself for passing it by.

She fell again.

The pain was blinding, starbursts and electric shocks. Immobile, she sagged into the limbs of a waxy-leaved bush. It was too difficult to carry on. Her chances of survival were too slim.

Except . . . Neena might also be injured and alone.

Josie's exhausted eyes peeled open, and her light shone a halo onto the next grouping of bottle caps. *One step at a time*, the voice reminded her. And she realized that it didn't matter who it belonged to. It loved her, and it would always be with her.

She picked herself back up. One blaze at a time, she continued through the woods, her bandaged foot bumping along behind her.

NEENA

NEENA REFLEXIVELY AVERTED her gaze before forcing it back to the decomposing man. His body lay supine with one arm bent outward at a warped and unnatural angle. Black flies and maggots teemed across stretched skin, which was marbled in bloated shades of gray and brown. Cloudy eyeballs protruded over a thickened tongue. The tent was ripe with the gassy stink of putrefaction.

Acid rose in her throat. She purged a mouthful of fluid bile, tasting the fetor of his rotting tissue. He had been deceased for much longer than the young woman.

We set up camp and slept beside a murdered man last night.

Her vision went white.

She blinked it, forced it, back into focus. The light of her headlamp exposed the cramped space. Dried pools of gunky blood. Gristly spatter, sprayed across everything—backpacks, sleeping bags, even the ceiling. The man himself was covered in so much that she couldn't even tell how he'd been slaughtered. The blood swallowed her beam.

Two backpacks, two sleeping bags. One body.

He looked to be about the same age as the woman. Beside an inflatable pillow there was a bra that looked as if it had been discarded before bed. *The man had been murdered so that his girlfriend could be abducted.* Neena saw the other man—the killer—wrap his sadistic hands around the woman's neck. With Neena's narrowed passageways, it felt as if he was choking her, too.

Overcome with an urgent need for water, she scrounged through a bloodied pack within reach. It was emptier than expected, and the haphazard mess within indicated that it had already been ransacked. She slipped an arm and foot inside the tent. Leaning toward the other pack, she dragged it over and discovered that its contents had also been dumped. She scoured the disarray until her lamp revealed a Hydro Flask that had rolled into a corner. The rest of her body entered the tent. Snatching up the bottle, she unscrewed the lid. Only about half a cup of water was left inside. She forced herself to drink slowly, but her hands shook so badly that some of the liquid sloshed out.

The corpse judged her endeavor in gory silence.

Sip. Her rib cage forced an inhalation and exhalation. *Sip.* Her muscles throbbed in agony. *Sip.* She repeated the effort until the water was gone. It was time to move again.

At least now she knew her location.

Neena plowed back out through the tent flaps. Psychosis engulfed her as the dead man chased her down the slope, pursuing her through the jagged darkness—arm crooked, elbow askew, fingers hooked. His figure morphed into the lean and rawboned killer.

She careened past the site where she and Josie had camped, disturbing the barrier of nightly fog. The pine trees disappeared into the vapors. Her boots crunched and bounced wildly against the spongy needles. She tore through the sagging curtain of vines out of Deep Fork and onto the Wade Harte.

She crashed into a halt. The trail was clear and exposed. Only now did it occur to her that the killer knew *exactly* where she was heading, because she had told him. He hadn't been chasing her through the woods all night. Most likely, he had returned to his campsite to eliminate the woman, and now he was waiting in the parking lot to finish the job with Neena. Or waiting somewhere else along this trail. It was easy to imagine him bursting out from the trees exactly as he'd done before.

There was another parking lot near Burnt Balsam, not far past their turnaround point. Despite their not seeing anybody yesterday at the overlook, it was the trail's busiest section. If she turned around and hiked back across the ridgeline, she was sure to run into somebody else eventually. It would take longer, but it would lead to help. She'd be safe.

But Josie would still be trapped.

And, because of Neena, the killer knew Josie's location. Maybe he wasn't waiting along this final stretch of trail, after all. Maybe he had gone to take care of Josie first. Maybe he was already there. The decision had to be made quickly. If Neena kept heading toward the Wade Harte trailhead, it was less safe for her. If she turned around for Burnt Balsam, it was less safe for Josie. The tunnel of mountain laurel loomed ahead—dark, descending, and ominous. The heavy leaves provided natural coverage to conceal and trap. Everything inside her shouted to run back toward Burnt Balsam and safety.

Neena chose Josie instead.

Girding herself, she headed toward the tunnel—as a second beam of light swept along the trail behind her.

Fear juddered her heart. She flicked off the headlamp and dashed behind the closest tree. Dirt clods and loose pebbles skittered down after her. Her lungs compressed tighter. Always, always, she couldn't breathe. With one hand cupped over her mouth, she tried to muffle the gasping wheeze. Her other hand gripped the fir tree for strength. The bark roughed her skin, but the branches smelled incongruously like Christmas.

The light was distant. The man was traveling slowly through the fog, but he was drawing near. Had he seen her? A mysterious, repetitive clink accompanied his form, similar to a prisoner being led in shackles. Each clink tolled a warning of danger.

Huffing one last time, Neena fell silent. The man was close now. Closer. Illuminated in the shimmering beam, a gun barrel struck the ground before her.

Terror exploded.

But the man kept walking. As his gun clinked away, the fog weakened into mist. In the receding light, she saw that the man's foot was dragging behind him. And then she saw that the man wasn't a man at all.

TOGETHER

THE WOODS WERE secretive. Trees older than death and saplings younger than spring watched over the creatures that slunk and scurried between them. The trees concealed. Shadowed. Obscured. Their trunks provided cover, their leaves bestowed shelter, and their limbs extended to make contact with fur and feathers, scales and skin. They knew everything that happened here, yet they did not take sides. They observed in silence. They offered these hiding places, but, predator or prey, it made no difference to them.

Neena burst out from behind a tree.

Josie shrieked and seesawed.

"It's me. It's me," Neena rasped as the same disbelief rushed through her—an unwillingness to believe it was actually Josie. Her best friend was nearly unrecognizable. Underneath the stark light of Josie's headlamp, her eyes were veined and bulging. Blood and dirt smeared her sallow skin. Bloody crusts rimmed her mouth and chin, streaked in vicious lines down her neck. She had one sleeve and one bare arm, and straw-like chunks of hair frazzled out from her braids and from underneath her hat. Her posture was stiff and broken, and, most alarmingly of all, she was grasping a gun like a bizarro crutch.

Josie floundered, lost to hyperventilating convulsions. Several fraught and raving seconds passed before recognition dawned in her eyes. Neena moved in for a sobbing embrace—and then discovered the missing right hand. She jerked back with a gasp. Josie's remaining sleeve had concealed the trauma. A crude bandage stumped her arm, and it was clear by the shortened length that the entire appendage below the wrist was gone.

"He shot it off." Josie sounded dazed. "There was a man."

Neena shuddered profoundly. "I know." In her mind, the man's helpful expression fell away as the gun swung in her direction. The woman lay dead and abused on the forest floor, the other man dead and bloated in his tent. Suddenly, she grew conscious of the brightness of Josie's headlamp. She lunged. "Turn it off!"

"It's okay," Josie said. "He fell into the hole."

This news stunned Neena. She dropped back again. "What?"

"He pulled me out, and I pushed him in. And then I shot him."

"*What?*"

Josie did not elaborate.

"Is . . . is he dead?" Neena asked.

"I don't know. But he wasn't moving when I left him."

Neena's breath hitched. The unexpected noise tuned Josie back into reality. With another wave of fear, she realized that Neena had been wheezing and keeping her words brief. Her skin was pallid, her lips dusky. They were both in critical condition.

"A man and a woman," Neena said. "I saw their bodies. He killed them."

The verb exploded like a bomb. Josie's ears rang. Her skin felt hot.

"Loaded?" Neena nodded toward the gun.

Josie shook her head. "I used both shots on him."

"How . . ." Neena couldn't finish the thought. She was staring at Josie in fresh amazement, and Josie understood this was a new question. *How did you get here so quickly? In your condition? How did you catch up with me?*

"The bottle-cap route," Josie explained. "Shorter. More direct."

They needed to move. Further discussion was unnecessary. Neena turned on her headlamp to double their light, and a murmur in the back of Josie's mind considered an argument about battery conservation. Just in case.

But the hell with that.

The girls began the excruciating climb down Frazier Mountain. They were severely compromised, so every downward step had become a potentially treacherous fall. Josie was still using the crutch, but now Neena was also providing support, gripping and lifting her up from the other side. It was a relief for Josie to lessen the weight on her armpit. The thin skin was rubbed raw and swollen, black and bleeding.

They entered the tunnel of laurel. The bushes confined, and the night tightened in. Together, however, their hope had strengthened. The parking lot felt closer, too.

A rifle cocked behind them.

Their chests seized. The girls turned around.

"Well, well, well." A man was framed at the top of the tunnel. "Look what we have here."

"You—you said you shot him," Neena stammered.

But this man was lean and wiry, and, even with her poor vision, Josie knew that she had never seen him before.

"I'VE BEEN LOOKING for *you* all night." The man seethed at Neena. His eyes were slits of rage. His muscles were as clenched as fists. "And look what I found instead. Two for the price of one."

Neena reeled with shock, which jostled Josie, who cried out in pain.

"I don't understand," Neena said.

"That's not the man," Josie gasped, her nerve endings throttled and whirling. "That's a different man."

The horrifying truth washed over them together. *Two for the price of one.*

The man inched over his rifle to aim it at Josie. "Now. I'm gonna need you to set down my friend's shotgun, nice and slow."

"I can't." Tears welled. Her good leg trembled. "I'll fall."

"I don't give a goddamned fuck if you fall."

Josie flinched and choked on a sob.

Fiercely, Neena held her grip. "I've got you."

Josie let go, helpless. The useless weapon clattered to the ground. It wasn't fair, she thought. Guns were *never* fair.

The man's rifle remained affixed to them as he moved to collect the shotgun, but the tension slackened from his muscles as soon as it was in his possession. Only the rifle had a strap, so he moved it onto his shoulder and carried the shotgun loosely in hand. Now that he held all the power, he didn't have to point it. Unhooking a flashlight from his belt, he shone it up and down the laurel tunnel until he located the desired swath. It looked the same as the rest. He held the branches aside with the full length of an arm.

"After you, ladies." The last word was witheringly simpered.

Josie curdled with revulsion.

Neena kept her grip firm as she adjusted herself to better support Josie. Her right arm wrapped around Josie's back. Josie's left arm and only hand wrapped around Neena's neck. Grappling with how to operate in tandem, the girls staggered toward the opening. Josie slipped, and Neena barely caught her in time.

The two halves of Josie's bad foot screamed with scissoring pain.

"*Move*," the man said. "I ain't got all night."

The girls hustled as best they could and ducked through the opening in the shrubs. A slight groove was worn into the forest floor on the other side, a pathway trodden by animals. Apparently, the men had been utilizing it for their own purposes.

The branches rustled back into place, closing like a door. Even with their three lights, the woods grew so much darker. The silence so much louder.

"Where are you taking us?" Josie asked as they stumbled forward.

Their abductor trailed behind them. Though his unhygienic stench reeked of violence, his manner distorted into something unsettlingly singsong. "Willie sure did a number on you. Hoo boy. You don't look so good, girl."

She raised her chin and hoped it carried into her voice. "My name is *Josie*."

"Well, Josie." Her defiance only seemed to tickle him further. "My name is Lyman. And I'm the last man you're ever gonna meet."

Josie's wounds pulsated inside their bandages. Lyman appeared to be a few years younger than the other man. He was taller and skinnier, and his features were all pinched together, while the other's had been wide-set. She couldn't smell his breath, but his body odor was worse. He was more talkative, too, although an erratic jitteriness undercut his relaxed demeanor. It seemed like an act, while the other man had been in full control.

"Where are you taking us?" Josie asked.

"Hey." He ignored the question for a second time, prodding Neena with the shotgun instead. An accusation. "You never gave me your name."

Neena knew *exactly* where they were headed. But since Lyman didn't know that she'd seen his campsite, she stayed quiet, trying to brainstorm any advantages this might give her. Concentrating was impossible. It was getting harder and harder to draw breath. Josie's unbalanced weight leaned into her, heavier than their packs. How much longer would Josie be able to survive without medical attention?

The muddy barrel pressed cold against her back. "I'm talking to you."

"You never asked for my name," Neena said.

"Well, I'm asking now. Like a gentleman. Which is more courtesy than you've given me. You know," he said, tone shifting to irritation, "fuck you. You're like my ex-wife, stirring the shit and then blaming me when the toilet clogs. Because of you, I've been chasing shadows all night. Because of you, Willie chewed my ass out. He's been blaming me for this whole goddamn mess like he had nothing to do with it. I *told* him he should have gotten you out of that hole straightaway, but he wanted to play."

Lyman was speaking to them individually, together, to himself, all at once. "Aw, man. I can't believe you fell for it. I told him it would work. I said if we covered that old sinkhole with branches— like one of them military booby traps—we'd catch us one. I can't wait to see the look on his face when I show up with both of you. Hey," he said, sharply interrupting his own stream. "How'd you get his gun?"

"I took it, and then I shot him," Josie said without emotion.

"Bullshit."

Josie didn't respond.

"So where is he, then?" he asked.

"Probably bleeding out inside the sinkhole," she said. "Or already dead."

"Bullshit. Bull*shit*," Lyman said, as if he was trying to convince himself. He probed her for more details, arguing with her and then denying her responses, growing increasingly worked up as they struggled through the forest. "He'll be there when we get back. He'll be there, you little liar."

They trekked for a long time yet still arrived sooner than Neena had anticipated. Perhaps because they had taken a shortcut. Or perhaps earlier she had only been traveling in circles. Perhaps she had never been far from this place. A dreadfully familiar glow lit the trees before them. The campfire was dim, but it was alive again.

Somebody was already here.

Lyman snatched the hood of her hoodie, holding her back. Neena lurched to a stop. Josie nearly fell beside her. Releasing his grip, he held up a silent, shushing finger, then waved the whole hand for them to turn off their lights.

All three went dark.

A flat clank issued from the shelter. Something metal hit something else metal, and moving shadows made scruffling noises. From the murky darkness of the campsite's edge, they watched a large and blundering creature emerge into the firelight.

"AW, SHIT!" LYMAN shoved the girls forward. "They told me you was dead, Willie." Getting a closer look at the injuries, he winced. "You *should* be dead, Willie."

Josie's tormentor was shirtless, although it took a moment for her to realize it. Willie was covered in an almost animalistic amount of hair, more like a grotesque coat of fur than regular body hair. The coarse curls were bloody and matted, caked with jellied gore around the areas where the shot had entered into his left shoulder and chest. He should have looked wounded and vulnerable. Instead, he looked dangerous and powerful.

She had shot him above his heart. Yet here he was, moving better than her and breathing easier than Neena, carrying a rucksack as though everything were normal. It made her question whether he was a man at all. Maybe he was something more. Something less. Something that could not be killed.

Willie was staring back at her, his eyes solid darkness as he slowly set down the bag. "You're still alive."

Josie's muscles went taut. "So are you."

Lyman held out the shotgun to Willie. "I told you I had every-thing under control." He sounded prideful and eager to show off his captures. "You remember Josie. And this one is"—his rangy frame snapped toward Neena—"hell, you still haven't said."

Neena screwed her mouth shut.

Willie grunted as he took the gun, the only indication that he was in any pain. Though he had the same accent as Lyman, his voice was deeper and measured. "Her name is Neena."

Neena startled against Josie, and Josie's shame reignited for hav-ing told him about her. Then again . . . Lyman had known about Josie. She and Neena had both been trapped in the same impossible posi-tion. This wasn't their fault. *None of this was their fault.*

The men were the only ones to blame.

Lyman glanced at the sack and then back up at Willie. "You were leaving?" He seemed hurt. "I told you I'd get her. I told you! Hell, I got both of them."

Willie ignored this, denying Lyman the praise he obviously wanted. "You'll have to dig it out." He gestured to his shoulder wound.

"Nuh-uh. No way. You need a hospital."

"No hospitals."

"Ugh." Lyman's nose wrinkled as his head turned aside. "Did you piss yourself?"

"Bitch threw it on me." Willie's voice tightened. Another indica-tion of pain.

Josie knew about pain. Her left foot was barely attached, her right hand had been blown off, and she had hobbled miles through the craggy darkness. Countless times she'd fallen, but she was still stand-ing up. For a moment, she felt triumphant. Pain meant Willie was human. But the reassurance vanished quickly. Because if she could still perform remarkable acts, then surely he could still perform un-speakable acts.

"Tend to the fire," Willie said, "then get this shit out."

It was an order, and he kept close watch over the girls as Lyman collected dry brush from a pile they couldn't see behind the shelter. The shelter wasn't big enough for the men to actually live out here, but the amount of work required to build it revealed that they had spent a lot of time at this campsite. This was a place they revisited.

The proximity of Willie's lecherous flesh was frightening. Lyman reappeared and hefted a large branch into the fire. The heat rose. Orange tongues licked at the night, revealing the ground to be littered with dozens of empty beer bottles. Firelight flickered and reflected on the brown glass like hazard warnings.

Neena trembled against Josie. Her gaze had locked onto something at the edge of the clearing. Josie craned her neck and felt the rest of her blood drain from her body. A long and misshapen lump was now visible underneath the dark boughs. It was a woman, dead and cast aside like another scrap of garbage. A portent of their own future.

Willie broke down his gun. The girls jumped at the noise, and the spent shells popped out, hitting the ground at Josie's feet beside a discarded bottle cap. She squinted down. Scarcely able to make it out, she was chilled to discover that the bottle cap was red with tiny white stars inside a blue X—Cataloochee Light. The same brand studding the trail that she and Neena had followed.

It didn't matter that they were inside a national forest. This forest belonged to *these* men. This was their territory. They hadn't just stumbled across her and Neena and made a split-second decision to abduct them. It hadn't even started with a chance encounter with the now-dead woman—or the man that Neena had found. Willie and Lyman had entered these woods with the explicit purpose of hunting for victims.

Lyman dropped another load of fuel into the fire. The flames hissed and sparked, startling Josie again, spiking her pain and making her cry out.

A depraved thrill rippled across Willie's face. An instinctive reaction of pleasure at her suffering. He dug into a pocket. Produced two new shells. Reloaded. His eyes remained fixed on her with feral intensity. The wind was cold, but he didn't seem to feel it. His body radiated heat. He was a predator, and he belonged in this forest.

He was going to shoot her.

But then he didn't. The distance between them closed in two heavy, steady steps. The full carnage of his injuries sharpened into focus. His repugnant breath made her stomach heave. With a feverish grimace, he grabbed her. His bulbous nose mashed into her cheek, and his sloppy lips opened against her recoiling mouth.

Josie tasted rotting gums, brown teeth, rancid tongue. She saw a ragged mother—angry from abuse, mean from alcohol and hard drugs—who liked to humiliate him. Called him names and made him watch when she was with her johns. He was filthy and unwashed and carried a bad odor. Kids bullied him. Teachers were repelled.

When he was six, his mother briefly married, claiming the man was his real father. He believed it back then, but he wasn't so sure now, even if they did share a name. William would take beatings from his wife, turn his rage inward, and then unleash it upon Willie. He once hit Willie in the head with the butt of a shotgun, the same one Willie carried to this day. Willie was knocked clean out for eleven hours before his mother's pimp drove him to the hospital. A dead kid would be bad for business.

Willie hated William because William was weak. But William's father—Willie's granddaddy—owned a tire shop, and, for a few good years, he took Willie out into the woods. Taught him how to drink and hunt. But when William was put away for armed robbery, Willie never saw him or his granddaddy again.

Willie's rap sheet for petty crimes grew rapidly. He did the seventh grade twice and dropped out in ninth. At least the food in juvie was warm. When he was sixteen, he raped a child in the neighborhood. She told on him—she'd said she wouldn't—and that got him sent to adult prison. They beat the shit out of him there, cracked his skull, and he vowed that he'd never get caught again. The girls would never again be alive to talk.

The full putrid sense of him overwhelmed Josie, which stunned her voluntary reactions into immobility. But one involuntary reaction remained. She vomited.

Fury threatened to burst Neena's lungs. "Get off her!" If she shoved Willie away, Josie would fall. She would never let Josie fall again. "Get off her!"

Lyman howled with laughter. "I told you, you gotta brush them nasty teeth."

Willie let go. His expression never changed, even as his hand wiped the puke off his face. But he grunted in brutal satisfaction. "Shut up and tie them," he said. With straining effort, he took a seat on one of the stumps that faced the fire.

Shock and sickness dribbled down Josie's chin.

"Josie?" Neena tried to say it gently, but her voice was too hoarse. She pulled the sleeve of her hoodie down over her hand and used it to swab Josie clean.

Lyman disappeared into the shelter. It emanated a menacing aura of masculine purpose, and Neena wondered how she had ever hoped it could belong to anyone else. The scattered equipment inside thunked and clanged as he rooted around, searching for something.

Glimpses of metal and glass and shiny plastic caught in the firelight. The materials gleamed as if the objects were new and expensive. Neena couldn't imagine either of these men being able to afford gear like this. Who had the camping equipment originally belonged to?

The ransacked yellow-gold tent. The footsteps in the fog.

Thunderstruck, she realized one of them had returned to the scene of their crime for a supply run. How many times had they done this? How many people had they murdered out here?

Lyman emerged with a length of polypropylene rope draped over a shoulder. He aimed the rifle at Neena's chest. "Over there." His head jerked toward a pair of trees behind the corpse.

Neena shivered but didn't budge.

Willie hocked and spit. The glob of phlegm landed on the toe of Lyman's right boot. "You never could make a bitch heel."

"Move," Lyman bellowed, in the natural transfer of human embarrassment: humiliation into anger into revenge on someone weaker. His rank body shoved between the girls, and he grabbed Josie from underneath the armpit of her good arm. The girls cried out as they were ripped away from each other.

His boot rammed into Neena, forcing her to stumble forward.

He dragged Josie. Leg scrabbling to keep up, she slid and fell. He hauled her across the ground. The pain was so extraordinary that she could no longer see or hear, only feel. She screamed, screeched, wailed. Lyman pushed her against a tree and then shoved her down into a sitting position, legs splayed out and arms at her sides. Using the hunting knife from the sheath on his belt, he cut the rope into two lengths and then held out the longer one to Neena.

"Wrap this around her, good and tight," he said.

Forced to obey, Neena wrapped it around and around, lashing Josie to the tree by her midsection. In Josie's condition, this was enough to secure her. Josie's screams weakened into gasps. And yet, through her pain, Josie sensed a purposeful slack in the binding. Somehow she held still enough so as not to give away the deception.

"Now." Lyman gestured with the rifle to the other tree. "Sit."

The second tree was younger and had less girth, so he was able to tie Neena's hands all the way behind her back, around the trunk. Picking up a third piece of rope that had been discarded nearby, he used it to bind her feet together in front of her.

He returned to Josie and tugged on the knot. His tongue clucked with reproach. "Well, that ain't gonna hold nobody."

Josie's hope shriveled. As Lyman began to unwork the binding, Neena released a macabre rasp. Josie understood that Neena's muscles were straining to exhale. The rope fell loose. Jolted by inspiration, Josie took a deep breath and expanded her rib cage as far as possible. Lyman tightened the binding. Josie held. He yanked and tightened. Josie quivered and held. Finally satisfied, he stood and picked up his rifle.

She exhaled, and the rope loosened—a titch.

He swaggered back around to gloat down at them. "My, my." His thin tongue licked his chapped lips. "Don't you two look pretty? Gonna have some fun with you."

"Stop fooling around," Willie yelled in a mushy garble.

Lyman's features screwed together like a child being berated by his father. He ironed them out quickly, aware of his spectators, but new wrinkles ironed themselves into the wrong places. The structure of his face turned demented. "Don't go nowhere, okay?" He barked twice with laughter—*what an original joke, what a comedian*—before striding away.

No doubt the rope around Neena's ankles had been previously used to bind the woman. Death had seeped into its strands. She felt it touching her, infecting her. She turned her head to look at Josie and rest against the tree. Dried blood in the bark, scratches in the trunk, and ruts in the earth further warned of a shared history with the dead woman. Her body was close, only a few feet away. Neena was close to Josie, too. If they weren't bound to immovable trees, they could have reached out and held hands.

"Are you okay?" she whispered, as Josie whispered, "Can you breathe?"

"Zip your lips, or I'll shoot one of you right now and make the other bury the body," Lyman hollered.

"It's in the—" Willie said.

"I know where it is." Lyman stormed past him and back into the shelter. He returned only a moment later, having fetched a small red box with a big white cross.

The first-aid kit infuriated Neena. They had no qualms about committing murder, yet they were still fearful of their own mortality. The corpse held a dark gravity that pulled her eyes again. Since she had last seen it, the body had entered into the stages of rigor mortis. The facial muscles appeared especially stiff and rigid, but no part of the body looked flexible anymore. Moonlight bounced off the bruised and battered skin. Neena wished that she could button up the woman's shirt to give her back some of her dignity.

Lyman took back Willie's shotgun and rested it out of the way, against the shelter. Then he set down his own gun at his feet before revealing a pair of tweezers.

Willie gave a derisive grunt. "You've gotta cut the shot out. An X over each one and *then* dig them out."

Lyman's brow furrowed, but he unsheathed his hunting knife. The huge blade glinted in the crackling light. He offered out a rectangular glass bottle—something stronger than beer—to Willie, who swigged and returned it. Lyman poured the liquor over the knife and then, with a wincing head shake, poured it over the open wounds.

Willie's scowl contorted into a huffing and lunatic grimace.

"You sure about this?" Lyman asked, handing the bottle back to Willie.

Willie swilled the remnants and then tossed the empty at the body. The bottle smacked the woman's thigh before thumping to the ground. Shining liquid droplets clung to his beard. "Just do it already."

Lyman's shoulders seemed to brace against an anticipated blow as he made the first incision. None came. His shoulders drooped with relief, and the surgery proceeded.

Slice, slice, dig.

The tools fumbled to reach each embedded shot. One by one, pellets dropped onto the forest floor. Sweat glistened on Lyman's forehead, and dark rivulets of fresh blood caught the light as they eked out pathways through Willie's chest hair.

Perhaps to maintain a tough appearance—or perhaps because he actually was that tough—Willie's cavernous gaze returned to the girls. "Morgan Shea Sullivan." His head inclined toward the body that lay between them. "Thought you should be introduced, since you're gonna have a lot in common."

Lyman chimed in. "That's what her driver's license said. We ain't stupid enough to take them, because that's evidence, but we always look."

"What was her boyfriend's name?" Though they came out in a croak, Neena's words were clear. "The man in the tent?"

Lyman snorted. "Now, that I couldn't tell you."

"Goddammit," Willie snarled as Lyman's hand slipped.

Cowed, Lyman finished digging out his current target. The shot dropped glumly to the ground with the others before his voice shored up with false bravado. "The guys are disposable, see. We ain't got no use for them."

The girls knew what *use* would come before their deaths. The taste of sick still contaminated Josie's mouth. It made her feel just as disposable.

Who was Morgan? Who *had* she been? Because of the similarities in their names and ages, Josie couldn't help but think of Win's girlfriend. Though new to backpacking, Meegan had taken to it enthusiastically. Josie had been angry to share her brother's attention, angry that it meant he spent even more time away from home. But Meegan had always been kind to Josie. She'd even encouraged Josie to join them.

Morgan's boyfriend was dead, too. Josie didn't know what Neena had seen, and she blocked out the gruesome possibilities. Imagining Win in his place was more than she could bear. Win and Meegan had always seemed so much older than her, but now she understood how young they actually were. They still had their whole lives ahead of them. Morgan and her boyfriend had none. Josie considered the boy with the deep voice and the girl with the milkmaid braid that they'd seen within their first hours on the trail, also so similar in age, and how close they'd come to being here instead. All of them walking through this same wilderness. All of it left to chance.

"How many?" Josie asked quietly. Just loud enough for them to hear.

Willie sneered. "We've been hunting these woods a long time. And we'll be here a long time after you're gone."

"Been here a long time," Lyman parroted.

"Others"—Willie winced as a pellet sludged from his skin—"they didn't tell nobody where they was going. Families and police think they're just missing persons. They don't know where to look."

"Our parents know where to look," Neena said. "They know exactly where we are."

Willie smirked. "But they don't know where you're *gonna* be. And it ain't here."

THE WOODS ARE ALWAYS WATCHING

"Where?" Josie asked. The men were bragging and trying to frighten them. This was wholly unnecessary because she and Neena had been locked in a state of terror for hours. However, if they did manage to get out of these woods alive, Josie wanted to be able to tell the authorities where they could find the other victims.

She also wanted to keep the men distracted while her hand stretched for something inside her pocket.

Relishing his captive audience, Willie surprised her by answering the question. "There are other sinkholes. Caves. Places where a body can drop and never be found."

Josie flashed back to the bottom of the sinkhole. Rocks and soil and branches dumped heavily onto her body, burying her, gravediggers filling their grave. Desperately, her fingers fished for the object inside her jeans pocket. Maybe she was only imagining the slight pressure. Maybe it had fallen out.

"You hear about those murders up in Hot Springs?" Lyman asked.

Willie hissed and shoved Lyman away with his good arm.

"I'm helping, you damn jackass."

"Help better," Willie said, settling back again.

After a sullen interlude, Lyman continued, "That story was big. Three dead hikers and a missing boyfriend. We was worried that one got out of control, but the dumb cops"—he laughed, and the sound was tight and jittery like a rodent—"they blamed the boyfriend. He had a record—possession or some shit—so they pinned it on him. But he's dead, too. He gave us a chase, so we had to dump his body someplace else."

Willie's temper ruptured again. "Finish the damn job!"

Lyman flinched. His knife hand trembled as it hovered over Willie's chest. Maybe Willie was mad because they had revealed too much. Or maybe he was just mad with pain. Josie wished that Willie's pain would kill him. *Morgan, her boyfriend, the four hikers.* Six people were dead, although clearly they were claiming more. Josie imagined Lyman slipping again. The knife plunging into Willie's heart.

Her fingers clasped around the object. *Yes.*

"There were others, too," Lyman said, resuming his work. Slicing and excavating. He'd hardened himself back into a braggart. "Whores we doped up and brought into the woods. If you've been arrested enough, the police don't believe it when you actually go missing. Ain't nobody miss them. Fucking addicts."

"You ain't any better," Willie said.

"I'm better than them!"

Willie shook his head in disgust before addressing the girls. "First time we met in prison, he was on that shit. Been on it since he was born."

"Those women have family and friends," Neena said. "Everybody does. People who love them."

"My mama was a whore," Willie said. "Ain't nobody misses her."

The object slid out from Josie's pocket. The tiny shard of her friendship ring had broken flat on one end, but the other end was sharp and jagged. Wriggling her hand into position under the rope, Josie began to saw.

JOSIE HAD TO be careful. It couldn't look like her arm was moving. The twisted nylon frayed slowly, strand by strand, the beginnings of a faint fuzz. Fearing the tip might break, she couldn't push too hard.

Lyman was done. Or, at least, Willie was. After Lyman's hands were shoved away with finality, Lyman strapped on the gauze and bandages, sticking the white medical tape to Willie's woolly chest. It wasn't a good job. It couldn't be a good job.

But if Josie had lasted this long, Willie could last longer.

Lyman cleaned the blood off his knife. Willie groaned and stood up, vertebra by vertebra. When he reached full height, he was larger than he had been before. Staggering aside, he undid his pants. Piss streamed into the bushes.

Neena noticed Josie moving around, doing something with her hands. *Hand, singular.* Neena fought a nauseating wave of lightheadedness. She owed it to Josie to stay strong. Josie, who was sawing. The action was suddenly, miraculously, recognizable.

How many hours were left until sunrise? It surpassed logic, but if they made it to sunrise, it felt like they could survive. These men weren't invincible; they were simply men. One wounded, both maybe intoxicated. Men made mistakes. What were their mistakes?

"I thought you were worried about evidence," Neena said.

The men, finishing up, turned toward her with perplexed expressions, as if they'd forgotten that girls could speak.

Neena sat up straighter against the tree. "Your DNA is all over that shot on the ground. You'll never be able to find every pellet in the dark."

The fire sputtered. Woodsmoke suffocated the air.

Willie slapped the back of Lyman's head, and Lyman skittered out of further reach. "Don't matter," Willie said, contradicting his act of violence. "Only my blood. Nobody else's."

"That first-aid kit looks new," Neena said, keeping their gaze fastened to her so they wouldn't look at Josie. "All of that equipment in there"—she coughed, smoke burning her impaired lungs, as she nodded toward the shelter—"is stolen. How is that different from taking a driver's license?"

Lyman crossed his arms. "That equipment is ours. Or it could belong to anybody. Or maybe we found it left behind after the murdering, and we didn't know no better, so we took it."

"All kinds of reasons why we have it," Willie said.

"The rope burns on Morgan," Neena said. "Those hikers at Hot Springs were bound in the exact same way."

"Yeah," Lyman said, "so they'll suspect the same missing boyfriend."

"No, they won't," Neena said, at the same time Willie expanded his chest and said, "Who says they'll find her body?"

"Why wouldn't they suspect the boyfriend?" Lyman asked.

Willie contorted with rage as he whirled on Lyman. "Why are you asking her? You think she knows something I don't?"

Lyman's hands twitched upward protectively, reflexively. As he lowered them, they clenched into fists. "I just want to know why she thinks that. In case we missed something."

"Stop trying to be smart, because you ain't." Willie lurched toward Lyman but stopped with another grimace of pain. "Just do as you're told, for once." Cradling his shoulder, Willie receded into the shelter. "Call me when you're done. And don't take too long." He gave a mean chuckle. "Then again, that's never been a problem for you."

Josie's sawing faltered. Halted.

Fear stabbed Neena—and then detonated into anger. "What, you guys don't like watching each other? *That's* where you draw the line?"

Lyman was stewing with fury, but this yanked his attention back to Neena. His posture righted itself. He made a show of sauntering over, his eyes glinting with the amusement of someone who knows more than the other person. "I like 'em alive." He paused for a terrible grin. "Willie likes 'em dead."

The words repulsed Neena to her core.

Harshly, Willie called out from the darkness. "It's your turn this time."

The smile collapsed on Lyman's face. A beat of silence blanketed the campsite. "Hey, man." Lyman swiveled toward the shelter. "I don't do that. That's your thing, not mine."

Willie exploded like a pressure cooker. "You fucked this up, so it's your goddamn turn!"

The silence following the outburst was deafening. Neena's terrified confusion over why they were still discussing turns upended, and her ears rang with the void of dread that opened around her. They weren't talking about rape anymore. They were debating who had the task of killing them.

Lyman's cockiness had vanished again. He looked deflated. Aggravated.

Lyman is afraid of Willie, Neena realized. Willie used threats and fear to control him, too. And even though Lyman seemed to be okay with murder, he didn't want to be the one who actually committed it. It was Willie. Willie had killed them all.

Neena glanced at Josie, trying to determine if her friend had reached this same conclusion. Josie was sawing frantically. Neena pivoted to a new tactic. Her heartbeat pounded through her skin, sweaty and palpitating, but her tone was calm and scornful. "Some friend, trying to drag you down with him."

Lyman's beady eyes narrowed even further. "What did you say?"

"He only wants you to kill us so that when you're caught"—he tried to argue, but Neena talked over him—"and you'll *definitely* be caught—you have no idea how hard my parents will look for you— you'll be held equally responsible for these crimes. That's a huge difference in sentencing, you know. Life versus capital punishment?"

Lyman hesitated, wariness muddling his forehead. But then he scoffed. "What the fuck do I care about your parents? Did it help the cops solve the case when the parents of those kids from Hot Springs boo-hooed all over the damn media?"

Neena imagined her own grief-stricken family on television, appealing for help in a press conference, all the distraught aunties and uncles of the local Bengali community supporting them in attendance. The clips would be recycled on crime blogs: Ma crying, supported in Darshan's arms, while Baba trembled bravely into the mic and pled for answers. Begged for anyone who might know something to come forward.

Neena's fear hardened into resolve. She and Josie would fight until the end. And if they went down, they would leave behind so much goddamn evidence that their families would get those answers.

These men would never have the opportunity to kill again. Improv wasn't Neena's greatest strength, but she gave it a go. "Okay, but even if you aren't worried about our parents . . . shouldn't you be worried about Galen's?"

Josie's sawing stumbled.

"Galen?" Lyman seemed to echo whatever Josie was thinking. "Who the fuck is Galen?"

Neena glanced at Josie. It was quick—quicker than the men's intellect—but loaded with meaning. "I mean, you said you didn't look at his license, but I thought that was a joke. You don't need an ID to know who that was."

"That guy in the tent?" Lyman asked.

"Galen *Cooper*?" Neena said. "Are you seriously telling me that you didn't recognize the governor's son?" Neena wasn't even positive if Roy Cooper was still the governor of North Carolina, and she sure as hell didn't know if he had a son named Galen. One of her loathsome coworkers had popped into her brain first.

"That's bullshit," Willie said, reemerging from the shelter. Neena had hoped that he'd already passed out. But not only was he conscious, he appeared to have heard every word.

"Yeah. You're just fucking with me," Lyman said to Neena. He glanced at Willie, but then his eyes bugged, and his hand flew to his forehead. His temper flashed again. "You're trying to play tricks with my mind."

"You guys killed the *governor's son*," Josie said, neatly picking up the thread. Though Neena doubted her own improvisational skills, she was wrong. The girls had had years of experience together. Josie understood exactly what Neena was doing, and she sensed Neena perk up as she went on. "You don't think the FBI will be all over you?"

"The CIA," Neena chimed in.

"The ATF," Josie said.

"The EPA."

Josie shot Neena a look, and Neena shrugged. The moment was so strange and off-kilter that they almost laughed. Thankfully, the men didn't catch it.

"They're messing with you," Willie said to Lyman, as Josie recommenced sawing. "Have your fun, and then shut them up for good."

Lyman was pacing. "I didn't kill nobody."

"No, you didn't." Neena's crosshairs locked on Lyman. "But do you think the feds will believe that? You need us. If you let us go, we'll tell them that you saved us. That Willie was the mastermind behind everything. If we turn on him, you might not have to go to prison at all."

Willie's muscles coiled and released, and he lunged like a snake, but Lyman reached her first. He was screaming as Neena's head smashed against the tree.

Lyman's scraggly fingers were gripped around her neck. Neena saw an addicted teenage mother who had given him up at birth. He was alone for the first three months of his life. His new mother, a Bible-thumping member of the Church of God, couldn't have children of her own. She was controlling, worrying, smothering. Always taking him to the doctor. The doc assured her that her son was fine, but she didn't believe him. Or the next doctor. Or the next.

His overworked father died from a ruptured stomach ulcer when Lyman was four. Lyman always wondered what his life would have been like if he'd had a father.

He made friends at school, but his mother chased them away. She chased away his girlfriends, too, so he married one of them at eighteen and moved out. Cayleigh was her own trainwreck, but she accused him of being insecure and immature and left him that same year. He went into the navy but was dishonorably discharged for sexual assault. While he was in prison, his mother—whom he both loathed and depended on—disowned him. When he got out, he was busted again several times for theft and possession.

Then he met Willie.

Willie had fantasies like he had. Willie had aspirations. Lyman felt lucky that Willie had even taken notice of him. Lyman would do anything for Willie.

"Stop!" Josie said. "Let go of her!"

Lyman released the stranglehold. His fingers transferred from Neena's throat onto his own, crawling up his neck like an infestation of spiders.

Willie shook his head in disgust at Lyman's failure to follow through.

"My father is a lawyer," Neena wheezed. "He can help you. *We* can help you."

Lyman was incoherent and unhinged, raging and cycling rapidly between emotions. Unbelievably, he appeared to be considering their bait.

"He's been calling you the fuckup this whole time," Josie said, "but he had me in a pit with no hand and no foot, and I got away. *You're* the one who captured us. He's the fuckup, not you." She was contradicting her own argument, praising him for being the one to catch them while also telling him that he was innocent, but Lyman didn't seem capable of catching the contradiction, so she pressed on. "We'll tell everybody that he's the murderer. That you kept us alive. Saved us."

"Willie will be sent to death row," Neena said, "and you'll be sent home."

The bark sloughed the skin off Josie's bare arm as she sawed, but the rope began to give way. It didn't matter how many times her ring had shattered; their friendship would always be powerful. Even the shards were strong.

"They're lying," Willie roared.

Lyman slapped his own head, trying to regain control of the chaos within. He was pacing again, agitated, unsure of what to do. Everyone was yelling at him.

Willie shoved him aside and lumbered toward the girls.

Maniacally, Josie sawed, bracing herself for the inevitable. Maybe she could stab Willie's injuries with the shard—or stab out an eyeball.

Willie's nostrils flared. He had noticed what her hand was doing.

"He was packing up to leave when we got here," Neena shouted at Lyman, pausing every few words for breath. "He was abandoning you! He thought we'd escaped, so he was leaving you behind with the bodies for the police to find."

Josie struggled against the weakened rope, trying to push through it with her torso. The shard slipped from her fingers. It dropped uselessly to the ground as Willie's eyes bore into hers with complete absorption, a pit that she could never escape.

His hands reached for her throat.

"You were leaving me!" Lyman yelled.

He barreled into Willie, pinning him to the ground, punches swinging in frenetic escalation. Though hampered by his injury, Willie was bigger than Lyman. He kicked up, dislodged the wiry man, and rolled on top of him. Almost as quickly, Willie grunted in shock. He fell back, palm pressed against his side as blood spilled out from a new wound.

Lyman's hand was clutched around his hunting knife. He was shaking—with sobs or laughter, the girls couldn't tell—as he crawled back on top of Willie.

"Push!" Neena said.

Josie strained against her ropes.

Snotty tears dropped down from Lyman's face onto Willie's. Willie's hand grabbed Lyman's wrist, blocking the knife, but he was expressionless as he forced the knife upward toward Lyman's throat. It was almost over. There was no doubt that if Willie won, the girls would not outlive Lyman by very long.

Lyman released a keening wail.

Willie huffed with steadfast determination.

Neena shouted at Josie to push.

Josie screamed as she burst through her bindings.

And then a fifth noise overtook them—a bustling of foliage and a powerful exhale—as an unseen beast thumped into a charge.

GIANT CLAWS TORE against the forest floor and whooshed through the firelit darkness. The bear was enormous. With an open jaw of gleaming teeth, it charged headlong at Willie, who released Lyman in shock. Willie's hands rose to protect his head. Lyman rolled away, scrambling onto all fours.

Time dilated.

The animal landed hard against Willie's chest, knocking him flat and pinning him down, tearing into his legs. Willie cried out. Snorting and snuffling, the bear let go for a better grip—to get a better angle with its jaws, those drooling white daggers of teeth—and then clamped back on, thrashing the body back and forth.

Lyman was shouting something, still crawling.

Josie sprang on her good foot toward Neena's wrists. Her teeth and hand tore at the binding as the bear backed its rump up against her. The bear felt *solid*. Its thickset muscles breathed and heaved. It smelled like a grassy wet dog that had rolled in pig shit, and, as she struggled not to be crushed, her fingers brushed its coarse and bristled fur. Willie was shrieking in abrupt bursts, but terror kept her muted as she clambered and tussled behind its haunches to free Neena.

"Shoot it!" Willie screamed.

Lyman lurched to his feet and grabbed the nearest weapon—Willie's shotgun, resting against the shelter.

The mauling was relentless, the biting and ripping. Willie flailed and punched, but the bear chomped down and tossed him as if he were a stuffed chew toy. Willie tried to scrabble away. A monstrous claw tugged him back.

Lyman swung the shotgun and aimed at the bear.

Behind the animal, Neena had a straight view down the barrel. It was still packed with mud from being used as a crutch. Lyman shouted as he fired. Neena braced herself, but the shot didn't blast outward. Mud trapped the shot, blowing it out the top of the barrel. The spray hit Lyman full in the face, and he keeled over backward.

Josie spit out the loosened knot.

The rope fell away from Neena's hands.

The girls darted away from the bear, both of them hopping, wide-eyed in manic disbelief. Neena's gaze snagged on the knife on the ground, near where Lyman had fallen, and she lunged. Blood gushed and pooled beneath him. Snatching up the knife, she sat down roughly to slice the bindings from her ankles. Lyman watched her, his face a surrealist nightmare. She couldn't tell if his eyes were open or closed, or if he even had eyes anymore. His body was unmoving.

Neena stood, and the rope dropped away from her feet. Still clutching the knife, she grabbed Lyman's rifle and slung it over her shoulder.

Scanning for Josie, the whites of Willie's eyes flashed at her through the chaos. A hulking paw was pressed into his back. The bear was winning.

"Shoot it," he said, struggling and huffing. A mutilated grimace tweaked his lips. His riven flesh was missing in chunks and hung in shining red peels.

"What about Morgan?" Josie asked. She was steadying herself against a nearby tree, berserk with fear. "We can't just leave her here."

"We aren't," Neena reassured her. "We'll tell everybody where to find her."

The bear growled and snorted with heavy, inspecting snuffs. It prodded the Willie-heap with its snout. Hot gore spilled out from punctured holes.

"Shoot it," Willie gasped, furious with desperation. His tortured limbs grasped uselessly for enough leverage to push the bear off his back.

Neena's arms wrapped around Josie.

The bear straddled Willie. His prone body was shredded and lacerated. The bear's colossal teeth ripped and thrashed. The ursine musk clung to the girls' nostrils, dominating over the iron-rich scent of blood—blood from the men who had believed themselves to be the most dangerous predators in these woods.

The beast roared, guttural and deafening. The entire forest shook.

Neither girl looked back.

THE GIRLS HOBBLED through the forest to their escape. Behind them, the slashing tears and shaking thuds indicated that Willie was about to die. The sounds were reassuring.

"A bear," Neena said.

"I know," Josie said. "A fucking bear."

The girls exchanged a look, a silent pause to acknowledge the irony. But where had the bear come from? And why had it charged Willie and not them? Or Lyman?

The animal had seemed huge, but maybe it was actually starving because the berries had yet to ripen, and it wasn't getting enough food. Maybe it was a mother with cubs nearby. Maybe it had been attracted to the smell of Willie's urine. Or maybe it had even stumbled across Willie's scent trail and tracked him through the woods after Josie had smashed him with the mason jar. This last notion was the most satisfying. Though the girls knew it was incorrect to think of the bear as an ally—it could just as easily have attacked them—the bear was a force of nature, and nature had chosen to let them live tonight.

The clash grew fainter. Their ears rang numbly.

The girls traversed back the way they had arrived, retracing the worn pathway Lyman had led them down, praying the bear remained occupied. To conserve energy, they didn't speak. It was still dark, but they had managed to hang on to both of their headlamps, and, as they approached Frazier Mountain and stepped back onto the Wade Harte, they could feel how close they were to dawn. The nearness of the sun thrummed. The daytime insects had yet to awaken, but the nighttime insects were quieting. Birds chirped lethargically as the mist transformed into dew.

Their passage remained slow, the descent perilous. Loose rocks shifted underfoot, and smooth boulders were scattered with slippery grit. They fell many times. They had adrenaline, though, and they had each other.

They also had fear.

They could still feel the ferocity of the bear as it snarled and thrashed. They could still hear Willie as he grunted, bashing its muzzle with his fist. They passed the deer's rotting corpse. Although they couldn't see it, the fumes were harrowing. These smells and sounds of death resonated throughout their bones long after they left them behind.

Were the men actually dead? It seemed possible that Willie and Lyman might be supporting each other, teetering down this mountain, too. For the rest of their lives, the girls would have to keep looking over their shoulders. It was the reason why slain villains in horror movies popped back up, still alive—because there would always be another man waiting to cause harm. It would never end. The girls would never truly be safe.

Their bodies continued to deteriorate. From the exertion of assisting Josie, Neena's condition grew increasingly dire, but the car keys dug sharply into her ass, spurring her on. She wished that she could set down the rifle. It weighed too much.

She did not set down the rifle.

They labored in the correct direction but waited anxiously for landmarks to prove that they were close. These final extreme hours were like struggling through a time loop. Were they traveling backward? Was this even the right mountain? A stream tumbled over rocks, and Neena imagined her body gliding smoothly down the slope with the current.

Dawn broke, at last. The first pink rays shimmered with soft warmth, and the water illuminated. Directly ahead, the girls' cairn was revealed in the light of the stream.

They ground to a halt to take in the miraculous sight. Their stacked stones were still holding strong. Suddenly, Neena understood why she had fought so hard to leave them standing. The decorative cairn was a statue, a symbol, a declaration: she and Josie would always be there for each other. Whatever they had fought about—tormented by the grief of separation and fear of their unknown futures—it no longer mattered. Moving forward was the only way to survive. To live. And even though moving forward meant moving apart, it would be in distance only. Not in spirit or support or love.

The girls tightened their grips on one another.

They moved forward.

Time accelerated. Josie's foot felt as if it were already detached. The intensity of her pain had become meaningless, but each of Neena's sucking breaths portended to her last.

They passed the ancient oak. Two days ago, its singular crooked branch and knobby forefinger had been ominous, pointing them back in the direction they had come. Now it was a guidepost, ushering them safely home. The final stretch of trail was a fog of color and sound. Grassy green, mossy green, leafy green, dying green. Rasping, shuffling, coughing, scraping. They passed the brown national forest sign and noticeboard—and then three feet crunched into the gravel parking lot.

The sun had fully risen over the vehicles: Neena's Subaru, the other Subaru, and a pickup truck. The other Subaru seemed harmless and nondescript, but a menacing energy vibrated from the truck. Its chomping metal grill was massive and aggressive, the angle of its mud spatter violent and severe. It was indisputable which belonged to Morgan and her boyfriend and which belonged to Willie and Lyman.

"Walk me to the truck," Josie said.

Neena did.

Josie glanced between the gun and the knife. She was sick of guns.

Reading her mind, Neena handed her the knife. Josie jammed it in to its hilt. The back right tire released an exhausted squeak and slowly began to leak. Josie struggled, one-handed, to pull the knife back out. What if the men kept a spare underneath the truck's locked bed cover? Her plan had been to destroy all four tires, but the rubber had clasped immovably onto the blade.

Neena placed a trembling hand over Josie's. *Enough.*

Josie let go.

The girls managed the last few steps to Neena's car. Neena dug out her keys and swayed, taking Josie with her in a hard lean against the door. She was close to passing out. Every ounce of her remaining fortitude had gone into helping Josie reach this point. A life-threatening asthma attack was well underway.

This time, Josie moved to support Neena. She aided her to the passenger's side, unlocked it, and helped her into the seat. Josie hefted the rifle into the back. With her hand anchoring herself against the car, she hopped around to the driver's side and climbed in.

"Do you remember how to drive?" Neena asked in a faint gasp.

"I've got this," Josie said. Because she wasn't afraid anymore. The road was a blur, but she could see more clearly than she had in years.

With her left hand, she started the car. It roared instantly into life. Her left hand crossed all the way over her body to shift into reverse, and her right foot hit the pedal. The car obeyed. She shifted into drive as Neena plugged her phone into the charger. Josie stepped on the gas, and the girls sped away, waiting for a signal.

Waiting.

Waiting.

ACKNOWLEDGMENTS

As with everything I write, Kiersten White read more drafts of this novel than anybody else, and, therefore, must be thanked first. If we went into the woods together, I'm sure we could overcome any dangers that crossed our path. But let's not tempt fate.

Thank you to my fearless agent, Kate Testerman, who works with a machete strapped to her thigh and pom-poms in her hands.

Thank you to my brilliant editor, Julie Strauss-Gabel, who sawed this story apart and found a smarter way to put it back together. Who does an infinite number of astonishing tasks behind the scenes and makes miracles happen.

Thank you to my badass publicist Vanessa DeJesús. Thanks to Lindsey Andrews and Sean Freeman for the marvelously eerie cover, and additional heartfelt thanks to Dana Spector and everyone at Penguin, including: James Akinaka, Anna Booth, Christina Colangelo, Rob Farren, Melissa Faulner, Alex Garber, Carmela Iaria, Bri Lockhart, Emily Romero, Janet Robbins Rosenberg, Kim Ryan, Shannon Spann, Felicity Vallence, and Natalie Vielkind.

Myra McEntire was my daily support team. Thank you for always answering your phone when it rings. Lauren Biehl, Manning Krull, Emily Maesar, Sandhya Menon, Kara Prahler, Heather Young, and Jeff Zentner also helped in tremendous ways with both story and research. Thank you, dear friends and dear sister.

My mother gifted me with her passion for books, but this one will be too scary for her to read. I'm thanking her anyway. And thank you to my father, who watched all the horror movies with me and popped all the popcorn.

Finally, to my husband, Jarrod: I'm sorry that I told you so many stories about bear attacks and serial killers before we went camping, but thank you for still dropping everything to go with me. Thank you for so many things. For all the things. There is no person with whom I would rather share a tent or house or planet. I love you the most, always.

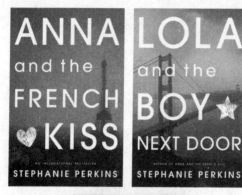
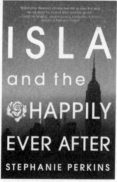

STEPHANIE PERKINS is the *New York Times* bestselling author and anthology editor of multiple books for young adults, including *There's Someone Inside Your House*, *The Woods Are Always Watching*, *Anna and the French Kiss*, *Lola and the Boy Next Door*, and *Isla and the Happily Ever After*. She has always worked with books—first as a bookseller, then as a librarian, and now as a novelist. Stephanie lives in the mountains of North Carolina with her husband. Every room of their house is painted a different color of the rainbow.

stephanieperkins.com

Instagram: naturallystephperkins